THE SHADOW WATCH

S.A. KLOPFENSTEIN

For Kaitlin, my partner in crime

CONTENTS

Watcher Magic
Corporeal Ordershifters

Regenero: the regenerators
Medici: the healers
Cerebro: the mentalists
Enduro: the ultra-swift
Metamorphi: the shapeshifters

Watcher Magic
Material Orders

Fieri: manipulators of fire
Conjuri: manipulators of matter
Lumeni: manipulators of light
Sonora: manipulators of sound

FOREWORD

It began with a gallows.

Well, actually, I suppose it began much earlier than that.

You see, I spent years writing and revising my first book. These days, I refer to that original work as the "Book that Taught Me How to Write." Dystopian novels were big at the time, and so my first book was also dystopian, but with supernaturally-gifted beings thrown into the mix. There were also zeppelins at one point.

In short, it was a hot mess, unsure of itself, trying to be too many things. It contained nuggets of potential. Faint traces of what would become the Watchers, and even a few of the characters you'll read about here. Kale and Kirra both existed in this dystopian world (though they were quite different), and there was a young girl and a young boy somewhat reminiscent of Tori and Darien (but with different names and very different fates).

But I was a new writer, and I could not put all the pieces of a good story together, and so that first book just didn't quite work.

After months of revisions, I finally decided to move on to a new story. Actually, several new stories. I wrote the beginnings of a number of novels that also didn't quite work. But I kept trying. And I kept learning about writing.

All the while, the concept of the Watchers—which originated from the basic question: *what if there were angelic beings, but they looked like everyone else?*—would not go away.

And then, one day, the image for a scene came to me quite clearly. In that scene, a boy and a girl were forced to build a gallows in a city square in a great wintry fantasy city. I didn't know why. I didn't know what would happen.

But I needed to find out.

I immediately started writing that scene. And then, the next.

I'd been entertaining the idea of writing an epic fantasy for a long time. And all at once, I saw the ideas from that first "Book that Taught Me How to Write" in a new light. Ideas and characters began reshaping themselves in a completely new story and setting.

With the gallows scene as a new starting point, the entire novel began to fall into place in a way stories never had in any of my previous attempts.

As I was writing, I started posting the chapters online, and people responded positively toward the story. I'd learned quite a lot about plotting and character arcs since the first novel was abandoned, and over the course of months, the momentum of this "gallows story" kept growing. Chapters formed into parts, and then many parts, and before I knew it, I'd finished my second novel. This time, I felt that I did, in fact, have something good, and I had the reader feedback to back up this feeling.

I kept at it. I edited and revised that book. It went by a number of titles—including the painfully cringeworthy *A Passage of Blood*—before settling firmly as *The Shadow Watch*.

The editing process brought more iterations of the Watcher story. I cut out entire parts that didn't end up matching the larger vision I was finding for the complete series. Eventually, it was finished.

And that second novel was published.

Eight years after the first iteration of that gallows scene, much to my amazement, people continue to discover and enjoy this book. Some think it's the best in the series. Most, like myself, think the books only get better as the series goes on.

But this is where it all started. This book will always hold a special place in my heart. And I'm still enormously proud of this tale. As I prepared this edition, I completed one final editorial pass. There were no major changes, but I wanted this version to be the best it's ever been. And so, if I found a clunky bit of prose, I tweaked it. A couple moments were reworked, knowing now exactly how certain questions are resolved in later books.

The edition you hold in your hands is the version I always dreamed of creating. With color illustrations and custom iconography, monster sketches and world lore, even a prequel story I always hoped to write.

It's the ultimate edition. But this never would have happened if not for an incredible sequence of people who read iterations of the book—as it was being written, or after it was published, or even when it was a different book entirely—and made it known that I was on to something.

Some of the people who funded this edition on Kickstarter have been around for those eight years and beyond. Some are brand new to the series.

However you've arrived, I'm indebted to you for believing in this story. *The Shadow Watch* will always be the book that started it all.

And now, once more, we begin a new iteration.

S.A. Klopfenstein
Salt Lake City, UT
Jan. 2024

THE SHADOW WATCH

S.A. KLOPFENSTEIN

THE SHADOW WATCH SAGA
— BOOK ONE —

DELUXE ILLUSTRATED EDITION

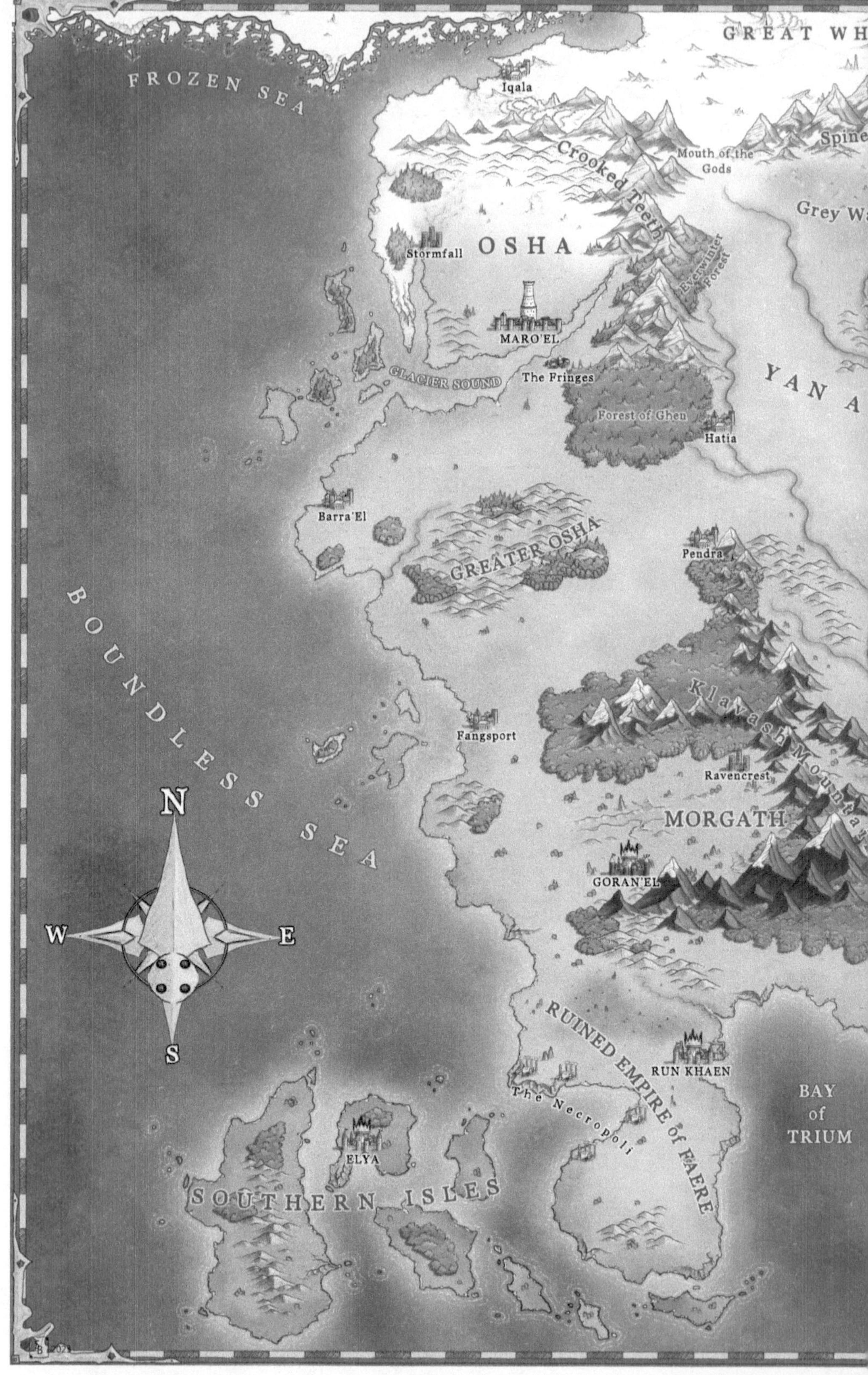

GREAT WH
FROZEN SEA
Iqala
Crooked Teeth
Mouth of the Gods
Spine
Grey Wa
OSHA
Stormfall
Everwinter Forest
MARO'EL
YAN A
GLACIER SOUND
The Fringes
Forest of Ghen
Hatia
Barra'El
GREATER OSHA
Pendra
BOUNDLESS SEA
Klavash Mountains
Fangsport
Ravencrest
N
MORGATH
W
E
GORAN'EL
S
RUINED EMPIRE of FAERE
RUN KHAEN
BAY of TRIUM
The Necropoli
ELYA
SOUTHERN ISLES

Map of the
New World
FROST ISLE
NORTHERN PASSAGE
Crimson Mountains
LOST SEA
JURKA
KERCIN
EPPE
NDERING
DUNES
ISLE of
JALLAA
BAY of JALLAA
Canyons
Dimh
KINGDOM of MALAI
SILVER PALACE
Southern Rim
Saltlands
Kerren
PARJHA
M'VEL
Bhalai River
Vel Tereth
Jhenai
BHALAI
MELANESIA
SILVER SEA
TH

PROLOGUE

The Year 312 N.W.
Sixteenth Year of the Reign of Aleksander Maro

The mother could feel the creatures in her mind. Searching, probing, scouring, desperate to unveil what remained hidden to them in the city of tents. She gripped her daughter's hand tight, so tight she could feel the throbbing of her daughter's heartbeat in her palm.

Little Astoria did not know why her mother had snuck her out of their tent in the middle of the night. She did not know what creatures might lurk behind the skin of any one of their tribesmen, waiting to crawl out and devour her.

Together, mother and daughter crept through the city, weaving from shadow to shadow. The mother prayed the creatures would not find her until her daughter was safe, but the sun goddess of the Yan Avii had turned her face from the world.

Astoria yawned, then covered her mouth with her tiny hand.

She's seen only seven summers, thought the mother. It pained her to think of what she had to do, but she could not keep her daughter a secret any longer. It was not safe.

Astoria did not know what hunted her because she did not yet understand the New World. She did not know of the ancient vows that had been sworn by ancient rulers, nor of the vile creatures that had been molded by them, molded for only one purpose—to eradicate Astoria's kind from the world.

Fear wrapped its fingers around the mother's throat, and she held still. She could sense the creatures again. They were searching all across the makeshift City Upon the Steppe. They had sensed magic, and they would not leave until their hunger was sated.

It did not matter that the Yan Avii were no longer part of the empire. The creatures did not abide by treaties or boundary lines. They knew only the purpose for which they had been bred. Astoria had used magic, and they had come for her.

A tenuous cloud slithered across the sky, shrouding the twin moons of the New World. A blessing from the gods. The mother imagined the Sisters were whispering to her as they cast the world in shadow. She could almost hear their voices on the wind. *Be brave, good mother, be swift.*

The mother seized the moment and hurried down the dark lanes through the labyrinth of tents, tugging her daughter along behind her.

Astoria shivered. Her tiny hand trembled in her mother's palm. Astoria wore only a cotton shift, which barely reached her knees and left too much of her bony shoulders bare. The mother wished she had thought to grab her daughter's cloak, but there had been no time.

Such a lovely thing, her daughter's magic, an innocent thing. Astoria had used her gift for good. She had saved the boy. But the creatures came for her, all the same.

The cloud passed, and the Sisters rejoined their thousand daughters in their nightlong dance across the sky, bathing the tent city in iridescent light. But the momentary darkness had been enough.

At the edge of the Yan Avii tent city, the mother reached the tent she sought. The flap fell behind them, shielding them from watching eyes, though the creatures relied upon another sense. The mother felt their minds again, but she would not have to ward them off much longer. Her daughter was nearly safe.

The merchant was so burly he seemed to fill the tent. His smile was crooked like his heart, the mother had no doubt. Her own heart shuddered at what she had to do.

Sweat beaded from the merchant's bald, fat head. Piercings lined the left side of his face from jaw to earlobe, threaded by a golden chain. His robes were blue like the glaciers of the mother's homeland, woven of fine silk, and she knew he had not attained that wealth from dealing in spices.

"Who's he?" Astoria muttered sleepily.

The merchant grinned, but he let the mother explain.

"He's… an old friend, my dear. He is going to look after you. You must go with him."

Realization dawned on Astoria's face. Her eyes widened. Her lips trembled. "Go with him where?"

"Somewhere safe."

"Y-you're coming too?"

The mother shook her head. The merchant's chest heaved with silent laughter. *How many times has he witnessed such treachery, to find the betrayal of a mother so amusing?*

"W-where are you going?" said Astoria.

The mother choked back a sob. She knelt and pulled her daughter close, and Astoria's tears soaked through her tunic. "Far away, my love," said the mother.

"I w-want to go with you."

"You can't. My friend will keep you safe. You must be strong, my love. You must trust me."

"I trust you," Astoria told her mother, straightening up bravely.

She's strong, thought the mother. *Too strong. This is the only way.*

Astoria did not realize that her mother did not even know the merchant's name. She did not understand when the man gave her mother a handful of coins in the exchange. The merchant took hold of Astoria's hand, and the mother let go, biting her lip until it bled to keep from crying.

"We move out at first light," the merchant said.

The mother handed him back the coins. "Leave tonight. Leave now."

The merchant raised a dark brow, but he did not question her. His golden tooth shone when he smiled. His fingers closed around the coins. "As you say. Come, little girl. We'll wake my friends, and then, we will go."

"Her name is Tori," said the mother. It was what the village children called her. It sounded unassuming and common. Her true name betrayed its Old World origins. The mother feared anything, even a name, might draw attention to her daughter.

"Come then, Tori."

Astoria held on to the merchant's thick hand, and they left to wake his friends. The chain on the side of his face jingled lightly. His friends would be wearing chains too, the mother knew, though not on their faces. Soon, her daughter would wear chains as well. Astoria looked back one last time, her tawny face streaked with tears.

The mother managed a feeble smile. "Be brave, my love."

The tent flap fell, separating them forever. Mother and daughter, blood of the same magical blood, no more.

"I'm sorry," the mother murmured to the vacant tent. Her heart collapsed inside the hollow cave of her chest.

Astoria was gone. But there was no time to mourn. Her daughter was not safe yet.

Her own magic was of the realm of minds, and it was important Astoria forget the things she could do. As she hurried from the merchant's tent, the mother reached out with her sense, found her daughter's mind, and reached inside. One by one, she removed the memories that made Astoria who she was, what she was. Each one brought tears. She was robbing her own daughter, but it was the only way.

She hurried to finish, hoping it was enough. Already, the mother felt the creatures coming. They had sensed her magic, as they had sensed her daughter's before.

But this time, the mother opened herself to their sense, and their minds washed over her, pulsing with hunger and anticipation. They had crossed the world for this.

The creatures changed their skins and flew toward her, soaring on black wings. The mother rose from the ground and flew to meet them, soaring with no wings at all. Only magic. Tears ran down her cheeks in cold, meteoric streaks as she flew across the city, as she flew to die.

Her blood rained down upon the city of tents. Her body fell like a star. The creatures fell like crows, and they sated their hunger.

But the mother greeted the gods with grateful tears.

Her daughter was safe. That was all she had asked of them.

Astoria was safe.

PART ONE
THE GALLOWS

In those days, the chancellors were the only gods. The old gods abandoned us long ago, and their Watchers along with them. Our gods were cruel, and they demanded blood. But all that changed the day of the Gallows.

—from *New Histories of the Old World*

CHAPTER ONE

The Year 322 N.W.
Fifth Year of the Reign of Cyrus Maro

The gallows loomed over them like a slaver's rod as the servants prepared the city square for the chancellor's drafting ceremony. The mighty towers of Maro'El cast long shadows over the square in the fading light, and Tori Burodai's breath hung heavy in the winter air, mixing with flurries of snow that lashed at her face with each gust of the wind. Her fingers felt like they might shatter as she hoisted the wooden beams upon her shoulder. The tips of her gloves were cut off so she could hold the beams in place while Darien Redvar pounded in the spikes. Her fingers were red and swollen, but the pain would end soon enough. The gallows was nearly finished.

Tori rubbed her hands together vigorously, then reached for another beam, muttering curses beneath her breath.

"You froze yet, Tori?" Darien pounded the spikes home with a mallet, which sent jarring aches through Tori's wrists as she held the beam still.

She bit down on her tongue. "I'll survive."

"Your fingers are icicles." Darien stopped her, wrapped her hands with his own, and blew warm breath on them. The sudden heat stung.

Tori pulled her hands away. "Look, the sooner we're done, the sooner we'll be beside the commander's fires. Let's just finish this bloody thing."

Tori hoisted another beam from the stockpile, and Darien retrieved more spikes. Darien was stronger—though Tori would never admit it to his face. He ought to have been the one holding the heavy beams upon his shoulders. Tori's muscles were firm, and she had always held her own in a scrap, but her body was small and her limbs slender. But the labor of hoisting the heavy beams warmed her up a little, and besides, she couldn't hold the spikes in place if she couldn't feel them. And the last thing she needed today was for her hand to slip and the mallet to shatter her fingers. Darien's hands never faltered. He was a native of the high peaks of Klavash, accustomed to bitter cold, and he pounded the thick nails in with calculated precision.

Tori and Darien had served Commander Scelero faithfully for three years, and for this servitude, they did not complain. Unlike many of the Oshan nobles, Commander Scelero was a decent master. But even he could do nothing when the chancellor required service. Every Lord House was required to send servants to prepare the city of Maro'El for the ceremony.

Tori was glad she and Darien had been sent to the square together. Last year, she'd been forced to work with a whiny housemaid named Ela. The taskmasters had threatened to whip her. It always amazed Tori the way a few months working indoors made the maids think they were somehow above hard labor.

Tori heaved another beam, but Darien paused, gazing up at the overhang that had taken shape.

"You all right?" she asked.

Darien shook his head, but returned to their task. "As if sending us to fight their civil war weren't enough. To make us build the very thing that keeps us in line, it's cruel." Darien had never been summoned for square duty before. There were times Tori worried her friend was too soft for a servant's life. His people were peaceful mountain folk who avoided conflict. Her own people, the Yan Avii, were warriors. They lived in the harsh climate of the Steppe, changing camps whenever the herds had eaten the grass down to dirt, or the weather turned too cold. The Burodai had fought with more than one neighboring tribe during her childhood.

But Tori did not like to think of those days. "That's the whole point. The nobles can make us freeze to stone out here, only to send us to die. And we'll thank them all the same. We've had it worse than this. You know it, and so do they." Tori's years in the Fringes had shown her far crueler faces than those of the Oshan nobles. She had it easy serving in Maro'El, and Darien's talk could land him back in the Fringes in an instant if overheard by a guard looking to gain favor with the nobles.

Darien drove in another spike, harder this time. Tori's shoulder ached with each pound.

Only four more beams, she told herself.

Tori had attended two drafting ceremonies since joining the commander's household, but she had never seen the gallows used. It was a symbol. Servants did the nobles' bidding, whether it was changing their linens or fighting their wars. Defectors would be executed. Darien paused again, as a servant from House Fedra fixed the noose of rope to the overhanging beam.

Tori brushed his shoulder. "We won't be drawn." She said it confidently, willing it to be so, more for him than for herself, but if she was honest, she feared the draft as well. Being drafted into the chancellor's Night Legions was as close to a death sentence as you could get. And even if they didn't die physically, the soldiers' minds were never the same. The indoctrination of the Legions was notoriously rigorous. Their expressions were always hard. Even their gait was rigid, as though they were automatons controlled by some dark spell. No one disobeyed orders, at least none that Tori had ever heard of.

Darien sighed. "If we're not drawn this war, then it'll be the next. What difference does it make?"

Tori glanced around nervously. *He shouldn't be talking like this,* she thought. But Darien always got bitter around the draft. They set back to work on another beam.

"I could never go on the chancellor's raids and slaughter innocents, conditioned to think it's right."

"You do what you got to survive," said Tori. "That's the way the world is." *I learned that much from my mum.*

Darien turned to her, his weathered copper face twisting into a dark grimace from beneath his cloak. "You don't believe that."

"I believe you alive is better than you dead."

"And what of the soldiers who killed my family? Were they better alive?"

Darien's family had been killed in a skirmish in Klavash four years before. Neither the chancellor's Night Legions nor the Morgathian rebels paid the mountain tribes any mind. Just one more casualty caught in the middle of the fire.

"The dead don't speak," Tori said. "We're survivors. We do whatever it takes. Most likely, the only people we'd face are Morgathians who wanted to shoot our heads off, anyway."

Darien stared past her. "You really think you could do it? Kill?"

If Tori had learned anything during her years in the Fringes, it was that death was a part of life, just like betrayal and injustice. Tori had accepted this fact. "I'll do what I have to, and so will you. But I'm hoping for plenty more years before we have to find out. We won't be drawn," she repeated.

"Hurry up!" bellowed one of the guards monitoring the gallows construction. Thom, a member of their master's personal guard, stood beside a simmering fire, his musket draped over the crook of his arm. Even amongst servants, there were hierarchies.

What's he got to hurry for? thought Tori. With raw fingers, she retrieved the final beam of the gallows. Darien pounded the last of the spikes, and then Thom led Commander Scelero's servants back through the city.

The sun dipped below the horizon and the shadows grew. All around, tall spires jutted up into the darkening heavens like bony fingers, and at the center of them all, the White Citadel towered ever higher. A remnant of the Old World, the crystal palace shimmered in the lamplight of the city and disappeared into the looming clouds. The citadel had survived countless wars and even the magical devastation of the age before; it was rumored to have been built by the Watchers of old, forged by magic, like in her mum's old stories.

Tori pushed the thought aside. Her mum had done nothing but lie to her. There was no such thing as magic. The citadel was nothing but an old tower, built to last.

Commander Scelero's estate sat on the northwestern end of the city, beneath the shadow of the White Citadel. Its grounds stretched several city blocks, and his mansion, located at the center, stood four stories. Of course, it revealed only a fraction of the commander's wealth. Like all Oshan nobles, he owned land across Greater Osha. Hundreds of servants tended his fields, and dozens of villages paid fealty for using his lands.

Thom ushered them through the wrought iron gates of the estate, and once the gates were closed, he hurried off to the warmth of the guard tower.

"You should've accepted Scelero's offer. To make you a guard," said Tori as they made for the servant quarters. Truth be told, Tori had thought him a fool for declining. She had labored to the bone to gain favor with Scelero with no such fortune. Sure, she had worked her way up from cleaning the privies, but she was still only a kitchen maid.

"Why?" Darien asked. "So I could sit by a fire and watch everyone else work?"

"At least, then, one guard in this city wouldn't be a complete horse's ass."

They laughed, and it made Tori glad to see Darien smile, if only briefly. His moods got so dismal on drafting days.

They went their separate ways. Tori hurried to change out of her damp breeches and into her serving uniform, a drab blue gown with a white apron. But it was made of wool and kept her warm, and so she did not complain. She tied her dark hair back, the act eased by the thawing of her fingers. She donned her woolen cloak, then returned to work, crossing the courtyard to the kitchens to help prepare supper. And after supper, Scelero would reveal who amongst his servants had been chosen to serve in the Night Legions. Tori tried not to think of it.

Ol' Merri, the head of the kitchens, and half a dozen others were already hard at work on the festivities when Tori arrived.

"You're late," said Ol' Merri, crossing her arms across her substantial bosom. Though only in her thirties, everyone called Merri old. It had begun as a jest long ago, after her auburn hair began specking with premature grey in her youth, and the name stuck. Probably because she had the sass of someone much older.

"Sorry, Mum," said Tori. "The gallows went slow today."

Merri scowled. "Ah, I forgot they sent you ter prepare the gallows again this year. Well an' good, dearie, but make yourself useful an' fetch them loaves out o' the oven."

Tori did. She minced fruits and boiled potatoes and set the tables in the great hall.

Ol' Merri flitted around the kitchen, snapping orders in her firm but kind way. But there was a razor's edge to her tone when Piper dropped a whole tray of loaves on her way to set the tables.

"S-sorry! It was an accident," Piper said, brushing away tears after Merri left the great hall in an angry huff.

"It's her last draft," said Tori, helping Piper gather the ruined loaves. "The last year she's eligible for conscription. Merri's nervous and ready to be done with it all, and no one can blame her for that. Got nothing to do with those loaves."

Piper nodded, but nevertheless, Tori handled the remainder of the food, and Piper stuck to setting silverware and tablecloths. *She wouldn't last a day in the Legions,* Tori thought darkly.

———

Before the draft, Commander Scelero let his servants eat like highborn Oshans. The servants were given a fine meal of baked bread, roasted pork, and potatoes. Always potatoes. They were the staple of the North. But on the night of the draft, Scelero pulled out a delicacy: pies loaded with fruits imported from the Trium'vel—apples and lemons and peaches that melted on the tongue, warm and sweet. The commander drew no attention to his kindness, but the meal occurred every draft like a ritual. A small gesture of gratitude to his servants and a grim farewell to those who would be sent to war.

The great hall teemed with feasting servants, and despite the coming draft, the mood of the room was generally amiable. They ate warm food at polished oaken tables set with fine silver. Colorful tapestries, normally reserved for honored guests, lined the walls, and a minstrel played humorous songs as he danced around the hall. But like a solemn reminder, at the center of the room hung the Oshan standard—a white tower set against a field of glacier blue. The same tower had been tattooed on Tori's left shoulder upon her arrival in Maro'El, yet another reminder that Tori was not her own. She belonged to a lord from a foreign power. That was her lot in life, thanks to her mum. Tori had always resented her lot, but she had quickly learned it accomplished little to resent something out of her control.

Darien arrived late from tending the horses in the stables, and he kept quiet during supper, which made it increasingly difficult for Tori to enjoy the delicious food. The rest of the room was abuzz, servants milling about the hall, slopping loads of food upon their plates, returning for seconds and thirds.

Commander Scelero sat at the head of the hall, accompanied by Fredrick, his estate manager, and Sergeant Keller, the head of his personal guard. Though young for his rank, Commander Scelero had still not married, and Tori sometimes wondered if that was why he treated his servants so well. They were all the family he had. Though only a few years older, Ol' Merri often joked that she'd practically weaned him herself, and he always smiled at the jest. Though kind, his smiles were rare. His pale face was shaved smooth, his dark hair trimmed short and neat. His features were rigid and calculated, the demeanor expected of a man who commanded legions, but on the occasions he smiled, the entire wretched world felt like it might one day turn brighter.

I'm lucky to serve here, Tori thought as she ate her pie. The other servants of Maro'El were likely feasting on stale porridge, not fresh meats and pies.

Darien stared at his plate, the crisp lemon pie growing cold. Tori touched his arm, and he managed a slight smile. His mood was worse this year.

"You've got nothing to worry about," she assured him.

Darien pushed away his plate. "You can't promise something like that, so don't."

"What's wrong?"

"I'm sorry," he said, holding her gaze. "I didn't tell you earlier. I didn't want you to worry. But I overheard Sergeant Keller this morning. The rebellion is getting worse down south. There's rumors the chancellor is taking double recruits from each Lord House this year."

Tori's stomach knotted up. Every draft, it was always two. That was how Tori and Darien had entered Scelero's household, chosen out of a long line of Fringe rats to replace a pair of servants who had been drafted.

After her mother abandoned her, Tori was sold to a spice merchant in the Trium'vel—the trade cities of the Far South. She learned the subtleties of a quiet housemaid, but her Trium master was the gambling sort of trader, and Tori and a dozen others were lost in a bad deal. Her new master brought her to the Fringes of Greater Osha, where she served in the textile houses, and where she received the spiraling thorn pattern of tattoos on her left forearm. Tori had survived that hellhole for four years.

At seventeen, this was her third draft, and one day, she knew Commander Scelero would journey to the Fringes to choose a servant to take *her* place. When the time came, she would hold her head high, and she would do what it took to survive. But Darien… she hoped his day was far off. "Double recruits?" she managed at last.

"There's only forty of us in Scelero's household. Not very good odds."

"I… I'm sure it's just a rumor." But Tori lost her appetite as well. The two of them sat quietly through the remainder of supper.

Darien was tall, and at eighteen, his muscles filled his loose servant's cloak. The draft was purportedly random among able-bodied servants between the ages of sixteen and thirty-five, but Tori feared for Darien more now than ever. If he had been born Oshan, he would already be training in the academies to be an officer. He was an obvious choice for the Night Legions.

"Ol' Merri survived all those drafts," Tori offered hopefully. "We can too."

"Merri's name is still alongside yours and mine," said Darien darkly.

"I hope we get drawn together, then." Tori whispered it like it was a dark secret, like saying it too loud might make it so. "We wouldn't let them mold our brains. We'd fight it. We'd survive, like always."

Darien shook his head, his golden eyes narrowing. "I hope you end up like Merri."

A soldier entered the hall, and the whole room fell silent. The man was bedecked with leathern armor, a red sash draped across his shoulders. Emblazoned on the scarlet field were two intertwining wisps of shadow, like twin black serpents—the emblem of the Night Legions. The man bore four scrolls that would decide their fates. He handed them to Commander Scelero, and just as quickly, he was gone again, off to deliver more conscriptions.

Scelero rose from his seat, and the servants followed suit. "Servants of House Scelero," said the commander solemnly, "I am grateful for your honest labor and your resilient spirits. The time has come for some of you to serve a cause greater than my own. Due to the intensifying threat of the Morgathian rebellion in the South, the chancellor's War Council has decided to double the recruits this year."

There were a few gasps. Darien looked at the ground, but Tori stood tall. She grabbed his hand. His fingers felt like the bodies of dead icefish.

"Four of you will receive the honor of serving our great empire," continued Scelero. "Tomorrow, at the chancellor's ceremony, you four will help form a new legion of Shadows to defend the realm. There is truly no greater honor."

The commander was not one for unnecessary words, so he went right into the names.

"Hollen Byndi." A member of the commander's personal guard, the young man rose to his feet. The other guards saluted him, and he joined the commander at his table. "Thank you for your service. May you serve the empire well."

"Gordon Duvre." The stable boy was slapped on the shoulder by the boys sitting near him, but his wide eyes betrayed his fear. "Thank you for your service. May you serve the empire well."

Commander Scelero paused at the third name. "Merri Kyrsted." Ol' Merri rose to her feet slowly. Her lips trembled. The woman was Morgathian herself; her greying red hair and sun-specked skin gave her heritage away at a glance. She would be fighting her own people in the chancellor's war. "You've served my household longer than any other in this room. Thank you for your service. May you... serve the empire well."

The commander straightened himself up for the last name. "Lastly, the Legions summon Darien Redvar."

Tori's body tensed all over. Something surged within her, fury and bitterness and sorrow... and something more. Something strange swelled deep inside her. She felt as though her veins might explode. She wanted to kill the guards, grab Darien, and flee. But Darien let go of her hand, and the feeling subsided.

Darien stepped forward to face his fate.

CHAPTER TWO

On the day Commander Scelero selected them for servanthood, Tori and Darien stood side by side in a much larger crowd of servants. The slumlands of the Fringes teemed with lowborns from all over the world. Thousands of them gathered in that cesspool seeking the hope of servitude for some noble. Most ended up slaving for the workhouses and salt mines, but on occasion, the nobles came looking for new field hands, and even guards and kitchen maids. So Tori and Darien's taskmaster cleaned them up and stood them in a great long line. One by one, the nobles passed them by for stronger brutes and prettier maidens.

But when Commander Scelero strode down the line, Tori could sense something different. The memory was engraved on Tori's mind. His eyes were green, like a meadow in springtime, like the eyes Tori had inherited from her Oshan mother. His face was hardened by years of war, but his expression softened when he saw her. She couldn't explain it.

"You look malnourished," he said gruffly.

Fourteen-year-old Tori stood tall. "I can work, milord. I can do anything you like. I learnt to live on little, and that's made me strong."

A hint of a smile crossed Scelero's face. "Made you stubborn, more like."

His gaze fixed on Darien then. Even at fifteen, Darien had been strong. He worked to the bone in the salt mines, and despite years of hunger and overwork, the commander saw his potential. "I'll take the boy," Scelero said to their taskmaster.

It took everything inside Tori to let go of Darien's hand. Her friend stepped forward, but then looked back to her.

"I-I can't go, milord," Darien said.

"That's not how it works, boy!" cried the taskmaster, a large grimy man named Kresta, who brandished a thick rod for unruly slaves.

"Afraid he's right, son," said Scelero, waving the taskmaster away. "If I want you, I can take you."

"Please, sir. N-not without—"

"Darien, shut your trap!" Tori cried. "Ignore him, milord. He's going. He *wants* to go. Please, don't change your mind. He's got to go with you!"

Warmth spread across the commander's face. "She your sister, boy?"

"Close to a sister as you can get, milord. I know she looks scrawny, but she's strong. Up here." Darien pointed to his head. "She'll learn to do anything you ask her, and do it ten times better than anyone else, I swear it."

The taskmaster gave the commander a querulous look, his rod resting on his shoulder. The line of nobles was being held up, and they were not pleased.

"I'll take them both," Scelero said.

———

Now, Darien had been chosen again, but there was no hope of Tori going with him this time. He made his way to the front of Scelero's hall. Tori reached for the empty space where his hand had been.

"Thank you for your service, Darien," recited the commander.

"May you serve the empire well." Scelero shook the hands of all four of his servants. Then, he addressed the room.

"Tomorrow morning, we will join all the Lord Houses in Maro Square for the drafting ceremony, where we will say farewell to them for the last time. Until then, enjoy the feast. Good night."

The commander left his servants alone in the great hall. There was a rush to greet the chosen four. The guards actually had the audacity to congratulate them, patting the new recruits on the back. The other servants expressed condolences and wishes for safety and victory, all the while inwardly thanking their gods that they had not been the ones chosen. That was how Tori had felt as well at previous drafts. But not this time. *I should be going with him.*

Darien pushed his way through the crowd, thanking the well-wishers, but he made for the door as fast as he could manage. Tori intercepted him across the hall.

Darien's face was empty. "Look, I… I don't want to talk about it, Tori."

Tori took his hand. "Then we won't talk. We'll drink."

She led him away from the hall. The rest of the evening, the servants would be feasting in the great hall. No one would mind them roaming the grounds. "You remember where we stashed it?" she asked when they reached the courtyard. The snow was starting to pile high. By morning, it would be past Tori's knees.

"The far stall." A smile teased at the edge of Darien's lips.

The stables were on the opposite end of the estate, and they trudged through the snow, careless of the tracks that marked their way. The far stall was always empty, generally used to store tack and feed. Darien stooped to the floor and pried back a board in the corner, producing a flask half-filled with wine. They had drunk much of it the previous year when their friend Ollie had been drafted.

Tori popped it open and took a long swig. It tasted a little sour, but it warmed her throat as it went down. She raised the flask. "To Ollie."

Darien took it and drank. "To Ollie."

For some time, they didn't talk; they just passed the flask back and forth, drinking it down fast so it would hit them hard. As the wine ran its course, they found words. Happy words. They reminisced about escapades and close calls in the Fringes. Like the time they inadvertently stole from a slumlord and nearly ended up skewered by one of his cronies.

Darien laughed. "It was your idea to hide in the funeral pyres."

"Gods, it smelled like—well, corpses!" The smell was forever imprinted on her memory, and it came rushing back anytime she smelled spoiling meat outside the butcheries.

"You were brilliant," Darien said, his shoulder resting against her own. "I'd have been dead a long time ago if it weren't for you."

Tori knew it was true. Darien had been scared and alone when he first arrived in the Fringes, but that was not what he needed to hear now. "Don't be an idiot. You were as tough as me. We helped each other. And anyway, you're not nearly drunk enough to be talking so serious."

Darien smiled. "All right, then." They reminisced some more. Darien joked about running away and swimming across the Sound, back to the Fringes, but Tori knew that even a soldier's life was better than that hellhole. Even death on some battlefield was better.

They leaned against a sack of feed, passing the flask. But far too soon, the wine ran out, and the effects dwindled like the coals of a fire. Tori laid her head against Darien's shoulder, wishing against the morning when they would say goodbye, likely for the last time. Again, she wished she had been the one to be drafted. *He's not made for a soldier's life.*

Ever since Darien had arrived at the workhouse in the Fringes, the two of them had been close. Tori had taught Darien to pickpocket, and he'd taught her how to hunt rats. They survived together.

They had never been more than friends, though. Servants in Maro'El were not allowed such pleasures. A pregnant servant was a burden no master, not even Commander Scelero, desired. But Tori always felt the odds of both of them being selected in the same year by the same nobleman were insurmountable. Coming to serve the commander had only drawn them closer. It was as though they were meant to remain together, to keep one another strong, as though the old gods themselves had paired them. Tori always wondered what they would have been in another life, in some other land, where they were the highborns with a say in their lives. Would they have fallen in love? Had a family?

Tori imagined it would still be a secret affair. She would be promised to some lordling, and Darien would be her midnight paramour. Even in her imagination, it was something forbidden. None of that mattered now. Tomorrow, he would be gone.

Darien's eyes were closed. He looked handsome in the lantern light, his cheeks ruddy from the wine, a bit of stubble specking his jaw. His hair would need to be trimmed, but he already had the stature and firm features of a proper soldier. Tori kissed his cheek.

"What was that?" he said, sitting up.

"For… another life," she said. She still felt warm from the wine. Or maybe it was Darien's warmth.

Darien shook his head with a smile. "In another life, we never would have met. I wouldn't trade it." He leaned forward, kissed her forehead, and that was all.

Tori knew it was for the best. As her head slowly cleared, sadness overwhelmed her. Darien was leaving. Leaving forever. But she couldn't let herself tear up. She had to be strong. Darien needed her to be strong. She pressed into his shoulder, and he wrapped his arm around her, and they fell asleep in the far stall.

———

When Tori woke, it was morning, and Darien had gone.

She hurried outside, worried that somehow she might have missed the commotion of the household leaving for the chancellor's drafting ceremony. But outside, the horizon was just turning with the colors of the rising sun. She made for the kitchens to find Ol' Merri already hard at work on the morning's porridge.

The woman looked weary, as though she'd not slept. "What's got you up so early, dearie?"

"Couldn't sleep, Mum."

"Ah," said Ol' Merri. "The draft, en't it?" Tori nodded. "You an' that boy're close. I could always tell that."

Tori managed a weak smile. "Why isn't someone else cooking? You're leaving too."

Ol' Merri's face tightened. "Well, why don't you help me, then? Stir this pot while I fetch them loaves out o' the oven. It'll take your mind off it, doing something useful."

Tori took a giant wooden ladle and slowly stirred the porridge, letting it thicken and curdle. "That why you're down here? To do something useful?"

Merri set down a hot pan of loaves to cool. "Always did love these kitchens. Sure, I could've had someone else make breakfast terday, but when it's something you love, well… might as well do it one last time." Merri cut up the loaves and tossed them in a basket to serve. "An' I was awake as a ghost all night, anyway."

"Will you go?" said Tori. "When they call you at the ceremony?"

"Will I defect, you mean? Rather than go ter war against my own people?" Merri laughed. "Nah! Tori, no one defects."

Tori hoped that would remain so. She kept thinking of what Darien had said, about not doing what was done to his family. Yesterday, it was talk. It meant something different now that he'd been drafted.

"I'm a white-knuckle survivor, dearie," said Merri. "An' I'll be damned if I don't keep right on clinging by my nails ter the bitter end. I'll tell you what, though, if I was going ter go down, I wouldn't do it at no drafting ceremony. I'd wait for the right moment, an' I'd take as many o' them bloody—oh gods! You'll burn it, stirring so slow! Gimme that!"

Ol' Merri snatched the ladle back and stirred the porridge herself. "Nah, dearie, I reckon I'll join up like the lot o' them. An' you'd be blessed ter do the same when your own time comes. If it en't you, it's someone else. But you can't do no one a lick o' good if you're dead—porridge is done." Ol' Merri poured some in a bowl and set it before Tori with a mug of goat's milk. "Check an' be sure it en't burnt now." She cackled to herself.

Tori took a small bite and then stirred the rest around the bowl aimlessly with her spoon.

"You want ter know why I really like it down here in the kitchen so early?" Ol' Merri said, taking up her own bowl of porridge. "Ah, now that en't bad. Reckon you didn't stir it too slow, after all."

Tori took another bite. The porridge warmed her body as it eased down her throat. She leaned over the bowl, letting the steam evaporate on her face.

"Every morning, I cook. An' down here in the quiet, it's just me for a while. I can be alone an' pray, ter the All Mother an' All Father. The high gods o' the Old World."

Tori tensed at the mention of the old gods. Oshans prided themselves on being devoted to no gods. They were above such Old World superstitions, and it was what set them apart from the rest of the world. If there was a god in Osha, it was the chancellor. Tori's people worshipped Arayeva, the goddess of the sun. The Morgathian rebels had their fire god, and there had been many gods in the Trium'vel. The old gods, though…

They stirred up dark memories from her past. Tori's mum had worshipped the old gods too, burning incense in their tent and kneeling on a woven rug. *And look where those gods got me,* she thought bitterly. But she didn't voice it. Merri had enough to worry about.

"You pray you'll survive the war?" Tori asked.

"Well, yes. But even more, I pray that one day—maybe in my lifetime, maybe in yours—their Watchers will return."

Tori jerked up from her bowl at the mention of the Watchers, nearly spilling her porridge. "You shouldn't speak of them, Merri."

Ol' Merri smiled. "The old chancellors may have killed 'em off in the War Between the Worlds, but they can't stop my prayers. One day, the Ancient Ones will send the Watchers back ter free us. Ter make things right in the world again."

"Don't waste your prayers." At the sound of Darien's voice, Tori and Ol' Merri leapt in their seats.

Ol' Merri spilled porridge on her apron and cursed. "Don't you sneak up on an ol' cook like that, son. I'll spill this down your shirt, next time."

"Sorry, Mum." Darien's voice was somber. "You want to pray for something? Pray the chancellor catches the plague, or a chandelier falls on his head. Something possible."

"The plague. Ha!"

"He's right," said Tori. "The chancellors banished magic. The Metamorphi killed all the… Watchers." Fearful tales of the shapeshifting magic hunters of Osha were told all across the New World.

Ol' Merri raised an eyebrow. "Mmmm… well, then your guess is as good as anything, en't it?"

Darien shook his head. "You don't really believe those children's tales, do you? The Watchers are nothing but myths. Like the gods and the shaman summoners of the White North. Stories the Fringe rats tell their starving littles to get them to sleep. If the Watchers ever did exist, they're long dead."

"An' what do *you* know?" said Ol' Merri. "Hmmm? You're barely a man!"

"I'm eighteen," said Darien.

"Ah, I stand corrected." Ol' Merri chuckled to herself. "Boy, you live as long as me, you get ter seeing there's things that can't be explained in this world."

"Way I see it," said Darien, taking up his own bowl of porridge, "you'll be called up at that drafting ceremony, same as me. There's no explaining needed about that."

Merri went quiet.

Tori could have hit him, but she held back. That was not how she wanted their last day to go. And besides, blunt as he'd been, she knew Darien was right. Hoping in gods and Watchers was useless.

"Rest'll be down in a minute," said Merri solemnly. "I got ter go set them tables for the last time. We report ter the square in an hour."

Ol' Merri hurried off, muttering to herself.

Tori and Darien ate their porridge and bread in silence, the weight of the day stifling any conversation they attempted. Darien stared off at the wall, his eyes blank, his mind elsewhere. Tori had the strange sense that she was eating breakfast with a dead man.

CHAPTER THREE

Snow rode upon the wind and bit at Tori's skin as Scelero's servants joined the throng in Maro Square. Thousands of servants in orderly lines, sorted by their Lord House, made their way to the stage they had helped build beneath the shadow of the White Citadel. The empty gallows loomed over every corner of the square. Darien never left Tori's side, but they both remained silent as they marched. It had been the same when Ollie was drafted last year. What could you say when the world revealed its true, cruel face?

Tori squeezed Darien's hand, wishing she were going with him. Her fists clenched as she pictured her friend in the Shadow Camps, learning to spar, to fire a musket. To kill.

The servants of Maro'El stood in the cold for some time. Tori stamped her feet to keep warm, watching as the stage slowly filled with lords and ladies dressed in thick fur cloaks. Lesser nobles and their families watched from towers above the square. And then, Cyrus Maro appeared.

The chancellor was clothed in thick white furs, and in his hand, he held a large scroll that had determined the fates of hundreds. Darien's life reduced to a scribble on a bit of parchment. The chancellor held up his hands, and Tori joined the rest of the city kneeling before their ruler.

It was the third time Tori had seen Cyrus Maro; nevertheless, the sight of him made her entire body tense. She was struck by how young he was for someone so powerful. The chancellor had only been sixteen when his father died, thrusting him into power shortly before Tori came to Maro'El. His hair was blond and drooped to his brow, his face was ghostly white and shaved perfectly smooth, and his teeth shone like snow-capped mountain peaks. There was something terrifyingly beautiful about him.

Histories claimed that the First Chancellor had rid magic from the world so that humanity could rebuild after the devastation of the legendary War Between the Worlds. Cyrus Maro was the sixteenth Chancellor of Osha, and he was feared more than any other ruler in the New World. Standing beside a roaring fire at a podium set before the gallows, the chancellor unrolled the scroll of names for the draft of Maro'El. Darien gripped Tori's hand tighter. She shivered, even in her cloak and woolen gloves.

"Good morning." The chancellor's greeting was so soft and casual, it was menacing. "Many of you, on this momentous occasion, will receive the honor of joining the valiant quests of the Night Legions. Together, we will continue to spread our grand empire across the New World. Together, we will crush King Hollsted's rebellion, once and for all!"

King Hollsted had once been a general in the Night Legions. Tori remembered the bitter murmurs among the servants when Hollsted joined the Morgathians to incite this civil war. War meant more servants would be drafted than usual. Now, as Hollsted's name left the chancellor's lips, he did not try to hide his own disdain for the traitor. The square shook with the angry cries of vengeance the chancellor expected. Nobles shook their fists from their balconies, and the servants shouted dutifully along with them from the snow-covered streets.

Cyrus Maro raised his hands for silence. "Today, it is *your* chance to rise, to serve our great empire, to make a name for yourself. Today, we raise up the next brave legion of Shadows. I thank the lords and ladies for their generous contributions." Tori hated the way the chancellor used soft, sterile words to describe the deathly fates of human beings the empire deemed lower in value—barbarians, tribals, peasants. No highborns were drawn for service. They served only as officers, trained at noble academies in the arts of military strategy. "Now, the time has come to welcome those who have received this great honor of service."

With that, the chancellor began reading names. The first, Tori recognized—a stableboy from House Fedra. The boy trudged to the front of the crowd and was greeted on-stage by his master, who handed him over to one of the generals in the Night Legions. A young girl, barely of age, followed. When Fedra was finished, it was House Dragonis, and then House Tindeir and House Wallis.

Tori spotted Commander Scelero on the stage, seated near the gallows. Scelero's face betrayed no emotion. He looked on dutifully. When his Lord House was called, Tori knew, he would shake his servants' hands, they would join the Legion ranks, and it would be done. In a few days, he would journey to the Fringes to purchase a new boy to take Darien's place. And so, the world turned on and on.

The stage was soon filled with new recruits. Over one hundred men and women had been called, and there were many Lord Houses that remained. Tori's feet were going numb inside her boots. Darien's hands trembled, whether from the cold or from fear, Tori did not know. She wanted this to be over, for Darien's sake more than anything.

Finally, the chancellor spoke the words: "From House Scelero…"

Tori stared forward, fighting back tears. She did not know how to say goodbye. The people she cared for usually just disappeared from her life. Darien's face bore no expression.

Hollen and Gordon were the first to be called, and then, Ol' Merri. Tori feared the portly woman would not last long in the Legions. Commander Scelero stepped forward to meet her, slower than usual. The commander shook Ol' Merri's hand, held it gently, and led her to her new master, a general of the Legions.

"Lastly, from House Scelero… Darien Redvar."

Tori stopped breathing. The old gods wrapped their hands around her throat. Darien's grip went limp on Tori's arm. Her gut twisted. He took hold of her hand, and she realized he was saying goodbye. Their eyes met for a moment. The last moment. *Say something,* she thought. *Anything.*

"Be brave," she said, unsure what compelled her to echo the last words her mother had spoken to her.

Darien nodded, his expression grim, but there was something off in his eyes. A strange fire. He still had not moved.

"Darien Redvar," the chancellor said again. It was eerie how calm the man was.

"What are you doing?" Tori said. "You've got to go!"

Darien shook his head. "I told you. I can't do what they did to my family."

"No," Tori hissed. "Don't you dare!"

Everyone in the city was watching them now. Tori felt like a great stone had been placed on her chest. The tears were starting to fall now. Darien squeezed her hand one last time, and then he stepped forward without another word. He weaved decisively through the crowd, no falter in his step.

This can't be happening! she thought helplessly. He would never defect if Tori were joining the Shadows alongside him, she knew he wouldn't. *We were supposed to go together. Keep each other alive!*

Darien climbed the steps to the stage, and Commander Scelero greeted him. He clapped Darien on the shoulder, thanking him for his service. But Darien shook his head. He stepped away to face the chancellor, and the crowd turned silent as death. No servant addressed the chancellor.

Nononononononononononono!

The chancellor remained calm, expressionless. He whispered something, but Darien shook his head, stood tall, and spoke the words Tori was dreading with everything in her. "I will not join the Shadows, milord."

The chancellor did not respond. He simply motioned to his guards, and they took Darien's arms and led him across the stage. To the gallows. The gallows he and Tori had built.

Darien wasn't even putting up a fight. He was like a sow going to the slaughter. He would be nothing. He would accomplish nothing through his death. The only person to be hung at the draft, that was all he would be.

Ol' Merri's words rushed to Tori's mind: *You can't do no one a lick o' good if you're dead.*

Darien could train with the Shadows, wait for his moment, like Merri. Maybe, one day, he could do something about the chancellor's cruelty. Maybe they all could. But not if he was dead.

The guards led Darien up the platform, bound his hands, draped the noose round his neck, and drew it taut. Darien's face was settled, his eyes closed. The guards looked to the chancellor for the word to drop the trap.

Tori felt something surging inside her. At first, she thought it was rage. But it was something more. Energy—like a river that had been dammed up for years and years inside her. Something within her screamed, *I have to make this stop!*

Suddenly, Tori became acutely aware of her surroundings, but not as she had always known them. She sensed the elements of the world. Tiny droplets of frozen water that made up each frame in the snowflakes that nipped her cheeks. Every splinter that made up the boards of the gallows. The little particles that made up the strands of rope around Darien's neck. She reached out with her mind, oblivious to how she was doing it. Yet it was true. There was energy at the heart of the world, and with a flex in her mind, she felt the world shiver.

The chancellor nodded to the guards—to drop Darien and snap his spine—and Tori reached out with her mind.

The trap dropped.

Darien plummeted through the platform.

The noose seized.

The stage shuddered, coming apart at the seams. Darien tumbled to the ground, unharmed; the guards went flying through the air. The spikes that had once held the gallows together shot out, veered direction, and pierced the guards. Dozens of nails ripped through each of their chests. The entire gallows launched into the foundations of the White Citadel with a cacophonous crash.

Darien was alive, kneeling on the stage, in shock; two dead guards lay beside him; the gallows was reduced to a heap of splinters behind them.

Maro Square was silent, as though the old gods themselves had drawn their breaths. Tori's knees went weak at the energy she'd expelled. The crowd dispersed around her, many knocked to the ground from the energy she'd released. Tori looked up, cold terror washing over her. *Oh gods, what have I done?*

The chancellor's eyes fixed upon her, and for the first time, an expression spread across his face. A smile. The chancellor was smiling at her.

Screams filled the city, shattering the stillness. Madness overcame the crowd. Everywhere, servants went running, scrambling over one another, trying to flee the square as fast as they could. But not because of Tori.

The creatures had come.

The chancellor's magic hunters.

The infamous Metamorphi.

Tori knew them only from horror tales, but she knew what they were the moment they changed their skins. The monsters moved nimbly amidst the chaos. One launched from the city walls, morphing from its human form in mid-flight. It soared on black wings protruding from its human back, bony arms outstretched, fangs flashing. The second creature morphed and bounded through the crowds, snarling, snapping its massive jaws, lumbering toward Tori with a body like a warg.

The Metamorphi were upon her before she could react. Tori did not run or fight back. Her entire body was spent from the destruction of the gallows, as though all her strength had been drained from her. A calm acceptance came over her. Somehow, this was meant to be. Tori only hoped that, in the madness, Darien might escape. That her death would not be for nothing.

Talons clamped around her shoulders, tearing her flesh. The flying creature descended upon her, knocking her on her back. The warg leapt and laid its claws into her sides. Pain rushed through her. Her vision blurred. Tori held her breath and waited to die.

But once the creatures had her pinned to the ground, they did not tear her apart. They held her still.

The chancellor stood over her. *How did he get here so quickly?* Tori thought dimly. Somehow, in the madness, he had crossed the entire square and come straight to her. The Metamorphi eased their hold at their master's command. Claws and talons and wings retreated, and suddenly, the creatures were two human men once more.

Blood seeped from Tori's shoulders and side, drenching her cloak, her wounds burning with excruciating fury.

The chancellor knelt beside her and smiled. "There you are."

And then, the world slipped away.

CHAPTER FOUR

Tori's limbs felt as though they were disconnected from her body by a vast sea. Sounds were muffled, rushing upon distant shores. Slowly, she swam back to reality, drawn by something real, something tangible. Drawn by pain.

Searing pangs shot up her right arm and into her bones, as though a blade were lodged there, weaving through sinew to her marrow. Tori reached out to remove whatever it was, but her hands were rendered immobile. There was a ringing clank, and more pain coursed through her. A pair of iron shackles bound her, holding her wrists fast to a ring in the floor by a length of chain. Cruel pain rushed through her body anew, and Tori cried out; it felt as though she were being hollowed from the inside out. She held still, terrified of bringing the pain upon herself again, and slowly, the pain subsided.

Tori saw nothing but darkness. The air smelled of gangrene and decay. She lay still, orienting herself to this dank reality. There was constant dripping somewhere behind her, each drop echoing off the stone. The cold seeped up from the ground into her bones and left her raw and aching all over. After some time, the pain ebbed enough she could remember how she'd wound up in this wretched state.

The gallows. The Metamorphi. The chancellor.

But why am I alive? she wondered. *Why didn't the chancellor let the Metamorphi kill me right there in the square?*

Tori realized with strange clarity that she had performed magic. She did not understand how, but the knowledge came to her like a haunting image that triggers the memory of a nightmare.

All of it—the power she released, the bodies flying through the air, the attack of the Metamorphi—took her back to the day her mother abandoned her. But there was something more, something buried deep in her mind, something nearly within her grasp…

But she couldn't place it. She felt as though she should be able to. And that feeling made no sense to her at all.

There was a clank and a screech of metal that made Tori's head throb. A pair of guards entered her cell, bearing lanterns. The sudden light blinded her, but she could not shield her eyes. One guard knelt beside her, setting down a large glass vial. He jerked at her right arm, and the pain returned full force.

The guard shoved a needle the length of her finger into the crook of her arm, and Tori screamed. Attached to the needle was a long tube made of something like animal innards. In the lantern light, Tori could see the tube turn dark as blood drained from her fragile body and filled the vial.

"Won't be working any more sorcery now," said the guard.

The ordeal lasted about a minute. When he finished, the guard tied a cloth around Tori's arm, tight, so that it throbbed, then he unlocked her chains from the ring in the floor and jerked her to her feet. Her knees buckled, and she slumped forward.

The guard yanked her up again, sending sharp pangs through her body. "You'll remain standing," the guard grunted.

Tori had never felt so weak in all her life. Her body felt lifeless, the detached fogginess returning to her mind, but she managed to slump against the walls of her cell and stay on her feet.

Another form entered. The guard handed the chain to the looming figure and left. The figure stepped toward her, a mere shadow against the flickering light, and a warm hand touched her arm, gently.

"D-Darien?" Tori said, delusional. The pain was wracking her in waves. It was all she could do not to keel over.

"I'm afraid I am not Darien," said Commander Scelero evenly.

"Oh, Master," she said. "H-he isn't…"

"No, Tori, Darien isn't dead." A rush of relief swept over her. She might have broken imperial law, but at least she had succeeded in keeping him alive. "He's on his way to the Shadow Camps. After the events in the square yesterday, he was taken away. He and the other drafted soldiers left the city this morning." The commander's voice sounded strained, as though he spoke through heavy cloth. His face was drawn tight.

One of his servants defected. And another destroyed the chancellor's gallows and killed two of his guards with magic. Tori was overcome with shame. The commander had rescued her from the Fringes, had been nothing but generous to her, and she had shamed him in front of *his* master.

"I'm sorry, I-I don't know what… came over me."

"I do," he said. And that was all he said for some time. Tori felt her mind drifting away again, separating from her body. Then, a hand brought her back. Scelero gripped her wrist and whispered, "I'm sorry, child, but this will have to sound convincing."

When her master's fist struck her gut, Tori felt as though she would pass out. She screamed as tremors swept over her.

"The gods damn your treachery!" Scelero shouted. And then, he struck again. Tori moaned and slumped to the ground, sobbing. He stooped beside her. She flinched away, but he took her hands in his own. Somehow, through the pain, Tori understood. Scelero had to save face, but he found no pleasure in this assault. The knowledge was strangely comforting.

"W-why am I still alive?" Tori whimpered. "What does the chancellor want with me?"

The commander shook his head. "I'm afraid you will find out soon."

The door rattled as the guard pounded from the other side.

"I must go." The commander stood, and then the final blow came, knocking her back against the wall. Tori shrieked in pain. "I wish I was the chancellor so I could kill you myself!"

Then, Commander Scelero helped her to her feet. "I'm sorry it happened this way." Scelero pounded on the door. The guard returned, and the commander disappeared. The guard yanked her forward, and Tori stumbled out of her cell.

"Come along, Gallows Girl," he growled. "It's time to meet the chancellor."

Tori was led up winding staircases from the dungeons all the way to the uppermost halls of the White Citadel, to the chancellor's inner palace. Before she was brought before him, she was led to a fine chamber, where she was stripped and bathed by beautiful maids. The girls were gentle with her, softening their touch when she winced. The wounds in her side and shoulder were dressed, and the aches in her arm from the bloodletting began to fade.

By the time the maids dressed her in fine silver linens and adorned her black hair, Tori could almost stand straight. There was still a sting in her arm where the thick needle had pierced her, but the blood had clotted quickly and the pain was fleeting. The maids touched up her tawny skin with cosmetics, which Tori had never worn before. All of it was much finer than anything she'd ever experienced.

Tori barely recognized her own likeness in the ornate mirrors that lined the room. The linens left her shoulders exposed the way the noble girls wore their gowns at palace balls. Tori felt conscious of the faded tan lines from her sleeveless summer uniform and the slave's tattoos that wrapped her arm. But otherwise, if not for her darker hair and complexion, she might have passed for a highborn girl. A look she did not like. *Why is the chancellor bothering to dress me up this way? Does he dress all his traitors in fine clothes before he kills them?*

Tori's stomach churned when she was finally led into the inner palace. She had heard tales of the White Citadel's splendor, but no tale could match the sight of it. Every inch of the inner palace glistened, pure crystal that shone bright with a million shimmers, reflecting and bending the light. It shone as though the palace were set in the heart of a star. Cyrus Maro, the sixteenth Chancellor of Osha, wore all white. In his halls, his pale skin shone with ruddy youthfulness, a stark contrast to his ghostly appearance in Maro Square. He descended from his crystal throne with long, resolute strides. He was smiling, and Tori's jaw clenched at the sight of him.

"Tori Burodai," a palace attendant announced, looking up from a scroll etched with elegant gold filigree.

"Astoria," said Tori, unsure why her true name had come to mind. Her mother had been the last person to call her that, but somehow, it felt right she should use her true name before she was executed. The attendant glared at her obstinance.

The guards escorting her halted and knelt before their ruler, heads bowed. Tori remained standing. When the chancellor reached her, he lifted her chin so their eyes met. His were blue like glaciers.

"Astoria," said the chancellor, examining her. "An interesting name for a servant. The name of an Old World goddess, the defender of the weak and the destitute." His tone conveyed mild amusement.

Tori thought it strange that the chancellor would know such a thing. Even she had not known the origin of her true name. She felt uneasy when he looked her over, as though he could see through her clothes and skin to her very thoughts.

The chancellor smiled, holding her gaze. "Green eyes. And yet the rest of your features are that of the Yan Avii horsemen."

"My mum was Oshan," said Tori. "She had an affair with a tribesman who came from tribe Burodai. We lived on the Steppe for seven years. Then my mum sold me into slavery."

Was that truly what happened? Something stirred in her memory. Perhaps it was the acknowledgment of her true name, of her old life. She could not be sure, but she suddenly recalled the image of a small boy with bronze skin and thick dark hair. A Yan Avii boy. *From my childhood?*

"You're a mutt, then," the chancellor said.

"Did you summon me to talk of my race?" Tori knew she shouldn't have said anything, but she was getting irritated with the pleasantries. If she was going to die for using magic, she would just as soon get it over with.

The chancellor smiled, his white teeth glistening in the vibrant light. "Spirited. I like that. Unbind her," he said to the guards. And then, "Leave us." His voice was steady, as though every syllable were set to an exact rhythm and tone. It was not harsh or angry. It was the voice of unquestionable power.

The guards removed Tori's shackles and left without argument about leaving their ruler alone with a sorceress. The chancellor held out his hand to her, still smiling. Tori stared at it.

The chancellor chuckled. "Bloodletting is painful, I know. But it renders you too weak to wield magic, which is necessary. You are still feeling weak, Astoria, are you not?"

Tori nodded, confused at his gesture, but she took his hand. His skin was warm, inviting, yet her fingers trembled at her ruler's touch—hands that could sentence her to death with a single motion. They had done exactly that to Darien yesterday. And soon, she would be next.

"You're trembling," the chancellor said. "You fear me?"

"Everyone fears you, milord."

The chancellor laughed again. Tori had only ever seen him on drafting days from afar. Up close, the ruler of Osha was strangely personable. "Good answer," he said. "Though I prefer the term *reverence*."

This was not the meeting Tori had expected at all. She should have been dead by now. "Why am I here, milord? Why am I still alive?"

The chancellor had not let go of her hand. "I want to show you something."

Cyrus Maro led her across the inner palace hall to a sprawling balcony that looked out across the city. In the streets, smoke rose from buildings in little pirouettes. The streets were in shambles, littered with splinters and upturned carts and bodies.

Dozens of bodies. A crew of servants was busy sweeping the square clean. Carts were being loaded with the dead.

"The servant uprising lasted only a few moments," said the chancellor. "But I think you know how much can happen in only a few moments, don't you?"

Understanding slowly dawned on her. "Riots... because of me."

"Because of the mere idea your magic represents. The Watchers... Of course, it's all futile. There are no Watchers, and they serve no gods. But weak people need something to keep them going, I suppose. At the sight of your power, the lowborns grasped for hope. But look where it got them."

The chancellor stared off at the great city, and for the first time,

Tori realized how exposed the Oshan ruler had left himself. She wielded magic. If she tried, she could cast him from this balcony.

But I can barely move, let alone summon the power I showed in the square. Tori had not felt that other sense since she awoke in her cell. Whatever power it was had left with her blood. "My magic…"

"You're the first to display it so publicly, and so powerfully, in quite some time." Still, the chancellor was smiling.

All her life, Tori had been taught to despise him. In private, the Oshan servants often let slip their contempt for the chancellor, yet here in person, there was something appealing about him, and Tori felt it was more than his beauty. He was fearsome, but captivating. It made sense the lords and ladies served him so faithfully. He treated them well, gave them power and wealth and glory.

And now, here she was in the inner palace, dressed in fine linens and cosmetics, standing on his balcony. She detested him all the more for his niceties.

The chancellor gestured to the carnage in the streets below. "For a moment, you became the symbol of the servants' hopes and prayers. But that hope was poorly founded. If you are the hope of the New World, then things are in a sad state, indeed. Oh, their precious Gallows Girl. Their Watcher sent by the gods." For the first time, the chancellor's tone turned dark. "You are nothing, Tori Burodai. A moment ago, you looked like a dog in the gutter. I made you beautiful. I drained your blood, and with it, your magic, and I can give it back if I choose. I am the source of hope. But weak people, for them it is not enough to see me capture you, nor to see you without your strength, as I see you now. No, in order to rule over the weak, you need something much more convincing to dispel their… hopeful notions."

Tori's body tensed. *This is it. He's going to kill me. Finally.*

The chancellor's grip grew firm around her wrist. A twinge of pain returned, and he led her to the parapet overlooking the square, stretching out from the citadel like a great tree limb. At the edge of the parapet stood a giant graven image of Cyrus Maro. The statue stood at least fifty feet tall and could be seen from all corners of Maro'El.

"This is the convincing weak people require," he said, gesturing up at his own statue.

There was something hanging from the graven chancellor's outstretched arm. A message for all of Osha to see—a body, strung up by the neck, swaying in the wind, the noose tearing into the flesh.

A girl's body. A girl with matted dark hair, trimmed at the shoulders like all servant girls. Like Tori's own hair. Pain surged through her again as she glimpsed the face. The green eyes and tawny skin.

The body did not belong to another Yan Avii servant girl.

It was Tori's body.

CHAPTER FIVE

Bile rose up in Tori's throat, and her knees buckled. She had seen many corpses during her years in the Fringes, but it was much different to see her own corpse while she was still alive to see it. Tori thought of the bizarre out-of-body sense she'd felt when she first woke in her cell. *Am I still alive? Or is the chancellor some sort of spirit summoner?*

The realization that she might in fact be dead did not strike her with fear, as she would expect. Tori was... enamored... and curious. It was beyond anything she had ever thought possible. She looked to the chancellor for answers, but he merely smiled. After a few moments, he took her by the arm and brought her nearer so she could get a good look at her hanging body. In the baking sunlight reflecting off the crystal palace, the corpse smelled like the heaps where dockworkers dumped fish innards in the Fringes. Stiff and grotesque, the skin—her skin—was already taking on the thready, hanging look of decay and the picking of crows.

Matted dark hair. Tawny skin. Pointed nose and thin lips. It was as though she were looking at her reflection in a nightmare. If Tori had not felt pain coursing through her body at that very instant, she might have thought she was a ghost looking upon her own corpse from the Aether.

"You've been dead a full day," the chancellor said. He chuckled. "In a sense."

"How?"

"Not all my Morphs are limited to beast forms. This one matched your figure perfectly, didn't she?"

Tori was speechless, and mortified by the chancellor's conniving brilliance. Cyrus Maro had squelched any hopes of rebellion before the thoughts could fully lodge in the people's minds.

"Yes, I killed one of my own soldiers. A brave and loyal woman, to be sure, but a small sacrifice to keep the peace. Already, the lowborns are doubting what they saw in the square, and their fear of the ruling class is restored."

"Why not *actually* kill me?" said Tori.

"Magic is a wonderful thing, isn't it?" As he spoke, the chancellor floated from the ground, only a few inches, but it still left Tori's mouth hanging open. Though his ancestors had outlawed it across the empire, though his Morphs scoured the New World hunting down sorcerers, the chancellor wielded magic himself.

"The First Chancellor feared magic," said Cyrus Maro. "So, he rid the world of it. And then he died, like all rulers before him. And then my forefathers ruled, and they too feared. The world all but forgot about the powers of the Old World. But what good did ridding the world of magic do them? Before he died, my grandfather lost half his realm. And my father lost half of that. I inherited a fragment of an empire. And now, this damned civil war threatens what little is left."

The chancellor's voice betrayed his disdain for his legendary forefathers. He gazed out beyond the city, toward the far reaches of his own realm. His eyes were focused and cool. "But I am different. I don't fear magic. No, I am fascinated by it." He took her hand again, still floating.

Tori didn't know what to say, but she found the tension leaving her. Was it possible the chancellor was not the monster she had always imagined? That this chancellor was different from his ancestors? He wielded magic just like her. He'd spared her life, despite her defiance in the square.

"Don't misunderstand me, Astoria. I do not believe tales of gods and Watchers. I believe in power. And magic, if one learns to trust it, is the greatest power of all." The chancellor returned to the ground. "Tell me, when your gifts came to the surface in the square, what was it like?"

The longer they talked, the more Tori felt comfortable talking to the chancellor. He didn't speak to her like a lowly servant girl. He spoke to her almost as an equal. "I became aware of the world in a... different way," she said. "I could sense things I'd never been able to see. I saw the world, but I saw something more—beneath it, I guess. Like I could see... the makeup of the world?"

"Yes! The makeup of the world! And what did you find in the makeup of the world?"

Tori struggled for the right word. "It was... energy."

"Yes! Yes, Astoria, there is a power at the heart of the world which cannot be fully explained. Despite my ancestors' attempts to exterminate it, it lives on. Some once attributed it to gods and Watchers. Now, we call it sorcery. Others have called it by many other names. This power threatened the Old World, and so the world moved on. But now, look at you and me. Here we are, three hundred years after the War Between the Worlds and the annihilation of magic. Yet that power lives on in us. We have access. We are special. We can harness this energy."

But Tori felt uneasy the more he spoke of this power. It was beyond her control. She had killed those guards in the square, innocent men, simply doing their duty. Servants just like her. And in the square below, the last cart of dead servants rode off in the streets. Tori felt a twisting in her stomach, as though the guilt were being wrung out of her. "You still haven't answered my question," she said at last.

"What question?"

"Why go to the trouble of staging my death? It would have been as easy to kill me. And you would not have wasted a loyal soldier."

"Wasted... no, Astoria, *you* would be the waste." Ever since the day her mother abandoned her, Tori had despised her true name. She had become someone different. She had become Tori. But now, she enjoyed hearing that name again from the lips of her ruler.

The chancellor smiled and took her by the hand. His skin was soft and warm and... enticing. She liked his attention. Throughout her life, Tori had walked in the background. She was not particularly strong or skilled. She was a hard worker, but she had never been special. Now, the greatest ruler in the New World was holding her hand. It was unfathomable how quickly her entire world had turned over on its axis.

"My dear, you are far too rare a phenomenon to simply kill," said the chancellor. "And so tenacious too. To defy me in my own city?"

Is he complimenting my rebellion?

"I spared you because I want you by my side. I want to learn from you, and you from me. Share your gifts with me, and you could have everything this harsh world has held back from you. Wealth, prestige, and power unmatched in the New World, unmatched even by those you've despised all your life. Those damned highborns..."

Tori imagined this future. Learning to wield her new, blossoming power. Playing the courtier. Attending balls with lords and ladies, as she'd seen so many highborn girls do. All of them would be envious; all of them would be oblivious to the secret she and the chancellor shared.

Tori *was* special. Perhaps she always had been, and she had simply not known it. And the chancellor admired it. He desired it—desired her. *Gods, to be desired by the chancellor! How many highborn girls would give their left hand for this moment?*

It was true. Tori did desire to rise above the lords and ladies. To slaughter the taskmasters in the Fringes who took advantage of poor and desperate lowborns. Tori stood up straight. Her strength was returning to her; she felt something surging in her again, an awareness of the world, the way she'd felt it in the square. Her magic.

"You want to collect me," Tori said.

"You might call it that," Cyrus Maro whispered. "I want you to share your gifts with me, and I will share with you as well." He took hold of her bare arm now, gently. Her skin tingled.

"What if I... refuse?"

"Refuse? Why would you ever want to do that? I want to share the world with you, Astoria. I want to discover this lost realm together."

Tori could feel his breath against her neck. His warmth washed over her. She imagined herself, one day, as his queen. Two sorcerers ruling over the world. She *did* desire it. Besides, she couldn't do anyone any good if she was dead. Look where Darien's resistance had gotten him. Tori was a survivor. And if this was what it took…

Tori leaned closer. "Okay," she said.

The chancellor smiled. "Of course, we will have to change you."

"Change me?" Her fingers suddenly felt colder in the chancellor's grasp.

"All the city knows your mutt face, Tori. Not to mention, have you ever seen a Yan Avii noblewoman in Osha?"

Tori shook her head. The nobles were all Oshan-born, from ancient families that had ruled the North since the ancient Elyan races had invaded the land.

"I want to raise a diamond up from the ashes, Astoria. But you must look like a diamond." His fingers traced her jawline, but now, his touch felt… less alluring. "We will construct a false identity. A lady from the southern reaches of the empire who has come to court. It will not take much magic to make you look Oshan. You already have the eyes."

Suddenly, as though coming up from the depths of a great sea, Tori realized something. Something that should not have taken her so long to understand.

This was the chancellor beside her, the tyrant whose line had reduced her and thousands more to slaves and peasants. The tyrant who saw her as a mutt, like all the other highborns. The tyrant who had sent Darien to slaughter in his name. Cyrus Maro's ancestors may have created this cruel world, but he perpetuated it, even took pride in it. And now, he wanted to change her skin so she could fit in with all the other nobles she had despised all her life. After Morgath was conquered, would the Yan Avii be the next to be absolved back into the empire?

Suddenly, Tori understood why Darien had chosen the gallows. If Tori served the chancellor, she would become the oppressor she had always despised, like the taskmasters, the nobles, the Legions who killed Darien's family.

"I think…" Tori pulled away from the chancellor's touch and pointed to the dead Morph dangling above them. "I think *that* is the future of those who refuse and don't refuse you, alike. I could never serve you, milord."

The chancellor's gaze turned icy. He seized her arm, where her blood had been drained. Tori cried out, and the pain surged anew. The chancellor shouted for his guards. Two appeared in an instant and took hold of her arms. *Now he will kill me*, she thought with morbid satisfaction.

Perhaps this was the way Darien felt when he'd walked to the gallows. Tori regretted using her magic then. She had stolen that rebellion from him, but now, she would die in his honor.

"You're right, precious Gallows Girl," said the chancellor. "I want to collect you. However, you are under the delusion that I need your consent. I have been a gentleman until now, but I will share your gifts one way or another. The draining of your blood allows me to do more than simply dilute your power."

The chancellor took a needle and tube from one of the guards and jabbed it into the crook of Tori's arm. Her blood drained into a chalice until it was overflowing, dripping down the chancellor's hands and onto the ground. The hollow, out-of-body feeling returned. Her body went numb as more blood trickled down her arm. Tori collapsed in a growing pool of her own blood.

Cyrus Maro lifted the chalice to his lips and drank until all her blood was gone. Tori clutched her arm. The numbness swept away, and waves of pain coursed through her bones anew.

The chancellor stretched out his hand toward the dead Morph dangling from the statue. The noose of rope trembled.

And then, the rope disintegrated in an explosion of fibers, and the Morph body of the Gallows Girl, the hope of the servants of Osha, plummeted hundreds of feet to the streets below. Tori realized with horror that he wasn't going to kill her.

"I hate martyrs," said the chancellor, turning to her. "And you will never become one, Gallows Girl. You will live in rot and pain for the rest of your short life, fueling my magic with your blood. You will serve me until the day you die. But always remember—as you cry out in agony, as you wish for the end—it was *you* who chose your destiny, not I."

Tori could not respond. She could only watch, helpless, writhing in pain, her blood forming tributaries on the crystal balcony.

PART TWO
WINTER'S END

The first flower to bloom in the North is the winter lily. Long before the thaw, it springs forth against all odds from beneath the snowpack. It gives hope to the people of the North, a sign that the harsh winters will always come to an end. It is the flower now known as "Astoria."

—from *Dawn of the Third World*

CHAPTER SIX

Tori's life—if it could be called a life—became a routine of blood and hunger and darkness. Her cell bore no link to the outside world. Light was perpetually dim and colorless, seeping under the iron door in bleak wisps. Day or night or whatever it was, the light remained constant. Her cell was buried somewhere deep beneath the White Citadel. There was no basis for time except when the slit at the bottom of her cell door would open, and a plate with stale bread, a fermenting apple, and a cup of water would come through. On occasion, there arrived a cold slop, which tasted vaguely of porridge. Tori guessed these meals came once a day, though there was no way of knowing for certain.

The meals were almost worse than true starvation. They dispelled the pangs for an hour or so, but then they would return with fury, and Tori spent the rest of the day with a crushing emptiness in her stomach, trying not to speculate how long it would be before her next momentary respite.

The little slivers of light provided enough visibility to know there was nothing in her cell to see. The room was about eight feet squared with no chairs, no drainage vents, nothing. Nothing but a small bucket in order to do her business, which reeked horribly and was switched out only when it had begun to overflow, and always while she slept. When this happened, Tori woke with a start to the sudden absence of stench.

As days passed, the bloodletting grew less frequent. At first, it seemed to follow a pattern of every two meals, but then it was three, and then it was more. It was as though the Morphs could sense the weakening of her body. No sooner would she begin to feel a little revived than Morphs would arrive with a needle and several glass vials. When they finished, they wrapped her arm in cloth and left her to lie in aching pain and hollow starvation.

Weeks went by, and the guards removed her shackles, as she barely had the strength to stand for the draining process, let alone to resist them. It was a small mercy.

Tori wondered how long she would last like this. How much blood and magic could her body continue to produce before her wells went dry?

A month passed before the chancellor summoned her to his palace. Once more, she was dolled up and dressed in fine clothes. She knelt at his throne, and the chancellor touched her jaw tenderly when he approached.

"You look terrible, Astoria," he said.

Tori felt terrible. As the servants readied her, Tori had seen the dark rings around her eyes, her yellowing complexion, the way her skin drew tight around the bones of her face. Tori did not respond. *I won't give him the satisfaction.*

"It's a shame to see you this way. Come along." Cyrus Maro held out his hand and led Tori, again, to his balcony. The square below was filled with nobles and merchants and servants going about business as usual. The snow was beginning to melt. Spring had come, but it all felt the same in her cell.

"No more riots," said the chancellor. "They've already forgotten about you. To think, your suffering is for nothing. I'd wager you don't last a year in the dungeons."

He said it as though this weren't a remarkable amount of time. Tori dreaded the thought. *A year of this hell?*

"What do you care?" Tori said. "You have my power, whether I serve you or not."

The chancellor did not smile. He took her hand, and his warmth spread through her, breaking through the numbness that had taken over her existence. His voice grew solemn. "Believe it or not, Tori, but I don't enjoy seeing you this way. I don't enjoy wasted magic. I don't believe in wasting anyone. Take your friend from the gallows. Darien, was it?"

Tori clenched her fists at the mention of him. She had destroyed his rebellion, and now, there was nothing she regretted more than the day she discovered her magic. "Don't say his name."

"Ah, yes, a tender subject… but Darien *is* adjusting well to life in the Shadow Camps. He may well become a fine soldier. He thinks you're dead, you know. Everyone thinks you're dead."

In a dark way, Tori wished it were true. Her fingers trembled, and it was not out of fear or cold. It was weakness. One month of bloodletting had left her feeling worse than any pain she had endured in the Fringes. She had known hunger and cold and agony then, but she'd had Darien. Though they had lived in a mere shanty with dozens of others, though she had worked all day in a textile mill and eaten little, Tori had still clung to the hope of better days. Now, there was no hope. Only wondering how long it would take to die…

The chancellor's touch grew warmer. His face radiated. Tori fought the urge to draw near. *That is what he wants.*

"There is so much for you to learn," said the chancellor. "So much potential. Why waste your magic, Astoria?"

Tori's mind had begun to clear, the most it had since she had last been on this balcony. But a month of suffering had not swayed her. "Serving you, milord, that would be the waste of my magic."

The chancellor did not grow angry with her. "Well, we will see what another month brings."

The guards returned with a chalice and tube, and the chancellor drank her blood on his balcony. And that marked the first sick cycle of Tori's existence.

———

Spring passed, and so did the short summer. Every month, Tori was summoned. Every month, she refused the chancellor, and every month, he drank blood fresh from her veins. As each month passed, Tori felt her body and mind fading farther and farther away. For most of her waking hours, she was barely cognizant of reality. When her mind began to clear—which usually meant she had less than an hour before the next bloodletting—her thoughts often returned to her mother.

Why did she sell me? Ever since the gallows, Tori had doubted the things she'd once thought were so clear. The memories did not return all at once. They slipped into her dreams, beginning with the boy.

A Yan Avii boy from her village. His warm, slightly pudgy face was so vivid, dark eyes stricken with fear. In her dreams, he was swept away by the surging force of the Great Spillway. The mighty river would have borne him to his death. Tori had to do something. Something raged inside her, like a sudden rising tide…

When she woke, Tori knew it was a memory. The images ran over and over in her mind, and she knew she had seen them before. It was a memory she had forgotten completely. *But how could I forget something so… real?*

Tori did not understand it, but she did not ponder long before the guards came and drained her blood, and she sank back into her blood-spent stupor.

But the dreams always returned.

She dreamed of the night her mum betrayed her. They sprinted through the tent city, Tori gripping her mum's hand. Her palms were cold and sweaty. Her mum was filled with fear. Tori had always remembered that. She had thought it must have been regret or guilt for selling her own daughter. In her dreams, the tent city was haunted by soaring, twisted shadows that seemed to choke the very life out of the city…

Why have I thought so little of that night? Why was Mum so scared?

Try as she might, Tori could not bring clarity to the memories, and soon enough, her blood was drained, and any clarity she'd managed would vanish.

Tori tried to recreate the sense that had come over her when she destroyed the gallows. To find that energy in the world. She reached out with her mind, tried to focus, to rediscover that inexplicable awareness of the world. Everything had seemed so vivid, so wondrous, so full of life. Tori longed for that feeling again, the way a drunk longed for another tankard of ale. But even at her strongest, in the moments right before the guards came, day after wretched day, the world of her cell appeared as it always had, blocks of cold stone stacked and mortared to form this cube of a reeking room. Astoria Burodai had no power here, and soon enough, her blood was drained and her mind fogged over again.

In those brief moments of lucidity, Tori also thought of Darien—what horrors he had to be enduring in the Shadow Camps, how she'd failed him, how she'd taken away the power of his attempted resistance. He thought her dead and, she supposed, he would likely be dead soon as well.

They would both slip away into the great void of those who resisted the mighty. And when they were gone, the chancellor's power would grow, and his dominion would spread from Osha to the far reaches of the New World, fueled by Tori's magic. The longer this realization sunk in, the more she wondered whether her resistance mattered at all.

———

Months passed, and the snow and the cold returned. The only constant was Tori's monthly trips to the chancellor's palace. She hated the way he doted on her, dressing her up, feeding her fine food, tempting her with little tastes of civility, as though she were some battered pup who would come running for the slightest form of reprieve.

"Your resilience is impressive," Cyrus Maro had said at her last visit. "Truly, I expected you to be dead by now."

It irritated her, the way he would speak so admirably of her. Tori might as well have been dead. As the months passed by, her body slipped from frailty into decay, and her mind drifted further and further into slumber.

It was horrible to be left alone with haunted thoughts, no one to dispel the fear, the guilt, the despair. Tori began to lose track of where her dreams ended and her consciousness began. In the dark stink of her cell, she lost herself inside her own mind.

One morning, Tori woke to the sound of swords clashing outside her cell. Then, Darien burst in. Her heart filled with joy. After all this time, he had come for her. Her resistance hadn't been in vain. Darien smiled, his copper skin glowing in the lantern light. He rushed in, cut off her shackles, kissed her forehead, and embraced her. His warmth washed over her, filling her with life.

"It's all right, Tori," he whispered in her ear. "We're safe now. Come away!"

And Darien ran out the door.

Tori stumbled across the cell only to find the door sealed shut and her room empty, and then the lock clanked and the Morphs came for her blood.

The hallucinations never turned dark, however. In her fantasies, Tori always escaped, things always got better. It was as though her mind were playing sick games with her, filling her with false hope. She dreamed of feasts and sunshine and green meadows while she lay in the cold, damp darkness. She dreamed her powers returned, and she killed the guards and fled.

Tori grew fond of the hallucinations. They kept her company, kept her mind off the reality that she was slowly dying. Every time her blood was drained, she felt a little closer to death…

When her mum came to her, Tori told her straight away, "I know this isn't real. You lied to me. Sold me. Abandoned me!"

"I'm sorry I left you," Celene Burodai said. Her skin shone like the sunrise.

"Why didn't you tell me what I was?" Tori sobbed.

Her mum smiled, her eyes sparkling bright like little pieces of night sky. "I had to keep you safe, my love. I have always been keeping you safe." She reached out and touched her face, and Tori pressed into her mum's touch. Oh, how she had longed for it, missed it. Tori was filled with warmth.

"I'm so sorry," her mum whispered.

"Y-you didn't… want to leave, did you?"

Celene Burodai stepped back. Her smile seemed to fill the room. Her hand brushed Tori's face, gently, so gently that it passed right through her.

Her mum disappeared, and Tori was left alone once more, lying on the floor of her cell.

Water was drip-drip-dripping rhythmically. When it splattered, it sprayed her with tiny droplets. Very tiny droplets. As though they were pieces of something much larger, something that composed the entire world.

Tori shot up from the ground. *It's the sense! My magic!*

She could feel it again. Feel the way it weaved in and out of everything, like so many threads binding the world together. So small, you could move your hand and it would pass right through without noticing.

But not for Tori. She noticed.

The Metamorphi were running late. If her senses were returning, they should come soon. Any moment, Tori feared, they would arrive and the sense would be gone.

Or worse, the sense itself might just be another hallucination.

But the Morphs never came. And the sense grew stronger, sharper. Her mind quickly oriented itself to her surroundings.

Minutes crawled by, and Tori barely breathed. She could feel her body gaining strength, clarity growing in her mind, the sense expanding.

Beyond the door, she could hear steady breaths, and there were hints of something potent on the air, like the wine she and Darien had drunk on their last night together. But there was something else as well, something sharp. Something that did not belong.

It came to her in a burst of final clarity. The steady breathing, the wine, the thing that did not belong.

Someone is helping me escape!

CHAPTER SEVEN

A trap! Tori thought, not daring to hope. *Of course, it has to be a trap.*

How else could it be explained? The Metamorphi were right outside her door, as they'd always been. This had to be the next stage in the chancellor's sick mind games. The same way he offered her fine food and clothes when she visited him. Now, he was teasing her with a little taste of her magic. And the more her senses swelled with that glorious awareness of the world, the more she longed for it to be true. But she forced herself to wait, to resist the temptation.

An hour passed and no one came, and Tori felt as though the spring sun was shining down on her after a long, dark winter. Her mind was nearly singing. Everything felt so real, so vivid, despite the dreary nature of her surroundings.

There came no sound from beyond her cell door but steady breaths. Even so, it was some time before Tori mustered the courage to test her abilities for the first time since the square. Finally, she could not resist it any longer.

It was as though her magic were willing her to use it again. In her mind, Tori sensed the intricate mechanisms of the lock on the other side of the door. Each one rang with a certain timbre, and if it was nudged just right, it rang more sharply, it rang true.

One by one, with a strange flex of her mind, Tori nudged the mechanisms with her sorcery. For a moment, the ringing got muddled, and she feared the Metamorphi would wake from their slumber and catch her. But of course, the ringing was only in her head. It was the sense. The mechanisms slid ever so slightly, and there was a soft clang, and then Tori pressed at the iron door. It groaned as it swung free. Strength and confidence rose up within her, and she stepped from her reeking cell. At the sight of the Metamorphi, Tori's heart leapt in her chest.

They were unconscious. Slumped against the walls on either side of the door.

Tori slipped out into the corridor. She could feel the creatures' rhythmic breaths. Between them lay a pair of goblets and a half-empty bottle of wine. *Drugged,* she thought. *Well, it's run or die, now.*

Tori shut the cell door behind her, took a lantern off the wall, and headed into the dark. Winding down corridor after corridor, her atrophied legs ached beneath her meager weight. She kept expecting her limbs to collapse from fatigue, but the more steps she took, the more her legs loosened up and grew stronger. Her stumbles turned into steady strides. Her mind soared with marvelous clarity. Tori winded down corridors for some time, marveling at how they continued on and on. *How many other cells are there in this place? Are there others like me? Other sorcerers being harvested by the chancellor?*

But she could not risk opening any doors to find out. She continued on, hoping as she turned each corner that she would not walk right into a guard.

The corridors seemed to stretch endlessly into the dark, and she began wondering if she would be found lost in this maze, days later, and then be put to death—or worse, kept alive for more months of bloodletting and agony. Perhaps it was still somehow part of the chancellor's games. But she could not turn back. She clung to hope.

After some time, she reached the end of the passage—a rounded room with no exits. And there had been no other passageways behind her. Tori cursed the gods and turned, about to head back and brave the staircase, when she felt a twinge in her mind beckoning her back.

There was a grate in the corner. Tori drew near. The opening was just large enough to shimmy through. A stench rose from the sewage vent, and it reminded her instantly of the waste fields in the Fringes after a hard rain. The horrid odor made her stomach lurch.

But Tori could either endure the stench or wander blind until she was captured and thrown back into an equally rancid cell. She just hoped the vent led out of the tower.

The tunnel was about four feet high, and despite her slight stature, it forced her to crouch low. She followed the slow seep of sewage, one hand holding the lantern, the other plugging her nose. Each footstep squelched, and the waste seemed to sink in and grab at her rotted boots. Something brushed past her leg and she jumped, covering her mouth to keep from crying out.

A dark blur scurried off down the tunnel. It was a rat, the size of a small dog. Tori recovered herself. Her hands were shaking. The farther Tori ventured, the more blurs scampered away. The place was infested, but they ran from the lantern light. Every twenty or thirty yards, small tributaries joined the main flow of sewage. Little shadows disappeared up the smaller tunnels. They were only rats, but with every squeal and sudden movement, Tori's heart quickened.

Legends told of other, more fearful beasts underground. It was said the beasts of the underworld were the only ones who survived the purge of the Old World. The Gurlag—a worm-like monster, with multiple heads and teeth the size of skulls, that burrowed deep below the earth and formed the cavern realms beneath the Crooked Teeth. The Kroqala—the demon faeries driven below by the Watchers of old. And the Nosferati—the cursed race of cannibals that feasted on humans who wandered too deep. Tori's mum had loved to tell tales of such beasts to the children of the Steppe.

Tori steadied herself and pressed onward, waving the torch. She could deal with rats.

But gods, the smell! It was a poison slowly numbing her mind the longer she breathed it in. Her head seemed to be floating somewhere above her body, as though she were looking down upon herself while she stumbled through the sludge.

Ahead, she caught a faint glimmer of the world above. Moments later, she tumbled out into glorious fresh air and scrambled out of the flow. Ducts bore the waste down to the harbor and dumped it into the Boundless Sea. From this viewpoint, at the base of a large hillside, Tori knew she was in the lowlands outside the limits of Maro'El.

She scrambled away from the ducts and lay in the snow, taking in fresh breaths. Towering leafless trees stretched out to the heavens like the fingers of Fringe babes grasping for their dead mothers. In the moonlight, Tori could make out her frail form. Her trousers were tattered and rotting around gangly legs, grey with grime and malnourishment. Her cloak was grungy and patchy. But she was alive.

Tori gazed up at the cloudless sky. She had never felt so grateful to see it in all her life, to lie upon snow and breathe sweet, frigid air. The stars fluttered, and the twin moons of the New World bathed the grove in a near daytime light. Tori felt as though the Sisters were shining down just for her.

Beside a small seedling in the grove, a lone purple flower poked through the snowpack. A winter lily. It was the first to bloom in the North. *Winter is coming to an end.*

The Northern winter had been nearing its end on the day of the Gallows. Which meant it had been a full year since Tori had breathed fresh air and felt anything but pain. A year spent bleeding, starving, lost inside her own mind. Yet here she was—free—gazing up at the war between dark and light waging in the heavens, and tonight, the light seemed to be winning.

But Tori could not rest long. An unsettling question stirred her from her reverie: *Who drugged those guards? Who helped me, and where are they now?*

Tori scanned the surrounding trees for movement. She felt helplessly exposed in the open grove. Would the Metamorphi come bounding through the tunnels in droves any second?

Her body tensed. But no one appeared. In the distance, the White Citadel was silhouetted against the sky. Tori could make out the outstretched arm of the chancellor's statue, where her body had hung for all the city to see. But her true body was feeling stronger by the minute; the effects of the chancellor were already wearing thin.

Tori needed to get moving. *But where?*

To the north, the craggy, snow-capped peaks of the Crooked Teeth loomed over Osha. It would be the last place the Morphs would look, but even if she survived the cold, there were the Crooked mountain folk to worry about. Half-crazed and half-starved, it was told, and there were the Rulaqs, if they truly existed.

The chancellors never bothered conquering the Teeth. The mountains formed the northern and eastern boundaries of the nation, a natural fifteen-thousand-foot wall secluding Osha from the world. No one would dare bring an army through its treacherous passes. To conquer Osha, an invading army could take only three paths: the Boundless Sea, avoiding the razor-sharp rocks, massive icebergs, and towering fjords lining the western coast; the chest-high grasslands of the Green Sea of Greater Osha; or the Haunted Forest of Ghen, where ghosts had been known to drive men to their own deaths.

The sea would involve bartering passage or stowing away. *But who knows when a ship will be sailing?* Tori did not have time to wait. The Green Sea was the path of the Night Legions. It would be filled with marching soldiers on their way to war against the Morgathians; it would leave her far too exposed, and food would be hard to come by.

The Haunted Forest, then. There was no other choice. The forest lay west of the Fringes, across Glacier Sound. The only way across the sound was by the Meridian, the immense bridge that spanned it several leagues to the east. But the Meridian would be teeming with guards. *Again, only one option.*

Tori set out at a swift pace, but soon slowed. Her head felt light from her journey through the waste. Or perhaps it was the fact she'd not eaten a decent meal since her last visit with the chancellor. Tori followed the ducts for half a league, then stole through the woods to the outskirts of a small harbor village. The dirt and pebble lanes were empty, save for the occasional fisherman or dock servant preparing nets and lines by lantern light, and Tori made her way easily to the abandoned docks. She was beginning to feel blessed by the gods again, until she saw the guard.

The tall, broad-shouldered woman paced the docks methodically. Her head wagged from side to side, keeping count of vessels. Anyone caught ferrying over from the Fringes was put to death. Tori had never heard of anyone ferrying the other way, though. No one desired to leave Osha once they arrived.

Tori hid behind a heap of nets and pondered her next move. Her first instinct was to kill the guard and toss the body into the harbor, tied to an anchor. But she couldn't help but think of Darien, training to fight the chancellor's wars. This woman was a soldier like he was. A servant like Tori had been. She could not bear the thought of someone killing Darien out of convenience.

After gauging the guard's pace, Tori waited until she passed by again, then made her way to the western end and chose an eight-foot *qayaq* made of socha and sealskin. The vessel was watertight, except for a small hole in the top for her body to slip through. Her legs extended down the length of the vessel, leaving her upper body exposed to row. She heaved off as softly as she could, using subtle paddle strokes to navigate her way from the docks. The guard made her way to the eastern end of the docks, oblivious, and Tori slipped into the night.

As she entered the open water, the waves grew larger and more violent. With every wave, Tori grew more nervous and more tired. *Am I making any progress at all?* The waves seemed to push back equally for every stroke. She dared not look back, but the shoreline of the Fringes seemed to get no closer. Already, the sky was turning grey with the coming dawn.

Tori paddled with all her strength, the nose of the vessel cutting through the waves. Salt water splashed in her mouth, reminding her how thirsty she was. Her strength was waning fast. Her arms ached. She'd had no food, and adrenaline could only take her so far.

In the distance, the silhouette of a patrol boat drifted past her, toward the Oshan shore. Tori paddled on, trying to move as fast as she could, despite her growing fatigue. At long last, the Fringes grew larger on the horizon. The waves shifted and began to bear her toward the other side. Steely skies were bleeding hints of yellow and orange.

Tori was a few hundred yards from the Fringes when a bell rang out from the Oshan shore behind her.

It did not ring once. Nor did it ring out the hour.

The bell rang furiously.

An alarm! Tori glanced behind her for the first time. To her horror, she saw the patrol boat bearing straight toward her. It soared across the harbor, leaping from wave to wave at the power of its rowers. With every stroke, they came nearer and nearer.

Tori had never worked so hard in her life. She paddled with everything inside her. Her breaths were desperate gasps, and her heart thundered in her chest. She could feel every beat, sense the contractions of her heart pumping blood to her paddling arms, sense the tiny liquid particles being fed air that coursed through her body. The world was large, yet it was small, everything a microcosm of the grander, larger thing. Infinitely complex particles composed everything. Between the particles, Tori could sense something binding them. *The energy at the heart of the world!*

It flowed in the water, danced upon the air, surged through her blood. Beyond physical plausibility, the paddles of Tori's emaciated body grew faster, and the swells of sea expanded. Her *qayaq* raced upon the waves. Tori crossed the final stretch of harbor, and the vessel caught sand. She leapt out and sprinted up the bank and into the Fringes.

Shanties formed a vast maze that stretched for several leagues in all directions, and Tori lost herself in the masses. At sunrise, the narrow lanes were already teeming with Fringe rats vying for a day's labor with the taskmasters. At first, Tori ran, weaving her way through the throbbing mass of scrawny bodies in tattered clothing, but then she realized her rotting clothes smelled of waste, her limbs looked more like dying willow branches than human arms and legs…

I look like any Fringe rat. Tori slowed her pace, pulled her hood up over her grimy hair, and blended in with the crowd. The shanties all looked the same—thatched roofs on a four-post frame. Some had the luxury of walls. Pyres littered the squares in the housing districts, where Fringe rats burned the bodies of their dead. This was a dark celebration in winter. Burning days meant the warmth of a fire. The poorest and most desperate rats would pile atop one another and sleep in the square near the warmth of burning corpses. Tori had not thought of this ritual in some time, and it made her queasy to think on the memories. The pyres were growing large. Fires would soon be lit.

There was commotion behind her. Shouts of guards and scrambling people. Tori pressed forward, trying with all her strength not to break out in a dead sprint. The crowds were thinning. The farther south she went, the fewer people there would be to hide her. Most of the workhouses were on the northern waterfront.

Tori's body grew weaker with each step. Her head felt light. She needed food desperately. Ahead, a small square teemed with vendor carts. She could not journey through the Forest of Ghen without provisions, but she had no money. She would have to steal them. *The vendors are crooks, anyway*, she told herself.

The square was crowded. A nearby cart was loaded with stale bread, probably overflow from Maro'El. The vendor argued with an elderly woman, though Tori knew it was likely the woman was little older than her own mother had been. The harshness of the Fringes aged people quick. No one lived long under those conditions.

"No, not enough," shouted the vendor. "Ten coppers apiece, no exceptions."

Tori inspected a loaf in the cart while the woman pled her case. "Please, sir! I need two ter feed me family. Please."

The vendor slapped her with the back of his hand. "Away! I do no business with beggars!"

The woman wailed. In the commotion, Tori snatched two loaves, slipped them beneath her cloak, and stole back into the crowd, unnoticed.

"One loaf, then. Okay," whimpered the poor woman.

"One loaf! And make it twelve coppers for begging!"

Tori wanted to kill the vendor right there in the square. The old woman's eyes filled with tears as she handed the vendor twelve coins and took her loaf. She trudged to the edge of the square, sat against a building in the thawing slush, and wept.

How many children will she be feeding with that one loaf? If their father was alive, he was likely working to death in the labor camps or salt mines. Tori was overcome by pity—as well as guilt, for having been chosen by Scelero, for having so easily forgotten how much worse it was in the Fringes. Even slaves had it better than a single Fringe rat.

Tori pressed her way through the crowd, knelt down, and handed the woman one of her stolen loaves. "Feed your family," said Tori.

Kindness was no virtue in the Fringes, for kindness did not exist. It was everyone for themselves. The woman eyed Tori for only a second, then she snatched the loaf and ran from the square without looking back.

Tori found a trough and scooped water with her hand. Probably she was sharing water with pigs and goats, but she didn't care. She nibbled at her loaf, resisting the urge to devour the entire thing at once. But with every bite, she felt more revived, and the loaf was soon gone. The Forest of Ghen would take a week at least to cross, and hunting and gathering would be scarce this time of year. She would need much more sustenance to begin the journey.

A cry rang out somewhere beyond the square. The soldiers were close again. Tori needed to be quick. She spied one vendor speaking jovially with a customer. This time, she did not pause to check out the vendor's wares; she walked right past, drawing as close as she dared. The vendor cocked back his head and laughed at something the customer said. Spit dribbled from his chin as he shook with cackling. With a motion so swift it was nearly invisible, Tori snatched a pair of apples off the vendor's cart and continued on her way. Weaving through the throng, she made for the southern entrance of the square.

"Yeh gods-damned thief!"

Tori kept her head down and pressed on. The crowd began dispersing around her. She looked back in time to glimpse the vendor's fist heading for the back of her head. She ducked, her senses flaring. The vendor missed and lost balance, but with his other hand, he latched onto her coat.

"Steal from me, will yeh? I'll ruddy kill yeh!" The man pulled out a jagged blade the length of Tori's arm and swung at her—missed. He jabbed it at her chest, and Tori dodged it. The man staggered forward with the empty motion, and Tori struck back.

Her palm connected with the vendor's nose, launching him off his feet. Energy rushed from her, and the man sailed across the lane, struck a shanty wall, and landed on his back in the snow, blood pouring from his face. He didn't move, but Tori didn't have time to see whether she'd killed him. As she turned to run, a shriek pierced the air.

Shadows streaked across the sky. Black wings loomed against threatening clouds. It was an army of Metamorphi.

Cries filled the air, and people ran in terror as the creatures bore down upon the shanties. Tori's heart raced. Her fingers shook from the memory of her last encounter with the monsters. A pair of wingless Morphs entered the square, sending anyone in their way soaring with a swing of their massive, mangled heads.

They turned without hesitance, and bounded straight toward Tori.

CHAPTER EIGHT

Tori did not freeze up as she had the day of the Gallows. She snatched up the vendor's shoddy blade from the snow and ran faster than she'd ever run in her life. Weaving between shacks and narrow passageways, fear and desperation propelled her on. Shrieks filled the sky, echoing through the Fringes as though the Metamorphi were attacking from all directions. Three Morphs circled high above, but they did not descend upon her.

It's only when they sense magic! Tori willed herself not to access the energy again. But her senses were on fire. She could feel the two wingless beasts closing upon her. The ground trembled with the jarring thuds of their massive paws. Hot, putrid breaths warmed her neck. The beasts were about to pounce. Tori dropped to her knees and spun to face them.

The creatures leapt through the air, and Tori thrust out with the vendor's blade. Blood sprayed from the first beast's chest, the blade lodged deep in its heart. The Morph collapsed, shifting back to its human form. But its comrade landed safely beyond, turning with a roar.

Tori leapt back to her feet, but now she had no weapon.

The beast stalked forward. A grin stretched across its wide mouth, revealing fangs the size of spikes. Tori knew she could not kill this creature, not without using her power and bringing the whole army of Metamorphi down upon her.

The beast leapt. Tori dodged to the side, rolling, and sprang back to her feet. It was all she could do to suppress the energy raging within her. It was as though she were denying every instinct inside of her. She sprinted down a narrow lane lined with empty crates, knocking them down behind her as she passed. The creature bounded after, barreling through the barricades. *If only there was someplace to hide, some nook where I could disappear.*

Tori recognized this place. She was in one of the poorest and most run-down slum districts at the southern end of the Fringes. One tall teetering structure towered several stories above a wide stretch of shanties. Tori remembered the tall building vaguely from her years here. She and Darien had been jumped by one of the many street gangs that lurked in the slums. Tori recalled looking up at that ramshackle tower from the ground as a vicious girl twice her size pounded her face and then snatched the few coppers Tori had and ran.

Tori had never ventured there again. All she remembered was the tower, but she knew she was at the heart of the Fringes. The muddy lanes were so rough they could barely be called roads, and so narrow it was hard to tell where one ended and another began. The lanes weaved nonsensically between hundreds of rusty dwellings. A few scrawny Fringe rats cowered in the corners of their homes and sank into the piles of rags they called beds as Tori shot past. Tori lost herself in the maze of shanties, hoping to find somewhere to hide. She rounded a corner, and her heart sank.

An impasse. A fifteen-foot wall isolated the slums from the factories at the heart of the Fringes. Tori had forgotten all about it. *There's no way I can reach the top,* she thought, eying the jagged surface of the stone. Factory walls were often lined with shards of glass and metal to ward off thieves. Even if she could leap that high, she'd cut her hands to pieces. Tori felt a swelling of energy inside her, ready to burst out. The warg paused at the end of the lane, blocking her only route of escape.

It laughed—a menacing growl, but it was unmistakable. "You can't escape me." The creature's voice was a seething, guttural purr. "You have no power over me, Gallows Girl. I can smell your fear."

Tori backed toward the wall, and the Morph crept forward, its head low, teeth dripping with thick, foaming spittle. "You will die," it said. "Just like your mother."

Tori's stomach sank. "W-what are you talking about?"

"I never forget a kill. It's not every day you find a sorceress on the Steppe. Your mother tasted like stale venison at the end of winter."

Tori's back brushed against the wall. The creature crouched, only a few yards away from splitting her open. Tori swelled with rage, the energy coursing through her veins. *The Morphs killed Mum?*

The beast shook with laughter. "I doubt you'll taste much better, but I am going to enjoy—"

"Enjoy what?" said a strange voice.

A man strode toward them from the end of the lane. He was tall, dressed in fine obsidian garb—the garments of a noble. He looked absurd in contrast with the drab surroundings. His hair was long and as dark as his clothes. His skin was pale as the snow—an Oshan noble. The creature turned to face the intruder.

"You won't be tasting her," said the Oshan man. "The chancellor wants her alive. Any fool can tell that." His voice was airy, as though he stared down Morph beasts every day. *What is this idiot's play? Is he here to turn me in? Collect a reward?*

The beast growled. "Perhaps you're right." It stalked toward him, turning away from Tori.

She did not move. Was this man crazy? He didn't even brandish a weapon at the creature. But perhaps she could get past while he distracted the Morph.

Suddenly, beside her, a second man appeared, leaping from the edge of the wall. He landed with the grace and precision of a hawk. He was dressed in ragged leathers. His long hair was dirty brown, and his eyes were like sapphires on a noble's amulet. His face curved in a permanent scowl, skin tight and weathered. He touched a finger to his lips and drew a silent blade.

The Morph was only a few yards from the cocky nobleman at the end of the lane. His rough-clad comrade crept toward the unwitting beast from behind. With all of them distracted, Tori considered leaping the wall and making a run for it, but something held her back. She watched the two Oshan men, curious.

The creature growled. "The chancellor may want the girl alive, but I think he couldn't care less about *you*."

The nobleman laughed, the beast mere feet from him. "Ah, but that is where you're wrong, my friend. We are *all* that matters to the chancellor."

The beast crouched, then leapt at the nobleman. But in the same instant, the rough-clad man dashed forward, swinging his saber. The warg's head severed from its body, inches from the nobleman's face, and rolled in the snow. The body collapsed in a steaming heap. Tori breathed with relief, her magic energy subsiding within her. She realized her fingernails had been digging into her palms.

"*Shenzah!*" The nobleman cursed in Yan Avii. A strange language for an Oshan. Was he some sort of merchant? "That was closer than I would have preferred, brother."

The rough-looking man inspected the Morph's head. Slowly, it shifted back to its human form, eyes lolled back in its skull, empty. "If you were worried, Ren, you'd have drawn your blades." He wiped his saber on his leathers and returned it to the sheath on his back.

Tori still had not moved from the end of the lane.

She was not sure if she should thank these men or make a run for it.

The noble-looking one named Ren strode forward, smiling. "There's no need to fear, Astoria. We've been waiting for you."

"You what?" She was certain she had never seen either of these men in her life. "How do you know who I am?" Her senses surged back to life.

A Morph flew high over their heads and shrieked. The three of them ducked into the shadows of the lane, crouching low in the muck of melting snow and pressing close to the shanty walls.

"We don't have time for pleasantries," growled the rough-clad brother. "And this kid is so tense she might explode with magic at the next sight of them."

How does he know? Tori thought, trying to calm her senses.

"If we move now, Kale, the creatures will spot us," said Ren. "We must wait for them to move on."

"That Morph sensed us. I told you we shouldn't have flown here."

A strange understanding dawned on Tori. In all her mum's tales, the Watchers had been able to do more than just wield magic. "Wait a minute! You can fly?" she said, picturing the rough-clad one named Kale landing effortlessly from atop that wall.

Kale granted her a nod. "And you *have* been locked up in a tower for a year, haven't you?"

"You'll have to pardon Kale," Ren said. "My brother wouldn't know how to greet a goat. Let alone the Saint of Osha. The Gallows Destroyer. The Last Watcher."

"What are you talking about?" said Tori.

Ren smiled. "That's what the common folk call you under murmured breaths. But I like to think of you more as the First Watcher. Or at least, the first one to be publicly known across the New World. Whispers have crossed the entire continent of what you did the day of the Gallows. Tales of the Watchers are being murmured all across the empire."

"I'm not a Watcher," said Tori.

Kale grunted, looking at the sky. "The Morphs have moved on. We should too."

"Yes, yes, you're right—he's always right, I'm afraid," Ren said, for Tori's benefit. "Even if he acts like an uncouth beast from the Old World."

Kale rolled his eyes and pointed down the lane. "Let's go."

"Where are you taking me? How did you know where I was? Why are you helping me? Were you the ones who drugged those guards in the citadel?"

Ren shook his head. "So many questions. I'm afraid we'll have to give you answers when we're out of this cesspool. Know that we are here to help, Astoria."

Tori did not like the idea of trusting someone she'd just met, even if that meeting had involved these men killing the Morph that was hunting her down. *But what choice do I have?*

Ren pulled a fine dagger out of a sheath on his hip and handed it to her. "This will serve you better than that nasty shard you used back there. Though you made fine work of that Morph under the circumstances."

"Ren, now!" hissed Kale.

The two brothers led the way down one narrow passage after another, and Tori followed. She felt wary about these men, and particularly their talk of Watchers—*Is that what I am? What this magic sense is?*—but she felt a need to follow, to find out more.

Avoiding the squares and the main lanes of the Fringes, they led her farther south. Two Morphs circled above, and in the distance, Tori made out the shrieks of lowborns. She wondered, darkly, how many were dying because of this hunt for her.

Kale led the way, moving lithely upon long legs, each footfall landing soft and sure. Ren kept by Tori's side, a long dagger in his hand. Tori liked the feel of her own blade. It was finer than any she'd held, perfectly balanced.

As they reached the edge of the Fringes, Kale slowed his pace. Tori and Ren followed suit. Before them lay the South Road, and beyond that, a wide stretch of field, and past the field, the Forest of Ghen loomed dark and ominous against the foothills of the Crooked Teeth.

"All eyes," Kale said, gazing up to the low-hanging clouds. The lane was empty, save for their footprints in the soggy spring thaw.

"Our tracks," Tori whispered. "Even if we slip past them, they'll know we went into the forest."

Ren nodded. "Morphs don't venture into the Forest of Ghen. It is full of spirits, the dead whispering on the wind, their fingers choking out the breaths of the guilty."

"I thought those were stories," said Tori.

Ren smiled. "I'm sure you thought plenty of things were stories. The chancellor's creatures will look for us on the other side of the forest. But we won't be venturing where they expect."

"We can yack about it when we're safe in the forest," said Kale, who had not once taken his eyes off the sky. "There are only the two sentinels now. The rest must be searching the northern Fringes. The sentinels will spot us as soon as we break cover, but we may have enough time to clear the field."

There was a mighty whooshing sound overhead, like canvas tents in a terrible storm on the Steppe, as one Morph made its pass. It soared near the cloud line. The other would be on the opposite end of the Fringes now.

Tori felt queasy, and gripped her dagger tightly. She pictured that wingless beast again, its fangs inches from her face. *Those Morphs killed Mum!* She wanted to kill them all, but she pushed the thought away. It would do her no good right now.

Kale counted to himself, then hissed, "Now!"

The three sprinted from the shanties. The field before them was barren grassland. No trees. Not even a hill. They were utterly exposed, and no sooner had they crossed the South Road than there was another loud whoosh behind them.

A Morph descended straight from the thick clouds, landing on a shanty roof. The four posts snapped beneath it. The creature arched its back and released an ear-piercing cry. Then, three more Metamorphi descended from the clouds. *The creatures were toying with us,* Tori realized, *waiting for us to come out in the open.*

"*Shenzah!*" Ren cried. "Run!"

Tori, Ren, and Kale ran as fast as they could, but the creatures were on them in seconds. One faced them head-on, its jaws wide, its talons flashing as they reached for Tori. Kale leapt forward, swinging his saber with finesse. The blade clanged off the creature's talons, and the Morph flew past and circled around.

Another came from the left, its talons tearing at Tori's cloak, but it could not latch on. Tori swung her dagger, and there was a splatter of blood from the creature's wing, but then another attacked from behind.

"We're surrounded!" Ren shouted as he clipped its wing with his own blade.

One by one, the Metamorphi descended from all sides. It was some sort of spiraling battle formation, and their blades had little effect on the creatures. They swooped down so quick that none could land a solid blow.

"Form up!" cried Kale. The three of them moved back-to-back, facing the creatures, exchanging blows deflected by talons. But the

Metamorphi could not snatch up Tori from any direction. Talons stretched out, only to be deflected by blades.

Ren tried a new tactic. From his cloak, he produced a satchel filled with iron balls. With a flare of magic, the balls shot through the air like a flurry of musket-fire. The first Morph to attack was shot in the wing and spun away, blood spraying Tori's face as she lashed out with her dagger. The Morph veered in the air, missing them, but its wing gave out, and it crashed to the ground nearby. Kale leapt to finish it off, and Ren sent another flurry of shots at the remaining three Morphs as they regrouped out of range.

The Morph leader let out three sharp cries, and the Metamorphi returned to the sky, flying in a tight circle.

"Well, if any of the Morphs didn't know we were here, they're on their way now." Kale glared at his brother.

Ren shrugged. "That's one down."

The Morphs remained high in the sky. Tori, Ren, and Kale crept toward the Forest of Ghen, staying formed up back-to-back so they could see the Morphs from all directions. Sharp cries echoed across the plains, and two more Morphs joined the others in the sky.

"And now, they have five," said Kale.

The leader let out a sharp series of cries, and the Morphs descended one after the other, in swift succession, straight down upon them.

Tori's grip went tight on her blade. *Was this how it ended for Mum too? Did she fight bravely, only to be overpowered in the end?*

The Morphs reached her, and Tori swung hard with her dagger, shrieking with rage, remembering her mum's face. It was deflected, but Kale swung his saber in the same moment and clipped the first creature's wing. Ren fired off another round of shots with a flare of his magic. The Morph came down hard, and Kale rolled away, entangled. Ren met the second in the air, leaping into flight with his dagger outstretched, a war cry on his lips. The blade met flesh, but the creature latched onto him and plummeted to the ground.

Tori was left alone to face the last three creatures. *This is it, but maybe I can take one down with me.* She swung her blade, but the three reached her together. She warded off her first attacker, but the leader of the Morphs came down from behind and latched onto her with bony arms.

Talons seared the flesh of Tori's shoulders, and she shrieked with pain as the creature lurched her heavenward.

Tori's dagger proved useless. Her arms were clamped to her sides. The fields blurred beneath her as the beast bore her higher and higher. Far below, Kale and Ren battled the other Morphs. One more creature lay dead, but the sentinels were circling back to join the fray. On the ground, a pair of wingless beasts bounded through the Fringes toward the clearing. Tori resisted with all her strength, but the Morph was too strong.

The creature spoke. Its voice was soft and sweet and familiar. "You are weak, little Gallows Girl. You have lost much blood this past year."

The chancellor! Tori's body gave up under his fierce hold. She knew, now, her escape was over. Even if she could manage to squirm out of his reach, she would only plummet to her death.

"You're a survivor, Astoria," he said. "And you're gifted. Why waste it? Why resist me?"

Tori did not answer. It infuriated her to have made it so far for nothing.

From this great height, the field seemed to roll past as though it were set on a giant wheel. Tori found the sensation exhilarating, as though she'd waited all her life to fly. The wind swept through her hair in currents and waves like the sea. Her senses came to life. The air, too, was composed of things unseen, coursing energy. And this realization gave Tori a trace of hope.

"You're right… I don't want to waste away," Tori admitted, a last desperate idea teasing at her mind. "I'm tired of resisting… I'm tired of hurting."

Even in his Morph form, Tori could tell the chancellor was smiling his alluring grin. "Of course you are, Astoria. You're weak. But I can make you great."

"I'll go," said Tori. "I don't want to fight anymore."

The chancellor was soaring north across the fields. He loosened his grip on Tori. He was confident. He thought he had won. But the chancellor was wrong, Tori was not weak. Her awareness of the world was stronger than ever. The chancellor underestimated her strength, and she would make him pay for it.

Tori flexed her mind, reaching out with her sense. The wind died down for a moment.

But then, a gust struck them, as though they had flown into an invisible wall. It was so forceful and unexpected that the chancellor spun on his wings, and Tori seized her opportunity. She thrust out her arms, and the chancellor lost hold of her. She plunged Ren's blade into his side.

The spinning stopped. The wind died down again.

And then, they were plummeting—

Tori wrestled free of the chancellor, and she plunged, her cloak flapping, her eyes watering. The ground raced toward her, and she knew she was going to die. She was a falling star about to collide with the world in an explosion of light. An explosion that would bear her on to see her mum again. That was what her mum had always taught her. *This world is but the first of many, and we are destined to explore them all, my little love.*

Celene Burodai's soft voice filled Tori's memory and gave her strength. Tori had been wrong about her mum, and she was grateful she had found out before the end. As she fell, her mum's face sprang from memory, so bright, so full of love, and Tori forgot all the bitter hatred she'd stored up over the years. In the end, Tori and her mum would have the same fate, and there was beauty in that.

The earth's jaws rose up to swallow her. But at the last moment, Tori felt a surge of energy spring forth from within her. Tiny particles of air—the energy that coursed through it, through all things—caught her up like so many tiny webs of rope, slowing her fall. Not much, but it was enough. Tori landed in a clumsy crouch. Her knees buckled, and she collapsed with a bray of sharp pain.

My legs! She thought she must have shattered them. But it didn't matter. She was alive.

The chancellor landed a short distance away. He stirred on the ground, to Tori's dismay, but as he tried to raise himself, he collapsed. The sentinels landed beside him, and wingless Metamorphi bounded across the field in their warg-like forms.

Ren and Kale flew to her; Ren helped Tori to her feet, and she realized, strangely, that the pain had dissipated, and she could stand. The three of them raced across the remaining distance of the field. The Morphs did not pursue, but instead tended to their fallen chancellor, who was screaming with pain.

The outstretched limbs of massive socha trees welcomed Tori, Ren, and Kale to the Forest of Ghen, and they disappeared under a thick shroud of foliage into the safety of the Haunted Forest.

They sprinted deep into the woods. Tori thought her lungs would explode by the time Kale finally paused to rest. Tori felt like she might retch, but Kale seemed to barely be breathing heavily at all. He stooped to his knees and held his ear to the ground.

"I don't think we've been followed."

"I told you as much," said Ren.

"We should keep moving, though."

"Please," said Tori, panting. Her entire body was pulsing from the throes of the attack, from surviving a fall from only the gods knew what height, and from running for her life for what felt like hours. Her energy was gone, and her body was spent. "Just… a moment's rest."

"Of course," said Ren, glaring at his brother. He handed her a canteen of water, and she lapped it up eagerly. "I feared you were dead." Ren touched her shoulder gently, but she still cringed at the unexpected touch.

"So did I," she said, taking another swig. "I would be if it weren't for both of you. Thank you."

Ren smiled, and Kale nodded, and for the first time in a year, Tori felt momentarily safe. But she knew it could not last long. "The chancellor…"

"I don't know how he managed to survive that fall," said Ren. "But I think it's safe to say he won't be on our heels immediately."

"He'll send scouts soon," said Kale. "We should press on. Our shelter is still a good distance away."

"Your shelter?"

Ren smiled. "As I said before, we've been waiting for you."

"We can talk about it when we're safe," said Kale. "Until then, we should move quick and keep silent."

Ren shrugged. "Afraid he's right." He touched her shoulder again. His hand was warm, but still it unnerved her. Tori became suddenly aware that she knew nothing about the men who had helped her. Ren seemed to sense her unease. "Breathe easy for a little while, Astoria. You're safe with us."

———

AFTER SEVERAL HOURS OF TREKKING THROUGH THICK undergrowth, Ren paused near an outcropping of boulders. He circled a mound of rock and, on the far side, found a thin crack just large enough to slip through. Tori followed and entered a small space about ten feet across, a cave formed by the leaning boulders, accessible only by the crack. Inside lay three rucksacks.

"Provisions, a change of clothes, and a bedroll," Ren said, handing her a pack. He opened his own and retrieved some strips of salted pork. "Eat. You look a bit haggard."

"Thanks for noticing."

"I'm not saying you're not lovely for someone who just spent the last year starving in the citadel. Because you are."

Tori regarded him querulously. Ren had saved her life, but she didn't even know why. *But he did risk his life to help me.*

For now, she was famished, and she dug greedily into the pack. Soft bread, nuts, salted pork. She slumped on the ground, leaned against her pack, and ate voraciously. Nothing had ever tasted so glorious.

"So, you were the ones who drugged the guards in the citadel?" said Tori.

"Actually, that was work on the inside," said Ren. "We wouldn't dare enter the White Citadel."

"The inside?" said Tori. "Who?"

"Who do you think?"

Tori had wondered it from the moment she'd seen the unconscious guards outside her cell. She thought back to the last encounter she'd had with him, when her master had embraced his rebellious slave. It had made no sense. "Commander Scelero?"

Ren nodded, though his smile waned. "Your former master has a... vested interest in your survival."

"I was only a servant."

Kale slipped through the crack in the rocks and huffed. "And I'm a horse's ass!"

Ren shook his head. "What my brother means is your master knew you were a Watcher. How do you think you ended up in his household? Blind chance?"

Tori pondered this, chewing on a large clump of bread. She had always thought it a strike of fortune, maybe even kindness from the gods. Certainly, Darien's pleading hadn't actually persuaded him.

"Don't eat it all now," said Ren, gesturing to her already half-devoured loaf. "However it may have appeared, Scelero chose you to be his servant because he knew what you were."

"But I didn't even know," said Tori.

Kale crossed his arms over his chest.

"The commander was trained to detect magic," said Ren. "Like all the other Morphs."

"Like all the..."

"Scelero is the commander of the Metamorphi," Ren said. "And without his help, we would have had far more Morphs on us in the Fringes."

Tori ate silently for a moment. She couldn't believe it. Her old master was a magic hunter?

"Don't be too surprised. The Morphs are a secretive army. I doubt even his close friends know."

"Then why would he help me? He should have had me executed years ago."

"Shapeshifting is a magic gift the chancellors of old fancied," said Ren. "They distorted it to make their very own breed of hunters to track down the surviving remnants of the Watchers. But the commander is not as loyal as our chancellor thinks. Just as I was not, many years ago. Just as many others in Osha are not. In secret, of course."

Tori gnawed on a strip of salted pork. "So, you work with

Scelero?" Ren nodded. "And you're an Oshan noble not loyal to the chancellor. So, who are you exactly?"

"Ren Andovier."

"Of…" Tori coughed, nearly choking on the pork. "Of House Andovier?" House Andovier was a fallen Lord House of Osha, often spoken of in hushed tones in Maro'El. "The Cursed House. I thought you died of a… plague, or something. The last of your line."

"And they hung your corpse from the White Citadel," said Kale. "Yet here we all are."

"For the past three hundred years, our family secretly preserved knowledge from the Old World," Ren went on. "Which is why they say we died. When the chancellor found out, he had to be rid of us. So now, I hunt down Watchers, but for different reasons than the Metamorphi."

"To recruit them," said Kale, but Tori sensed that he did not quite share the same fervor his brother displayed. "To join his army of Watchers."

"An army?"

"A resistance," said Ren with a smile. "We call ourselves the Shadow Watch."

"Shadow…" said Tori. "Like the soldiers in the Night Legions?"

"A play with words, of sorts. The chancellor has his Shadows, and he has forced the Watchers to live in shadows for centuries. Soon, shadows will be his undoing." Ren beamed as he spoke of this hoped future. "We have a fortress, deep in the mouth of the Crooked Teeth, where many more Watchers are hiding. That is where we're headed. We'll start north tomorrow."

More? How is that possible? Though, Tori supposed if she and her mum had remained hidden from the Morphs for so long, perhaps others could as well.

"There's no sign the beasts pursued us into the forest," said Kale, glancing back out the opening to the cave.

"Why don't they come?" Tori asked.

Ren spread out his bedroll. "Morphs are responsible for so much horror, the ghosts would torment them into insanity. But they will be watching from above, and waiting on the other side. We must go unseen, travel in darkness. We'll rest till nightfall. Sleep, Astoria. You deserve it. You've had one damned day for the ages."

Tori spread out her bedroll beside Ren's, and Kale stalked away to take the first watch. Tori did not sleep immediately. She could not calm her mind.

It was overwhelming to take in. Her master had been a Morph. He had known what she was. And now, he had betrayed his master and assisted in her escape.

Tori could not let herself dwell on what that might mean for him if he was caught. He had likely risked his life to free her.

Tori thought of her mum. It was strange to think of her. Since the day of the Gallows, she had suspected that the events of her mother's betrayal had not been what they had seemed, but the Morph had confirmed it. Her mother had died at the hands of the Metamorphi. *How did it happen? Was it because of me? Was that why we were running through the tent city that night?*

Tori had blocked it all from her memory for so long. She had not wanted to think of it, because it only brought sadness, bitterness, and rage at her mother's betrayal. But now…

When Tori finally drifted to sleep, it came in fits. For it was in her sleep that the ghosts of Ghen first appeared to her.

PART THREE
A SHADOW AMONG LEGIONS

We are not many.
We are one.
The chancellor's hands and feet.
His boots on the ground.
The blade in his hand.
The Shadows in his Legions.

—a mantra of the Night Legions

CHAPTER NINE

The Night Legions marched across the Meridian and south along the coast of Greater Osha, streams of movement in perfect, organized unison. They were not many. They were one. A magnificent mechanism. One shadow that spread the Oshan Empire's influence farther and farther across the New World.

Darien Redvar did not know if the world had ever been another way. There might have been no Old World at all—no War Between the Worlds, no Watchers, no gods—nothing but tales to make the chancellors appear more and more powerful for defeating them. Darien had never believed in gods; however, he had not believed in Watchers either. Yet there was no other explanation for why he was still alive. He pushed the thought from his mind and marched on, matching the rhythm of Jujen, the young Faerish soldier in front of him. Darien never dwelt long on thoughts of Tori. He could not afford to.

She was dead, of course. He had seen the creatures descend, seen them morph, before he'd been dragged away from Maro Square. The chancellor had strung up her corpse for all the city to see, and the new Legion recruits had been marched right past the tower, a solemn reminder of the fate of defectors. All defectors but Darien, that is.

Darien shifted his musket on his sore shoulder and pressed forward. The thought of Tori's dead body drove him mad, but hope drove him madder. He could not hope, could not listen to rumors. *Damn Ol' Merri for spreading rumors!*

How could Tori have escaped? It couldn't be true! Even if, by some miracle, she was alive, it was impossible she could have escaped the clutches of the chancellor's Metamorphi. Darien would not believe it, and he would never speak of it. Ol' Merri would get herself killed spreading such nonsense among the troops. General Thrain would not hesitate if he overheard. Still, Darien was glad he and Merri had been assigned to the same regiment.

A cry rose up ahead, and the units spread out to make camp. Jujen sidled up beside him. "When we gonna make war, ey? I'm sick of all this marching. When we gonna slit some Morgathian throats?" Jujen was from the Ruined Empire of Faere, and his people hated the Morgathians nearly as much as the Oshans did. Jujen's light brown skin flushed with fierce anticipation.

Darien smiled a practiced smile, lowering his pack, relief spreading through his aching shoulders. "Ooh, rah! Soon enough, comrade, soon enough, we will have blood."

"Not soon enough. We been training and training and marching and marching. I'm worried I'll lose my touch. En't shot my musket in weeks."

"Why don't you practice your aim on Fran Dosen's fat ass?" said Valeria, a tall, fierce soldier from the Southern Isles. She shook out silvery-blonde hair from her fur hat. "I'm sick of watching it jiggle all damn-long day."

"Wouldn't be no practice, would it?" said Jujen. "I could shoot with my back turned. Gods, I could toss a rock across Glacier Sound, and I'd hit her."

Darien laughed, though he didn't find Jujen particularly funny. It didn't matter—Jujen was joking, and so he was supposed to laugh. The three young Shadows set to hoisting the poles for their bunk tent. The field became a temporary city, a forest of tents on the plains of the Green Sea. Fires were lit, provisions checked, muskets cleaned. Then, Ol' Merri served stew.

Darien filled his bowl and took a seat by the fire as he ate his supper. Thrain's regiment ate better than all the Legions, Darien felt sure, and Ol' Merri always gave Darien a little extra portion. *If only she didn't risk rumors…*

They were spreading. Darien had overheard soldiers murmuring at night about whether another War Between the Worlds was coming; whether the chancellors hadn't truly rid the land of the Watcher curse; whether the Gallows Girl wasn't truly out there, somewhere. Three days previous, the marching army of Shadows had been joined by a band of Metamorphi. Darien wished it was Scelero's regiment. He had not seen the commander since he'd been taken away to the Shadow Camps.

Darien hadn't been altogether surprised to learn Scelero was the commander of the creatures. There had always been something different about him. His duties more sporadic, his ways more secretive than most officers in the Legions. But when he let his mind wander, Darien sometimes wondered how Scelero hadn't known what Tori was all those years she had served him. *Did* she *even know what she was?*

The thought angered him, and yet his very anger angered him as well. He shouldn't be thinking of it.

"Redvar, why you so bloody solemn?" said Valeria, squatting beside him around the fire. "You been staring at that fire like it's gonna speak to you."

"Just anxious for some combat is all," he recited.

Valeria nodded and patted his shoulder, but there was something off about her eyes, and it unnerved him. It almost felt like… suspicion.

Jujen hooted. "Ooh, rah! We'll blow right through 'em bloody Morgaths! Wait till we get to their townships, comrades. Then we'll really have us some fun, won't we?"

"Ooh, rah!" cried Darien mechanically.

"Ooh, rah!" cried Valeria.

Soon, the whole camp was crying out, "Ooh, rah! Ooh, rah!" The warrior's chant rumbled across the plains like a roll of thunder, and then their cries transformed into a braying song of conquest and honor in battle. Darien sang along.

He had learned to blend in quickly. Indoctrination was rigorous during the Shadow Camps, and since he'd been the Gallows Boy, he was closely watched. He'd been smart, though, and learned to look like the others, to think like the others. Sometimes, he wondered if he wasn't starting to *believe* the mantras. Too often, he found himself reacting less and less by practice and more and more by instinct. Found himself thinking about how Osha was mightier and altogether superior to Morgath and their pagan fire god, how the Morgathian rebellion deserved to finally be vanquished. Darien found himself chanting words from deeper and deeper memory, without having to think what the words were.

He had survived the Shadow Camps with what he thought was his sanity, what he thought was a remnant of the boy from Scelero's estate, but more and more, he had trouble recalling what life had been like in those old days. When he thought of Tori, he thought of a fleeting shade of a person. He could barely remember the timbre of her voice. For some time, this was a torment. But he had moved on.

Whatever the rumors might be, Tori was long dead, and he was left to live, to march to the borderlands of Osha and drive out the Morgathians. Soon, they would take back Morgath for the empire, and the chancellor would rule over more and more of the New World, and Darien would have helped him. And more and more each day, this felt right.

As the troops left the cook fires, Ol' Merri caught him by the arm and demanded he help her finish scrubbing the pots. Darien obliged, and Valeria and Jujen left them alone.

"Whispers been telling o' the commander," said Merri, when it was safe to speak. "Say the chancellor placed Scelero in some sort o' reclamation."

"What in the Abyss is that?"

"For reclaiming his mind. Locked him away in the dungeons. On account o' her escape, I reckon. How bad you s'pose the chancellor's wrath would be for breaking her out?"

"She's dead, Merri. The rumors came from the Fringes. Lowborns say that stuff because they need something to cling to."

"I refuse ter believe she's dead."

"You saw her dead, same as me. We marched right beneath her

bloody corpse when we left for the Shadow Camps. She's been dead for a year. And if the chancellor was angry with Scelero, he wouldn't reclaim him. He'd execute him. Rumors, all."

But was it absolutely true? *He didn't execute me…*

Merri responded as though she'd not heard a word he'd said. She touched his arm in a motherly fashion. "Heard tell there's still no sign o' her. Reckon they lost 'em Morphs in the Forest o' Ghen. Bloody clever ter go there."

"Don't start, Merri. You're gonna get yourself killed, and me too, if you don't shut up about these rumors."

"She's free. I believe it."

"Believing en't brought the old gods back to save you, and believing can't bring back the dead neither."

"She's coming back one day, and by the gods, she'll be raising an army."

"It's a gods-damned fantasy!" Darien pulled away from the base of the pot he was scrubbing, the film thick on the brush.

"You can't let go o' hope," Merri whispered. "You can't let the Shadows take you over. You were spared for a reason, Darien. So one day, you'd finish what you started on that gallows. You survived so much! Don't let 'em steal your hope!"

Darien threw the brush on the ground and cursed. "Finish your own duty!" And he stormed off.

He did not make for his bunk. Darien trudged through the thick grass and perched himself on a rock at the outskirts of the tent city. The sun slid over the edge of the earth, but the colors did not stir him. Beauty meant little to him these days. It served him no purpose. Beauty reminded him of other days, days when he was a boy with a mum and father, days when he was a slave for Scelero and life had been bearable, working hard alongside Tori and Ollie and the others. But memories served him no purpose, and he had learned to measure every deed, every thought, according to its usefulness.

Darien pushed the useless thoughts aside, turned from the sunset, stared off at the sea of grass for a time, then returned to the encampment, unsure why he'd gone. He weaved amidst the throng of men and women howling round fires as the night descended and the flagons of ale came out.

The chancellor treated his soldiers well. Sure, they marched long hours and kept a rigorous training regimen, but Darien ate better than he'd eaten in all his life. Every meal included hearty cuts of meat, and every evening brought ale and wine. Life in the Legions was not nearly as bad as he'd expected. Not at all.

The week previous, for the first time, Darien had entertained the thought that perhaps his parents had somehow deserved to be killed in the raids those years ago. Darien had shown merit—that was why he'd been chosen by Scelero, why he'd been spared the noose by the chancellor. He was a fine shot, and he had grown stronger and faster by the day. The closer they got to Morgath, the more he found himself longing for the chance to prove himself in battle.

Even so, Darien did not relish the prospect of killing. He'd never killed a man in his life. *But if they deserve it…*

No, blood spilled was always wrong. Suddenly, he felt ashamed of himself. What would Tori think to see him now?

Damn it, she's dead! Dead dead dead!

As Darien lifted the flap to his tent, he caught a flash of blue and silver that set his heart racing. Valeria Sardona withdrew quickly from behind a neighboring tent, where she'd been watching him. She disappeared into the night, the flash of her silver hair in the firelight imprinted on his mind like a flare of the sun.

Darien froze, guilt eating at his insides. How long had she been watching him? Only the moment? Had she followed him to the edge of camp? Seen him shouting at Ol' Merri? *Why was she watching?*

He shook the thought away. It was nothing.

Darien entered the tent, and as he lay awake on his mat deep into the night, he told himself over and over again that it was nothing. He had nothing to hide from Valeria or anyone else. So what if he'd gazed out at the Green Sea and the setting sun? He had told Ol' Merri off about the rumors. He was loyal to the chancellor, a Shadow in his Legions, ready to slit some Morgathian throats any day now. Darien had nothing to hide.

It was nothing.

CHAPTER TEN

Through another week of marching, Darien dispelled any possible notions of suspicion from Valeria or anyone else. He didn't talk to Ol' Merri; he didn't wander off by himself; he enjoyed himself in the company of his regiment.

They were fine warriors, and fine men and women, all of them. Even the fact the chancellor recruited women was a testament to the superiority of Osha. The Morgathians were a barbaric patriarchal nation. Darien would meet no women in battle except at his side. The Morgathian women were weak, left home to tend frail children. When the men died, the women and children would be helpless. They deserved to be overcome by the inevitable future—casualties in the progress of the human race.

Round the fires at night, Darien drank ale and laughed and relished the prospect of battle. There was no fear among the Oshan troops, only anticipation.

When they reached the edge of the Green Sea, crossing the border into Morgath, the excitement approached a boiling point. They had only to cross the Klavash Mountains, and there would be blood.

When General Thrain's regiment was chosen to venture to the far eastern ends of the range, to circle round and surprise the Morgathians from behind, Darien cried, "Ooh, rah! Ooh, rah!" like never before. Such a sensitive mission was entrusted only to the very best of the best, and Darien, the Gallows Boy, was among the finest soldiers in the Legions. Like a plague, they would descend upon Morgath.

Thrain's regiment marched deep into the mountains. Darien led the company at the general's side, hand chosen, because he knew the Klavash peaks. He had grown up in them.

"Must be strange to come back, comrade," said Thrain. The general had always been cordial toward Darien. Thrain was stern, yet not above his troops. He trained them himself. The final test of swordsmanship was to spar with Thrain. When the fighting came, he would be in the middle of the fray. Darien admired his leader, yet he had never once carried on a personal conversation with the general. He noted a resentful glare from Jujen as Thrain addressed him. Darien could not help but swell with pride.

Something deep in him stirred, though, at the general's question. He tried to suppress it. "No, er, not strange at all, sir."

"You cannot fool me, comrade," Thrain said, not angrily, but with an air of bestowing wisdom.

Still, Darien found himself gulping, a pain forming in his gut. It *was* strange to return to the mountains of his boyhood. He had striven to displace those thoughts, for the sake of his duty. *Why would the general try to stir them up?*

Thrain went on. "Most of us harbor sentiment for the place, and the people, that raised us, even if that sentiment be falsely founded. I was sixteen when I joined the Legions myself. Raised on the Steppe. My father was a tribesman. Barbarians, the tribesmen. The *soltaynes* and their heathen goddess and barbaric hierarchy. My father was a cobbler for my *soltayne*'s herd, and he would have been his whole life, and I would have been after him. Anytime he wanted, my *soltayne* could take my mother or my sister for his pleasure, and he took many mothers and sisters. I was glad to claim an Oshan name when I was promoted to general.

"The world is a cruel place throughout, comrade. But I could never have risen among my people the way I have in the Legions. My first battle was with the Yan Avii. Many years ago, a band of tribes rose up to take back the Western Steppe. I was torn, but I did not let it sway my duty. It would have been wrong for the Yan Avii to triumph. It would have been wrong for them to be spared. So, in my first battle, I slew a dozen of my kinsmen, my *soltayne* among them."

"Ooh, rah, sir."

"I did not relish it, at first, but I knew it to be true. As I think you do now. You were meant to begin your duty in these mountains. You were meant to be spared the gallows so you could lead us through to attack Morgath and end this civil war. The chancellor himself may have foreseen this. We could not complete our mission without you, comrade."

Darien was speechless at the general's forthrightness. Thrain was voicing the very things he had been wondering, the very things he needed to hear to keep his courage and resolve up. His upbringing, his parents' deaths, slavery, Tori, the gallows, the rigors of the camps, all his hardships—it had all brought him here. It had all been part of his progression, his destiny.

A calm settled upon him as the air thinned and the vegetation grew scarcer. The Legions marched high into the heart of the mountains Darien remembered so well; it was as though they had been mapped in his mind during his Klavash boyhood. He embraced the feeling, he did not deny it, and he found that once he owned it, the power of his past lost its grasp on him.

The higher they climbed, the freer he felt.

———

THRAIN'S REGIMENT TREKKED THROUGH THE MOUNTAINS FOR three days. Jujen and Valeria joined Darien at the front of the line, while the general brought up the rear. The three were talking of the glorious battle soon to come, when the child appeared.

A tiny, spindly thing, as most Klavash girls were, she couldn't have been more than five or six years old. Brown doe eyes shone from behind her fur hood. Bits of long black hair poked out in messy strands like a frayed rope. Snow coated her parka, as though she'd been rolling in it. When she stumbled into the clearing—giggling and then, at the sight of the soldiers, hushing to a whimper—the whole regiment froze.

They had not seen a single soul in these mountains, but they knew what was expected if they did. A single cry could alert a Morgathian ranger. Darien had been all eyes for men at the edge of their path.

But a little girl?

She could have been no older than Darien's own sister had been the day the Legions came.

"What do we do?" Valeria whispered to Darien.

What does she mean, what do we do? Is she testing me? There's only one thing we can do! Darien glanced around, but the general remained at the back of the line, nowhere in sight. By the time Thrain reached the scene, the girl would have shrieked or run for help. The call was on Darien, and he had but fractions of a moment. All were looking to him. He had been the one chosen to lead them through the mountains. He was the one Thrain spoke to, as to a son.

The girl was ten yards off, trembling silently like a fawn spooked by hunters.

Without an order, Jujen raised his musket. "You know what we gotta do!" The Faerish boy was grinning.

"No, it'll alert the whole—"

But it was too late.

Jujen fired.

The mountains echoed with a strike like thunder, and then a thud resounded across the woods like an axe head against the heart of a rotting tree. Jujen's aim had not faltered during their long march from Osha—it remained truer than a preying falcon's. The ball of lead collided with the Klavash girl's chest, launching her off her feet, no time to make a sound, not even a dying whimper. She fell dead on impact, spilling red upon the snow.

The shot reverberated off the walls of the peaks, as though a dozen shots had been fired. The noise faded into a moment of heart-wringing silence.

And then, a shriek.

At the edge of the clearing, a small boy's shaggy head stuck up from the ground. Probably the girl's brother, or village playmate, the boy was no older than four. He scrambled to his feet, tripped, then dashed for the cover of the forest.

Vaguely, Darien felt his musket being wrenched from his hands. He was helpless to resist, as though he were caught in another world.

Jujen aimed Darien's musket, and the boy painted the snow in red as well.

The peaks rumbled with the last wisps of the boy's screams, mixed with the sound of thunder. They faded, swallowed up by the falling snow. Darien felt as though his entire body had been left out naked in the cold. He moved his lips, but no sound was emitted. His head told his arms and legs to move, but it was as if the messengers had been taken out by the enemy.

Darien was in shock.

Jujen whooped and cried, "Ooh, rah!"

"Oh gods!" There was a shuffle and someone rushed past. Ol' Merri knelt beside the young girl. "You bastard!" she hissed at Jujen. "They were only children!"

"Who fired those shots?" It was the general, shoving his way through the ranks.

"Jujen, sir," answered Valeria. Her face bore no expression. *Would she have been the next to fire? Or was she scared stiff too?*

The general paused for a moment, staring forward, eyeing Ol' Merri and the bleeding dead girl in her arms. His expression hardened. He turned on Jujen and punched him in the jaw.

"Firing a shot in these mountains, you incompetent son of a whore? Their entire village will have heard those shots. You just compromised our entire mission!"

The general turned to Darien, and he flinched. But the general did not hit him. "Comrade, how far is the next village?"

"Harrivral, sir. A league, maybe two, due south."

"There must be outlying homesteads as well. No children would venture that far on their own."

"Aye, sir."

Thrain cursed under his breath, muttering, "Be swift. No delay. No unnecessary combat. Arayeva!" He swore by the sun goddess of the Yan Avii, an uncharacteristic slip. Thrain addressed the troops.

"LEAVE NONE ALIVE, SHADOWS. NO ONE ESCAPES. TAKE NO PRISONERS. OUR MISSION DEPENDS ON THIS. YOU'VE LUSTED FOR BLOOD, WELL... NOW YOU DAMN WELL HAVE IT!"

Darien helped Jujen to his feet like a good comrade. He jerked him close and hissed in his ear. "Next time, throw a bloody knife!"

Thrain's regiment became a perfect machine, cogs and wheels moving in precise order through the woods, and Darien led them, the general at his side. There was a moment—the briefest moment—when Darien considered the possibility he could save the village of Harrivral. Only *he* knew exactly where it lay, where the small trodden path wended between the meadow of boulders and then snaked between the kissing cliffs. He could lead the regiment to the east, maybe let them stumble upon a smaller settlement. A family or two would be slaughtered, but all of Harrivral—all of Darien's people—need not die.

But that would compromise the mission, his purpose, his comrades.

Darien let the treacherous thought slip away. Forgotten, as though it had never entered his mind. He found the hunter's path within a few minutes. The first outlying settlement lay past the boulder field, a small mountain farm in a clearing. Thrain sent Jujen and three others to deal with the farmers, and Darien was relieved to be rid of the boy's idiocy.

Darien led the remaining troops down the path between the cliffs and down into Harrivral Valley. The Klavash were a peaceful people. They had been caught in the middle of many wars between Osha and Morgath, as well as the Old World nations that had preceded them. It was raw, hard country that tested the limits of a people. The Klavash lived in the mountains, boldly facing harsh winters and short growing seasons, because they longed for peace and loved nature. They had a respect for the land the greater civilizations had forgotten; they grieved over needless death—they were Darien's people.

It was fitting his first mission should be among them.

His final test.

Contrary to what Darien expected, the people of Harrivral had mustered no army to face the attacking horde. They were going about their morning as usual when the Shadows arrived. Thrain's regiment stole silently from the woods, descending upon the village from all sides without warning. The general did not leave Darien's side. It was Darien, Thrain, Valeria, Hollen, and Uraa. They entered the village from the south in single file, slinking behind thatch-roofed dwellings.

The first to oppose them was barely a man. His long dark hair was pulled back and tied up in a small bun, and Darien knew the boy had just come of age. Klavash boys left their hair down until the day they turned fifteen and became a man grown. Filled with a thirst for honor, filled with a love for family and loyalty to his kinsmen, the boy was the first to face the invaders, and he would be the first brave one to fall.

As the boy approached, Thrain stepped back, as though declaring it Darien's opportunity to prove himself, once and for all.

The final test.

Darien lunged forward, unsheathing his saber with a flourish. The Klavash boy was armed only with a crude hunting blade, a jagged work of the mountains. The boy brandished it boldly, crying for his god, Rivka, to curse the Oshan hordes.

The blade was out of his hand with a pair of thunderous blows, and the boy—the brave defender of his kinsmen, the man grown—fell upon his back, grimacing, his fingers bleeding.

It was at this moment that Valeria Sardona caught Darien's eye and nodded, her eyes cold and heartless.

She was watching all along! Perhaps at Thrain's command. Of course, Darien had not been trusted. He was the Gallows Boy. But now he would prove himself.

The final test.

Darien did not hesitate. He plunged his blade into the boy's chest. He felt the blow as though his own hand had entered the boy's flesh, as though his saber were *part* of his arm, attached by tendons and muscle, the blood pumping from his heart and filling the saber with strength and precision. He sensed the pierce of skin, the crunch of ribs, the tearing of organs, and the grinding thud as his blade struck the ground beneath the boy's body. He felt the life leave the boy in a shudder of rasping breath.

Darien would not remember the others so vividly. But this was his first.

The first kill.

The final test.

The Gallows Boy—the boy who had once stood against the cruelty of the Legions, the boy pardoned by the chancellor in spite of his rebellion, the lone Klavash boy spared in the raid that had slaughtered his family—had redeemed himself at last. He'd earned his redemption. Darien had become the chancellor's hands and feet, his boots on the ground, the blade in his hand.

A Shadow in his Legions.

PART FOUR
INTO THE TEETH

Death is but a crossing between worlds.
Our world is the first of many,
And we are destined to explore them all.

—an ancient saying of the Watcher order

CHAPTER ELEVEN

*M*urrrderrrerrr...
Murrrderrrerrr...

The words echoed through the wood, whispers ferried upon the breeze. Branches stretched out like bony fingers and then retreated with the dying of the wind. Everything went still.

Tori stood alone in a small clearing in the wood. It was twilight. The Sisters bathed the forest in a silver glow, and their thousand daughters began their nightlong dance across the sky. *Where did Ren and Kale go?* Tori wondered. *How did I get to this place?*

She had no memory of the journey. Was she still in the Forest of Ghen? The world was still. Then, a flutter. A leaf trembling. And then, the wind hissed with voices again, rushing through the snowpines with fury.

Murrrderrrerrr...

Murrrderrrerrr...

Murrrderrrerrr...

More whispers joined, building upon one another, growing louder and louder with each breath of the wind.

Murrrderrrerrr...

Murrderrerr...

MURDERER!

As though rising from cracks in the bramble and snowmelt, the spirits arrived. Tori fell back, cutting her hands on a rock. First, it was the soldiers from the gallows, their translucent bodies riveted with a hundred holes, blood drenching their chests in a hundred splotches, dripping silver splatters upon the earth. Their blood glowed like constellations on the forest floor.

"I'm sorry," Tori murmured, scrambling back to her feet. The guards walked slowly. Their feet never quite seemed to touch the ground, as though they were not fully present. They reached out their rotting arms as they neared. The trees reached as well. Tori sprinted away, tripping over an outstretched tree root. There was a rush of the wind, and then the soldiers appeared again, directly in front of her. A chill shot across her skin. There was no escaping them.

Only doing our duty, hissed the ghosts, drawing near again. *Like all the others.*

Tori held still, her fingers grasping at her belt for Ren's dagger, but it was gone. But what good would a blade be, anyway?

Murrrderrrerrr...

"I didn't mean to!" Tori backed away.

Murrrderrrerrr...

You enjoyed it! It made you feel powerful. Made you feel complete.

Murrrderrrerrr...

Tori turned again and ran. Another spirit appeared—the vendor from the Fringes, his neck cock-eyed, snapped from when she threw him across the square. Tori screamed. The sound was muffled, as though someone were smothering her voice with a blanket. The vendor hobbled toward her. Tori backed into a dead tree.

Just trying to make a living. And you stole my wares. What'd I ever do to you?

"I didn't mean to, I was only trying..."

You know how hard life is in the Fringes, you little whore! You stole my wares.

Murrrderrrerrr...

The wind rushed, and there was a great groaning sound. The dead branches came swinging forward, and Tori leapt away just in time.

One of the branches came free and flew over her head. Tori sprinted through the woods, weaving between boulders and snowpines and socha trees.

A voice resounded through the woods—a voice Tori knew all too well.

It was her mum. Celene Burodai stepped out from behind a tree, and Tori froze, a sick feeling rising up in her stomach. Her mum's curly dark hair floated upon the breeze. Her pale skin was glowing. She was beautiful, even in death, until she lifted her head to speak. Tori cried out in shock. Her mum's neck was split open. Silver blood dripped down her black gown. Her head wagged as she spoke in a cold, even tone that seemed to come from a thousand directions, wailing with the wind.

It was you the monsters came for…

"No!" Tori shouted. "I didn't know what I was!"

You just couldn't control your magic. For some stupid little horse boy. The monsters came for YOU, but instead they killed me…

Her mum disappeared in a wisp of something like fog, joining the other ghosts, their voices building and echoing to a crescendo. Tori felt the coldest touch at her neck. It was like a blade left out in the snow. It passed through her entire body, and she spun around.

Darien stood before her. His broad chest was bare, glistening in the soft light of the Sisters. His face was shaved smooth, his dark hair neatly trimmed—a proper soldier. Darien wore the dark grey breeches of the Night Legions, a red stripe lining the outer thigh. Tori had forgotten how handsome Darien was. She'd forgotten the look of him, if she was honest. His memory had become more an idea than a person. Darien's face was etched with sorrow, his gaze never leaving his hands. They were drenched in blood, and this blood was crimson.

Tori leapt back, felt at her neck. Blood left behind from his touch, still cool on her skin, dripped down her neck, down her back.

Why couldn't you let me die? I never wanted this, Tori. Blood. Blood on my hands, because of you.

Murrrderrrerrr…

Darien looked up. His eyes were dark chasms that seemed to suck her in like a whirlpool. Tori could not look away. She felt herself drawing nearer, unable to resist. "No! I wanted to protect you! I wanted to save you!" Tears dripped down Tori's cheeks, mixing on the ground with the blood from Darien's hands.

You call this saving me? Darien turned to reveal his naked back. Tori's knees went weak. His back was nothing but shreds. Muscle and bone shone through the gashes—a thousand stripes on his back, copper skin hanging in threads.

Murrrderrrerrr...

Murrrderrrerrr...

MURDERER!

All the spirits were there now. They fell upon Tori, whispering their mantra, clawing at her, hands passing through her body like icy vapor, clutching, grasping, pleading. Darien's fingers clamped round her throat, constricting and constricting, until no breath entered her lungs and no breath escaped. They were going to kill her, and Tori knew she deserved it.

A shrill scream pierced the night, rushing across the treetops, spreading like wildfire...

Tori shot up from her bedroll back in the Forest of Ghen. She brushed frantically at her neck, the chill of the spirits' hands still cool upon her skin. Sweat drenched her face, but the spirits were gone. She sat still, her whole body trembling.

The sun had begun to set. Tori had slept through the day. Five settings of the sun they'd spent in the woods, and each one had followed the same routine: travel by night, so they'd be unseen from the sky, and sleep by day. Ren Andovier slept soundly beside her, his chest rising and falling with serene constancy.

Tori breathed. It had only been a dream. Every slumber in these woods, she had been tormented by nightmares, all of them playing upon her darkest fears and regrets. Tori's fingers were clammy. She couldn't shake the dark feeling that she had no business wielding magic. She was a murderer. *Everything I've done with magic has only caused pain and suffering for the ones I love.*

"You are haunted by many spirits, for one so young."

Tori started at the voice. Kale Andovier stood watch at the edge of camp, all eyes for Morphs. But the enemy was not out there, Tori knew. It was in her dreams. Tori walked over to join Kale. "How did you know?"

"Don't worry, you will learn to discern their lies. In time."

"The ghosts… they're real?"

Kale nodded. "Though the form they reveal may not be. Spirits play by no rules. They feed on your guilt and your fear. Bits of truth shrouding lies. Nevertheless, I, too, sleep little in the Forest of Ghen." Kale glanced down at Ren, still dozing in peace. "Not all sleep as easy as my brother."

"I saw a ghost in my dream… but he's still alive. At least, I hope he still is…" Tori trembled at the memory of Darien's shredded back, of the blood dripping from his hands. She felt at her neck again, but it was clean. *What is the truth and what is the lie? The blood on his hands… is it real?*

"Who was this ghost?" said Kale.

"The boy… from the gallows. It's been a year since he was sent to the Shadow Camps…" Surely if he were dead, the chancellor would have told her so. He had so liked to update her on Darien's progress in the Legions. *Unless all that was a lie as well.*

"If your friend is alive, pray he remains so. Do not listen to ghosts."

"How much farther do we have in this gods-forsaken place?"

"If we move quick, we may reach the edge of the forest by daybreak."

"What are we waiting for, then?"

Kale shoved his sleeping brother. "The sun has fallen. We should go."

Ren stirred. "Gods, I was in the middle of a glorious dream. I was king of a dozen kingdoms. Beautiful lords and ladies were at my sides. And I wake to this damned forest, and *you*, brother. Dressed like some common hunter."

"Reality is a wench, isn't she?"

Tori smiled in spite of herself. For a moment, she tried to forget the phantoms and the guilt and the blood on her hands.

———

KALE LED THEM AT A FAST CLIP, BUT TORI DIDN'T MIND. SHE HAD recovered remarkably since her time in the citadel. Each morning, she felt stronger. The forest was silent but for the soft crunch of their footsteps on the melting snow. The memories of Tori's dreams kept sifting back to her mind. *Was I truly responsible for Mum's death?*

Ren's chatter was a welcome distraction. "You will love the Watchtower. The chancellor has no sway in the Teeth. You'll be able to develop your magic gifts in safety, with dozens of others like you."

"There are that many Watchers still alive?" said Tori. It was incredible enough there were two walking with her right now.

Ren smiled. "There may be hundreds more hiding throughout the New World. We just need to find them."

"I thought the First Chancellor killed them all."

"Yet here we are," said Kale drily.

"Even if that were true, it wouldn't matter," said Ren. "Magic does not pass on solely by heredity. It is in everything. It is the fabric of life. All the Watchers in the world could be hunted down, but more would keep turning up."

"Were your parents Watchers?" said Tori, thinking again of her mum.

There was an awkward pause. Kale would not meet her gaze, and Ren's face turned to an unnatural scowl. "Our family is a… rather unpleasant subject, I'm afraid," said Ren. "But yes, they were Watchers. They suppressed their gifts, like many others in Osha."

"People never had good things to say about House Andovier in Maro'El," said Tori.

"Yes, the Cursed House, they called us. They blamed our demise on a plague. It wouldn't have gone over well if it got out that an Oshan Lord House practiced sorcery, would it?"

"I guess not."

"When I betrayed Cyrus Maro to form the Shadow Watch, three years ago, they made up all that *shenzah* about the plague. They murdered my cousins and aunts and uncles, and called it a bloody sickness."

"You betrayed him," said Tori. "And where were you, Kale?"

"Gone," he said curtly, "years before any of that."

"You're the one they called the Exiled Lord," said Tori, recalling the old rumors. The Cursed House had always been a point of gossip among nobles, and the fact they had fallen from favor in Maro'El made them especially interesting to the servants as well.

"Exiled myself actually…" Kale's voice drifted off. His eyes appeared sad. "Couldn't be in that city anymore."

"And now here we are," said Ren.

"So, this resistance… it's about revenge, then," said Tori.

Ren shook his head. "No, Tori. This is about liberation. For our kind. For the lowborns. The chancellors are evil. They sit in their citadel while their Morphs, who were created by magic, hunt down and kill those blessed with the gift. And the High Council is filled with corrupt nobles, who live in their luxurious estates while thousands of lowborns toil in their fields and workhouses. This is about much more than revenge."

"But they killed your family," said Tori.

Kale looked away, and Ren scowled. "Yes," said Ren. "As they killed yours… and many others."

The brothers were silent for some time. There was more, Tori could tell. Something Ren and Kale were hiding about their past. And Tori was struck with the unnerving realization that she was entrusting her future to complete strangers. *Yet what other choice do I have? Where else would I go?*

Tori had known few friends in her life: a pair of young serving girls in the Trium'vel, a thief or two in the Fringes—if anyone in the Fringes could be called a friend—and Darien… But out here, Ren and Kale Andovier were her only allies. Scelero must have trusted them, and Commander Scelero was about the only person in the world Tori had left to trust. *I wish he were here. I wish I understood why he helped me. Why he chose me when he knew what I was… Is he even still alive?*

"Tell me about the Watchtower," Tori said when she'd tired of the silence.

Ren spoke, and Kale seemed content to let him. "The Watchtower is like no place in the New World, Astoria. Not since the ancient days have so many Watchers been united. There, you can become the

Watcher you're meant to be. We are the future of the New World. The chancellor is not nearly as invincible as he believes."

"He may not be as weak as you want him to be," Tori muttered. She had told the brothers about the source of Cyrus Maro's power. They did not imagine hers was the first Watcher blood to be harvested. Tori might have been only one of many locked away in the depths of the citadel. If there were dozens at the Watchtower, there could be dozens elsewhere for the chancellor to hunt and feed upon.

"But he has lost *you*," Ren said. "And that makes him weak. Perhaps not physically, but there is a power far greater, even than magic. Your act of defiance was a sign of hope the New World has waited centuries for. The lowborns are angry and defiant. There are Lord Houses tired of the corruption of the High Council. The empire is thirsty for a new government. The time is ripe for revolution."

Tori recalled the riots in the square after the day of the Gallows. The time was ripe for revolution then, as well. The lowborns had revolted, and they had died. *Am I a source of hope?* she wondered. *Or a pathway to destruction?*

"What if I don't want to join your army?" said Tori. "I'm grateful for all you've done. But I never asked for this. What if I don't want anything to do with this revolution?"

Part of her was torn. She was free. She could run off to the Southern Isles, or Parjha, or the Trium'vel. She could forget about magic altogether. A notion that seemed more and more appealing each night the ghosts came to her. After all, Tori had lived most of her life in ignorance of her gifts. She could run far away, live free from any memory of the chancellor.

But what about Darien? She pictured him in the Night Legions, blood on his hands, as in her dream. To run away would be to leave him to rot in the chancellor's service.

And could she really run off and pretend to be something else, now that she knew what she was? Her senses had only been growing. The past few days she had longed to use them, like a child learning to talk who can barely resist the urge to babble on and on.

Tori wished her mother were alive. She wished she had anyone left she could confide in.

"Long ago," said Ren, "the Watchers were the aides to kings and queens across the Old World. The Order helped keep peace, helped protect the world. My mother believed in the creeds of the Order. She used to tell me that we were given these gifts by the gods. And since they are gifts, we must give back. We are fighting the cruelty of the empire. Soon enough, the chancellor's time will end, and the Watchers will rise again." As he spoke, Ren looked up at the stars, his voice strong and determined. "If you do not wish to bring justice to the world, Astoria, then you are free to go. But I've a feeling you want the chancellor dead as much as anyone."

It was true. Tori hated Cyrus Maro. He was cruel, and he perpetuated the system of violence and injustice Osha held so dear. Tori thought of Darien and Ol' Merri suffering in the Legions, and she longed to free them. But she also thought of her mum's head wagging limply. The vendor, the guards from the gallows. The images made her sick.

Kale kept silent through the conversation. He did not seem to possess his brother's enthusiasm for the rise of the Watchers. Though, in truth, Kale did not seem to possess enthusiasm about much of anything.

"How have so many Watchers remained hidden from the Metamorphi?" Tori asked, happy to change the subject from revolution.

"The Watchtower is protected by ancient enchantments," said Ren. "The Metamorphi cannot detect the use of our power there, even if they cared to venture that far north."

"Isn't it dangerous in the Crooked Teeth?"

"We live in a stronghold leftover from the ancient days. Near the village of Ytala, in the central Teeth."

"Crooked folk," said Tori warily. She had heard tales of them impaling Oshan soldiers on stakes if they marched too far north. Ancient savages, gone mad with cold and starvation, it was told.

"It is true the mountain folk show no kindness to Oshans. But neither do we. We are mountain folk ourselves in their eyes. And the monsters of the mountains live on only in legend. The Rulaqs died out with the Old World. There is nothing to fear for us in the Teeth."

The Crooked Teeth filled Tori with nervous excitement. Even

Oshan nobles spoke superstitiously of the monstrous, two-headed Rulaqs of the Old World. The Teeth were a realm of mystery and terror, but Tori felt strangely eager to see it. When Tori was a child, her mum had told many stories of the creatures of the Old World. It made more sense now, why her mum had known so much.

"You said there are other Lord Houses involved with this Shadow Watch."

Ren nodded. "Like Scelero, they have been biding their time. No one knows of their treachery. Even I did not know of Scelero's until shortly before your escape. But when the moment arrives, the others will join us."

"Are they like your House? Are there others in Osha who are Watchers?"

"She is wondering about her mother," said Kale, suddenly.

Tori nodded. *How did he know?*

"Your mother was Oshan," said Ren. "But sadly, I do not know what House she came from. Just as no one knew about our House until things unraveled. I wish I knew, truly. But you were named for a goddess of the Old World. I imagine her House also held on to the old stories, the old ways."

Tori said no more. She did not want to think further about her mum just now.

As the Sisters set and the horizon began to glow with the approaching dawn, they reached the eastern edge of the Forest of Ghen. The Fields of Pendra welcomed them from the realm of nightmares and ghosts. The open fields stretched for leagues in all directions, and Tori had never been so happy to see a wide-open plain. It reminded her of her childhood, her people, her mum. Beyond the fields stretched the windblown hills of the Western Steppe. And to the north lay the jagged foothills of the Crooked Teeth.

At the tree line, Kale held up his hand. He crouched, focusing, his head down. The wind shot up from the plains, tossing the tall grass to and fro. It sounded like waves crashing. After several moments, Kale stood. "The way is clear, for now."

"Of course it is," said Ren. "The creatures expect we'll flee south. It is the quicker journey through the forest. No one would expect us to flee to the Teeth. They'll be watching the ports along the western coast and the roads across the Green Sea."

Kale shook his head, but Tori sensed a disgruntled fondness toward his brother. "We must be swift, nonetheless." He waded through the thigh-deep grass.

"Do you listen for them?" Tori asked Kale. "The Metamorphi?"

"He's a Cerebro," said Ren. "The order of minds. He can sense magic across leagues. That is how we found you back in the Fringes."

"And what about you?" said Tori. "What's your ability?"

"Besides being fiendishly charming?"

"Well, that's more a curse, isn't it?" Tori shot back.

Ren laughed, his mouth gaping. He grasped her shoulder. "It is, yes, it *is* a curse! Finally, someone who understands. It's a heavy burden, in fact. You hear that, brother?"

"Sorry, I tend to tune out *shenzah*." Kale smirked.

Ren laughed all the more, and Tori let a smile spread wide. She enjoyed sharing the brothers' company, even Kale's, despite his somber disposition. But there was something very disarming about Ren—youthful confidence, courage, lightheartedness. It was a welcome change from the darkness she had known so long.

"Besides my charms, though, Astoria, I am a Conjuri. The manipulators of matter. We are paired in this ability." As he spoke, Ren summoned his dagger from its sheath. It floated alongside him as he walked and then flew to his hand. This was followed by the satchel of lead balls. As Ren continued walking, he fired them at a lone tree in the distance, hitting his mark every time. Then, all of his weapons returned to their place on his belt.

Kale glared at his brother. "We are not nearly far enough north for such carelessness. The Morphs are still searching for us."

Ren nodded, though with a smirk. "If they were near, you would sense them."

"Why didn't you use your power when you faced that Morph in the Fringes?" said Tori. "The one that had me trapped in the streets. Surely you could have simply shot it."

"Well, for one, that would have drawn more Morphs to us, using magic. And it wouldn't have been as much fun." Ren grinned mischievously.

"Conjuri," said Kale, "have a reckless thirst for theatrics."

"And I'm a Conjuri?" said Tori.

"Only a Conjuri could do what you did on Gallows Day," said Ren. "And *that* was theatrical in any sense of the word."

"Gallows Day," she muttered.

"The rumors have spread all across the New World," said Ren. "Your act of defiance has given many a brief bit of hope. Imagine the hope when word spreads you are still alive?"

Tori did not like the thought that she was some mythic sign for the masses. "Hope of what? More war? More bloodshed? Another War Between the Worlds?"

"Restoration," said Ren. "In the Old World, the Watchers were the last link to the gods. The thought that they may not have been vanquished... Tori, you are the first Watcher to reveal power so publicly in over three hundred years."

"There are dozens of others."

"And we have lived our entire lives in fear of being tortured and killed by the Metamorphi. You were the first to reveal your power, and you survived the chancellor's wrath. This is something larger than you, whether you like it or not. You've given hope to *us* as well."

They traveled on in silence for some time. Tori kept thinking back to her fall after stabbing the chancellor. The pain that had smothered her, and then, the almost immediate relief. "Do Watchers only have one gift?" she asked.

"To wield more than one was rare in the Old World, and unheard of in the New," said Ren.

"You both can fly," Tori ventured.

"All Watchers can fly," said Ren. "*You* flew in the Fringes. Enough to survive your fall, that is."

Did I fly? It had all happened so fast. Thinking back, nothing seemed clear. Only that she had survived. She'd felt searing pain for a moment, and then it was gone, and she had sprinted to the Forest of Ghen as though nothing had happened. But it made no sense. The magic of the Watchers seemed to be so ordered. A Conjuri would not be able to heal.

Kale turned back to her briefly, and Tori felt uncomfortable in his gaze, as though he could sense she was hiding something. A scowl creased his brow, and he turned away.

"Haven't you heard the tales of the Watchers?" Ren went on.

"I heard them," Tori said, trying to recall her mum's stories, but they were all faded, as though they had been told to her in an old dream. Ever since she became a slave, she had tried *not* to remember anything to do with her mother. "But you never know what's myth and what's truth as a child. I thought the Watchers were only legends from the Old World. Something to give children hope."

"Well, Tori, let me assure you. The Watchers are no lost legend. We have endured the chancellor's purging. The time has come for the world to remember us. Soon, we will not need to hide in the Crooked Teeth like thieves."

———

At dawn, they neared the village of Hatia, set amongst the craggy foothills of the Teeth. Kale ventured alone, and Ren waited with Tori outside the village, so not to spread rumored sightings of the Gallows Girl. It was at Kale's insistence.

"Your face was well known amongst the lowborns after Gallows Day," said Ren after his brother had gone. "The girl from the Steppe with green eyes. It's been over a year, and I doubt the chancellor has publicly admitted your escape, as it would expose the lie of your execution, but I suppose it *is* better to be safe." But he spoke with some reluctance, and Tori could tell he did not like to be the one waiting around.

The Hatian horseman could only spare two steeds, no matter the price, which meant Tori was left to ride double. "I think Ren may have that honor," said Kale as he led the steeds from the village. "I don't think he'll mind."

Tori did not mind either, if she was honest. She wrapped her arms around Ren's waist, noting the clearly defined muscles beneath his tight-fitted tunic. She found her gaze falling upon his sharp features more than once as they rode on. But this distraction was remedied as they climbed into the foothills. The air grew thinner and much colder, and they all quickly donned heavy cloaks.

They traveled by day and camped by night. For the first couple days, Tori could tell Kale was tense. He often closed his eyes, sensing for signs of their hunters. Once they entered the high mountain passes, he relaxed. His scowl softened, and he stopped riding with one hand at the hilt of his saber. The wild mountains appeared to be his element.

Though Tori had felt excited a few days ago, the mountains had the opposite effect on her. The higher they journeyed, the more she thought of her mum's tales of Rulaqs and Nosferati. When night fell and they huddled together for warmth inside a canvas tent, every sound made her tense. More than once, she was certain she heard howls echoing off the towering peaks, though Ren insisted it was only the wind.

On the fifth day, they reached the mountain village of Ytala. Even in spring, the lanes were thick with snowpack. The villagers were bundled in thick fur-lined parkas, and the men all bore voluminous, nest-like beards. Mountain folk were a mixture of races that fled to the mountains at the dawn of the New World. Their skin was coppered and weathered by harsh high-altitude exposure, and this spread to their countenances. The Crooked folk were known for no kindness in Osha. But at the sight of Ren, their expressions softened. Children pointed and grinned at them, running alongside their horses. Ren waved them off with a charming smile. "I told you, we are mountain folk."

"You offer them blessings from the gods," said Kale.

"Blessings?" said Tori.

"To the people of Ytala, our tower is a monastery devoted to the old gods," said Ren. "And on occasion, the High Priest will come down and offer blessings to the Crooked folk."

"That surely helps their dispositions." Kale did not seem impressed.

Ren grinned. "Undoubtedly, brother, undoubtedly. Helping them construct a glass house so they can grow crops year-round surely helps, as well. I'm a regular saint among the mountain folk."

Tori was still trying to read Ren. For his talk about the injustices of lowborns, he sure didn't mind fooling them. Though she had to admit, these people lived in better conditions than any in Osha, and he had helped them grow more food. Ren gave the impression that he was some sort of idealist, but Tori still could not shake the sense that this revolution was personal for him.

They rode for another hour, leaving the village and ascending a steep, narrow path cut into the side of the mountain. *How high have we climbed since Hatia?* Tori wondered. *Thousands of feet?* And yet, still, the peaks towered thousands more above them. At the edge of a clearing, they approached a sheer cliff wall. Tori saw no path until they faced it straight on; a narrow cleft was cut into the rock, and they filed through one at a time.

"We call this the Birth Canal," said Ren. "I swear it gets narrower with each passage. In the Old World, the Teeth were known to shift when the gods became angry. That is how this passage was formed, they say."

The path weaved through the mountainside for half a league, then spread wide into a hidden valley, surrounded on all sides by towering peaks. At the far end of the valley, carved into the side of the mountain, was the Watchtower. Three narrow spires rose over a hundred feet from a vast granite fortress. The towers were coated in a thin layer of snow that left Tori marveling at their sheer magnificence. The snow-covered Teeth towered above, as though the castle were being devoured by the gaping jaws of a Rulaq.

Ren spread his arms wide. "Welcome to the last refuge of the Watchers."

CHAPTER TWELVE

The Watchtower appeared to have been carved straight from the mountainside and looked just as ageless—the way Tori imagined a fortress of the Ancient Men might have looked. The stonework blended in with the mountain, as though the two had always coexisted. Tori guessed it would be near impossible to spot from the air, if a Morph ever were to fly over the Teeth. Majestic though it was, the fortress appeared empty and felt dead. There was no sound but the clopping of their horses' hooves resounding off the face of the mountains. Tori felt uneasy as they approached.

Kale led the way across the clearing, and as they neared, the iron gates spread wide, seemingly on their own. Tori realized it was Ren's gift bidding them open. Once they entered, the aura of the place transformed, as though a lever had been triggered. The air in Tori's lungs seemed to grow lighter. The three towers basked in warm light. Sounds of life filled her ears in a jarring instant: people bustling in a wide square, a pair of young girls hovering several feet off the ground, holding one another's hands for balance, giggling. It was strange to hear something so light and frivolous, as though the world were some bright, happy place. *Have I ever giggled like that?*

Yes, she had, but it was long ago, when she and her mum lived on the Steppe among the Yan Avii, when the world had been bright and simple, a child's world.

A short, muscular woman with olive skin and bushy obsidian hair greeted them, along with a lanky man with deep brown skin and thick dreadlocks that fell to his shoulders. The man took hold of their reins as they dismounted. Ren took Tori's hand and helped her down. Her legs felt clumsy on the ground; she had gotten used to riding over the past five days. The aches had subsided on the third day, and now, as she moved, it felt like there was still the ghost of mount blankets and muscle beneath her.

"Dajha," Ren addressed the lanky man, "why don't you show our new recruit to the stables? I've a few things to discuss with Sahra." He gestured at the woman, dismounted, and handed his reins over to the man.

Dajha handed a pair of reins to Tori and ushered her to follow him. The stables were around the corner, and inside, a lone bay horse nibbled at the floor of straw. "Where are the others?" Tori asked.

"Yeh brought 'em." Dajha grinned. "We don't 'ave much need fer horses round 'ere." His voice floated on the air with the lilting accent of the Parjhan seafarers. "Seeing as we all fly?"

Tori chuckled. "I suppose not."

"Meself, I 'ope we keep these two round, though. Poor Rothbert 'as to pull our sleigh on 'is lonesome anytime we make for the village. I don't reckon 'e'd mind the assistance."

Dajha removed the mount blankets and led the horses to a stall, then heaved mounds of hay after them. "Yeh're the one they been talking about. The one who blew up the bloody gallows."

"That's me."

"Gods, what a way to find out yeh're magic, ey?"

A pang of guilt tugged at Tori. She felt sick, but pushed the notion away.

"Me, I tripped on a bit o' rigging. There was these giant 'ooks all set out on deck. I would've landed straight on 'em and skewered meself."

"What's your gift?"

"Mum called it being shifty. But round 'ere, they call it Enduro. I can be ruddy quick when I need to be. Managed to slide past them 'ooks with barely a scratch. One time, I lifted the purse off a Morgathian admiral when they boarded Mum's ship, wagering we was pirates."

"Your mum *was* a pirate." Ren stood in the door and laughed.

"She was a bloody privateer! Gods save 'er! Aha!"

Ren shook his head, still chuckling. "Daj, tend to our gear, will you? I'm going to show Tori around."

"Yeh're the cap'n," Dajha said. Though, Tori noticed his jolly expression turn slightly at the request. "Pleasure to meet yeh, Gallows Girl," he said, recovering himself.

"Just Tori."

"There is no *just Tori* anymore," said Ren, wrapping his arm around her shoulders. "You are Astoria Burodai. The Gallows Girl. Come, let's get you cleaned up. A year in bondage, a journey through sewers, battles with Metamorphi, two weeks on the run, and it's nearly dinnertime."

Tori laughed. She was quickly finding that Ren had a way of triggering laughter. Kale stayed back with Dajha in the stables, and Ren led Tori across an open courtyard to the three central spires of the fortress. Within, there was a great wide hall leading to extravagant rooms—a ballroom with a crystal ceiling that made the light dance around the walls, a vast dining hall with tables that could have served a hundred people, a library filled with ancient scrolls.

"Where did all this come from?" Tori asked as he led her toward the three winding staircases to the spires.

"Much of this was here when we arrived. This place went untouched for hundreds of years. The scrolls were collected by my family, our secret library of the Old World." Ren took her by the arm and led her up the central tower. They stopped outside a room halfway up.

"These will be your quarters. I trust they'll suit you." Ren pushed open the door.

As they entered, there was a shriek. A young woman with bronzed skin and dark curly hair spun from a vanity, a hand mirror crashing to the floor. She clutched at her bathing robe. And then she cried out again, this time staring at her bare feet. There was blood.

"*Arayeva!*" The girl swore by the sun goddess of the Yan Avii. She lifted her foot and a piece of glass worked its way out, and the skin closed over—a healer. "Captain Andovier! I did not realize you would be visiting my bedroom the moment you arrived." The girl's cheeks had turned crimson.

Ren smiled. "My apologies, I should have announced myself. Thank the gods—and the Sol—you are a Regenero. Vashti Burodai, this is Astoria. Though, you know her as the Gallows Girl. Tori will be taking the third bed in here with you and Mischa. If we find many more Watchers, we'll have to build more towers."

"I, er, yes, of course, Captain. As you wish." Vashti bowed again, then stooped and gathered the shards of her mirror.

"Excellent," said Ren. "Astoria, I'm afraid I *must* discard these dreary traveling clothes before dinner. I will see you shortly." He took her hand. His skin was warm and her fingers tingled at the sudden touch. "I'm glad you're with us."

Tori smiled. "Me too. Thank you for everything… Captain," she added.

Ren opened the door, then glanced back. "Vashti, give her something to wear for dinner, will you? *Terasi!*" He thanked her in Yan Avii and whisked away, apparently oblivious to the look of death on her face.

Vashti muttered curses in her native tongue, looking herself up and down, standing in her robe, still blushing. She turned back to the vanity and returned to powdering her cheeks. The room was silent but for the dabbing of cosmetic brushes.

The bedroom was much larger and more ornate than the room Tori had shared in Scelero's estate. The walls were decorated with fine tapestries, the bedsheets made of exquisite linen. There were hand-carved cabinets beside each bed, and a full-body washbasin steamed with soapy water beside the vanity. Tori couldn't wait to wash.

In silence, Vashti finished her cosmetics and donned brightly colored silks.

"I'm, er, sorry I embarrassed you," said Tori, taking a seat on the bed.

Vashti had begun braiding her hair in the intricate star design of the *soltaya*. Tori remembered it from her childhood. The women in the chief's family all wore it. This girl had been Yan Avii royalty once, and she certainly acted the part. She scowled in the mirror, but did not turn to respond. "Embarrassed?" said Vashti eventually. "Do not insult me."

"You're a Burodai."

"Yes," she said coldly. "I was."

"Daughter of the *soltayne*."

"What do you know?"

"I was a Burodai too," said Tori. "My mother ran away with a tribesman. I spent my first seven years on the Steppe. We might have seen each other long ago."

"How touching." Vashti got up to leave.

"Vashti? You told Ren I could borrow some clothes?"

Vashti huffed, eyeing Tori up and down. "You are oblivious, aren't you? Here's some garb." Vashti tossed Tori her damp bathing robe.

The door flew open just as Vashti was about to exit. A spritely girl with short black hair and olive skin rushed in, smiling. "New room-mate, have we? Is that what smells?"

There was an awkward pause. The girl smiled up at Vashti, who did not seem sure how to respond. The girl glanced over at Tori, still smiling. Vashti left, shaking her head and muttering in Yan Avii. It had been long since Tori had spoken the language, but she remembered the curses well enough.

"Gods, what's her problem?" Tori muttered after Vashti had gone.

"Vashti and the captain were… involved. She hates your guts. But don't take it personal. She hated you long before she met you. And now you're sharing our room. Should be loads of fun, eh? I'm Mischa, by the way."

"Tori."

"I know who you are. Everyone knows who you are. Astoria Buro-dai. We've been waiting for you. Ever since we got news you were alive, the captain hasn't been able to shut up about bringing you here."

"I'm sick of hearing that. It was nothing, really. I just happened to discover my gifts in front of the chancellor."

"Nothing, ha!" Mischa crossed the room and began sorting through her wardrobe. She wore breeches and a white blouse, which was apparently not dining attire. Tori also noted a strange pair of stone bracelets around her wrists. "What you did that day—no one reveals their power like that. That'd be tough for a Conjuri with three years' training. The captain has never gone after a recruit like that. Always sends his brother. He thinks you're special. Gods, even the Crooked folk have been whispering about what you did."

Mischa picked out an elaborate turquoise evening gown, the sort the highborn ladies of Maro'El would have clamored to wear. She stripped out of her clothes where she stood.

"The people think it's the start of a new age," Mischa went on, lacing herself up. Mischa moved to the vanity and touched up her face. Her odd stone bracelets remained. "You should get ready, you know. Dinner will be in an hour, and I'm sure the captain will be making a big thing about your arrival. So wear something nice, and, er, wash up."

"I don't have any clothes!" said Tori. "Except Vashti's damn bathrobe!"

Mischa laughed. She bent over and clutched at her stomach. "Sorry, but you must see the irony of him asking her to lend you clothes. Not to mention, you smell like *shenzah*. Take a bath, Tori. I'll find you something to wear, don't worry."

The basin was in the middle of the room. Tori eyed it, contemplating for a moment.

Mischa laughed again. "Don't be shy. Get out of that filth and wash up."

Tori peeled off her clothes. The smell had been less potent during the days on the road, but in the warmth of the bedroom, the stench was seeping back out.

"Here." Mischa held up a rough-spun sack. Tori pitched her clothes in. "I'll send them to be burned. Gods, the smell's getting worse, I think." Mischa tied the sack tight and disappeared down the hallway.

Tori slipped into the tub. The luxury of a bath had never felt so wondrous. She wished she could lie in the warm water for hours, but dinner was approaching. She scrubbed herself vigorously. And then, a second time, and a third. Slowly, months of grime slipped away. By the time she was done, Mischa had selected a violet evening gown and draped it on Tori's bed. It fit a little loosely. Tori had never been so skinny in all her life.

"How does the bath stay warm?" said Tori. "There's no coals."

Mischa smiled. "Look closer, underneath."

Tori stooped and peered at the underside of the basin. Tiny flames hovered in midair, licking at the ceramics.

"I'm a Fieri." Mischa flicked her stone bracelets together, triggering a spark, and then it transformed into a ball of flame that hovered above her skin. She tossed the flame in the air, and it vanished. "Just a little trick I came up with. Coals are so finicky. It's either cold or scalding. Don't tell the captain. He'd fret at the thought of marring this Old World basin. Gods, he's funny."

Tori smiled. Perhaps her living arrangement wouldn't be so bad. "I think it's brilliant."

Mischa waved her hand and the flames disappeared. "Please, you turned a gallows into splinters and sent all the hardware through the guards' chests. Or is that only hearsay?"

Tori shuddered, remembering the ghosts from the Forest of Ghen. She took a seat at the vanity, reaching for the powder Vashti had been using. "No, not hearsay."

"Whoa! Hold on there."

Tori put down the powder. "What?"

Mischa grinned. "Yan Avii princesses may pull that off, but your skin is too light."

"I'm half Yan Avii."

"Really? Well, I suppose you *have* been living underground for a year. Let me help you—use this to dab your lashes—we'll deal with those bushy eyebrows some other time—and for your cheeks, a little blush is all we want. You know, in Melanesia, fairer skin is a sign of royalty. Means you don't work in the hot sun. The highborns wear nothing to cover up their fair skin."

Tori had no desire to look highborn. "Were you royalty?"

Mischa laughed. "Gods, no! My father was a merchant. I was no peasant, but hardly royalty."

In a few minutes, the cosmetics were complete, and Tori's wavy black hair had been tied back in a braid. It was longer than it had been since she was a girl, reaching well past her shoulders. Tori barely recognized herself in the mirror. Not just because of the gown and the cosmetics. She felt different all over. So much had changed. It seemed like a lifetime ago she had been in Scelero's household with Darien and Ol' Merri. *Would they even recognize me if they saw me now?*

"Let's eat! I'm starving," said Mischa. Then she looked Tori's rail-thin body up and down. "Sorry, no I'm not. Don't worry, Tori, you won't stay skinny long around these halls."

PART FIVE
THE ASSASSIN'S DEN

We are the dark cast away by the light,
The night that comes before dawn.
The Sol shines not upon us, but within.
Her secret bidding.
Her whispered will.
Her last true seekers.

Take solace in our watching eyes,
O, people of the Red City,
But look upon us and despair.

—found scrawled on the sandstone walls of Vlyanii
(a message of the Ilya, assassins of the Red City)

CHAPTER THIRTEEN

When Astoria Burodai entered the hall, every eye fell upon her, every eye but Kale Andovier's. Kale watched his brother's eyes, watched them widen and focus on the slave girl, watched him rush from the head of the table to greet her, watched him fawn and dote before his followers.

Tori cleaned up well for someone who, three hours ago, had looked like she'd been raised in a pig stable. Her tussle of black hair glistened in the lamplight. Her light brown skin, paled from months in the citadel, had been touched with hints of cosmetic that made it radiate. Dressed in her violet satin gown, she was captivating. All eyes followed her about the room. This quality was exactly what Ren wanted, and it was exactly what made Kale feel uneasy. Things were moving forward for the Shadow Watch, and though Kale should have been pleased, he was not.

Ren introduced Tori to the host of Watchers, his hand on her bare shoulder all the while. He made a rousing speech about their coming glory—the rise of the Shadow Watch—how they would return to power and the world would be made new again. Tori smiled at all the right moments, and when Ren took her by the hand to lead her to the head table, Kale noticed her flush. What was it about his brother's charisma that made Kale feel this way?

It was not jealousy. Well, not exactly.

Kale did not fancy Tori. But it was always Ren the gentlemen and ladies gravitated towards, and Tori was the latest example of this truth. Kale was a mere shadow, cast into notice at the whims of his brother, and left in the corner when it did not suit him. It had always been this way.

Usually Kale did not mind living in the shadows. He was not one to long for thrones and great halls; he did not seek the doting of lords and ladies, nor the following of an army of Watchers. In truth, he already longed to return to the road. He had much more pressing matters, even than the Gallows Girl.

Tori took her seat between Kale and Ren. "You look nice," Kale managed. He was not one for speeches either.

Ren laughed. "She looks gorgeous! Stunning!"

Tori smiled. "Yes, yes. Thank you. Now, I know this isn't ladylike, but this is the first real meal I've had in months, and right now, I want nothing more than to eat." And Tori dove into the feast before them: roasted alkine, stewed vegetables, potatoes, and steaming bread. Tori ate voraciously. She'd proven so strong on the journey, Kale had nearly forgotten she'd spent a year starving and bleeding out in the White Citadel, that she'd lived her entire life in poverty and slavery. This, too, for some reason, worried him about her. He sensed a buried rage, shrouded by guilt and insecurity. The combination left a bad taste in his mouth.

"Gods," said Ren, brushing Tori's shoulder again. "You'll choke yourself if you don't chew more."

"Sorry." She blushed.

"I'll say it again. I think it would be best if you rested a few days before joining the others in their training regimen. Eat up and sleep in a bed for a change. You're weary and you've been through so much."

But Tori shook her head. "Things are moving forward for your resistance, correct?"

"Well, er, yes…"

Kale liked to see his brother stumbling over his words.

"If I've stirred up the makings of a rebellion, and if you've been waiting for this moment, we don't have time to waste, do we? I have no control over my gifts, and I need to learn."

Tori did not strike Kale as the revolutionary sort. She was soft-spoken and small. She was undeniably fierce, a survivor. *But the face of a rebellion?* Kale sensed she was driven by something much more personal than a magical revolution. Not unlike himself.

"Very well," said Ren, smiling. "Your point is made. I will inform Sahra you will join the others tomorrow morning."

"Sahra?"

"You met her at the gate this afternoon." Ren gestured to the Alyut woman, who was conversing with a pair of younger children.

It had always worried Kale that children so young were learning the ways of war. But he, of all people, knew that even youths were not spared by the chancellor.

"Sahra oversees all drills and leads the morning exercises," Ren went on.

Tori's expression turned slightly, and something stirred in Kale's Cerebro sense. "What about you?" she asked.

"I am the captain," said Ren. "I oversee everything. Now, please, it is not healthy to eat so quickly. You will not go hungry again, I promise. Replenish yourself, slowly."

"What about you, Kale? Will *you* be assisting in my training?" Tori turned to him. Her green eyes flickered in the torchlight.

Kale cleared his throat. "I'm afraid not. I set out at first light. There are more Watchers waiting to be found."

"So soon?"

"Exactly what I said," said Ren.

I am the Exiled Lord, after all, Kale thought.

"Walled life has never suited me much," said Kale. "There is much work to do before we entertain thoughts of a revolution. As you said, there's no time to waste."

Mischa came by the table and whisked Tori off to meet the other Watchers. Ren watched her, and Kale watched them both. Ren was grinning, leaning back in his chair so it balanced on two legs, cheating gravity with a subtle flare of magic. There was a certain beauty to this place, Kale had to admit. The ability to use their gifts without fear of discovery.

"The rumors *are* spreading, Kale. Sahra says word has already reached Ytala of the Gallows Girl's escape from the citadel. More Watchers will be coming to us. More will believe and more will discover their gifts. You will sense them by the day."

He had sensed them already.

"We will have our army," said Ren. "Mother would be proud."

Mother would be proud of YOU. And she would berate me for my lack of fervor, for losing Kirra, for the Isle of Jallaa, for the day I discovered what I could do with my mind...

"It is a good day for us, Kale. You should enjoy it, and a few more like it."

Kale shifted uncomfortably. He lowered his voice. "She is more powerful than you let on, brother." Ren held his smile, though Kale sensed he'd been caught off guard. "Did you think I hadn't noticed?"

Ren let his chair back to the floor, still smiling. "I would be a fool to think I could keep secrets from a Cerebro, wouldn't I? Yes, Astoria Burodai is more powerful than I ever could have dreamed."

Kale shifted uncomfortably in his seat, his uneasiness making him restless. Mischa Sufai was escorting the Gallows Girl around the room. Tori looked so innocent, yet he sensed a desperation inside her, something beyond her control.

"Look at her," Ren whispered. "Shaking hands and smiling, as though *she* should be honored to be here. She has no desire for power. And that is just what we need."

"You think she is a Mage."

"She exhibits Conjuri *and* Regenero skills at the very least, one from both the Material and Corporeal realms. I've never seen someone heal so quickly, and with so little training. Her legs were obviously broken when she fell with the chancellor. The girl healed so fast, even she doesn't know her own power."

Kale watched Tori for a moment. He was not so sure this was true. Somewhere deep, Astoria knew she was powerful, but she was afraid of it. He had shared her dreams; he had seen her ghosts in his mind. "She trusts you, brother."

"Should she not?"

"You want to use her."

"For the good of our kind. The good of the world."

"And you're content to leave her in the dark about her power?"

"For the time being," said Ren. "Astoria must learn to accept her strength. She must grow in knowledge of herself. Then, she will be ready to embrace who we want her to be."

"Who *you* want her to be."

"Who the world needs her to be, brother. This is bigger than you or me or the Gallows Girl."

He was sounding more and more like their mother every day. "All the more reason I should go, then."

"At least take someone with you. Dajha would do well."

Kale shook his head. "No, I must go alone."

Ren set his goblet down, hard, but he maintained his smile in the presence of his soldiers. "You're not rushing to search for Watchers at all, are you? You're looking for Kirra!"

Kale cursed him. It was a rare secret Kale could keep from his brother. "I journey where I please," said Kale. "I may have come to help your cause. But you are not my captain."

For a moment, Kale thought Ren might explode, but after a breath, he calmed himself. "I wish there were hope for Kirra as well, but do not build up hope where none should be built. She fell into the hands of the Morphs months ago. You know what they do to—"

"She escaped. And I must find her. I can send others to track down your recruits for a week or so."

"And how do you know she escaped?"

I just know. Kale was silent.

"Tell me, brother, if she truly escaped, why hasn't she returned? How can you be sure Kirra wants to be found?" Ren was always dependable for putting words to the fears Kale did not wish to voice.

"If Kirra has abandoned the Shadow Watch, she can speak it to my face." Kale and Kirra had tracked together for years. They had been partners before Ren found his long-lost exiled brother, before Ren had recruited them in a gamble to restore the old ways. And Kirra believed in the cause, oftentimes more than Kale did. *If Kirra is hiding, there's a reason.*

"You think she's gone after the godstones," said Ren. He was not pleased. "It was that damned fantasy hunt that got her captured in the first place."

"You know this revolution will not be won with a handful of Watchers."

"Oh, yes," Ren said scathingly. "Our salvation belongs to little magic stones from the Old World, the ones that created the New, the ones that created the Morphs."

"Mother believed they existed."

"Our mother is dead, and this revolution will be won with men and women. Watchers. Not mythic weapons from the Old World."

"The chancellor is harvesting magic from Watcher blood," Kale said. "How do *you* suppose he's doing it?"

"You think he's using the stones?"

"How else could he keep up his army of Morphs? They're not immortal."

Ren sighed. "I don't know."

"I think Mother was right, that the chancellors always had one. And I think Cyrus Maro is looking for the others. When the Morphs attacked, Kirra and I were close. I think there was a reason they followed us to Jurka on our last expedition."

"They're myths, Kale. Has it ever occurred to you that our mother's stories were *shenzah*? You want them to be true because you think finding them will relieve your guilt about what happened to her."

"Don't!" Kale nearly shouted. They had fought this fight before, and Kale was tired of it. He lowered his voice. "Do you trust me, or not?"

"I trust you, but not your heart, brother," said Ren, clapping his shoulder like patronizing elder brothers had since the days of the Ancient Men. "You were always the soft one."

"Godstones or not, I have sensed Kirra, and I am leaving. Whether with your blessing or not, I fly at dawn across the Steppe."

"You think Kirra is among the Yan Avii?" said Ren, his tone growing lighter. "Well, that is convenient, at any rate. While you're there, you can gauge that army the Great Soltayne is raising across the Steppe. The timing of his next move will be critical to our own."

"An army?" said Kale skeptically.

"Vashti may have been banished for her sorcery, but she knows her father. Soltayne Burodai has been biding his time for years. With the Legions marching south, and Morgath soon to fall, he will be readying the twelve tribes for a counter-resistance to take back the Western Steppe, maybe even Greater Osha. If he does, it will provide our perfect moment to rise up in the White Citadel. Scelero says the High Council is tired of Cyrus Maro, and there are more who would welcome back the old ways if given the opportunity."

"Does Vashti know you wish to use her people to initiate your own rise to power?"

Ren glared. "Vashti hates her father. Just find out what the Great Soltayne is scheming. And then you may search for Kirra and your silly stones as you please… with my blessing."

Ren always had to have the last word, but Kale was glad for his blessing nonetheless. "Very well."

"Before you go, tell Dajha where he can find the next recruits. You've sensed more, I trust?"

"Several, but Dajha? You think he can bear the responsibility?" Truth be told, Kale did not wholly trust the privateer's son. Parjhan seafarers were not known for their moral code. They blew wherever the wind took them.

"Someone has to do the tracking while you're galavanting with those herdsmen. Dajha is quick and ruddy sharp at getting out of a bind. And he's itching to prove himself. Didn't you see the glare he gave me when I asked him to tend the mounts?"

"If you say so."

"I do." Ren raised a glass of wine, smiling, though his eyes had narrowed. "You're right, brother, there is much work to do."

Kale excused himself and made for his quarters. He was so focused on his thoughts that he nearly trampled the girl as he turned a corner. Astoria roamed the halls alone.

"You should return to the feast," he said.

Her face fell a little. "It feels wrong to… celebrate… while there is so much suffering elsewhere. I've never known comforts like this place."

Kale could sense her thoughts dwelled on the people of the Fringes, and the Gallows Boy who haunted her dreams.

"It is good not to forget those who suffer." Kale knew this well. "It is also not wrong to enjoy comforts. Otherwise, you lessen the hope of everyone else."

"What do you mean?"

"Don't forget those who live as you once did. But don't cheapen what they themselves long for and die for—comfort and freedom."

"You should speak more, you know," said Tori. "You're wiser than you look."

"Well, that stings."

Tori smiled. "Have a safe journey, Kale. I hope you find more Watchers. But… don't stay gone too long. You deserve some comfort yourself."

Kale nodded, and Tori left to rejoin the festivities.

When Kale reached his bedchamber, he found himself unable to consider the possibility of sleeping on a feather mattress in a stonewalled cell. He had spent so many years on the run, terrified to use his powers lest he be hunted down and murdered by the chancellor's creatures. If you ceased to use an ability long enough, you could believe it did not exist, like an old prisoner who, after a lifetime underground, believes there is no such thing as color and light. There had been times Kale could not have used his Watcher gift, even if he'd had the nerve to try.

That was his existence after his self-appointed exile—until Kirra.

Kirra Fehn had reminded him who he was. In the outer realms of civilization, on an isle in the Bay of Jallaa—in the Far East, beyond the reach of the chancellor and his Morphs—they had rediscovered their gifts. There had been seventeen of them, a commune of Watchers rediscovering their true selves, led by a Watcher as ancient as the orders of the Old World. It was a place not unlike the Watchtower. But no place was truly safe from the reach of the chancellor.

The Morphs had come in the early hours of the morning, descending in grey light upon blurry, waking eyes. Kale and Kirra had spent the night in the gardens, and they were rejoicing in their triumphs and their awakening love when they heard the screams.

All the others were slaughtered, even their leader, whom Kale had thought could never die. Only one Morph was slain in the process. Kale and Kirra, the lone survivors, were left alone to walk among the dead and wonder what might have happened had they spent the night with the others rather than indulging themselves in love.

Kale had hardly spent a night in the same place since. It did not matter that his brother had lived safely in the Crooked Teeth these past three years. No place was outside the creatures' reach. One day, Kale feared the Watchtower would fall, and the Shadow Watch would endure the same fate as the commune on the Isle of Jallaa.

———

Kale flew through the night from the Watchtower and the Crooked Teeth, but was forced to rest on the shore of the Steppe as the sun crawled its way back to the world. He slept during the day and flew three more nights to cross the great sprawling hills and plains, before he landed outside the capital of the Yan Avii—Vlyanii.

Sandstone spires jutted from within the central palace walls like daggers caked in dried blood. Rising above the entire city was the central dome of the Red Palace. Surrounding the city, portable kela-skin yurts spiraled in all directions. The Yan Avii were a nomadic people. Even the Great Soltayne spent less than half the year in the confines of his palace, preferring to sit a horse over a throne. It was a sentiment Kale respected about Soltayne Burodai, though the only one. The twelve *soltaynes* roamed the Steppe with their herds and their tribesmen, waging small wars amongst themselves and, at times—now, if Ren's suspicions proved true—banding together under their Great Soltayne for larger and much longer wars. If this massive city of yurts was any indication, Ren was right. The Yan Avii were preparing for war.

Kale entered the inner walls of Vlyanii to the blaring horn call for the rising ritual of Arayeva. As the sun goddess began her daily journey across the sky, the people faced east and asked for her blessing upon the day to come. Kale made his way to one of the countless rooftop shrines of the Red City, doused his forehead in oil, and bowed his greeting to the Sol.

It was then, amidst a host of twenty kneeling men and young boys, that Kale realized the Yan Avii were in mourning. Every male was dressed in ceremonial sackcloth with a smear of ash upon the bridge of his nose. Their prayers were not a greeting of the sun, but a wailing lament.

When the prayers ended, Kale stopped a young man as he left the shrine. "I have just traveled many leagues," Kale said in Yan Avii. "Tell me, what evil has descended upon the Red City?"

The young boy had tears in his eyes. "Our Great Chief has gone to join the Horsemen Among the Stars." The boy wiped his eyes, oil and tears smearing with ash.

"How?"

"A shadow blade stole his breath," said the boy's father.

The Great Soltayne had been murdered. Kale cursed, then he said, "The Sol will have her justice."

"The Sol will have her justice," the boy and his father repeated.

Kale joined the throng of Yan Avii tribesmen as they made their way to the palace. The sun was particularly crimson as it ascended from the depths of the Wandering Dunes. The Yan Avii would see this as an ill omen for days to come. The mourning would go on all week. Perhaps longer, as so many had gathered for the Festival of the Rising Sun, when it was believed Arayeva walked among her chosen people. At the dawn of spring, she blessed the seeds of earth, of herds, and of men. On the final night, she caroused with the Great Soltayne himself and ushered in another year of plenty on the Steppe.

This would be a cursed year unless the mourning rites were especially long and fervent, in hopes the Sol would bring swift justice and bless the Choosing of her new Great Soltayne.

The Yan Avii would not be going to war anytime soon. Ren would not be pleased. But Kale's true purpose was also cast awry in the wake of the Great Soltayne's death. In the vast crowd, he could not sense Kirra anywhere. His mind was clouded. The Yan Avii minds, with all their sorrow and fear, descended on him like crows upon a rotting corpse. He could not discern one from another in the madness.

He was about to depart Vlyanii—before he was pressed into the heart of the mourning city by the crowds—when he felt a stealth blade at his throat.

Extending from the sleeve of a dark cloak, it was the signature weapon of the Ilya.

The assassins of the Red City.

The blade pricked Kale's skin, and blood dripped warm down his neck.

"You are not the first Sky Blood to enter our city on this dark day." The voice was feminine and confident, which took Kale by surprise. In Vlyanii, women were not known to carry blades.

Kale was about to abandon stealth and fly from the earth. He could disarm the assassin and flee before the woman knew what had happened. But suddenly, he felt weak. His limbs betrayed him, and he collapsed in the street.

The Ilya's blade had been laced with a draught.

More dark cloaks joined the Ilya woman, and many arms hauled his limp form into the narrow lanes between the sandstone towers. The last thing Kale saw was the woman's razor smile, teasing from the depths of a dark hood, as he was dragged underground.

# CHAPTER FOURTEEN

K ale woke lying upon fine pillows in a lamplit room. Oil was pungent on the air as it soaked the wicks and slowly ebbed away with the lapping of soft flames. He lay alone and, to his surprise, unbound. His strength and power were returning, the last effects of the draught wafting away. There were no guards in the room, but voices stirred from beyond the arched entry. With his sense, he recognized a familiar presence. Kale roused himself and left the bedchamber.

Several round tables littered the vast domed chamber beyond. Around them sat men in dark cloaks, laughing and drinking wine and sharing joints of roasted lamb. When Kale entered, their leader stood and addressed him.

"I trust you slept well, old friend."

"I trust you are still a bastard, Salla," said Kale, recognizing the man instantly.

The woman beside him tensed. The only woman in the room, Kale noted, and the one who had put him to sleep in the city. In his mind, he could sense her fierce loyalty to her prince.

Prince Salla Burodai—Vashti's brother, the commander of the Ilya assassins, and son of the late Great Soltayne—laughed so that his entire body shook. "All is well, Ashi," he said to the Ilya woman. Salla rushed forward and took Kale by the arm in greeting. "A bastard, indeed. But no one sees the pathway to the Den of the Ilya. Not even you, Sky Blood. I heard you were in the city, and I knew we must speak."

"Word travels quick," said Kale.

"Ah! We are not all blessed with eyes in our minds that see the depths of the soul, old friend. But I have been blessed with many hundreds of eyes in the Red City. No one comes or goes without my knowledge."

"Not even the murderer of your father, I venture to guess." Salla did not laugh at this. "Your father lies dead but hours, and here you are, bothering with an… old friend?"

"My tribesmen believe I am mourning in my chambers." Salla gestured to his table. "Come, share a cup and a meal, and we will speak."

Kale took a seat. The other Ilya moved across the room, giving them the appearance of privacy, but Kale knew Salla kept no secrets from his followers. The Ilya continued their festivities, though in hushed tones, while Salla served up a plate. But Kale could feel their eyes and their concentration fixed upon him, Ashi's in particular.

"You've come seeking her, have you not?" said Salla, pouring Kale a goblet of wine. For a moment, Kale was puzzled, his thoughts still fixated on the Ilya woman. Then Salla added, "Kirra."

Kale tried not to let his excitement show. "Yes, though I sense she's left the city already. Thanks to you?" He had guessed it the moment he'd heard of the Great Soltayne's demise.

Salla patted Kale's arm and sat beside him. "Eat, please." Kale did. As he ate, Salla explained himself. "The ability to become as a shadow is one quite desirable among assassins. We may go unnoticed, but to disappear entirely, as Kirra can… I have longed to recruit a Sky Blood for some years. I tried to recruit *you*, not so long ago."

"Yes, and Kirra is wiser than I."

"I helped her escape the Morphs."

"In exchange for the murder of your father?" Kale's tone was dark and cold. He tore the lamb's roasted flesh off the bone. He could sense Ashi's fierce gaze.

Salla sipped from his goblet. "Do not blame *me* because you failed her and now you feel emasculated. I aided Kirra out of honor. I requested her help in return. And she obliged, perhaps because she sees the values of the Ilya."

"Or perhaps it was because you had something she seeks. You know something of the godstones." There could be no other reason Kirra would walk into Salla's snare.

Salla lifted a dark, trimmed brow. "Perhaps. You should know this about me by now, old friend. I do what is needed to accomplish what needs done."

Kale did know. Salla had discovered the Shadow Watch, after all, in time to save his sister's life. He was resourceful, and not at all like his father. Though still, Kale could not say he trusted the man. Certainly not when he wanted something.

"My father was a bastard," Salla went on. "He deserved to be murdered long ago. It was out of love for my people that I arranged his death. Do you know why my father feared Vashti's power, Kale? Why he put his own daughter to death?"

"She was a woman. It was an abomination for her to seek power."

"Seek power? Arayeva! Is it seeking power to be true to yourself? But you are right, that was part of it. She was a woman seeking to discover the power within her. Which *is* an abomination among my people. And yet we worship a woman, don't we? A powerful goddess."

"That was always a puzzle to me."

Salla tore a strip of meat and chewed slowly. "My father values women he can control, or who bring him pleasure. Arayeva is our provider, and yet she enters his chambers during the festival. It's all *shenzah*, of course. But the Great Soltaynes allow a goddess because even a goddess seems beneath them. A male god would make the Great Soltayne seem inferior and weak. A goddess, though, they can control.

"When Vashti began to reveal her ability, my father knew what would happen. The people would have come to see her as a goddess, descended from Arayeva herself. A goddess he could not control. The women had already begun whispering prayers in secret. As Vashti's power grew, the men would have had no choice. It would have been undeniable. In time, there would have been an uprising. So, my father accused her of blasphemy and put her to death before the rumors spread."

"Yet she lives," said Kale, recalling the harrowing plan Salla had concocted to save her. "And you would—what?—have her now ascend the throne?"

"You do not know my people, Kale. Ghosts do not bring good omens. The Death Walkers of the Old World were a cursed race. Your brother hoped to make her a queen and rally my people. My sister survived the stake, by a miracle of her healing power, but she could never return from the dead. Not to her people. She would be marked a scourge of humanity, and she would be put to death. Properly, this time. They would send her into the belly of Xa'Rila."

Kale had heard tales of the Old World monster beneath the Wandering Dunes. During their years of desert exile—in the wake of the War Between the Worlds, after the First Chancellor had conquered their nomadic ancestors—the monster had taken many Yan Avii lives, it was said. Giant whirlpools formed in the sand from nowhere and swallowed men whole. They could spring up anywhere in the shifting desert, without warning. No one knew whether Xa'Rila was many beasts or one—or if it was merely an anomaly of nature, and no beast at all—for no one had survived an encounter. A fact that made Kale doubt its existence. Nevertheless, the monster was still greatly feared by the Yan Avii.

Salla stood. "I long to create a world in which my sister would never have been executed in the first place. When the mourning for my father has ended and the lots are cast for the next Great Soltayne, I will be chosen and things will change."

"Now the Ilya can manipulate fate?"

"I will be chosen. And Vashti may return. Not as who she truly is, not as Vashti, the princess of the *soltaya*. But she may return to her home and to her people."

Kale was growing tired of the conversation. And he could sense Kirra's presence drifting farther and farther away from Vlyanii, like a cloud on the horizon about to slip over the edge of the world. "If you are such a saint, Salla, why didn't you resist your father, then? When it mattered?"

Salla lost his cool demeanor for the first time. He pounded the table. "Do not piss upon my love for my sister! You know nothing of honor, Sky Blood!"

The Ilya stood, but kept their distance. Kale remained calm and gestured for the prince to return to his seat. Salla caught his breath, ran fingers through his slick dark hair, and then sat. His Ilya did the same.

"Nevertheless," said Kale, "Vashti is dead to the Yan Avii. She is with my brother now, and there, she *can* be herself. She can become what she was meant to be. She could never come back and hide in the Red City. I do not doubt your love, but you do not know your sister's kind. We have been in hiding for far too long. The future is not in thrones, Salla. The future of the Yan Avii, and of the New World, lies in the return of the Watchers. If you truly care for your sister, then become Great Soltayne. And then, gather your tribesmen and join us in war against the chancellor. Then, Vashti may truly be able to come home. Not as a goddess, but as a Watcher of old."

"Ah, those are Ren's words. You do not think in such absolutes. Your few dozen Sky Bloods—your Shadow Watch—they are no army. The chancellor has his Metamorphi, and the tribes are no match for his Legions."

"Your father thought differently. No Festival of the Rising Sun has drawn so many tribesmen before. Your father was planning an attack on Osha, while the Legions are focused on Morgath."

"And my father would have led my people to slaughter. Why do you think I killed him when I did? We have kept peace for many years. And we will continue to keep it."

"How long do you think that peace will last?"

"Longer than if I ride to war in the wake of my father's death. A blood red sun rose this morning. The people already fear a cursed year. I will not ensure it comes upon them. We will not ride to war."

"I have said what my brother would wish me to say," said Kale. "And I will deliver your answer. Now, where is Kirra?"

Salla took a long drink from his goblet. His assassins suddenly sat at attention. Ashi had her hand at the hilt of her blade.

"Do not worry, Kirra is being kept safe, old friend. Until she completes the last task I have for her. And until you complete your own task."

"My task?"

Salla smiled. "I need your help obtaining my throne. When I am chosen as the next Great Soltayne, you and Kirra may go free. But until then…"

Ashi's blade moved so fast, Kale could not react. The draught worked quickly, and Kale's world faded to nothingness.

PART SIX
THE SHADOW & THE MORPH

All the chancellor's servants were Morphs, one way or another. Some showed the change in their physical bodies, but all of us were morphed in the soul. We all ceased to be human. We all were creatures, molded and warped to do the chancellor's bidding.

—the Last Commander of the Metamorphi
as quoted in *Dawn of the Third World*

CHAPTER FIFTEEN

The Battle of Morgath raged around the Gallows Boy. Darien's world was a whirl of musket-fire and explosions, blood and ash melding with the bitter rain that poured down upon the battlefield. The fray had reached a tipping point, like a cauldron seething, about to spill over in the fire.

If the plan worked, after three days of combat at the walls of the Morgathian stronghold of Goran'El, the Night Legions would finally break through.

The Morgathian walls had proven impenetrable. The Legions had hardly been able to get near them, let alone find any weaknesses. The fortress of Goran'El was shaped like a crescent moon, with a sheer cliff at the rear. Thousands of Shadows had died already as they stormed the walls from all sides. They could not last the carnage much longer.

It was Darien's idea to send the Metamorphi, but it would have been impossible without the turbulent storm raging overhead. As the thunderheads sailed in from the Klavash mountains, Darien rushed to tell General Thrain his plan.

While the Legions created a violent and deadly diversion, the Morphs would descend secretly from the thunderheads and take on the form of Morgathian soldiers within; the cauldron would spill and unleash the fury of the chancellor upon all the Morgathian rebels.

THE OUTER MORGATHIAN HOLDFASTS HAD BEEN WEAKER AND fell by the sheer mass of Shadows in the early days of the attack on the rebel nation. Thrain's troops began the first phase of the invasion, surprising Morgath with an unexpected attack from the east, while the majority of the Legion horde was camped one hundred leagues away at the border of Morgath. After the slaughter of Harrivral, Darien and his comrades had successfully stolen their way through the mountains of Klavash unnoticed, and without warning, they dealt the chancellor's wrath upon Ravencrest Tower and the nearby village of Eigal with the loss of fewer than a dozen soldiers. Nearly all Morgathian regiments had been sent west to face the main Legion horde, leaving the eastern holds hopelessly vulnerable. The eastern victories were small in scale—only one Morgathian regiment, the rest women and children and old men—but the losses struck up an infectious heart of fear across all of Morgath. Where else might the Shadows come from?

The seahold of Fangsport and the northern tower of Vulcan Rock fell soon after in a brilliant coordinated attack from land and sea, accomplished with the help of a fleet of ruthless Parjhan privateers sailing from the Boundless Sea in the black of night. Within mere days, the terror-stricken Morgathians retreated to their central fortress, the capital city of Goran'El. It seemed nothing could stop the Legions. But that confidence proved to be their downfall.

Darien knew they should have taken their time, laid siege to the fortress over the course of weeks, while the troops recuperated and replenished their supplies, while the heart of fear festered within. They should have waited for their cannons to arrive. But the Legions had been lured into a false sense of victory and bloodlust. They felt invincible, and that was exactly what the Rebel King, Hollsted, had been hoping for.

That was when the explosions began.

In secret, the Morgathians had devised a cannonball that exploded in midair, raining down lead and fire upon the attacking horde. Combined with the skill of the Morgathian sharpshooters, this new horror proved devastating for the Legions. Despite their far greater numbers, the Legions could not ascend the walls with ladders nor breach the gates with battering rams—they could not come close to Goran'El from any direction without crippling losses. The band of flying Morphs managed marginal damage on the walls, but musket-fire was thick, and they, too, were forced back.

———

Now, with Darien's plan in motion, the Night Legions pulled back and reformed ranks, beyond the range of the Morgathian cannons. The Morphs would need a distraction, and all the Legions needed to be close when the wall was breached. They would not attack from all sides, but would focus all strength on the main city gate.

Fiery arrows soared like meteors, pinging of the walls of the city with showers of sparks. It was the first wave of the Legion attack. Arrows would do no damage, as the entirety of Goran'El was composed of obsidian star rock—the arrows were a show, drawing all eyes and all men within toward the King's Gate.

The second wave of the attack was men. Wave after wave of them.

Lightning crackled overhead as Darien rushed the gates beside General Thrain, their regiment close behind them, their sister companies on all sides. The Shadows stormed the King's Gate, fired a volley, and then retreated to reload while the next wave took their place. Two Legion regiments carried battering rams, and after the first volleys of musket-fire, they drove forward with massive socha logs borne upon their shoulders.

It was suicide. Every Morgathian musket was trained on them, but Darien knew it was a necessary sacrifice. With all Morgathian eyes fixed on the storming of the King's Gate, the Morphs took flight from the north, invisible in the darkness of night and storm. Within Goran'El, disguised as Morgathian soldiers, the Morphs would bring down the walls. If all went according to plan.

Thrain's regiment surged forward again, fired upon the walls, and then retreated to reload. Bodies fell all around Darien. He had never seen so much annihilation. Men and women he'd marched with, trained with, shared ale and stories around the fire with, lay dead all around him. He'd lost sight of Merri and Jujen and Valeria by their third charge, and could only hope they were not among the fallen. He kept close to General Thrain and reloaded his musket for the next wave.

A nearby explosion rocked the earth and threw him to the ground—

His ears rang—

His vision was a white flare—

And his back seared with pain—

A cannonball exploded in the midst of Thrain's regiment. Shards of lead pierced Darien's skin, penetrating his thick leathern armor. For a moment, he was rendered immobile. Darien lay in a daze. His brain seemed to be tumbling around in his head. A shrill ringing was all he heard, like a hive of hornets. He did not hear the shots and explosions, nor the cries of his comrades dying in agony.

One thought brought him back: *The general!*

Darien did not see Thrain anywhere in the madness. All was a blur. The ground beneath him pooled with blood and rain. Smoke from musket- and cannon-fire hung over him like the fogs over Glacier Sound, and the air smelled of gunpowder and death. Darien scrambled forward, head still ringing, but he could move, which meant his wounds must not be deep. He managed to stand, but he could see none of his comrades in the chaos. Nor the general.

There was a thunderous crash as the battering rams reached the gate. They would not be able to break through. It was amazing they had not all been shot down already. A war horn resounded from the wall, followed by a flurry of musket-fire.

Another rocket exploded to his left, and dozens of soldiers fell. Darien was on his hands and knees again, the ringing worse than ever. He covered his head with his hands.

Gods, what is taking the Morphs so long?

A sudden hand touched his shoulder, and Darien jerked away instinctively, reaching for his saber. But he caught a glimpse of silver hair shimmering in the light of the explosions. It was Valeria Sardona, and relief swept over him.

"Are you all right?" she shouted above the din.

He nodded, his hearing still muffled. He drew nearer. "Where's the general?"

"I don't know! I lost everyone after that first blast! Gods, you're bleeding!"

"I'll be all right," he said. His voice sounded distant, as though coming from outside his own body. "It's not deep."

Valeria pulled him to his feet. His back ached with pain, but it was bearable. The second blast had only jarred him.

A regiment marched past and fired on the wall, hitting only a couple Morgathian marksmen, who tumbled over the side of the towering wall. Screams filled the air, and the surviving Legions retreated from the gates at full speed. The thud of the battering rams ceased.

Darien grabbed a musket from a dead comrade and loaded as fast as he could manage. Valeria did the same. They were about to rage ahead with the next wave of muskets, when they were thrown back to the ground in the worst explosion yet.

The air filled with bodies and parts of bodies.

But they were not the bodies of the Night Legions.

A stone the size of a small hut landed a few yards off. A titanic piece of the wall of Goran'El. *The Morphs did it! The wall is breached!*

A cry rose up from the Night Legions—"Ooh, rah! Ooh, rah!"—as the walls of Goran'El exploded in all directions, leaving behind a gaping hole the width of a city street. The battle cry turned into a deafening roar. The Morphs took flight, letting all of Morgath know how their rebellion had been undone. Shots fired into the haze to no avail. The Morphs disappeared in the clouds and then descended in glory, soaring over the cheering Legions.

"Ooh, rah! Ooh, rah! Ooh, rah!" they all cried triumphantly.

The Legions stampeded forward. Any memory of the pain in Darien's back vanished. Adrenaline surged through him as he and Valeria sprinted across the battlefield to the chasm in the wall. Nothing mattered but ending the Morgathian rebellion once and for all.

The onslaught of Shadows broke through like water through a breached dam. They poured through the opening and spread through the streets of Goran'El—a deluge, taking out all who stood in their way.

The first wave of Shadows was shot down, but in the chaos, the Morgathians lost all order to their musket-fire. Carefully coordinated volleys turned into a flurry of desperate shots. Too many fired. Too many were left to reload at once. And the Shadows stormed past.

Darien fired his musket only once, hitting his mark in a soldier's exposed neck. Then, he pitched it aside and drew his saber from the sheath on his back. The Night Legions wore leathern armor and moved swiftly. It made them vulnerable in the open field, but in close combat, it made them quick and deadly. The Morgathians wore plates of cumbersome forged-steel. It made their men fiercely difficult to kill from a distance, but left them bulky and awkward in close quarters. The Morgathian muskets were fitted with long bayonets, but they were no match for the speed of the overwhelming number of Legion sabers.

Darien parried a bayonet jab and thrust with his blade. He missed, drew back, warded off another jab, and another. How long might they continue this way? The longer his attention was fixed on one soldier, the longer he was exposed to the thousand others swarming around him. But then, Valeria appeared behind the Morgathian. Her saber sliced open the soldier's exposed neck in a spray of blood and sinew.

Her face was cold and set as she pulled away. Darien nodded his thanks for coming to his aid yet again.

Without a word needed, Darien and Valeria became one vicious mechanism. Four arms, four legs, and two flashing blades working in unison, surging forward. One deflected attacks while the other sought the death blow. It was like their minds had synced, anticipating every move of the other seamlessly. Morgathian men fell all around the whirlwind pair, bathing the streets in blood.

Bodies were soon strewn so thick, it was like moving through a felled forest, as the Legion force drove forward. The Morph beasts bounded in the midst of the fray, mauling men to pieces with their massive claws. Taking Goran'El became suddenly easy. *Too easy,* Darien thought.

The streets were thinning of Morgathian men. Darien and Valeria and their comrades rushed into an open market square located deep within the city, when a company of spears strode to meet them. The spearmen each stood nearly seven feet tall, and one at the front quickly fixed on Darien and Valeria. The spearman's lance was ten feet long. Darien had never seen a man move so lithely with such an unwieldy weapon. They lunged into their attack, but neither Darien nor Valeria could get close enough to land a blow. The man whipped the lance through the air like a sea dragon snatching its prey. It was all they could do to ward off the violent thrusts.

As he parried, Darien's sword was wrenched from his grasp, and he fell to his knees. Valeria blocked the spearman's deathblow, but the force knocked her back. She stumbled over a corpse in the square, leaving Darien exposed and without his weapon. The spearman stepped forward, grinning. He shifted his lance in his hands, then thrust at Darien's lightly armored chest—

A shot rang through the street—

The lance fell short and dropped to the ground—

The spearman's neck splayed open at the impact of the rocketed ball of lead, and he collapsed.

"Ooh, rah!"

Darien glanced back. Jujen was grinning madly from a Morgathian wall, pumping his fist. A host of Legion sharpshooters had taken a central Morgathian tower within the city. While Jujen reloaded, the others fired, picking off more spearmen. They were left with no choice but to flee the square. As the Morgathian spearmen retreated, the Legions fired another volley, and a dozen more spears fell. Darien had never been so relieved to hear Jujen cry out in maniacal victory.

"Ooh, rah!" Darien shouted, pumping his fist at his comrade. Valeria and Darien scrambled to their feet and left the open square behind. The streets were soon emptied, and the Legions proceeded cautiously, wary of an ambush. But it never came.

The Morgathians had fled for the innermost keep of Goran'El— their last line of defense before King Hollsted's central palace and the final victory.

Battering rams were brought forward, but the star rock gates would never be breached with wooden rams. The obsidian stone was several feet thick. The central palace was not built for offense. It was built to be impenetrable. No shots rained down on the Legions, but they could not fire any themselves. Of course, the end was inevitable. The Morgathians were routed and weak. They might survive a few days, maybe even a month under siege, but there was no doubt the rebellion was crushed. If Hollsted was wise, he would surrender and spare the women and children the agony of starvation.

The Legions swarmed around the thick palace gates. The rams ceased their onslaught as a cry rose up from the rear. Jujen and the company of sharpshooters came forward, rolling three of the Morgathian fire cannons to face the gate. The Legions cried, "Ooh, rah! Ooh, rah!" like never before.

The rebels' secret weapon became their downfall. The star rock did not give at once, but after several volleys, the gates began to crumble. The Legions braced for attack, but there were no Morgathian forces beyond the gate. They had retreated deep into the inner fortress.

General Thrain stepped from the masses and approached the devastated gate. Darien was filled with relief. He had not seen his commander since the rocket that tore apart their regiment outside the city.

"Hollsted!" Thrain shouted to the towers of the palace. "You are undone! There need be no more bloodshed! End this civil war, and save the people who yet live!"

There was no answer from the tower.

The storm had ceased, Darien noticed for the first time. The sky was beginning to turn grey with the coming morning. Commander Zamel rode forward on his ebony courser. He spun at the gate and faced his Legions.

"You have fought valiantly, Shadows! You have crushed the rebellion!"

"Ooh, rah! Ooh, rah!" they roared.

"Now we finish this civil war once and for all! Kill anyone who stands in your way, until Hollsted comes groveling before me! May Morgath never forget the day they rejected our chancellor's mercy!"

There was sudden movement in the palace tower. One after another, thick sacks came hurtling from the precipice.

Firebombs!

Valeria grabbed Darien and pulled him to the ground along with her. The explosions decimated the Legions. They had all gathered thick in one place, and the bombs ripped through them like they were made of lace. Limbs and blood filled the air. Commander Zamel was launched from his mount when its legs were blown out from beneath it. The earth shook with blast after blast. Seven in all.

There was a palpable silence as the smoke settled. The surviving Shadows did not dare move, bracing themselves for another explosion. But it did not come.

General Thrain was the first to stand. He helped Zamel out from under his dead horse. Darien helped Valeria to her feet, grateful they had survived, knowing many of their comrades had shielded them with their own lives. The other Shadows stood in the settling smoke and waited for the command.

"Kill them all!" Zamel cried, raising his saber high. "Leave none alive!" And the Legions stormed through the gaping palace gates to end the Morgathian rebellion. Once and for all.

CHAPTER SIXTEEN

Beyond the gates, it was a slaughter. Hollsted's inner palace was buffered with Morgathian women and children, packed tightly in the narrow, pillared lanes. The rebels launched their last desperate firebombs, which killed Shadows and civilians alike, and then, the Legions broke down doors and spread through every room, slashing through any Morgathian who dared stand in their way.

Darien had lost sight of Ol' Merri long before the walls were breached. From the beginning of their march, he had wondered how she would fare in the heat of battle, with her piety and hope. But when the first Morgathian had shot at her, during the sneak attack on Ravencrest, Merri fired back at her kinsman without hesitance, and finished him off with a slash of her saber. Darien had been proud of her. Despite his efforts to distance himself from any suspicious activity, he was still fond of Merri. He hoped she was still alive somewhere in the madness.

The halls of Goran'El filled with the shrieks of old and young, helpless and strong alike. The remaining Morgathian soldiers fired desperate shots at the heartless invaders before being cut down. Civilians ran for their lives, making for the innermost depths of the palace. But there were few places to hide and too many vying for them. The marble floors of the palace were rendered invisible beneath the thick layer of bodies.

Darien and Valeria stuck close together, scouring every corridor for King Hollsted. Only his capture would end the slaughter of his blind followers. Darien kicked open a bedroom door and shut it quickly behind them.

Within, Ol' Merri faced off with a young boy, maybe twelve, wearing fine robes and wielding a musket far too large for him. Merri's saber was raised, but she spoke softly to the boy. "Please," she said. "Lower your weapon."

The boy waved the musket dangerously. "I-I'll kill you!" the boy cried, his voice croaking. "Y-you Oshan bastards! I'll take as many of you down with me as I can. I-I am my father's son, a servant of Nafta, god of the Flame, and I will not go quietly!" Darien noted the iron crown upon his head.

"Kill him!" hissed Valeria.

Merri was close enough she could easily knock the musket away with her saber. It waved wildly between Merri and the new intruders. The moment Darien and Valeria arrived had been her opportunity—while the boy was distracted—but Merri held back. Darien knew she could not stomach the slaughter of a child. Not even one willing to take her life. Not even Hollsted's own son. Darien's hand went to his belt.

"N-no!" the prince cried. His musket fixed more steadily on Merri's head. His finger pressed the trigger.

With near-invisible speed, Darien snatched the throwing blade at his belt and let it fly—

The musket fired—

The blade lodged in the boy's throat in a spray of blood—

Bits of stone crumbled from the wall at the impact of the boy's shot—

He had missed Merri. The prince collapsed, blood gurgling between fingers clasped at his slender neck. Darien rushed forward, removed the blade, and returned it to his belt. Merri was shaking. She could not take her eyes off the dying prince. Darien left her, without a word, and turned to Valeria.

The girl's face was expressionless. Fear struck him as she watched him cross the room. He should not have been the one to kill the boy. The old fear of being watched, of doing something treasonous, returned like a winter plague. He had covered for Merri, and now Valeria knew it without doubt.

"Leave none alive," she said carefully, eyeing Merri.

"And none live," he said firmly.

Valeria paused, considering the situation, but then nodded and said, "Then we should move on."

They returned to the halls and cleared the next room. Darien took no pleasure in the slaughter of women and children, but there was no way around it. Hollsted had even left his own son to face the soldiers while he retreated deeper within the palace. It was said that the Morgathian god, Nafta, left the world of men dying in his own flames as he destroyed his enemies, and it was Nafta's last words that Hollsted had taught his followers to live by: *Do not go quietly.*

The Morgathians had been fools to serve such a heathen ruler. Darien performed his duty and slew any man, woman, or child he encountered in the palace.

Hollsted had barricaded himself in his innermost court with his elders and generals. It was not until the Legions brought the battering rams to the door that Hollsted finally surrendered. The Rebel King opened the door himself and held out his saber, still bearing the insignia of two dark interweaving wisps of shadow. The traitor still carried the saber issued him by the Night Legions so many years before. General Thrain stepped forward to meet his former comrade.

Hollsted had pale, freckled skin and fiery red hair, a sign of special blessing from Nafta. To the end, Hollsted wore his iron crown of flames. Looking upon the river of dead bodies that lined his halls, Hollsted bore no expression, no remorse, no sorrow. His face was empty as he spoke. "I surrender."

Thrain grabbed Hollsted's saber and threw it to the ground in anger. "You son of a whore! You have destroyed these people!"

Hollsted laughed and stepped closer. "I knew this rebellion was doomed the day my troop defected from the Legions. I knew, one day, I would hand you my sword, and you would lead me back to the chancellor in chains. So go on, comrade, take me to him." Hollsted held out his hands arrogantly.

Thrain retrieved a pair of shackles from the ranks and stepped forward.

Hollsted's next movement was so quick the general had no time to react. Thrain reached for Hollsted's hands, but at the same moment, from his robes, Hollsted produced a dagger, and he thrust it into Thrain's side. The general gasped as the blade plunged in deep, and Hollsted pulled him close.

"We never fought to win. We fought to take as many gods-damned Shadows down with us as we could!" Hollsted pulled the blade out viciously, then sliced at Thrain's neck. The general fell to the floor of the throne room, blood pouring into the cracks between the marble tiles. Hollsted started laughing.

Darien could not bear that this despicable traitor would survive—because of some ridiculous custom of warfare—laughing, while the general bled out before him. It was unfathomable that kings should live, after letting so many die on their behalf.

Without thinking, Darien leapt from the ranks, drawing his saber, and attacked the Rebel King. Hollsted was not prepared for the attack. He stumbled backwards and fell as he deflected Darien's first blow with his dagger. One of his elders slid him a saber, just in time to deflect Darien's next blow. Hollsted scrambled to his feet and faced off. The king was a better swordsman than Darien expected. Hollsted did not see much battle, preferring the safety of halls and battle camps, it was said. It had been many years since Hollsted had trained in the Shadow Camps, but it was clear he had not forgotten his training.

Darien had never fought so hard in all his life. He was filled with bitter rage. Every blow was stronger than the last, but Hollsted deflected them all. Then, the king delivered blows of his own, and Darien was on the defense. Hollsted was a madman, each blow pounding like a shipwright's hammer. He twisted his blade with a flourish, and Darien's saber was out of his hand. Darien fell to the ground, fearing what was about to come. But he did not regret his choice. It would be an honorable death. A Shadow's death.

Hollsted laughed. "Now I get to kill one more Shadow before I meet the chancellor."

Hollsted leapt forward, his blade aiming for Darien's neck.

A shot rang out in the hall—

A bullet ripped through the king's cheek and out the other side of his face—

His saber clattered to the throne room floor, and Hollsted fell back. Darien turned to see who had fired the shot, relief swelling within him.

Valeria Sardona stood apart from the Legions, smoke pouring from her musket, which was still aimed at the king's head.

Hollsted spluttered on the ground, blood bubbling from his frayed mouth, but Darien could still make out his last words. "Do not go quietly."

The Rebel King's elders and generals rushed forward to make their last stand, to take as many Shadows down with them as they could.

Just like their god.

CHAPTER SEVENTEEN

When all was told, the Battle of Morgath—Hollsted's Last Stand, the Battle of Fire and Fury, the Great Rebel Slaughter—lasted three and a half days, leaving six thousand Morgathian soldiers, women, and children slain, along with five thousand Shadows, largely found in the Goran Fields outside the fortress. No Morgathian soldiers surrendered. All went down in a bloody fight until their last breath. Though many were slain, the old men, women, and children who survived were given the option to swear allegiance to the chancellor, so long as they forsook their pagan god. Most obliged. The survivors would see the chancellor as a kind master in contrast to Hollsted. They would become loyal subjects, all notions of rebellion quenched. It was a mercy they did not deserve, but the chancellor was wise and gracious. Darien could only hope his ruler would be so gracious when he and Valeria arrived back at the White Citadel.

Bound by the wrists, the two war criminals were escorted from Goran'El by Commander Zamel. Darien mourned General Thrain's death as he had his own father's—in chains and in silence. If given the chance, he would attack Hollsted all over again. He did not regret his actions. *Damn the traditions of warfare.*

The Rebel King had not deserved to live. Though it might mean flogging, banishment, or worse, he would never take back that choice.

Threading carefully through the mass of bodies that stretched across the Goran Fields, Darien and Valeria were led to the Legion encampments at the edge of the King's Forest. Valeria had not spoken a word. It had been folly to fire that shot. She should have let the king run him through, but Darien was grateful she hadn't. Because of her, Hollsted lay among the slain, and the Rebel King's betrayal of General Thrain—and of the chancellor himself—was avenged.

Zamel led them through the Legion encampment to a large black tent at the very center—the Metamorphi camp.

One of the flying Morphs descended from the sky and landed before the entrance to greet them. He morphed back into his human form, and Darien, Valeria, and Commander Zamel all went to one knee instantly. The Morph was Cyrus Maro—the sixteenth Chancellor of Osha. Darien trembled at the sight of him. The last time he had been this close to his ruler, Darien had defied him. And now he had defied the Oshan laws of warfare.

"Rise, please," said the chancellor evenly. He pulled back the flap and ushered them into the tent. The place was lit by a circle of lanterns surrounding a small throne made of pale snowpines.

How long has he been in disguise? Darien wondered with horror. *Did he march with us the whole way? Fight in the battle?*

"Zamel, leave us for a moment," said the chancellor. And before Zamel could protest, he added, "Do not fear, I am in no danger in the company of these comrades." He flashed a thin smile at them, which made Darien feel queasier than he had the entire battle. Zamel nodded to his master, handed him Darien and Valeria's chains, and left.

"Gallows Boy!" said the chancellor.

Darien sheepishly met the intense gaze of his master. "Aye, milord."

"Last time I saw you, you were defying me in front of all my lords and ladies."

Darien nodded dutifully. He had not thought of that day in weeks, and it made him cringe, particularly in the presence of his ruler. He felt as though he were sinking into the ground. "I was a fool then, milord."

The chancellor cracked a sly smile. "And not now?"

"Only a slightly wiser fool, milord."

"Slightly? You attacked a king in the wake of battle, in front of all his elders and all *my* generals. That is beyond slightly foolish!"

For the first time, Darien felt a twinge of shame at his defiant act. His body tensed, anticipating the chancellor's coming wrath.

"Comrade, you have the cunning of a general!"

"Milord?"

"As I understand it, it was *your* idea to send me and the other Morphs across the wall in the midst of that storm last night."

I sent the chancellor into the middle of the Morgathian fortress? Darien gulped. "It was, milord."

"Brilliant!" said the chancellor. "I haven't had that much fun since I was a young boy. And you bloody well won us this battle and, in many ways, singlehandedly crushed the rebellion. Well, perhaps not quite singlehandedly." His gaze moved to Valeria. "Valeria, is it?"

Valeria nodded. "Yes, milord. Valeria Sardona, once of the Southern Isles. Now a loyal Shadow of Osha."

"Loyal, indeed. You shot off Hollsted's head! Tell me, what did it feel like to see that bastard's face torn apart by your bullet?"

"It felt... very satisfying, milord."

The chancellor laughed again. "I would call you a liar if you said anything to the contrary. I wish I could have seen it!"

"I'm sorry, milord, but aren't you... angry with us?" said Darien. He knew he shouldn't have interrupted the chancellor, but he bore no love for games. They were here to be punished, likely executed, and he would just as soon get on with it. "Isn't that why we're here, in chains? We broke the Oshan laws of warfare."

"Ancient laws for ancient fools," said Cyrus Maro. "There are no laws in war, comrade. A true soldier understands that. There are only those with the guts to do what is necessary to achieve victory. And the two of you have proven to be of such quality. I am not angry with you. I spared you after your rebellion last year, and I spared you for a reason. To some, it might have seemed a fool's pardon, but I saw a spark in you, and you did not disappoint me. The Gallows Boy has redeemed his rebellion, as I knew he would."

Darien swelled with pride, the way he had when General Thrain had first spoken well of him, but he tried not to show it. "I was... only doing my duty."

"Well, I would have more of your duty, comrade. And yours also, Valeria. I fear when the draft comes next, there may be more need of the gallows, if these damned rumors continue to spread. You have heard the rumors, have you not?"

"Of the Gallows Girl," said Darien. "Y-yes, milord."

"And do you believe them?"

Darien did not hesitate. "I saw her body hanging from the citadel on the day of my conscription, milord. And even if the rumors were somehow true, I would wish they were not. Sorcery is an abomination. Her rebellion was deserving of death."

The chancellor's grin stretched wide. "Was it, comrade? Now, of that, I am not so sure."

Darien and Valeria both bore puzzled expressions, and Darien felt uneasy. Was this all a game? It was surely no coincidence the chancellor mentioned Tori and her magic. Was this a test?

The chancellor waved his hand, and Darien's and Valeria's shackles, magically, fell from their wrists. The chancellor was more than a Morph. *He wields magic himself!*

"The Gallows Girl's folly was not her magical prowess, but her defiance. It was the same folly that led to your old master's downfall."

"Commander Scelero?" Then, Merri had been right about the chancellor's reclamation of his mind. Did that mean she'd been right about the rest of it? About Tori?

"I am in need of new Morphs, seeing as Scelero assisted in the escape of my most treasured prisoner." The chancellor paused for effect.

"Milord?"

"What if I told you the rumors were true, comrade? That the Gallows Girl's death was a fraud, and now, with the help of Scelero, she has escaped and is in the company of a remnant of Watchers bent on a magical revolution. What would you say to that?"

"I would say again, *I wish it were not so*. I have no desire to return to the heathen ways of the Old World."

"And you, Valeria?"

"In the Southern Isles, many still hold to the pagan practices of the Old World. It is even said that a Witch Queen now rules the Veil. I fled that land, and I hold no love for the old gods, or their Watchers of lore."

"You answer wisely," said the chancellor. "But do you answer truthfully?"

As the chancellor spoke, Darien felt a rush of air behind him and a chilling presence. He and Valeria both turned, and what they saw snatched away their breath.

The tent filled with a dark cloud, and seemingly from the air itself, a woman appeared, translucently at first, and then she took on full form. The cloud dissipated around her, revealing a short, slender woman with skin paler than any Darien had ever seen, paler than Valeria's, paler than the snows of the North. The woman bore a wild nest of dark hair sticking out from all sides in thick, tangled locks. Her clothes were made of thin silk that was nearly transparent and billowed from her body. Her face was contoured with discreet lines of age.

"H-how did you..." Darien stammered.

"Where did you come from?" said Valeria.

"From beyond," whispered the woman. Her voice was airy, as though spoken in a dreamworld. Her misty eyes wandered the tent, yet never seemed to fix on anything entirely. Darien had the unbidden feeling she was not wholly present, but he couldn't explain it. Absently, the woman handed the chancellor a pair of glowing gems. Then, she stretched out with great branchy fingers and latched onto Darien's head, and then Valeria's, and her warm skin felt suddenly *very* present, her grip like a vice on his skull. Yet Darien did not desire to resist it.

The chancellor smiled. "Beyond—that is all you would understand presently, comrades. The world is much larger than our small corner, though few alive still know it. The knowledge has been lost to us since the fall of the Old World. Medea comes from a land too far to reach by sail, nor even by flying. But there are other ways to travel. And so... here she is."

Darien felt warmth, an otherness, that seemed to tease from her fingertips like wisps of smoke, and his head felt weightless.

"In the Old World, Medea would have been called a Watcher of the Cerebro order. She can see into the mind, delve deep, and find what is hidden in the darkest crevasses. I have high hopes for the two of you, but first, I must know where your loyalties truly lie."

"High hopes?" said Valeria.

"The two of you have proven yourselves beyond all your comrades. And so, it is to you I bestow a special honor. We lost many Morphs in the Battle of Morgath."

"You want us to become Morphs?" said Darien. The idea was strange, but then, everything that had happened to him in the past year was strange.

"My personal army of sorcerers. Of course, if you do not wish such an honor, you may return to your regiment. There is no shame in a soldier's life. I have full confidence you would both become generals of your own regiments, someday. But that, in my mind, would be a waste of your cunning. I have greater plans than you could dream up your-selves. But you must desire those plans."

Darien and Valeria made eye contact. She nodded to him. Darien felt the warmth of Valeria's fingers weaving between his own, and he knew this was what he wanted. The feeling of energy increased from Medea's fingers and seemed to pour into their minds as though her magic were a tangible thing.

"We want your plans for us, milord," Darien and Valeria said in unison, as though suddenly possessing one voice.

The chancellor smiled and knelt, clasping his own hands around their intertwined fingers. "In the Legions, your minds were known and molded outwardly. But my Metamorphi must be known inwardly."

As one, Darien and Valeria said, "We are your servants, milord. We have nothing to hide."

The feeling of warmth filled Darien's senses as Medea's energy poured into his mind. He had never known such lightness, such knowledge, such meaning. He could feel the woman, her innermost essence, binding to him, and he could feel Valeria's as well, as though they were parts of the same being.

And then, in the midst of everything, he felt the chancellor's presence, and he realized who that being was, binding them together.

The chancellor.

He was the center of it all. The meaning to Darien's existence.

There was nothing else.

PART SEVEN
THE WATCHTOWER

In the Old World, the Watchers were believed to have descended from the gods themselves. Though the magic beings counseled countless kings, the Watchers did not seek power for themselves. They devoted their powers and their lives to preserving peace and protecting the weak...

Once, a faction of Watchers sought power. That was shortly before the fall of the Old World.

—from New Histories of the Old World

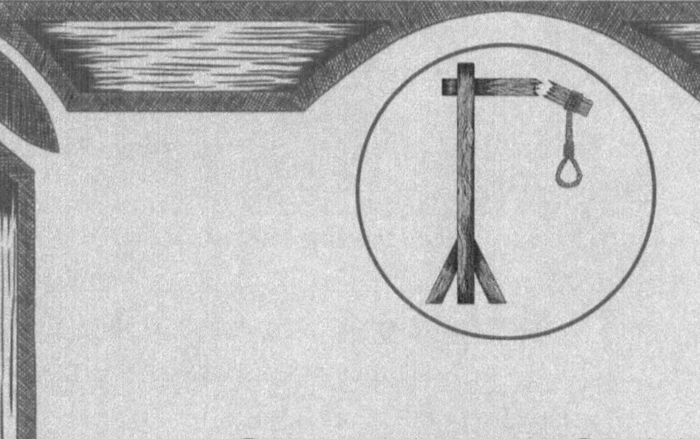

CHAPTER EIGHTEEN

Acandle seared the darkness and a hand grasped Tori's wrist. She jolted awake, and Mischa Sufai laughed.

"Why?" Tori complained sleepily, shielding her eyes from the jarring light.

"You're the one who demanded private lessons. Get dressed. The captain's waiting."

"Arayeva! Shut up, both of you!" moaned Vashti.

"Sorry, sorry," said Mischa, not sounding sorry at all. "Had a little too much to drink last night, did we?" Vashti cursed and rolled over.

It had been only a month since Tori arrived at the Watchtower, and already there had been three new arrivals. The latest was a young boy named Jann, no older than twelve, whom Dajha Bhati had found in the Trium'vel. The welcoming banquet had not been as extravagant as Tori's own, but everyone had been generous with the wine. Vashti, most of all, though this was likely because Ren had seated Tori at the head table, which was apparently not common if you were not the new recruit being welcomed. Vashti had sat brooding while Mischa and a Medici named Zaya flirted the night away, and Tori caught Vashti glaring up at the head table more than once while she chatted with Ren. Tori didn't see why she was jealous of the attention. Ren had been discussing her struggles in Conjuri training, which was when she'd asked for private lessons. This morning would be the first.

"Be quick," Mischa whispered to Tori, shaking her playfully.

Tori rolled from bed and slipped into a pair of woolen breeches, a tunic, and a thick cloak lined with kendrak fur. Ren had supplied her with an entire wardrobe of fine clothes—tunics and cloaks and dining gowns—finer than any clothes she'd owned in all her life.

"Gods, it's still dark out!" Tori muttered, rubbing her eyes as she gazed out the window.

"The captain is waiting in the courtyard," said Mischa. "Have fun!"

Tori slipped out the door, but not before she heard Vashti muttering more demands for silence. Tori found Ren standing alone in the snow, his cloak shifting in the breeze. The courtyard was lit only by the pale light of the Sisters. A sharp chill nipped at her nose and cheeks. Even the summers were cold in the Teeth, especially at this hour.

"Are you certain your strength is returned?" Ren said. "In truth, I was not surprised you've struggled in the exercises thus far. You've been through so much."

Tori did not wish to be doted on. She was frustrated, and she was still waking. One month, and she had not been able to summon so much as an apple from across the table with her Conjuri power. "I am recovered plenty!"

"Very well, then," he said. "Show me what you can do."

Tori had never used her powers at demand. The sense always came of its own accord, and this was her problem. She could not control it. It was as though her body was rejecting the abilities, like fighting off a sickness. Tori reached out with her mind, trying to re-create the sense that had come so easily during her escape from the White Citadel. Now, in the safety of the Watchtower, with Ren's sparkling eyes watching her every move, she sensed nothing.

"That bench," said Ren, gesturing across the courtyard to a wooden bench toppled on its side. "Raise it."

Tori focused and held out her hands toward it.

Ren laughed. "What in the names of the gods are you doing?"

"Trying!" Tori clenched her fists tight, then released them.

"Do you expect a rope to fly from your hands and move it for you?" Ren was smirking.

Tori glared. "When Mischa uses her flames, she waves them away. Several of the Conjuris use their hands as well."

Ren laughed again. It was getting annoying. "That adds nothing. Your power does not come from within your body, Astoria. It is out there"—Ren gestured at the sky in a sweeping motion—"you have access to the forces behind the world. Use your mind. Reach out with your senses."

Tori focused again on the bench and tried to recall her magic awareness, imagining what it had been like back in the Fringes. Ren hovered above the ground, watching her intently. Tori gritted her teeth and concentrated. There was no awareness. She could not make the bench move. How could she do anyone any good if she couldn't replicate that sense?

Already, the enthusiasm of the other Watchers was waning. Tori's first few weeks of training had been a letdown for all. Two days previous, Tori had overheard Vashti whispering to a Faerish girl named Calla about the folly of the Gallows Girl. And Tori did not despise Vashti for it, so much as herself. Tori cried out in frustration, and a pair of ravens started across the courtyard and flapped away, squawking. Tori dropped to her knees.

"I am not the girl you were hoping for."

Ren remained silent, floating a couple feet in the air, eyes closed, as though in meditation. Then he said, "You are what you think you are, Astoria. Failure is nothing but a game in your mind. Just like the ghosts of Ghen."

Tori shuddered at the memory of the ghosts. They still entered her dreams, still plagued her thoughts, still left her wondering what was truth and what was nightmare. *Does Ren know this? How Scelero and Mum and Darien torment my dreams?*

Ren had been absent the past two weeks, gone to Maro'El to meet with nobles conspiring against the chancellor. Last night, Tori had asked for news of Scelero at the celebration, worried that he had been imprisoned—or worse, executed—for helping her escape. She had also asked about the Gallows Boy. During her imprisonment, the chancellor had gleefully updated her on his progress as a soldier. Now it killed her not to know what had been truth and lie. But Ren said he had heard nothing of either of them. A fact that frustrated Tori nearly as much as her failure to make any noticeable progress in over a month at the Watchtower.

To make things worse, the only news Ren had brought back from Osha was bad. The Legions had ended the Morgathian rebellion, which did not bode well for persuading nobles to turn on their chancellor.

Ren returned to the earth and knelt beside her, brushing her shoulder. "What was it like, the day you destroyed the chancellor's gallows?"

Tori thought back. It seemed unfathomable that it had been so sudden, that her abilities had surfaced by some necessity to save Darien, that in all the years since her mother sold her, not once had her powers emerged, not even for a second. But her memories were dark and empty, like looking back into the depths of a cavern, and she feared what lurked in the past. How was it possible her powers had remained dormant for so long? Even the new boy, Jann, had traces of Fieri power.

There was the memory of the Yan Avii boy, but Tori did not know what had happened that day. Had she used magic? It was as though the details were blocked from her mind. *But something happened, didn't it? That's why Mum was scared that night. That's why she sold me into slavery.*

Or perhaps all of it was wishful thinking. "Far as I can remember, I never sensed it before that day," she said finally. "It came over me like a wave crashing, and suddenly, I was filled with energy. I could sense it. I could see it. It was as though a shroud had been lifted from my eyes, and I could see something that had been there all along. I could sense the energy at the heart of the world."

Ren smiled. "And what did you feel in that moment?"

"I was desperate. The Gallows Boy… he was my best friend. I was so angry!"

"And the Gallows Boy, he is a soldier now."

"Or else, dead." Again, she thought of Darien's ghost, his shredded back, the blood dripping from his hands.

"I am sorry I did not hear anything while I was away. I'm afraid the nobles' interests have moved on in the past year. The Gallows Boy was all the talk in the wake of that day, but I'm afraid he's been forgotten in Maro'El."

Tori did not know what to say, so she remained silent. It angered her to think that his defiance had been forgotten. *Because I stole it from him.*

Ren thought a moment, then said, "Go on. You were so angry…"

Though it was painful, Tori replayed the events in her mind. "As they led him to be hanged, I had to do something. He was the only friend I had in Maro'El. And then, I was able to do something. I became aware of the energy, and suddenly, the gallows was exploding. I didn't control it. It just… happened."

"Because it needed to," Ren mused. He stared off at the mountains looming in the growing predawn light, then he strode across the courtyard toward the gates of the Watchtower. "Come along, Tori."

They left the confines of the castle and walked across the snow-covered meadow toward the tallest of the mountains surrounding them. Winding up the steep slope was a narrow path cut perilously into the face of the stone. Tori looked up. "W-we're going up there?"

"The mountain folk do not venture to this valley because of superstition," said Ren. "This mountain is sacred. This staircase is believed to have belonged to the god Orran in the ancient world. To receive his blessing, peasants had to brave the treacherous passes of the Teeth, and then, the Staircase to the Clouds. Most turned back, many fell to their deaths, but those who reached the top received riches and lovers and plentiful harvests. It is said that Orran left the ancient world in a rage. His temple crumbled to ruins, and he left the mountain cursed. The mountain folk believe we are monks devoted to the old gods. They think we are a blessing, but they do not dare approach the mountain. I, however, find the view marvelously inspiring."

Ren led the way up the face of Orran's Mountain. At first, the climb came easy to Tori. Over the past month, her strength had increased incredibly. A flush had returned to her skin and her eyes seemed brighter, according to Mischa. She'd put on weight and her muscles were growing taut with Sahra's rigorous training exercises. Tori was proving adept with a saber, and she had always been able to hold her own in a scrap.

But Orran's stairs went on and on. They were so steep she had to scramble on all fours, the sharp stone cutting into her hands. Soon, Tori fought for breath and had to will each limb forward. She looked down and nearly slipped, clutching at the step in her hands. The stone sliced deep. They were at least five hundred feet above the Watchtower. Far below, the courtyard was bustling as the Watchers made their way to breakfast. From this height, they looked like bees scurrying around a hive.

Still, the mountain rose hundreds, perhaps thousands, of feet higher. Tori paused to regain her composure. The skies had turned bright with morning, though the sun would not be visible for some time over the towering peaks. Ren urged her on.

They had still not made it halfway up the face of the mountain when the sun crested the peak and painted the valley with color. Ren led her to a small niche in the mountain to rest. The ledge looked down upon the Watchtower. There was a sheer drop for hundreds of feet before the mountain eased into the gentle slopes of the valley. Tori caught her breath, one hand clutching the mountainside. Ren stood at the edge and breathed calmly, his eyes closed—as though he were not at the edge of a looming cliff, as though he had not climbed a mountain for the past hour. His chest eased in and out with perfect rhythm. After some time, he opened his eyes and said, "Beautiful, isn't it?"

Trying not to gasp, Tori managed, "It is."

"I must confess, there are times I think it wouldn't be so bad to stay here at the Watchtower. It's beautiful and safe. Maro'El is conniving and dangerous, and I wonder if we might do all this, only to run straight into our own demise. But it is only my mind playing tricks with my heart, just as your mind is playing with you now. Telling you that you have no more strength. That you have no control over your gifts, or perhaps that they are *shenzah* altogether."

Tori did not respond. Perhaps because she was still dying from lack of breath, or perhaps because she knew Ren was right.

"My mind tells me things too, at times," Ren went on. "Fear and doubt and guilt have a hold on us all. But some of us step out to the edge and face them." Ren held out his hand to her. "Step out to the edge, Tori."

It took all her willpower to let go of the mountainside, but she did. Her legs were so weak, she did not trust them to steady her, but she forced herself not to think about it. She looked out at the valley, rather than at the sheer drop below. It was beautiful. The valley was painted with a warm glow in the morning light. Summer grass poked through patches on the hillside where the sun shone the most.

"Now breathe," Ren said.

Tori breathed, slowly, acknowledging the chilling sensation as the frigid air filled her lungs and reappeared in a warm cloud.

"You are strong, Astoria. You have always been strong, though you have been taught not to recognize it. But your body knows. It has proven it over and over again, in spite of your mind. When it is forced to… it reacts!"

There was no warning. Ren did not even have to touch her. He simply reached out with his Conjuri sense. Tori felt the ledge disappear beneath her boots, and she plummeted over the edge of the cliff.

CHAPTER NINETEEN

Forces at the heart of the earth pulled on Tori's body, as though a thousand invisible hands had emerged from the ground, and all their strength was focused on drawing her to her death. Tori shot towards the earth. The weight of the world seemed to be contained in her chest, the forces pulling harder and harder, as though she might be torn apart before she even reached the earth below. She did not have time to think. Her mind shut off. The world was a blur. But her body reacted.

At the last possible moment, her body lurched upward. Tori missed the rocks and landed in a heap upon the scree. She tumbled down the face of the mountain, scraping her face and hands raw. Finally, she latched onto an exposed tree root and stopped her fall.

Nothing but pain filled her senses. Her head felt like it might burst. There was blood everywhere. Shards of rock specked her skin like gruesome freckles.

Ren landed gracefully beside her. Tori tried to raise herself up, but her arms gave out and she collapsed, screaming in agony. *How many bones did I break? That insane bastard!*

But then, before her eyes, blood retreated from Tori's bare hands back into her body; skin closed over; her leg shifted beneath her, straightening itself out; bones pieced themselves back together. It was incredible. The pain subsided and then disappeared altogether. Ren was smiling at her, undisturbed at her healing.

"Y-you knew that would happen?" Tori stammered. She was still shaken from the fall, and from her regeneration.

Ren took her hand. "My family survived the purges of the First Chancellor. Our House preserved the tales of days when Watchers did not have to live in secret, when we counseled kings and kept peace across the entire Old World. You do not know how rare it is to wield two gifts in our world, but I do. You are *exactly* the girl I was looking for, so I will not stand to hear you voice your doubts to me." Ren helped her to her feet. "You are strong, Astoria. I know you don't like it when I call you by your true name. But it is only one more proof of your fear and your doubt."

It was true, as though Ren could see her thoughts. She did fear it. When she met with the chancellor it had felt like she was being true to herself, but now Astoria, the Gallows Girl, felt like some other person. Who was she to be the hope of the lowborns? Who was she to lead a rebellion? "I'm just a slave. All this, my magic, it's all an accident. A mistake."

Ren shook his head. "My mother used to tell me that there are no accidents in this world, only those too afraid to embrace their own destinies. Your mother named you after the goddess of the weak and the destitute. The defender of the poor and the downtrodden. Astoria gave them hope and strength, and it is believed she gave humanity its first awareness of the magic behind the world. Tori, you are strong. Even when you don't feel it. Even when others call you a sham. Even when your mind tells you lies. Look at what you just did! You fell hundreds of feet, and you do not have a scratch."

Suddenly, Tori understood. *Two gifts. This was how I survived the fall with the chancellor in the Fringes. I didn't fly. I healed like the Regeneros.*

"I... healed," she said. Ren nodded. "But what does it mean?"

"It means that while you may not have control over your abilities, or your fears and doubts, you are still incredibly strong. In here." Ren pointed to his chest. "And you will become much stronger." Ren held onto her hand, but he did not lead her down to the Watchtower. He turned and faced the mountain.

"Now," he said. "Again."

And they began the arduous climb up Orran's Mountain once more.

———

"Three times?" Mischa Sufai exclaimed over the noonday meal. "He made you jump off the mountain three times?"

"Well, technically he pushed me off the first time," said Tori. She had missed breakfast and spoke between eager mouthfuls of warm stew. A bit dripped down her face, and she wiped it with her sleeve.

Zaya Shalvar laughed and handed her a cloth. "No wonder you missed the morning run."

Run was an inadequate word, making their morning fitness regimen sound like a leisurely jog. For beings who could fly, the Watchers did precious little of it. Sahra believed that in order to make proper use of their gifts, they first needed to grow strong and disciplined without them.

The morning run consisted of hauling weighted sledges behind them as they trudged through the thick snow with webbed Alyut *muluqs* strapped to their boots. Tori never came close to a running pace, but Sahra would run the course, then come back and spur the others on with unfathomable enthusiasm. Tori had never seen anyone with as much stamina as their Alyut trainer.

Tori was unsure which was worse, the morning run or climbing the Staircase to the Clouds. "Yes, I'm sorry to have missed *that*."

Zaya chuckled, leaning closer. Her sparkling golden eyes reminded Tori of Darien. The Medici hailed from the Klavash mountains of his childhood. "So how was it?"

"How was what?" said Tori.

Mischa smiled, locking her arm around Zaya's, and whispered, "Spending the morning with the captain, of course."

Just then, Vashti brushed past, bumping Tori's chair as she maneuvered past their table. More stew dripped down her chin.

"Excuse you," Tori hissed. But Vashti did not respond and chose a seat across the room with Calla. "Gods, I am sick of her *shenzah.*"

"Yeah, she's a cold one," said Zaya.

"You're telling me," said Tori. "I've never been anything but decent to her."

"Probably makes her hate you all the more," said Zaya.

Mischa had gone quiet. Her eyes lingered after their roommate, but not with the anger that Tori felt. Mischa looked… sad.

"You okay?" asked Zaya, touching her arm.

But before Mischa could answer, Dajha plopped down to join them, his bowl spilling over, as he had filled it so high. He followed their gazes to Vashti. "Ah, don't mind 'Er 'Ighness. She en't used to being second in line."

"What do you mean?" said Tori.

"The cap'n don't exactly give private lessons all around, yeh know."

"Vashti was the only other one," said Mischa. There was softness in her voice. Mischa teased their bunkmate, but Tori realized Mischa was fond of her. Tori couldn't understand why. Vashti did not seem to be fond of Mischa, or anyone else.

"En't you 'eard 'ow she came to the Watchtower? There's a bloody tragedy, what 'er father done to 'er."

"I thought she was royalty. A princess," said Tori.

"Princess only means so much to the Yan Avii when you're a woman," said Mischa.

Tori didn't carry vivid memories of this from her childhood on the Steppe, but she had heard the notion uttered often enough in Osha.

"Vashti always had fine things, of course," Mischa went on. "Had servant girls and porters and all of it. Would have been married off to one of the *soltaynes*. If she hadn't been special."

"Couldn't stand to 'ave a daughter more powerful than 'im. The Great Soltayne saw 'is own daughter as a threat."

"So he burned her at the stake," Mischa finished. Her gaze still lingered on Vashti across the room. Vashti faced away, whispering back and forth with Calla.

"But Vashti's alive," Tori said incredulously.

"Bloody miracle, en't it?"

"Her brother stole her body," said Mischa. "She survived the execution. Just barely. It was a remarkable show of power for someone with no training. The captain trained her personally for nearly a year. Wanted her to be his queen when the Shadow Watch rose up. She fell in love with him, but... Ren thought she might be able to rally her people to our cause, but it was more complicated than that... He moved on when the hope of an alliance with the Yan Avii fell through."

"And now you're here," said Zaya.

"Now I'm here," said Tori.

"The symbol of the revolution," said Mischa.

Dajha chuckled darkly. "Gods! En't seen this much drama since me mum took me to court in the Silver Palace of Malai."

Tori didn't laugh at the joke, and neither did Mischa or Zaya.

"Yeh know? Where the princes 'old that contest to choose their brides? If that don't breed drama, I don't know what else—"

"We *know* what it is!" Mischa cut him off.

Zaya took her hand. "Come on. Let's go forget about sad things for a while."

But Mischa shook her head. "I can't... I, er, promised Tori I'd spar with her."

Tori raised a brow. Mischa was lying to her.

"Okay, well, I'll come find you later, then." Zaya left them.

Dajha soon scurried off to another table, muttering about how Tori and Mischa needed to learn to see the humor in tragedies, and something about how they would die crying in their sleep. But Tori was not really listening.

Ren caught Tori's gaze from the head table in the dining hall and smiled, his eyes twinkling in the lamplight, and Tori could not help but smile back. She longed to prove herself to him. She looked forward to the next climb up the mountain, and yet...

What does he want from me? she wondered. *To be his queen, like Vashti?* Tori did not want to be Ren's queen, or symbol, or anything else. But then, what did she want exactly?

———

THE COMING WEEKS FOLLOWED THE SAME ROUTINE EACH DAY. Tori and Ren would climb Orran's mountain three times in the mornings. Tori would nearly fly, just enough to slow her fall, but not enough to land the way Ren did, and she would heal from her wounds. The pain was arduous, but the more it occurred, the more it became strangely bearable. In the afternoons, Tori joined the others for the remainder of their daily training, and the others muttered behind her back as she failed to show any evidence of giftedness whatsoever. At first, Ren took these failures in stride, but as the failures mounted, Ren began to lose his cool demeanor.

After several weeks of private lessons, Tori took a particularly hard fall. The crunch of her own bones filled her ears. The healing took longer than normal. She groaned in agony while Ren watched her body repair itself.

"That was the worst attempt yet," Ren said as she finally managed to raise herself from the ground. "The point is not to prove how well your body can heal itself. We've damn well established that! The point is to fly, Astoria!"

A bone in her arm righted itself with a snap, and Tori cried with the pain. "I can't fly!"

"Nonsense! I've seen you! Gods, I swear your flying has gotten worse the more your body proves it will heal no matter how hard you land. What are you afraid of?"

"I'm not afraid!"

"*Shenzah*! You have fear dripping off you like sweat. You have to face it. Embrace your power. Rule over it!"

"Don't you think I want to? I don't know how!"

Ren watched her for a moment, his chest heaving. Tori had never seen him this frustrated. Usually he was so calm and collected. But it had been weeks of this, and Tori had only regressed since her first fall.

Ren's heaving breaths subsided. His expression softened. "I'm sorry, Tori. I expect too much of you. You've been through unfathomable horrors. Seen things far worse than I could believe. It is no wonder you are afraid." He took her by the arm. "Enough for today. You should rest."

Ren turned to head down the mountainside, but Tori shrugged away his hand and spoke through gritted teeth. "No, again!"

———

"I don't know what's wrong with me," Tori confided to Mischa that night. The two of them sat on their beds. Vashti was in the library. The princess spent a lot of time there lately, probably because she knew Tori couldn't read old scrolls, and so would have no reason to go there. Zaya was off studying anatomy with the other Medicis. Sahra insisted this was as important as any healing ability, and it kept Zaya busy most evenings.

Alone, Tori felt she could speak more openly. "I can't control it. I've never been able to."

"You expect too much," said Mischa. "This is normal. The captain knows that."

"But I'm the Gallows Girl. You're thinking it. Everyone else is thinking it. I'm supposed to be different. I'm supposed to be strong."

"You *are* strong."

"I'm letting everyone down. I'm letting… *him* down. Ren tries to hide it, but I can tell. He wanted me to rest today!"

"Maybe you *need* to rest."

Tori sighed and flopped back on her bed. "I'm not a resting sort of person."

"Who are you trying so hard for?" Mischa asked. "I've been trying to figure it for a while. You just don't strike me as the revolutionary type. All this… it's personal for you, isn't it?"

Tori thought of Darien. Pictured him marching, killing in the name of the chancellor, because of her. She pictured Ol' Merri. Her mum. Commander Scelero…

Their ghosts would not leave her dreams. They taunted her failure, her weakness.

"I don't know, Misch. Maybe that's the problem. What are any of us fighting for? The return of the Watchers? None of us were alive then. So, what's it matter to us? For safety? We could hole up in the

Teeth forever, and the chancellor would never find us. You tell me, what are we fighting for?"

"We're fighting to be true." The answer did not come from Mischa. Vashti had slipped in and leaned against the doorframe. There was a flash in her eyes and an edge to her voice. "We are fighting because our world tells us we have to hide who we really are. And that is *shenzah*! You never knew what you were. You didn't have to live your whole life pretending to be something you're not. You didn't live in suffering every single day, fearing Morphs or watching eyes… or jealous fathers."

Suddenly, the frustration that had been building up inside Tori exploded. Vashti didn't know the first thing about Tori or what she'd suffered—or how she'd made others suffer.

"Don't talk to me about suffering," said Tori bitterly. "You strut around here like the world owes you some damn thing. You think you're the only one who's had a hard life?"

"Tori!" Mischa said, appalled.

"No, please, let her finish," Vashti said scathingly. "Share your wisdom, Gallows Girl."

Tori fumed. "I spent most of my life hungry and cold. I never knew fine clothes until I came to this gods-forsaken place. My father never cared about some bastard daughter. And my mum sold me into slavery. But you don't see me moping about it. I suffered. You suffered. We've all suffered. The *world* suffers! That's the way the world is. So spare us all your sob story."

Vashti did not respond right away. Her expression remained cold as the face of Orran's mountain. She spoke each word like it was an arrow, drawn slowly and methodically. "Well, we've all wondered what it was that drew the captain to you. Obviously, we knew it wasn't your abilities. Turns out it was your way with words."

Tori shot to her feet, ready to pummel the sneering princess, but suddenly, there was a great ball of flame separating them. Tori and Vashti leapt back from the searing heat.

Mischa stood with her hands raised, tears streaking her cheeks, little flames fluttering around her skin like butterflies. "Enough, both of you!"

The flames went out, and all three of them were silent for a moment. Tori had never seen Mischa get emotional like that, and she felt guilty, not for saying what she'd said, but for upsetting the one true friend she'd made at the Watchtower.

Vashti stood. "I should go." She opened the door and then stopped. "Oh, I nearly forgot. The captain asked me to fetch you, Gallows Girl. Looks like he has something… special… planned for you in the courtyard." With that, the Yan Avii princess left.

"The courtyard?" said Mischa, wiping at her eyes.

"I've no idea what she's talking about," said Tori.

The two of them descended the spiraling staircase of the central spire. The courtyard was lit by torches, and at the center, an immense gallows had been erected. It was nearly identical to the one Tori and Darien had built for the chancellor's drafting ceremony. Tori felt like she might retch. Dozens of other Watchers had gathered around, all wondering what was going on.

Ren stood upon the platform, a noose wrapped around his neck. All eyes were fixed on Tori as she approached.

"What is this?" Tori shouted.

Ren motioned her closer. "I've been thinking long and hard about what to do about our situation, Astoria. You are powerful and strong, but your mind is bent on convincing you otherwise. And all the other Watchers doubt you too, and to be honest, I can't blame them. They have not seen you in action, as I have."

"D-don't do this, Ren!" Tori stammered. Her whole body was trembling. She clutched Mischa's arm in a death grip. "I-I can't do this! D-don't make me do this!"

The little Fieri, Jann, was on stage with Ren. His hand was on a lever connected to the trapdoor of the gallows.

"You are afraid, Tori. Afraid of the things you've done. Of what you might do, what you might become. Who might get hurt, who might… die—because of you. You're afraid to have any other life in your hands because even when you've tried to help those you love, you believe you've failed. And I think it all comes back to this." Ren gestured at the rope around his neck.

Tori pictured Darien hanging from the gallows, his neck cockeyed, his legs stiff. She pictured his ghost in the Forest of Ghen, blood dripping from his hands. She had saved him from one terrible fate, but she had turned him into a soldier, a killer. She knew the ghosts had spoken truth. Every night, she dreamed of it, and it ate away at her insides.

"Captain, please," Tori managed at last. "I-I can't—there's no way I—"

"You don't have a choice," Ren said. "My life is in *your* hands."

"Ren, no, please. I can't—"

"Don't think. Just react!" Ren nodded to Jann.

"THREE!" Jann counted down.

"No, please!"

"TWO!"

"Ren, no! Gods!"

"ONE!"

"I believe in you, Tori!" Ren shouted.

Jann pulled the lever.

CHAPTER TWENTY

For the first time, when she desperately needed them, Tori's powers failed her. There was no time to focus or harness her power. It was supposed to be instinct. That was what Ren was counting on. Every other time, desperation seemed to compel her abilities, like a dog compels a hare to run for its life.

Every other time but this—

Ren shot through the trapdoor, and the courtyard filled with a splintering sound as the rope drew taut around Ren's neck.

Tori screamed, helpless. For a moment, she froze. Surely Ren had foreseen this possibility. Surely he had rigged the noose somehow, or had used his Conjuri powers to prevent the rope from actually drawing tight. *Any moment now,* Tori thought frantically, *he'll open his eyes and demand someone get him down.*

But Ren did not move. His body hung at the end of the rope, still swaying with the momentum of the fall. No one in the courtyard dared even to breathe. All eyes were on the Gallows Girl.

Tori snapped from her catatonic state and rushed forward. "Cut him down! Somebody cut him down!"

But no one moved. It was as though a spell had been cast over the entire Shadow Watch. They were in shock, all of them, even Sahra, their trainer, the toughest of them all. Jann had collapsed to his knees upon the gallows platform; he stared blankly at Ren's head, floating in the open space of the trapdoor. Ren's eyes were still closed. His face was contorted from the pressure of the noose. It reminded Tori of the way dead bodies became bloated in the summertime in the Fringes.

Tori snatched a blade from a nearby Watcher and rushed up the gallows steps. It took her two hacks at the rope before it frayed and released Ren's body to the ground. Tori leapt from the platform and landed hard, pain shooting up her leg, but she didn't care. Ren's eyes were wide, unblinking, his limbs lifeless. She felt at his neck and tilted her ear over his mouth, but there was no pulse and no breath.

"Ren! You can't die!" Tori pounded her fist on his chest, as though somehow this might shock him back to life. She was shrieking, her words drowned in sobs, but still, no one had come to help her. "What's the matter with you people? Somebody help him!"

But they all stared at her in shock.

Tori's tears drenched Ren's tunic. "Why? Why would you do this? I told you I couldn't do it!" She pounded his chest a few more times and then slumped over him, her body shaking with sobs. "Gods damn you! You can't die! You can't die! You can't die!"

His body was limp beneath her. In time, her sobs slowed and her breathing steadied. She had remained slumped over Ren's body for some time, when she noticed the awareness.

It was as though she was connected to Ren. She could feel inside him, feel life. Blood did not run through him, and his lungs drew no breath, but still, there was… a sense coming from his mind.

Her own senses honed in on Ren's body. She became aware of the makeup of it—the organs and tissue that filled him—and she could feel something wrong. She could feel where his spine had snapped, and she knew that if only this could be undone, he could live. She focused her sense further, to a more complex level, and she felt the tiniest elements that made Ren who he was, the infinitesimal components of his bones, his blood, everything. And then, it came to her: *If I can manipulate the rest of the world, I can manipulate Ren's spine. I can make it right again!*

Slowly at first, and then all at once, as a trickle becomes a downpour of rain, the elements of Ren's body began to rearrange themselves with her Conjuri power. It was subtle. There were no jarring movements, as when Tori healed after a fall from Orran's mountain. It was strange how such diminutive changes could take or grant a life.

Carefully, Tori righted what had been wronged until all the parts were aligned as they were meant to be. But still there was nothing. No pulse. No breath. But Tori was no longer frantic. Peace had settled over her, a deep inner focus. Ren needed breath in order to breathe, and so, she needed to give it to him.

Tori leaned over, spread open his mouth, and blew breath into his lungs. One, two, three breaths. His lips were cold, but with her sense, she could feel life spreading, air filling his lungs. She reached out with her Conjuri sense and, knowing his heart needed to beat, she compressed his heart from within. His chest spasmed as it brought air and blood to his body once again. There was spluttering and a desperate gasp.

He's alive! Tori sobbed with joy. She brushed his cheek with her hand. She had never been so relieved in all her life. "Oh, thank the gods!"

Ren coughed. There was a trace of blood. But he managed to speak in a whisper. "I-I thought you wanted the g-gods to damn me." Ren shook with coughs again. Or was he laughing? A sly grin stretched his swollen face.

"Even in death, you're a bloody idiot," said Sahra, kneeling down beside them. Sahra ran her hands over the captain, checking him over. She was a Medici, checking to be sure he was all right. Tori filled with rage. Sahra could have helped. She was a healer.

"You were going to let him die?"

For a moment, Sahra did not answer. She was focused on Ren. When she was content, she sat up. "You did well, Tori. Not the work of a Medici, but a few days with me, and his spine will heal."

"Why didn't you do anything? What if I hadn't saved him? What if your captain had died?"

Before Sahra could respond, Ren spoke between violent coughs and deep, wheezing breaths. "I... commanded them not to... help you... I... believed in you, Tori... though I... expected to be saved...

before the rope got me." Ren chuckled, and then he was thrown into another violent coughing fit.

"You need to shut up for once, Captain," said Sahra sternly. "Your body needs rest. Your spine is back in place, but the bones and tissue still need to heal. Or your neck will snap right back again."

Sahra called for Zaya and another young Medici to retrieve a stretcher from the infirmary.

"Tori, that was… incredible," Zaya whispered as they prepared the stretcher. The Klavash girl brushed her shoulder and smiled with wide golden eyes.

"Thanks."

Ren was loaded up with a brace fixed firmly against both sides of his head, though not without protest.

"Come now… I can get myself to my own… chambers. Sahra, I don't need… to be ferried around like some… cripple."

Sahra seemed to find satisfaction in the captain's weakened state. She shook her head. "Captain, you were just a moment from death, and your spine is fragile as a porcelain doll. Until my healers are finished, I don't want to see you out of your bed. For three days."

"Three… days?"

"At the very least. And I will hear no more of it. Medici orders."

"Perhaps the gods are… damning me after all," he muttered to Tori as the young Medicis carted him off. He chuckled, then fell into another coughing fit.

Tori was still for a moment, finally catching her own breath, overwhelmed by the energy she had used up. She stirred at Mischa's hand upon her shoulder.

"You should rest too," Mischa said, kneeling beside her. "You're trembling."

It was then Tori realized that the entire Shadow Watch was still staring at her, their mouths gaping.

"What are they gawking at?" Tori asked as Mischa took her by the arm and helped her up.

"The Gallows Girl," Mischa said, smiling.

Tori had been so overcome by relief about Ren that it hadn't sunk in exactly what she had done. Or how she'd done it. She had worked her magic, at her own will, for the first time since she had arrived at the Watchtower. She had saved Ren.

And all the Watchers had seen her do it. There could be no denying Tori's abilities now—not by Tori, or anyone else. Tori smiled with relief. Even Vashti's mouth hung wide as the Gallows Girl left the courtyard.

PART EIGHT
THE SLAVE'S BLADE

The Great Soltayne was chosen by the sun goddess, Arayeva. The chieftain who was chosen became like a god in the eyes of the people of the Steppe, with unquestionable influence and power. The chieftains of the twelve tribes vied ruthlessly to become the Chosen of Arayeva. Anyone who stood in their way gambled with death.

—from *Dawn of the Third World*

CHAPTER TWENTY-ONE

Get up, Sky Blood!"

A jarring kick to his ribs startled Kale from sleep. His senses were on high alert. In his dream, his brother had nearly died, and he had been overwhelmed by the darkness surrounding Ren's mind. Kale shot up, hands reaching for the attacker. But the Ilya woman was too quick. She snatched his wrist and twisted ruthlessly.

"All right, all right," said Kale. "*Sorenyi!*"

Ashi let go of his arm with a shove. Kale cradled his wrist. She had nearly broken it. Kale was not the strongest Watcher, but he could usually hold his own in a man-to-man fight. This Ilya woman was something else altogether.

"Get dressed. My prince has need of you."

Kale stretched out his strained wrist, then rose to his feet. *At last,* he thought.

It had been over a month of waiting for the Yan Avii to complete their arduous mourning rituals for the Great Soltayne, over a month of living beneath the city in the secret Den of the Ilya under Ashi's vigilant watch. She was the lone woman in a man's world, and it did not make her pleasant. She always seemed to be out to prove her worth.

The host of assassins in the Den changed each day, coming and going from the gloomy tunnels at all hours of the day, but each day, the Ilya woman remained.

Kale had not seen Salla since the prince had revealed his plans to use Kale's and Kirra's gifts to ensure his place as the next Great Soltayne. Though Salla, by inheritance, took his father's place as *soltayne* of the Burodai tribe, the leader of all the tribesmen was chosen by lots, and the honor had never before passed to the son of the previous Great Soltayne. Salla would need more than the help of fate, or Arayeva, to gain the throne. He needed Watcher magic.

Salla had remained in the world above, performing his princely duty in the palace, and in the short time they'd spent together, Kale had been unable to discern Salla's true schemes. Salla was practiced in the art of protecting his mind, and Kale had been too preoccupied with thoughts of Kirra.

Though Kirra was part of Salla's plan, Kale had not seen her. He had not sensed her since the day he'd arrived in the Red City. This fact drove him nearly mad, but as long as Kirra was in Salla's hands, Kale was forced to comply with Ashi's brusque nature.

"Dress quickly," said Ashi, holding out a set of clothes. "We must be to the palace before evening prayer."

Kale took the bundle of clothes, but Ashi remained where she stood, arms crossed over her chest. "No privacy?" he muttered.

"I will not take my eyes off you today. My prince trusts you, Sky Blood. But I do not."

"No to the privacy, then?"

Ashi did not smile. The set of clothes was nothing but a pair of faded brown *xadjar* pants, which were billowier than Kale preferred, and a pair of leather sandals.

"You forgot my tunic."

"I did not forget. You are a slave," said Ashi, smiling for the first time. "To the eyes of the palace court, you are an exile from Osha, and one of Salla's personal attendants. So, you will dress the part."

The Exiled Lord rises again, Kale thought darkly. He faced away as he stripped off his Oshan garb. Ashi's stern, unwavering eyes made him feel vulnerable naked. Though, truthfully, she made him feel vulnerable at all times. She was Salla's most trusted and loyal assassin, so far as Kale could sense, and she had made sure he knew it over the past month. He slipped into the *xadjar* pants quickly. When he turned, Ashi picked up a jar and lathered its thick contents in her hands.

"The bodies of palace slaves are oiled. The *soltaynes* wish all their attendants to be strong and as pleasing to the eyes as possible. You are strong, at least. The oil will help deceive their eyes with the rest."

Kale smirked, but did not argue as the Ilya woman oiled his bare upper body. When it was finished, Ashi led him to the central hall of the Den, where a dozen assassins dressed in black waited for them. Ashi handed him a black hood. "Or, if you would prefer the sleeping draught again, I would be happy to oblige."

Kale draped the hood over his head. Ashi took hold of his wrist and led him forward. Somehow, the darkness of the hood managed to increase as they entered the tunnels.

"The Ilya don't believe in torches?" said Kale.

"These tunnels are a part of our very being. We are creatures accustomed to darkness. Ilya do not need light."

And it allows them to easily appear and vanish within the Red City, Kale supposed. *Just a dark cloak in the shadows.*

"You Ilya, in many ways, act like the Watchers of old, you know."

"Do not compare us to your sorcerers! My people value honor, unlike Osha."

"I am not like most Oshans," said Kale.

"And this makes you honorable?" There was a bitter edge to Ashi's voice. "I know what your kind did to the Old World, Sky Blood. Not all have forgotten so readily. The Yan Avii remember why our people roamed the desert for so many years. You caused the War Between the Worlds. Somehow, you endured the war and the chancellor's purgings of old. Are you going to tell me your kind survived all these years because of your honor?"

"No," Kale said. "I am like you, Ashi. Willing to do anything necessary for the one I care for. Nothing more."

Ashi said nothing after this. The Ilya marched on through the winding passageway. It was half an hour before Kale sensed the absence of the other assassins. A rush of light and heat seared through the thick fabric of his hood, and he felt suffocated by the onslaught of Yan Avii minds teeming around him.

The hood came off. He and Ashi stood alone upon a narrow street in the heart of Vlyanii. Beyond, there was the bustle of crowds, chanting as they made their way to the shrines for evening prayer.

Without a word, Ashi removed her dark cloak and tucked it into a nook in the sandstone brickwork. Beneath, she wore a scanty leather *lynti* that left her shoulders and midriff exposed, along with a pair of *xadjar* pants identical to Kale's. Her skin was a deep bronze and smooth with oil. Her beauty surprised him—a proper slave of the Red Palace.

Ashi grabbed hold of his wrist again. "We must be quick."

They entered the Red Palace through a slave's entrance, greeted by the captain of Salla's personal guard, an Ilya named Jerrah. Kale recognized him from the Den. The captain ushered them in, with a smirk at Ashi's attire. "The slave has returned from the underworld," Jerrah said, his eyes hovering unabashedly over her cleavage.

Ashi's mind became unguarded beneath the captain's gaze. Salla had seemingly trained his Ilya to resist the invasion of a Cerebro, for Kale had been able to detect little from the assassins, least of all from Ashi. But now, Kale sensed a deep animosity toward Jerrah that sprang forth unconcealed. "I serve my prince in whatever way suits him," Ashi said.

"Yes, well, hurry along. While you've been playing nursemaid, we men have been setting pieces into place. Our prince is in his chambers and has need of his Sky Blood. And I may have need of my Sweetling before the night is done." At this, Jerrah squeezed Ashi's face between his immense fingers—hard, though she hid the pain well. Kale detected it only in her mind. "I trust you haven't forgotten the way."

Ashi shirked his grasp, but nodded. "I am a servant of the Red Palace, and I am at your command, Captain."

"I am glad to see you have not forgotten your place during your time in the Den. Our prince may be entertaining your little play at assassin for now. But once a slave among the *soltaya*, always a slave. Once a woman, always a woman."

"I have not forgotten what does not lie between my legs, Captain," said Ashi.

"Palaces are the realms of men, Sweetling. Welcome back." Jerrah pinched Ashi's cheek once more, then he left them at the gate.

Without a word, Ashi led Kale down a labyrinth of halls to Salla's chambers. When they came to the door, Kale stopped her.

"You are a slave," he said, the surprise evident in his voice.

"And you must be a *scholai*."

"Surely Salla would not let that brute treat one of his Ilya—"

"Salla does not *know*!" Ashi hissed, shoving Kale up against the sandstone walls. "And he must never know! I am a servant of the Red Palace, Sky Blood. All my life, I have served the *soltaya* as I am required. It was a great honor to be chosen to serve my prince among the Ilya. I will not piss upon that honor by renouncing my other duties. I am still a slave."

"But surely if he—"

Ashi slapped Kale across the face. "Do you Sky Bloods all think your magic gives you some special sway over my people?"

"All?" said Kale. Did Ashi speak of Kirra? Or had Salla encountered other Watchers?

She slapped him again. "We never needed Sky Bloods! Not in the Old World, and not now. When the time is right, I will win my freedom, on my own terms. Do not pretend to care for me now that you know my tragedies. I do not need your help or your pity."

"As you wish."

"You will speak nothing of what you've seen. You will shut your mouth and do as you are bidden, and then you will leave us. Not soon enough, in my opinion."

Kale nodded his assent. The woman had struck him first as a blind follower, but he realized she was calculated and honorable for all her fierceness. A lesser woman—or man, for that matter—would never put her prince's cause above her own suffering.

Ashi knocked, and two Ilya ushered them into Salla's chambers. The place was immaculate. Every sandstone wall was intricately etched with the dune wave patterns of Yan Avii artwork. Elegant tapestries and ornate statues of Great Soltaynes past lined the halls. At the end of the room before the eastern window stood an immense statue of Arayeva in all her glory, a blazing sun held at her waist. Somehow, the stone itself seemed to radiate. At the base of the statue was a small shrine.

"So that even when she is shrouded by clouds, I may say my morning prayers, basking in the light of the Sol," said Salla, emerging from his bedchamber. A young servant boy stood at his side, matching his every stride. "She is beautiful, isn't she?"

Kale nodded. "An elaborate facade for a nonbeliever." He reached out, but Salla's mind was closed to his sense.

Salla grinned, but his voice was stern. "Careful, old friend. There are ears everywhere in the Red Palace."

"Even in the prince's chambers?" Kale asked, scanning the empty hall.

"I am no longer a prince. Only another chieftain vying for the Great Saddle." Salla motioned for Kale and Ashi to follow him into his bedchamber. The guards remained at their post.

The servant boy closed the great doors behind them. Salla pointed to an immense rug at the foot of his bed. The boy strained with all his might to roll it back. Salla smiled approvingly when he finished and clapped him on the shoulder in a fatherly fashion. Beneath the rug was a lone stone without mortar, which Kale and the boy inched out of place, revealing a space just large enough to shimmy through. Salla went first, dropping straight down.

"It is only a six-foot drop," Salla said from within.

Ashi followed, and then Kale dropped into the dark. The servant boy remained above.

"Close it up, Pelah," said Salla. "We will exit another way. If anyone comes, tell them I have gone to the temple to pray."

Pelah shoved the stone back into place. There was a loud unfurling as the rug rolled back over the entrance. Salla lit a candle, revealing a long tunnel that stretched between the levels of the palace.

"I feel safe only in the Den of the Ilya, but these tunnels are as close as I can get. This month-long mourning ritual has been torture, believe me, Sky Blood."

"And yet you seek permanent fixture in this place," said Kale.

Salla smiled in the glow of his candle. "It would seem I am fated to live a double life, wouldn't it?"

"Fated by whom? The Sol?"

"Fated by myself."

"And by Kirra. And me, it would seem."

"Fate is but a game, old friend. Do you know how the Great Soltaynes are chosen?"

"I cannot say I have had the… privilege… of participating in the process before, though I imagine it has as much to do with fate as your double life."

"And that is why I like you, old friend. No *shenzah*. You are right. I have found, behind most things attributed to gods and fate, lies nothing more than ambitious men. And women," Salla added with a glance at Ashi. "Ashi knows better than anyone. We choose our own fate. Even slaves."

"If that is so, then my fate is to see you to the throne, my prince," Ashi said.

A tender touch passed between the two. Salla gripped her fingers briefly, and for the first time that Kale had seen, the Ilya woman smiled with true pleasure. Her loyalty was not fueled by blind faith in her prince, Kale sensed. Nor was it pure honor. It was fueled by love. Whether or not Salla felt the same passion, Kale could not tell, but in Ashi's mind, it was unmistakably clear.

"Yet," said Salla, releasing Ashi's hand, "I wonder how ambitions do happen to cross. What do you think, Sky Blood? Is it blind fortune you and Kirra have come to me?"

"If there is blind fortune, then there is also blind misfortune," said Kale, his thoughts on the innocent Watcher lives lost on the Isle of Jallaa. Was *that* simply misfortune? That the night he and Kirra had finally welcomed their budding love, the Morphs had come like a curse? Slaying their ancient master and all his followers. Leaving only them behind to wade through the guilt. "I do not trust in fortune," Kale finished.

"Then what do you trust in? Ancient gods, like the Watchers of old?"

Kale pushed away thoughts of the Isle of Jallaa. "I do not trust in anyone."

"I pity you, old friend. Life is a sham without ones you can trust. Ashi is my truest servant, and I would trust her with my life. If it was fortune that brought her to me as an attending slave in my youth, then I count myself blessed. And if it was the Sol"—Salla met Ashi's gaze—"then I thank Arayeva immensely that our ambitions have crossed. I trust Ashi treated you as I would have during your stay in my Den, Sky Blood."

As he spoke, Kale thought of his wake-up kick and smiled. If that was from Salla, then Kale was correct in his continued distrust of his *old friend*. "I believe Ashi treated me just as you would, Salla."

"Very good. Now, follow me into the deep, old friend." Salla blew out the candle and led the way down the tunnel in the dark. "It is time you learned how fate works in the Red Palace."

Dark tunnels and narrow staircases ran through the entire Red Palace. The twelve *soltaynes* occupied the three lowest levels of the main palace spire. The remaining two levels, including the great pointed dome, belonged to the Great Soltayne. When time came for the Festival of the Rising Sun, even if the tribes were warring, the *soltaynes* took up residence in the Red Palace. But that did not mean all wrongs were forgotten. More than one *soltayne* had been found mysteriously dead in his bedchambers. But never before had a Great Soltayne suffered such a fate. Salla was the first to commit *that* crime.

"How is it these tunnels have passed unknown all these years?" Kale asked as they descended a spiraling staircase.

"They are not unknown," said Salla. "I told you. There are ears everywhere in the Red Palace. All the *soltaynes* know of these passages, and they keep their own guards posted at the entrances to their own chambers. No chieftain has been murdered by use of these tunnels since the days of our second Great Soltayne. Which is why they are empty now. They have become rather useless."

"Then why are we down here?"

"Because we are not trying to kill anyone. And I have a Cerebro. The other *soltaynes* have not paid me any mind over the past few weeks. I am not a threat, since I am a Burodai, and no successor has ever been chosen by the Sol to succeed his father as Great Soltayne. The eleven are busy bribing priests and temple maidens and plotting assassination attempts against one another. They will not see me as a threat at the Choosing tomorrow. But there is one chieftain I yet fear. An age-long adversary of my family. One I believe may suspect my ambitions, and may try to kill me before I have a chance to manipulate the lots. I need you to get a sense for what scheme Xander Mynah is concocting."

Minds flitted in and out of Kale's senses—quarrels between princes, whispered prayers of dutiful wives, the ecstasy of men and the defeated inner cries of accommodating slave girls as their masters had their way with them.

Kale tensed, reminded that Ashi would be among them come nightfall. Why this bothered him so much, he could not truly say. These slave rites were not so different from those of other nations. Oshans had their nighthouses. The Trium'vel was famous for its pleasure barges. But Jerrah's lustful gaze sprang back to mind, and Kale was glad when they reached their destination, and the minds of the slave girls passed on.

But when Kale's senses filled with two new minds, his anger flared all the more. In the chamber above, he heard Jerrah's cool voice.

The captain of Salla's guard was speaking with the *soltayne* of tribe Mynah. Their voices came through the stone clearer than Kale expected, almost as though they wanted to be heard.

"My chances are good, yes?" said Xander Mynah.

"It has been three generations since our people have sat in the Great Saddle," said Jerrah. "Your chances are good, indeed."

So, Jerrah comes from tribe Mynah, Kale thought with interest.

Each man spoke his words with great care, but Kale soon detected a code beneath them. The words themselves were not altogether clear to him, but Kale could piece together their hidden meaning well enough.

Everything is in order? meant Mynah.

The pieces are set in place, meant Jerrah.

"Three generations!" said Mynah. "Pah! It should have been two!" *Those Burodai bastards stole the throne from us last Choosing.*

"Ah, but if it had been two, my chief, then you would stand no chance at the throne." *Unless you were a Burodai.*

"Yes, of course," said Mynah. *Then, my suspicions about Salla's aims are well founded.*

"No chieftain has been as blessed as you. Your lambs are strong. Your crops are abundant. The Sol shines upon you, my chief." *You will be Chosen.*

"Yes," said Mynah. "Well, let us thank the Sol that this will be the last night we must endure Burodai rule, however the lots fall tomorrow."

"Indeed. Well, I have overstayed my welcome," said Jerrah. "I should make myself seen elsewhere." *Salla trusts me yet.* "Perhaps I *will* go thank the Sol."

Mynah laughed. "You? Utter prayers?"

"Not all prayers are uttered at shrines, my chief. They say it is poor luck to bed a woman the night before the Choosing, but we have no need of luck, do we? Our fate rests… with the Sol."

"And Arayeva shines whether we go to bed or not. Let us pray, indeed!"

The two men roared with laughter as they left Mynah's chambers. Even when their voices had gone, Kale could sense Ashi's tenseness lingered.

"Your captain of the guard…" said Kale carefully.

"Has played his part well," said Salla. "The Ilya are bound by ideas, not tribes. Jerrah has spent months winning the confidence of his chieftain. But even Mynah is not fool enough to trust him with the whole of his plan. Now, what did you sense, old friend?"

Kale chuckled out loud at this. "Do you take me for a fool?"

Salla scowled. "Hardly."

"Then you should know you will not get your information until I have seen that Kirra is safe. I haven't been able to sense her, but I trust she is close. She will be casting your lots tomorrow, will she not?"

Salla was silent for a moment, then he chuckled. "Very well, Sky Blood. As you wish." Salla led them silently back through the tunnels, down below the quarters of the *soltaynes*. They slipped into a vacant hall, inching a stone out from behind a large tapestry. "I will meet you both back in my chambers shortly. With Kirra." Salla disappeared down the hall.

Ashi led Kale up the spiraling central staircase of the Red Palace to Salla's chambers, her teeth still set on edge as she slammed the great doors behind them. The place was empty except for the servant boy, Pelah, who stood dutifully at the door. A table was loaded with bread, wine, and cheese. Kale went to it.

"I would not eat that," said Pelah.

Kale stopped, a slice of cheese between his lips.

"Many *soltaynes* have taken their last breath with cheese still on their tongues."

Kale smiled. "Ah, but Salla is not a threat to the throne, is he, son?" *Do all Salla's servants know their master's ambitions?*

"The boy is right," said Ashi. She remained by the door, anticipating the next person to enter.

"I can assure you," said Kale, "Xander Mynah's plot is more clever than poisoned cheese." Kale replenished himself, with no ill effects. He offered some to Ashi, but she shook her head, without a word, her gaze fixed on the door.

It was several minutes before there was a loud knock, followed by, "Sweetling?"

It was Jerrah. Ashi paused to collect herself. She breathed, and her body relaxed a little. Accepting her fate, she opened the door to him. "I am attending my prince this evening, Captain."

Jerrah chuckled, looking around the room. "It would seem he is away at the moment. Perhaps praying? Why don't we pray, you and I? We won't be gone long, Sweetling. You will have plenty of time to attend our prince tonight. Or would you deny a man of the Red Palace?"

Ashi released a labored breath. "No, Captain, of course not. I will meet you for prayer in a moment." And Jerrah left them.

"Pelah," Ashi said, turning to the servant boy. "I must attend to other… duties. Please do not take your eyes off our new slave."

"I know what he is, *sera*." Pelah addressed Ashi formally, as servant boys addressed free women of the Yan Avii.

"Do not call me *sera*. I am a slave just like you." Though Ashi feigned contempt, Kale could tell she longed for the title to be true.

"We are alike. Both of us will not be slaves for long," said Pelah. "I will look after the Sky Blood until my prince returns, *sera*."

Ashi shook her head, but Kale sensed a fondness for the boy. She clapped him on the shoulder, then turned to Kale.

"Don't worry, I'm not going anywhere without Kirra."

"He's a good man, Sky Blood," said Ashi. "Salla is a man of his word. If you do what he asks, he will do as he's promised. Don't play games with him."

"You speak to *me* of playing games?" Kale said.

Ashi glanced away. "I must go."

He felt a surge of pity for the woman. There was fear buried deep within her spirit, though she strove hard to walk with her head high.

Kale called after her. "I hope for your sake, as well as mine, that you are right about Salla."

"I do not hope, Sky Blood. I trust." And Ashi left for Jerrah's chambers.

"Did Salla promise you freedom too?" Kale asked the servant boy once she'd gone.

"There are many things wrong with the ways of my people," said Pelah. "Much corruption. Salla will make the Yan Avii better than we've ever been. He is a good man. And he will make a fine Great Soltayne."

Kale smiled and nodded. He would not squelch the poor boy's dreams, but truth be told, he was coming to trust Salla less and less by the hour.

The longer he waited, the more anxious he became. How was it that Kirra had remained hidden from his sense all this time, if she was truly nearby? And how had Salla so conveniently learned of the godstones they sought? Had Salla learned to use them? Kale could think of no other explanation for Kirra's absence from his sense. It was said they could be used to travel long distances in moments. And there was much darker lore associated with the legends of the godstones, which Kale dared not let his mind linger upon.

His fears and suspicions were forgotten quickly at the sight of Kirra. A young soldier led her through the great doors. Shackles bound her wrists behind her back, but she looked well enough. Her short black hair fell into narrow, nearly black eyes. Her olive skin was clean and smooth, and Kale wanted to rush to her, to unbind her wrists and clasp her hands in his own. But he resisted, standing still, hands at his sides, showing cool composure.

Salla followed the young soldier and Kirra into the room, accompanied by two Ilya wearing Red Palace ranks. Salla nodded, and Kirra's shackles were removed. She rushed forward and pulled Kale into an embrace.

Kale was startled at first. Kirra was not usually the type for such unabashed affection. A surge of anger rose up in him. What had they done to her? Kale recovered himself quickly, noting Salla's scrutinizing gaze, and wrapped his arms around her. She felt weak, clinging to him for support. It was unnerving to see her this way.

"Are you well?" Kale whispered, stroking the hair out of her eyes.

"Still alive." Kirra's voice was barely a whimper.

He reached out with his sense. There was no hidden meaning behind her words that he could tell. Kirra's mind seemed locked away from him. She had never liked him prodding around. Especially after the Isle of Jallaa. She always resisted when he tried, and he respected her privacy, and so, he rarely tried to break through. But even now? Had she been commanded to hold back her mind? Kirra had never felt so distant in his presence.

But it was a relief to hear her voice, weak as it was. Kirra's frailty broke him. Suddenly, Kale forgot about Salla and the Choosing and his own rage. He did not care. He would do what was expected of him if it meant Kirra would be safe. He let his emotion show, both because Salla wanted to see it and because it was a strain to hold it back. With Kirra in his arms again, relief swept over him—and guilt. "I am so sorry, Kirra. All this is my fault. The Morph attack, and now this. I shouldn't have—"

"There's nothing you could have done." Kirra pulled away from him, slowly, clutching her arms to herself. Her sleeves pulled away from her wrists, revealing fresh, swollen wounds. Kale fought to hide his rage, glancing down at the floor, hoping Salla didn't notice. He would not give that bastard the satisfaction.

"Don't resist him. Don't play games," Kirra said, fear evident in her voice. And then, she whispered, "He knows what we're looking for. He knows of the godstones. If we get him his throne..."

But there was another meaning hidden beneath it, released in a brief flash.

Things are not what they appear, Kale!

Out loud, for Salla to hear, Kirra claimed Salla would keep his end of the bargain, but inwardly...

Kale was ready to fight, ready to take Kirra and flee. Forget the godstones. But something held him back. There was something strange about the whole encounter, and Kale paused, forced himself to seize the glimpse into Kirra's mind. Much as she hated it, he prodded for more.

And it was the momentary flash that broke down the whole facade. Suddenly, Kale realized why Kirra kept her mind walled from him now —why she had remained undetectable from within a half hour's walking distance—why she had rushed to his embrace—why she had flashed the scars.

It was not out of fear. Though that was what Salla must have hoped Kale would come away with. Though the woman before him looked and sounded exactly like the woman Kale loved, his glimpse into her mind had revealed the truth.

This woman was not Kirra.

CHAPTER TWENTY-TWO

Kale tried not to let this revelation show in his eyes. The woman who was not actually Kirra was eyeing him, awaiting a response, and Salla was watching them both.

If this was not Kirra, then who could it be?

There was only one real explanation. The woman was a Watcher, a Metamorphi, feigning Kirra's likeness. Kale and Kirra were not the only Sky Bloods that Salla had enlisted. But if she was working with Salla, why had this Morph woman let Kale into her mind at all? Surely Salla knew a glimpse into her mind would be enough for a Cerebro to realize what was going on.

Say something! It was the Morph again. *Or Salla will suspect something is wrong.*

The Morph was letting him into her mind. Intentionally opening herself to his sense.

You have to keep playing his game, Kale. Now, say something about my wrists. Make it good!

The Morph was still standing with her arms clutched to her chest so Kale could glimpse the fresh wounds Salla wanted him to see. He hadn't acknowledged them.

"Your arms!" Kale managed, his gaze moving to her wrists.

Wounds that were not real on a Kirra who was not real. What was this Morph up to? He sensed fear in her every time she opened her mind to him. Fear she was trying to mask. Fear of whom? Kale had to keep playing along until he could figure out what her motive was. "You're hurt." He whispered it, then let the anger rise up in a flare. "What has that bastard done to you?" His icy gaze met Salla's across the room. The prince's expression was hard, but Kale could sense pleasure at his response.

That's better! Kirra the Morph touched her wrists again, then pulled her sleeves down. "Don't play games, Kale. We have to do what he asks," she said aloud.

"W-we will," said Kale, choking up now. "We'll get out of this. I promise." He stepped forward and pulled the woman who was not Kirra into his arms once more.

"Where is she?" he whispered in her ear. "Where's Kirra?"

I am sorry, Kale. She is gone. She was gone the day you lost her... but you can still do some good yet.

Kale pulled her tight, true tears forming. It couldn't be true. It couldn't be. It couldn't be. He kissed her forehead, and then her ear, imagining it was real. That this truly was Kirra's soft skin at his lips. But no. She was gone. She had always been gone. His grip went tight around the Morph.

You must kill him, Kale. You need to kill Salla. Tonight!

"All right, lovebirds," said Salla, smirking. "That's enough affection for today."

The young soldier came forward with Kirra's shackles. He bound Kirra's wrists roughly and led her away with a shove.

You must kill him! You must!

This was the last thing Kale caught from her mind before the Morph disappeared with a final shove from the soldier.

And he *did* want to kill the prince. Salla had fooled him. He had never had Kirra. Kale eyed the blades of the Ilya in the room. If he was quick, he might be able to do it. But something held him back.

Kale made a show of his response, storming forward without any true intentions. An Ilya moved between them, sword drawn, and Kale stood down. "You bastard, Salla! If your brute touches her again, I'll—"

"You'll do what? Withhold information again, old friend?"

Kale switched from anger to desperate pleading, giving Salla just what he wanted to see. Wringing his hands before him, he said, "Please don't harm her. I'll do what you want."

"I know you will," said Salla. "But before you try to play games again, remember that I hold the stakes in this bet."

Kale nodded. But he knew better. Salla held no stakes in this bet at all. Mynah had been playing Salla for a fool. Kale realized it, then. He had known there was something more to Mynah's plan, but he had thought it would play out during the Choosing ceremony. Now it made more sense.

Kale was the last piece to Mynah's plot. Kirra had been a ploy all along, and he and Salla both had been fooled.

"If you betray me," said Salla, "do not think for a moment that my men will hesitate to kill her... or you."

Kale nodded obediently. But the prince's words held no weight any longer.

Salla came near, his voice softening. "Now, tell me, what is Mynah's plan, old friend?"

———

It was the encounter with Kirra the Morph, and the revelation of Salla's true stakes, that decided Kale's plan.

"You're sure the assassin is *him*?" said Salla softly.

"As you've made clear, you hold the stakes. I have no motivation to lie," said Kale. "Mynah's first assassination attempt will be poorly executed, and it will be unsuccessful by intention. Tell me, do you always eat in your chambers?"

"No *soltayne* dares to eat or drink in public on the eve of the Choosing. All chieftains, including me, will have food sent to them, first tasted by a servant."

"This tasting servant will be the first assassin," said Kale. "He will fall easily into your hands. He will make you feel strong and triumphant. You will think you have thwarted Mynah. And it will be then that the real assassin will enter, the one you have foolishly trusted. He will come to your aid at the commotion. But you must not hesitate when he enters. You must not let a sliver of doubt waver your hand. He does not expect you know his intent, and that is your advantage. But that advantage will not last long."

Salla clapped him on the shoulder. "Very good, old friend. You and Ashi will stand watch in my chambers tonight, until all this is over. Where is she?"

"Ashi was called away for… other duties in the palace," said Pelah.

Salla cursed. "I am her only duty this night! Who called her away?"

Pelah was about to answer when the doors to Salla's bedchambers eased open. "It was the kitchens," said Ashi, slipping in. "They wanted to know your breakfast preference."

Salla breathed a sigh of relief at her return. "Yes, very well then. Send Pelah if they require anything else, will you? I want you here by my side until I am chosen. Now I must rest for as long as I can manage. Surviving the night is only the beginning."

Salla drew the silks around his bed, and soon Kale could hear the rhythm of steady breathing. Even in dreams, Salla's mind was locked away. Kale could know nothing for certain. He could only trust his instincts.

It had seemed a marvelous coincidence that Kirra had been rescued by Salla Burodai. But perhaps it was not. It seemed Salla had fallen right into Mynah's schemes. The Morph wanted Kale to think Kirra was dead, to use his rage to Mynah's advantage.

But there was one problem with that. Kale did not believe she was dead. If Kirra was truly dead, he would feel it to be true. He would sense her absence from his mind. But she lingered still, and he had to believe she was alive.

Kale and Ashi stood watch by the doors as the world went dark. Pelah remained dutifully by Salla's bedside. Kale could sense Ashi's tenseness. It seemed to fill the air in the room like a fog. Her head was held lower than usual, and though she tried to hide them, he noticed the thin dark lines around Ashi's wrists, how often she dabbed her lip with the cloth draped on her arm.

"Ashi…" he said when she raised her gaze from the ground.

Her eyes were cold. "You have nothing to say to me, Sky Blood." Ashi dabbed at her lip again, and the cloth flashed a stain of crimson.

And Kale knew he had chosen the right path.

———

It was an hour before morning prayers—while Arayeva yet turned her gaze from the world and the deeds of men—when there was a soft knock on Salla's door. Kale had told Ashi about the tasting servant, but withheld what would follow. That was when he supposed Mynah wanted him to kill Salla.

The tasting boy entered with a tray of roasted lamb, buttered *ylkii* bread, and a bowl of egg and rice, along with a golden goblet and a decanter of wine. The tray rattled in the boy's trembling hands.

Pelah stirred the prince as the tasting boy approached. Salla rose, spreading the curtains wide, and the tasting boy set the tray on the bedside. One by one, the boy took each item from the tray and took a small bite of it. Lastly, he sipped from the decanter. All proved safe to consume.

"*Terasi*," said Salla, dipping his head.

The boy bowed, still trembling, and began to pour the wine. Salla leaned forward to take a sip from the goblet, and it was then the boy made his move.

But Salla was ready. As the boy lunged with the long cutting knife, Salla pulled out a blade of his own—his Ilya blade, which sprang forth from his sleeve. Salla blocked the boy's stab, sending the knife flying across the room.

The boy cried out in fear, falling to his knees. "*Sorenyi! Sorenyi!*"

"I am sorry you were involved in this dark game," said Salla grimly, and he plunged the Ilya blade into the young boy's chest, pulled it out and jabbed again and again, crying out with each attack. Salla set the boy's body gently on the ground. His expression was hardened, angry, as though he detested what he'd done. He looked up, anticipating what was to come.

Kale and Ashi had not moved from their post at the door. Pelah rushed and knelt beside his prince and the dead tasting boy.

When Jerrah burst into the room, Ashi remained still. It was expected for the captain of Salla's guard to keep watch on the eve of the Choosing. It was expected for him to rush into the room, saber drawn, at the cry of his prince.

Kale, however, sprang into action, attacking the captain from behind as he surveyed the bloody scene. Kale disarmed him with a flourish of the blade Salla had provided him.

"Arayeva!" Jerrah cried. "You filthy Sky Blood!" He lunged at Kale, his Ilya blade shooting out from his sleeve.

Kale dodged the attack, spun round, and slashed out with his saber, shredding the back of the captain's knees. Jerrah roared with pain and collapsed to the floor. Ashi gasped in horror.

"You bastard!" Jerrah cried. Blood streaked the floor as he dragged himself, still, toward Kale. Kale finished his attack with a thrust clean through Jerrah's back.

Ashi rushed forward, kneeling beside the captain as his blood pooled on the floor. "What is the meaning of this?" she wailed at Kale.

"This is our true assassin," said Salla, rising to his feet and crossing the room.

"He was playing a part!" said Ashi. "He is one of us! An Ilya!"

Kale marveled that, even yet, Ashi remained loyal to the men of the Red Palace, Ilya or not. He set down his bloody saber and stood to face Salla.

"No," said Salla. "No, it would seem my captain learned his part a little too well."

Blood gurgled from his mouth as Jerrah tried to speak.

"What was that, you traitorous bastard?" seethed Salla. "Speak! And let me hear your dying words."

Jerrah reached out with a bloody hand, pointing with a long, trembling finger. "Boy!" Jerrah cried. "Boy!"

Salla turned, too late, to see Pelah rushing at him, the tasting boy's knife in hand.

Kale realized with horror that he had been wrong. *He* was not the final piece to Mynah's assassination of Salla.

It was Pelah.

Kale reached for his blade, but he was too late. The boy would run Salla through. But just before Pelah reached him, Ashi let her own blade fly.

It lodged in the boy's neck. Pelah's dagger slashed his prince's robes as he fell.

As Jerrah and Mynah's two assassins bled out in Salla's bedchambers, the room filled with Ilya. And Kale found himself pierced, once more, by an Ilya blade laced with a sleeping draught.

CHAPTER TWENTY-THREE

When Kale woke, he found himself in Salla's chambers, chained to the statue of Arayeva at his eastern window. The sandstone room was radiating with the light of the rising sun. With Ashi at his side, Salla watched as Kale stirred. Salla's eyes lit with rage, and he was upon Kale in an instant. His hand gripped Kale's chin like a blacksmith's clamp and shoved his head back against Arayeva's stone thigh. Pain shot through his skull.

"You are a bastard, Sky Blood!"

Delirious from the fading draught and the jarring impact, Kale's body did not resist but merely tensed, anticipating the next blow. Would this be his end? Bludgeoned to death in the Red Palace?

Ashi must have told him everything. How Kale had fabricated Jerrah's treachery. How he'd not known—or not revealed—the identity of the true assassin, Pelah. Salla would kill him, right here.

The next blow, however, did not come. Salla stepped back, breathing heavily, but his anger seemed to have subsided. "You should have told me there would be a third assassin, old friend. But Ashi assures me it was all part of your plan, so that Pelah would not suspect anything. And since it worked, I suppose I cannot be too angry, can I?"

Behind Salla, where she had remained statue still while Salla assaulted him, Ashi now met Kale's gaze and nodded curtly. *She lied for me?* he thought.

"Pelah was by your side every moment in your chambers," lied Kale. "If I had asked to reveal the third assassin in private, the boy would have suspected, and Mynah would have changed his plans."

Salla knelt before him, his eyes boring into Kale's. Then, he clapped Kale on the shoulder. "You damn well cut it close enough last night, old friend. Look at my robes!" Salla held up his tattered, bloodied robes from when Pelah fell upon him with the knife.

"But you survived the night," said Kale. "That is all that matters."

Salla nodded tersely. "Yes, well, that is one task complete, at least. The Choosing will begin shortly. And I must ready myself. Ashi, cut him loose, and both of you, get cleaned up. The day is far from done."

Salla retired to his bedchambers, accompanied by two Ilya, leaving Kale and Ashi alone. Ashi fiddled with the lock on Kale's shackles, and then she stopped and met his gaze. The slap was sudden and unexpectedly forceful, throwing his head back against Arayeva's thigh once more. His head throbbed.

"Gods!" Kale moaned.

The lock released, and the shackles fell from his wrists. As he stood, Ashi jerked him close. Her breath was hot on his ear, each word like a hissing snake. "Did you know?"

"About Jerrah?"

"Pah!" Ashi glared. "About Pelah!"

"No, Ashi. I did not know he was the third assassin."

Ashi eyed him for a moment, and then her gaze softened. "Third assassin? You are a fool. And even more to take me for one. You knew Jerrah was never working for Mynah."

Kale did not react. His head began to clear, and it was his turn to grab hold of Ashi's wrist. She tried to wrest herself free, but he held tight. "Did *you* know that Kirra was a Morph, Ashi?"

"A… a Morph?" Her voice sounded puzzled, but her eyes betrayed her.

"I thought that Morph was part of Mynah's scheme to turn me into the second assassin. I bear no love for your prince, but it would have done me no good to kill him. So, I let Jerrah take my place as the second assassin in Salla's eyes. I never saw Pelah coming. But if the Morph was not Mynah's, then she was Salla's. Which means you knew Kirra was a Morph all along."

Ashi nodded. "Yes, I knew, and I am sorry."

Kale released her arm and leapt to the edge of the window behind Arayeva's statue. "Well then, there is nothing for me here. You might tell your prince, he should know better than to trust the chancellor's creatures."

Kale looked out at the vast city and readied himself. The draught had mostly faded. He ought to be able to reach the edge of the city at least. It would be enough of a start to evade pursuit. He crouched, ready to fly.

"Wait!" Ashi shouted. She looked up at him, desperate. "Why shouldn't Salla trust the chancellor?"

Kale smirked. "Because Salla's little Morph asked me to kill him last night. I thought it was Mynah's scheme, but if not, then whatever alliance Salla has managed with the chancellor appears to be crumbling."

Ashi's face went ashen. "You cannot leave, Sky Blood."

"Oh, I am leaving. And I will never return to the Red City, I promise you."

"If you leave, then you condemn Kirra to death!"

Kale froze. Even at the thought, Kale's hope surged anew.

"You are right," said Ashi. "The woman Salla brought to you last night was not Kirra. She was one of the chancellor's servants. But that does not mean Salla does not have the real Kirra."

"You expect me to believe that? On good faith?"

"How do you think that Morph matched her likeness so convincingly, if it had never seen her before?"

Kale had not thought of that, but still, he was skeptical.

Ashi approached the window. "There is a way you can know without doubt that I speak the truth."

"You would let me inside your mind?"

"I will hold nothing back, if it means you will stay until Salla is chosen."

Kale dropped from the window's ledge and took hold of her outstretched hands. Ashi's mind swept over him like a rush of wind. Kale saw everything:

He saw a young slave girl, clinging to her mother's apron. Her mother being taken away by men of the soltaya, *and young Ashi whimpering until she returned. He saw Ashi taken away to pleasure highborns for the first time. He saw Salla through her eyes. Her prince was like a ray of light. He kept her close, but did her no harm. Salla protected her. Kale saw the time Ashi saved Salla's life. Saw her help him fake Vashti's death. Saw the day Salla welcomed Ashi to his Ilya.*

And then he saw Jerrah. Felt her hatred, and the deep struggle within her to remain loyal to her prince without defying his vile captain. Kale saw a secret meeting between Salla and the chancellor. And finally, he saw Kirra, the real Kirra, being exchanged with the Morph in a dark passage. Kirra was unconscious, but alive, and being carried away by a strange woman.

Kale released Ashi's hands, and she stumbled back. She was trembling. Her face was hardened. "Salla is, above all things, devoted to his people," Ashi said. "Believe me when I tell you that he made an alliance with the chancellor only to preserve the Yan Avii. If what you say about the Morph is true, then the chancellor has betrayed him, and I fear for my prince's life now more than ever. We need your help, Kale. And if you help us, I promise you, Salla will keep his word."

Kale leaned against the window's ledge for a moment, taking in all that he had seen in her mind. "I believe you," he said, wishing he did not.

"Thank you." Ashi moved away from the window. "Come along then, Sky Blood. We must prepare ourselves for the ceremony. Kirra is yet a part of Salla's plans for the Choosing."

Kale did not argue. He followed the Ilya woman to a small servant's quarters. The room was but a nook filled with a single washbasin beside a pair of stacked bunks.

Ashi handed him a rag. "There are fresh clothes on the bottom bunk. We are slaves, so we are afforded no privacy. But if you will show me the courtesy of turning away while I wash Jerrah's blood off me, I will do the same for you."

Kale nodded. As hardened as the woman was, he had come to respect her.

"You first," said Ashi, turning away.

Kale stripped his bloodied slave's garments. He grimaced as he washed his hair. The back of his head was tender from when Salla and Ashi had hit his head against the statue of Arayeva. "Why did you lie?" He glanced over as he dipped the rag in water. Ashi remained with her back to him, arms crossed.

"I will answer your question once you've answered mine, Sky Blood. Last night, you thought Salla did not have Kirra. You should have fled. Yet you delayed your escape. You knew Jerrah was not a traitor. Which means you stayed to kill him. But why?"

Kale finished scrubbing and donned fresh slave garb. "Your turn," he said.

Ashi turned around. Their eyes met briefly, and she stared at him as though his eyes would let her inside his mind. She motioned for him to turn around. He faced the wall and heard her clothes fall in a heap, followed by the trickle of water from her rag. "Well?" she murmured.

"I have made the mistake of letting one too many bastards live in my life."

"You've got to do better than that," said Ashi. "Jerrah may have deserved it, but you are no hero, Sky Blood. You killed him for you."

"You remind me of her," said Kale, staring off at the sandstone walls. In here, there were no carvings, no designs. Only enough room for two slaves to sleep and wash. Ashi had lived in such conditions all her life. As Kirra had for so many years before he'd met her. "You remind me of Kirra. I killed Jerrah because I wish I could have done the same for her. I did it because she would have wanted me to."

Ashi's hand brushed his bare shoulder. Kale wished it was *her* hand. Kirra's skin was warm, and when he had felt her touch on the Isle of Jallaa, it had felt like the world might one day be made right, that his past might finally be forgotten. Ashi's touch, however, was cold... and wet.

"You can turn around." Ashi was clothed, and holding a jar. She began oiling his upper body for the second time. It stung his shoulder, and he realized that he had been cut by Jerrah's blade. When she finished, Ashi handed the jar to him. "Believe me, Sky Blood, I wish someone else were here to do it."

Kale managed a slight smile. He rubbed the oil in his hands and spread it on her shoulders. "Why did you lie to Salla?"

Ashi did not hesitate. "I lied because if Salla knew you'd wrongly killed Jerrah, he might have killed you on the spot. Which would be unfortunate, since I suspect there is more to Mynah's plan than you have revealed so far."

Kale had to hand it to her. There *was* one final piece that he had withheld. "Since Salla survived the night, Mynah's final plan takes place during the Choosing."

"I couldn't very well let Salla kill you, then, could I? And if the chancellor has broken our alliance, it is even more fortunate I kept you alive."

Kale finished the last of Ashi's oil and set the jar aside. "You'll have to do better than that."

Ashi turned to him, but her face had hardened again. "Jerrah paid me little attention until I was made an Ilya. Then, suddenly, he was relentlessly in need of my… services. For two years, I endured him. I am glad that Jerrah is dead, Sky Blood. But that is not why you are alive. I am not ruled by emotion like you."

The door flew open, and Salla entered the slave's quarters. "You're ready?"

Ashi and Kale nodded.

"Good," said Salla. "The Choosing is about to begin."

Ashi nudged Kale in the side, hard. "Go on, Sky Blood, tell us what Mynah has planned for the Choosing ceremony."

PART NINE
CREATURES OF THE NORTH

Few people believed in gods or monsters in those days. They were lost tales from the Old World, passed down through the generations from ancient superstitions. They were tales told to children. Fables. Ghost stories. Nothing more...

—from *New Histories of the Old World.*

CHAPTER TWENTY-FOUR

While Ren recovered in his chambers after the gallows incident, Tori joined the rest of the Watchers for their regular training exercises. Long forgotten were the whispers of her inadequacies. She continued to struggle with midmorning flight lessons and her afternoon practice with the Conjuri, but after she saved Ren from death, the other Watchers had all developed an evident respect for her, perhaps even more so because she struggled. It made the Gallows Girl seem less like an ideal and more like a fellow young Watcher. At least, that was what Mischa Sufai claimed.

Either way, things began to go more smoothly at the Watchtower for Tori. The other Watchers spoke to her more freely in the dining hall. Vonn Elra—the Conjuri leader, and Sahra's husband from Malai —offered Tori tips from when he had learned to focus his own senses. A few days after the gallows, Tori managed to move a clay jar several inches across a table, to cheers from Vonn and the other Conjuri.

That was also the first day Sahra would allow Ren to have any visitors. Ren's chambers were located at the very rear of the castle. Ren sent for Tori as soon as the Watchers finished their evening sparring session after supper.

He was out of bed when she arrived, kneeling on a woven rug in the cool air of his balcony, which overlooked the courtyard. Wisps of incense smoke swirled from three burners on the ground. *He's praying,* Tori marveled.

Tori stood in the doorway and watched for a moment. She had only known two people who actually prayed to the old gods. Ol' Merri had prayed to them in her closet at Scelero's estate, though she'd burned no incense. Tori's mum had prayed the Old World way, the way Ren was praying now, burning incense and reciting ancient prayers in their tent back on the Steppe. As a child, this had seemed normal, but thinking back, Tori realized how odd it was. Her mum had been Oshan, after all.

Serving the old gods, or any gods, was strictly forbidden in Osha. Many swore by them still, though this seemed to survive out of tradition more than belief. They were spoken of in the same way mothers scared their children with tales of Rulaqs. No living person had seen the great white monsters of the North, as no person had seen gods come down from the heavens to answer prayers. They survived in myth. Yet here was the captain, praying as dutifully as Vashti prayed to Arayeva each morning and evening. It surprised Tori. Ren had never struck her as a particularly religious man.

Without turning, Ren broke the silence. "Are you going to join me, or are you going to spy on me while breathing like a winded horse?"

Tori chuckled and entered the room. She was still worn from sparring. She'd been matched against Dajha, which was exhausting, as he was so swift with his Enduro gifts. "I'm sorry, er, I didn't want to interrupt."

"There's another rug at the foot of the bed. Join me."

Tori found the roll and spread it on the cold stone. The smell of incense reminded her of her mum, a thought that filled her with guilt. For so many years, Tori had despised her, only to discover that Morphs had killed her long ago. Her mum often haunted her dreams. Celene Burodai was always mortally wounded, torn apart by the Morphs. An image that fueled Tori's fears that, somehow, she had gotten her mum killed. She could not remember the details, but she was convinced she had practiced magic that day so long ago. The day her mum sold her into slavery.

Tori knelt on the rug and took in the scent of incense with deliberately slow breaths, and her body began to relax. Ren stared out at the valley, his breaths calm, his back straight. Tori tried to match his form, but she was too distracted. She had been dying to speak to Ren ever since he had come back to life, and now he just wanted to pray?

"I've never done this before," said Tori, shifting awkwardly, a little annoyed. Her knees seemed to be sinking into the stone, sending pangs up her thighs.

"You kneel in humility and pray with sincerity. My mother taught me to always begin with thanks. It reminds us all is not within our control, and it reminds us of times the gods have been good. Since the gallows, I have begun each prayer by thanking the All Mother and the All Father that I am still alive. And I thank them that you are here with us at the Watchtower. So start there. What are you thankful for, Tori?"

Snow-capped peaks towered on all sides of the Watchtower like a crown. The evening skies glowed orange and red, making it look like the Teeth were ablaze. It was beautiful. Tori kept her eyes open and spoke to the open air.

"I am, er, thankful to be alive and free from the chancellor's dungeons. I'm grateful to be here at the Watchtower with other Watchers like me... gods, this sounds stupid."

"My mother also said the gods are not impressed by fancy words. They already know what's inside you. They know what you think before you say it."

"Then why pray?"

"Prayers are more for us than they are for the gods."

"Your mother say that too?"

"That was my own witticism."

Tori smiled. Ren turned to her for the first time since she'd entered. His dark brown eyes were bright amidst the wafting incense smoke. He took her by the hand, and her skin tingled. "Nothing sounds stupid to the gods, Astoria. Now, what do you want to ask them?"

Tori pondered a moment. Of course, she knew what she hoped for. And wasn't that rather like praying? She let go of Ren's hand and looked out at the majestic mountains. *Does Ren really believe the gods made humans, like in Mum's old stories? Shaping them like clay in the hands of children? Why would gods mold the world and then leave it?*

Tori had believed the stories when she was a child. But belief in gods had disappeared with the betrayal of her mother. She had never renounced their existence the way Darien used to, but she had stopped thinking of them. If she needed something, she had trusted herself, and she had trusted Darien.

But Tori supposed it couldn't hurt to try. Her prayer was short and feeble, but it was true, whether anyone out there was listening or not. "I pray that Darien and Merri are alive. That they'll escape the Legions. And that I'll see them again. That I can… rescue them from the chancellor someday." When she finished, she realized Ren was studying her. His eyes locked with hers, and he smiled.

In return, Tori managed only a crease of her lips. Her thoughts lingered upon Darien.

"You loved him, didn't you? The Gallows Boy."

"He was… my friend," Tori said. *My only family. More than family.* Tori recalled their last night together, Darien's lips on her forehead, falling asleep against his shoulder. It felt strange to think on it now—it had been so long ago, another lifetime—especially here at the Watch-tower, with Ren.

So much had changed in the past year, the past few months really. Did Darien still think of her? *No, of course not. He thinks I'm dead.*

Ren's eyebrows rose. "You are very reserved, Astoria."

Her true name still felt strange to her. Her mum was the only person who'd called her Astoria. And yet her old name also felt truer than ever. As though Tori was some forgotten slave girl, and Astoria was the Watcher. She knew that was why she had used her true name before the chancellor, when she had thought she was about to die.

"I cannot force you to share your troubles with me," said Ren. "But you should know, fear is a witch of a mistress. She takes and takes and never gives anything in return. The only way to deal with her is to send her away."

Tori breathed deep, taking in the sharp air, paying attention as the cold filled her. She wanted to be the Watcher that people expected. She wanted to be powerful. To help lead this revolution. To free Darien and countless others from the chancellor's tyranny.

Ren touched her shoulder softly, and Tori turned and met his gaze.

"Darien wasn't just my friend," she finally began. "He was… my whole world back in Osha…"

Tori opened up to Ren in a way she had opened up to no one since she'd been with Darien back in Scelero's household. At first, it felt strange to voice everything that had been knotted up inside her mind, but as it all came unraveling, she began to feel comfortable, and things made more sense.

"When I saw you hanging from that gallows, it brought it all back. I failed Darien. I killed his rebellion. He hated the Legions, and I turned him into a soldier, a killer, just like the ones who killed his family."

Ren thought for a moment. "Do you really think Darien blames you?"

Tori didn't know. Darien was always the softer one, though, so perhaps he would understand. Perhaps he would forgive her.

"You saved his life. And you ignited a spark seen across the New World. Your friend strikes me as someone who longs for peace and justice. And even if he does resent what you did, this is bigger than him. You brought hope to lowborns across the empire. Just this morning, I received word of slave uprisings in Pendra and the Fringes."

"And how many of those slaves died?" Tori asked, the familiar darkness creeping into her thoughts.

"That's not the point, Astoria. Lowborns never fight back. In the history of Osha, there have never been uprisings of this magnitude. Will people die? Of course they will. But change will not happen any other way. You grew up in the midst of Osha's oppression, and I know you long for freedom for other lowborns."

Tori sighed. "I know you're right, but… it's a big burden to bear. To be a symbol for all this. I'm no one. I never asked for this. It just… happened."

Ren clasped her hand, gently. His fingers were warm. "You know, a few years ago, all I wanted was a noble's life in Maro'El. I longed for power, to serve on the High Council. I longed to expand my family's influence, but it wasn't until my house was undone that my priorities changed. Sometimes I feel like the Shadow Watch was thrust upon me. I'm no military man. I don't know how to start a war."

"Then why did you do it? Why did you start the Shadow Watch?"

"My family kept the old ways hidden for hundreds of years. We worshiped the old gods in secret, read ancient scrolls, but for our own preservation, we resisted the temptation to discover the gifts we possessed. We blended in. We vied for power. We were full of ourselves and our ambitions. But I realized that there was more than my own family's preservation at stake. I realized that the corruption in Osha affected all my kind, that we had been murdered for centuries at the whims of rulers who thought we were a threat to their orderly system. And I couldn't let the fear of what might happen hold me back. As a result of my pursuit of magic, I was forced to flee Maro'El, and my entire family was wiped out. It was a terrible tragedy. But it led us all here. It led to the Shadow Watch."

"But how do you live with that?" said Tori. "The dark effects of your magic?"

"Not easily, I promise you," said Ren.

Tori gave him a querulous look. "You make it look easy."

Ren shook his head. "I've learned to guard my mind from those dark thoughts because… they would rule me if I let them. I know it was good to pursue magic, even if my family died as a result. And I know that all good things require sacrifice. You cannot let your regrets about failing to save a few people stop you from saving anyone else."

Ren had not let go of her hand. He squeezed it tight. And Tori knew Ren was right. She did long for justice, and not just for the Watchers. For lowborns in Maro'El, the Fringes, all across the empire. Sorcerers were not the only ones who lived under the oppression of the chancellors. The world needed to change, and if Tori was some sort of catalyst for that change…

Tori smiled, a little sad as Ren let go of her hand. "All right. I'm ready."

"Ready for what?"

"I'm ready to face my fears. I'm ready… to be the Gallows Girl."

Ren's smile stretched wide, and Tori wanted to bask in that blissful gaze. She was filled with warmth and hope for what was to come. She felt like she could do anything—fly, lead a rebellion, whatever.

"I don't want to be a queen, though," she added.

Ren's brow curled with bemusement. "Who said anything about being a queen?"

Tori fought back a blush. "Never mind."

When Tori finally left Ren's chambers, the Sisters had risen high in the night sky. Although Sahra would be furious that he'd left his room, Ren insisted on walking Tori to her room. Before she closed the door, Tori turned back and watched him walk away. Ren's movements were feeble still, but he should have been dead.

She called back to him. "How did I do it, Ren?"

Ren smiled as he turned. "Perhaps you just couldn't bear not to see my face again."

Tori shook her head, but couldn't hold back a slight smile in return.

"It's only a theory," he said, drawing near again. Very near.

"Well, I wouldn't put much stock in it." Tori could feel each of his breaths on her neck. His own neck was still bruised from the noose, a dark line that looked like an incision in his skin. "I'm glad you're alive, Ren Andovier."

"Me too." Ren laughed. His hand found hers again, and his touch sent shivers up her arms.

"When you first pushed me off that cliff, I thought you were insane, you know. When I saw you on that gallows, I *knew* you were insane. But… well, it worked, didn't it?"

"You can call me a mad genius if you like."

Tori shook her head. "Goodnight, Captain." Without thinking, she kissed him on the cheek, then slipped away and quickly shut the bedroom door behind her, her heart thundering in her chest. She leaned back against the door and breathed. *I shouldn't have done that,* she thought. *That was stupid. He's my captain, and you heard him. He's not looking for a queen. And there are far more important things to worry about. Like how we are ever going to launch a rebellion against the chancellor!*

The lamps were out, but Tori could still make out the form of Vashti turning over in her bed to face away. Even so, Tori couldn't help smiling as she slid beneath her sheets.

———

THE NEXT AFTERNOON, REN TOOK TORI ASIDE DURING COMBAT training. "If I spend another day in that bedroom, I'll go mad," Ren said. "I couldn't convince Sahra to let me take you up the mountain for a few more days. So, we will have to try something different."

He led her to a long and narrow hall lit by oil lamps. At either end, there were tables spread with an assortment of throwing knives. He handed her a blade, and she tensed at what she guessed was to come.

"Throw it. Directly at my head."

"Ren, you're still healing. Maybe it'd be best if I—"

"Just throw it."

Tori gripped the handle in her fingers.

"Hold it by the blade, loosely, like this." Ren grabbed his own blade and showed her the technique.

Then he crossed to the end of the hall. He stood still and calm. His broad chest rose and fell in perfect rhythm, his shining eyes met hers, and he nodded.

Tori cocked her hand back and threw the blade with all her strength. It sailed high, a little too high, nearly hitting the ceiling, but just before it brushed the stone blocks, it arced and flew right at Ren. He reached out. Just as it was about to hit his face, it slowed slightly, and he caught it by the handle.

Tori huffed. "Don't make it look so easy!"

"It *is* easy. It's like breathing, Astoria. Vonn told me you were making progress in your Conjuri lessons."

"Vonn was too generous with the word *progress*."

"Or perhaps he believes in the Gallows Girl, just as I do."

Ren pitched the blade she'd thrown on the ground. "My turn."

Ren chose a longer, larger blade. He made a show of stretching out his arms, giving her a moment to calm herself.

Tori concentrated, but she was trembling. Of course, she could always heal, but since the first plunge from Orran's mountain, she had worried that, someday, it might not occur by instinct. She gritted her teeth, determined to show Ren what she was capable of.

"Relax," said Ren. "You are a Conjuri! You manipulate the matter around you. You make it do what *you* bid it to do."

Tori nodded and tried her best to relax. She closed her eyes and breathed deep, in and out, in and out, focusing her mind on her surroundings, letting herself become aware of the intricacies behind the world.

She opened her eyes, and immediately Ren let the blade fly.

He did not even throw it. It flew from his fingers with a flare of Conjuri power, shooting end over end, directly at Tori's face. Her hand shot out in front of her instinctively. *Better to heal a hand than an eye!*

But midair, the blade seemed to slow, and Tori's sense came to her like eyes spreading wide—a new world opening up. She could feel the vibration of each knife rotation on the air. She could sense the minuscule particles that composed the metal of the blade, all of them tumbling right at her face. Over and over they turned. And then, the rotations slowed. The blade met her grasping hand, as though it had been passed across the table. But it was the blade she caught, not the handle.

Pain shot up her arm, and Tori dropped the knife. "*Shenzah!*" The knife had sliced through the length of her palm. Blood spewed out for a moment, painting the stone floor, and then the wound closed over.

Ren came running over, howling with excitement. "Excellent! Excellent! Excellent!"

"I nearly cut off my hand!"

"Nearly! That's the important word. That blade should have sheared your hand clean off. You summoned! You manipulated the world around you. The blade did *your* bidding. Remember that feeling, Astoria. Memorize every success. Play it over and over again in your mind before you fall asleep. Visualize yourself mastering your power. When the doubts and fears creep in, replace them with this memory.

You have opened up the gates. Now, let the flood come pouring in. Vonn was right! You are making progress, indeed!"

Tori filled with pride at his praise, watching with wonder as her skin weaved itself back together. *Now, if I can just focus my sense a little earlier*, she thought, anxious for another chance.

Ren picked up the bloodied blade, wiped it on his trousers, and handed it to her healed hand. "Your turn."

CHAPTER TWENTY-FIVE

Over the next few days, Tori managed to land her first jump from Orran's mountain without breaking any bones. She caught five knives in a row without injury. She managed to hover a foot off the ground during flight lessons, then flew several feet across the courtyard.

Her nightmares continued, but they held less sway over her mind. Tori faced her ghosts, and when they derided her abilities and poked at her fears, she told them to leave her. And the more she faced them, the more her magic swept over her, like a monsoon over the tidal walls of the Trium'vel. Every day Tori felt stronger and more in control of her gifts, and she craved a real opportunity to prove her abilities. She found herself longing for the revolution to begin. A week after flying across the courtyard, she flew the entire distance from her tower window to Ren's balcony.

Ren beamed at her as she landed, and he pulled her close. It took her by surprise at first. She felt stiff in his arms, but she recovered and returned the embrace. His warmth filled her up, and suddenly, she felt short of breath.

The captain had not mentioned anything about her kiss on the cheek the previous week, and since that day, he had seemed more focused on her training than ever. And she had been relieved, in all honesty. Her emotions were a twisted mess, particularly toward Darien.

When she thought of Darien, she felt strange. She loved him, yes. She always would, but he was gone, only the gods knew where. *And did I ever truly want anything to happen between us?*

It had always been something forbidden in Maro'El, and even entertaining the notion felt odd. One day, if he was alive, Tori hoped to free him from the Legions. But first, Ren's revolution would have to overthrow the chancellor.

As her power grew, Tori's contempt toward Cyrus Maro increased. She hated the chancellors and all they had done. They had eradicated her kind, hunted them down, and as if that were not bad enough, Cyrus Maro had harvested their blood.

The Watchers would return to the known world. Tori felt sure of it. And she would help Ren lead them. She and Ren. Somehow, it felt like something beyond her. Something the All Mother and the All Father might have orchestrated all along. How else could she explain the events of the past few months?

Tori had been trying to deny it ever since the night she kissed him. She had thrown herself into her training as hard as she could. It was silly to consider such things now, on the brink of a revolution. But it was becoming increasingly difficult to renounce her attraction to Ren, and her hope that he was attracted to her as well.

Her favorite parts of the day were their morning climbs up Orran's mountain and evening lessons in the courtyard. The past couple months, Tori had grown physically stronger than she ever could have dreamed. She could climb the Staircase to the Clouds three times a day without feeling winded, and then make it back for the second leg of the morning "run." Meanwhile, her Watcher abilities were coming more and more naturally every day. Through Ren's belief in her, she was learning to believe in herself.

Ren did not take any credit for her progress, though without his persistence it would have been impossible. Ren was not making her what she was, he was helping her see the powerful Watcher she already was inside, helping her become more herself than she had ever been. And that was what attracted her most to him.

But the captain was difficult to read. Sometimes, Tori felt as though he might be warming to the connection they shared—times like now, after her successful flight—but other times, he felt like her captain and nothing more. His concern was always with what would make her a better Watcher. Their talk was always focused on her abilities and what was helping or hindering her progress. He did not share about himself. In a moment, he would pull away and become hard to read again.

Still, Tori had never seen Ren as excited as when she landed on his balcony after flying across the grounds of the Watchtower. Tori could feel Ren's breath on her neck, and it sent shivers through her. She pulled away slowly, and his fingers traced the bare skin of her arm.

"We are getting close," he said.

"Close?"

"To the revolution…" The enthusiasm waned from Ren's voice, and the shivers left Tori at once. The embrace was only his excitement, and nothing more. And now, he spoke what should have been exhilarating news with an air of reluctance. "The Watch is growing larger and stronger. You are getting more powerful every day. You will be ready to announce your survival to the New World soon. If only…" Ren leaned out from the balcony and gazed out at the valley. But his gaze was empty, as though seeing the world but not looking at any of it.

Tori touched his shoulder. "What's wrong, Ren?"

Ren did not speak for some time. "I received news… news that the Great Soltayne is dead."

"Vashti's father?" she said with a slight fall in her voice. *Why is he concerned with her father?* Ren nodded wordlessly. "Have you told her?" Tori asked.

Ren looked up, puzzled. "Er, no. Gods, you're right, I should speak with her. I hadn't…"

"So, it's something more than Vashti?"

Ren sighed. "We cannot accomplish this revolution alone. Before he died, the Great Soltayne was raising an army. He was going to ride to war against the chancellor while his Legions were weak from their war against Morgath. It would have been the perfect time to reveal ourselves to the New World. The perfect time to turn the nobles against their chancellor. The High Council of Osha is filled with unrest. The nobles are tired of Cyrus Maro. But with the Soltayne dead, that opportunity is lost."

"Then perhaps now is not the opportunity the gods want you to take," Tori said.

Ren did not seem to be listening. He continued on, consumed by his own thoughts. "I have not heard from Kale in weeks… not since he left for Vlyanii. It's not like him to be gone so long. Something has gone wrong."

"What is he looking for among the Yan Avii?"

"He and his partner, Kirra, have been searching for a very powerful weapon—one that they believe may be the key to our rise—called the godstones."

"Godstones?" Tori had never heard of them.

"A mythical weapon from the Old World. According to lore, there were two sets. One belonging to the All Father, one to the All Mother. It's been said the stones could wipe out entire cities with the right wielder. Legend says they did as much in the War Between the Worlds."

"That's horrible."

"Yes… and there's more I've been pondering since my brother left. When Scelero sent word of his plan to break you out of the citadel, he warned us that the chancellor had accepted the company of a strange sorceress. He said that Cyrus Maro was dabbling in dark Old World magic."

"Have you heard anything more from Scelero?" At the mention of his name, Tori grew worried again for her old master.

Ren looked away. "I'm sorry, Tori, I should have told you earlier, but… I was worried you would feel guilty, and you were just overcoming your fears…"

"Guilty about what?" she demanded. Her stomach sank.

"When I returned from Maro'El a few weeks ago, I told you that I had not heard word from Scelero. But that was not entirely true."

"What do you mean?"

"There were rumors circulating amongst the nobles. It seems, since your escape from the citadel, the commander has not been seen anywhere in Maro'El."

"You mean h-he's… dead?" Tori did feel guilty. Scelero had helped her escape. *This is* my *fault!*

"The chancellor doesn't like to waste," said Ren. "I would wager that Scelero has taken your place in the citadel, another supply of magical blood."

Tori did not know what to say. She was not sure whether she should feel grateful that Scelero had sacrificed himself, or horrified. "He… he was a good master," was all she could think to say.

Ren's face hardened at this, however. "In truth, my relationship with Scelero has always been complicated. After my mother was killed for practicing sorcery, I renounced her. Yes, it ran in the family. But mine was not the only family to have magical prowess in Osha. Many of the chancellors themselves were said to have possessed the seeds of magic in their blood. The sin was not having the ability, but using it… But I rose up amongst the nobles, and eventually discovered that a certain young prince did not approve of my mother's execution. That prince was Cyrus Maro. This was before his own family died, before he was chancellor, but even then, he was ambitious.

"In secret, he was massing followers, followers who wanted to return to the old ways. And Commander Scelero was among those followers. We both served the chancellor as he began experimenting with magic. We had not yet realized the chancellor's dark intentions for it. But we were both powerful and ambitious. Perhaps too ambitious. Everyone was vying for a seat in Cyrus Maro's circles. Many believed that he would be the chancellor to return Osha to its former glory.

"It was a dark game. Nobles turned on one another for a little more power. Scelero betrayed me, convinced the chancellor that I was a traitor, and… I was forced to flee."

Again, Tori did not know what to say. She knew Ren had come from a noble family, but he had helped the chancellor rise to power? He and Scelero both?

"I don't claim to be a saint, Astoria. And truth be told, had Scelero not cast me out, I might not have learned Cyrus Maro's dark intent until it was too late. The Shadow Watch might never have formed. I thank the gods it happened the way it did. But for many years, I hated Commander Scelero more than any other."

This was hard to comprehend. Scelero had been good to Tori. Her last memory of him was the moment in her cell, when he'd come to visit her. He had cared for her, sacrificed himself to free her. A lowly slave girl in his household.

"Scelero was not always a Morph," said Ren. "He betrayed me to gain the chancellor's good graces, to rise up, to become the commander of the Morphs. For years, I thought him one of our greatest enemies, but a few months ago, I received word from one of my spies in Maro'El. Scelero had turned against the chancellor, and he had a plan to break out the Gallows Girl, who was coincidentally not really dead. Scelero turned his cloak because he believed Cyrus Maro's lust for power was growing out of control under the influence of this dark sorceress."

And now Scelero has disappeared because he helped me escape, Tori thought.

"I've been thinking of it often," said Ren. "For Scelero to give up all he'd worked for, it must have been something great he feared."

"You think the chancellor is after these godstones?"

"My mother used to tell us stories of Old World magic. I never believed in the godstones. But if the stones are real, I fear Kale may not be the only one after them. I think Kale has gotten into trouble among your people, Astoria."

"What sort of trouble?"

"My brother is not driven by dreams of power, nor even the restoration of the Watchers. He fights to redeem his past, and that is always a volatile motive. Kale's story is dark and filled with ghosts. And it drives him to make… foolish decisions."

"What happened to him?" Tori asked.

Ren's gaze became distant again. "Our mother's death… ah, but we were boys, and it doesn't do anyone good to dwell on old tragedies. Kale has spent enough time doing that for a lifetime."

Just then, there was a rap on the door. Ren and Tori moved apart as Mischa entered. She saluted the captain before she spoke. "Captain, we are ready to head to Ytala. Is Tori ready?"

"Ah, *shenzah*," said Ren. "I forgot that was tonight."

"Ytala?" said Tori. "What for?"

"The next phase of your Watcher training," said Ren, with a slight chuckle.

Mischa's eyes were sparkling with anticipation. "The taverns! I'm so excited. Come on, Tori. You need to get changed."

Tori was irritated. Ren was just beginning to open up to her, and Tori wanted to stay and hear more about the Watchers, and Ren and Kale's past. She wanted Ren to want her to stay. "Taverns? Can't it wait for another time?" she said.

"No, no, you should go," Ren said, moving farther away from her.

"I want to finish our conversation," Tori insisted.

"We will have plenty of time for tales. Besides, I've got things I need to take care of here."

"It's the next phase of my training, but you're not coming?"

Ren shook his head. "I'm sorry, but as you said, I should speak with Vashti about her father. Vonn will tell me all about it. Enjoy yourself. The Crooked boys are mighty handsome, I hear." And Ren turned and left them.

Crooked boys? Tori thought, fuming. Again, Ren was pulling away. *Or maybe his nearness is only in my head, only some other aspect of being the Gallows Girl.* But Tori knew it was no use defying the captain. Mischa hurried Tori away at a swift pace, leading her to their bedroom.

"You'll want to change into something a bit, er, grungier," said Mischa.

"Why?" said Tori, annoyed.

"Because fights are messy! You'll ruin that nice silk tunic."

"Fights?" said Tori.

Mischa's eyes sparkled with a devious glint. "Crooked fights."

———

THE CROOKED MOUNTAIN FOLK WERE A HARDY AND FIERCE people—anyone who lived in such a harsh land had to be—and the village of Ytala was no exception. One of their favorite pastimes was to get drunk on a fermented potato concoction called *gnasch*, and then they would send two people into a thick iron cage called the Tomb. There, the villagers would watch the pair fight until one surrendered or was rendered unconscious. Usually, Tori soon discovered, it was the latter, for the mountain folk were fiercely conniving and stubbornly proud. Surrender was the greatest shame. So they won at any cost.

According to Dajha, many a Crooked man or woman had been bludgeoned to death because of their unyielding pride. The matches were a test of what a human person could endure, and the Crooked folk placed bets on the victor. Dajha claimed a dark stain on the floor of the Wolf's Fang tavern was from the time a Crooked woman had bet her husband's right arm on a fight and lost. The fights were an all-village madhouse. So, naturally, the Watchers had made it part of their training to journey down to join the festivities. The rules were simple: no magic and no surrender. A test of their mettle, combat training, and physical endurance.

The Tomb was a domed cage set in the village square between two taverns that pit patrons against one another. After several pints of *gnasch*, the fights began.

Tori was the first Watcher sent in after a pair of bloody village fights, the second won by the fiercest woman Tori had ever seen—the man she'd faced was barely recognizable once the villagers peeled him off the ground.

Tori was matched against a giant beast of a man, who fought barechested and barefoot, even in the snow. He entered the cage first and danced around on the balls of his feet, throwing massive punches into the air to loosen up, which aroused raucous cheers from the crowd.

"You got this, Tori!" Mischa shouted over the din, clapping her on the back.

"My bet's on you!" said Zaya.

Dajha guffawed. "On 'er first go? No magic? Not a chance. My bet's on the brute."

"But she can heal," whispered Zaya mischievously. "She can't help that." The Klavash girl glanced at Mischa, but she seemed unamused.

"Don't mean she can't get knocked cold from one o' them clubs," Dajha said, pointing to the size of the brute's fists. "If she wins, I'll take your stable duty *and* your kitchen duty next week."

"You're on!"

Tori tried to steady her breaths as she entered the Tomb. The gate slammed shut behind her. *There is no going back now.*

Though she was irritated that Ren was not there, a host of Watchers had come down from the Watchtower, and Tori was determined to show them what she could do. Vonn caught her eye from the crowd and grinned. Zaya cheered, and Dajha howled about how much he was going to enjoy getting out of his duties. Mischa simply nodded to her.

Tori shifted her focus inward. She did not match her opponent's warm-up antics. Instead, she practiced what Ren called *shevanya*—an old Watcher discipline of self-awareness—focusing hard on her own body, what it felt like, what she knew it could do. It was a gateway to her magic sense, but it was also key to controlling her physical body.

She could use no magic in the fight, but her body had grown strong and quick without it, thanks to Sahra's emphasis on physical ability before magical ability. Tori's speed would be her advantage over this brute. She focused until her world was her opponent and nothing else. Just her body and his.

The beast was pumping his arms. The crowd formed around the Tomb roared and pounded on the iron grates of the cage with violent anticipation. The crowd parted for the clan leader of Ytala, who carried a long musket with a jagged blade fixed to the muzzle. He hefted the musket in the air and fired.

And the fight began.

The Tomb was about twenty feet across and ten feet tall at the peak of the dome. The two combatants faced off from either end, circling around, always facing one another, waiting for the other to make the first move. The beast gestured for her to come to him, but Tori held her ground. He was smiling. He was used to this, and he knew this was her first time. Tori's senses felt like they were on fire, but she tried not to let her fear show.

She narrowed her focus, analyzed the beast's every move—the speed of his steps, the length of his reach—and waited patiently. *Never make the first move.* She'd learned that in the Fringes. The man's cocky grin turned into a fierce grimace. His eyes lit up with rage. Finally, with a vulgar cry, the brute launched forward.

He moved quicker than Tori expected for someone so large, and she barely dodged his first attack in time. His momentum carried him into the side of the Tomb with a crash, while Tori scampered to the other end of the cage to face off with him again. The next time, the beast controlled his strength better. He stopped and swung with immense paws. Tori ducked and cut to his right, but as she moved, the beast's foot swung out from under her and took out her legs.

Move lightly, Sahra had taught her. And Tori was, if anything, light and quick. She landed in a tucked roll, letting the motion absorb her fall, and sprang back to her feet with ease. The beast grunted angrily, then sprinted forward again with another empty result.

After a few attacks, his chest was already beginning to heave. Tori's plan formed in her mind. After a couple minutes, she barely felt a thing. She could dance around this brute for hours. All her training had given her endurance. *I'll wear the beast down, bit by bit, before I—*

As he thundered over for another attack, a hand suddenly grabbed Tori's tunic from behind—

It was one of the villagers. The unexpected grab broke Tori's focus and pinned her back. As she tried to wrench free, the beast's fist met her gut. The air escaped her lungs all at once, as she was launched back into the iron cage. Tori slumped to the ground, only to be lurched back up by a brutal kick to the face. Her jaw rushed with pain.

More hands reached for her from outside the cage. The villagers were shrieking with drunken laughter. Tori twisted away, scrambling on all fours, cursing, blood dripping from her mouth and nose.

The beast was pumping his fists in the air to cacophonous cheers from the Ytalan villagers. Tori looked desperately to the Watchers, but they just shook their heads.

Dajha was laughing. "Anythin' goes in the Tomb, love!"

"Keep away from the edge!" cried Mischa.

With arms reaching into the cage from every side, Tori had even less space to maneuver. Luckily, Zaya was right. Her Regenero abilities kicked in unbidden, and she spat the last of the blood out on the ground. *Anything goes*, she thought, with a smirk directed right at the beast.

He charged. Tori didn't let him get close enough to land a blow. She darted to the side, and he lumbered past. She danced around the cage, dodging his attacks easily, which only made him angrier. His moves grew erratic, his focus moving from the fight to his frustration, and it was then Tori finally changed her tactics.

She let him get close, ducking a massive right hook. As he tried his sweeping foot trick again, she arched back into a kick of her own, landing a solid blow to his nose. He stumbled back. Tori seized the opportunity, landing a punch to his gut and blocking his own jab with her right fist, and then offered another left punch to his face.

The brute staggered away from her and began circling, trying to catch his breath. Blood was pouring from his mouth, but Tori was nowhere near letting up. She charged again, mixing her attack up with a sweeping kick that knocked him off his feet. He didn't land as lightly as Tori.

As he struggled to stand, she was tempted to take the fight to the ground. But now was not the time. If she had learned one thing in her scraps back in the Fringes, it was that her smallness made her quick and agile, but it also made her useless once she was pinned by someone bigger. This beast could wrap her up and use his mass against her. She let him regain his feet, and waited for his next move.

The beast was spitting blood like a well pump. His steps were unsteady, and he was deathly angry. He lurched forward.

Tori forced herself to hold back, letting him use up his energy on empty attacks. She let him get close, enough to keep him coming back for more, to keep him hoping. She threw some weak jabs that did little damage to his immense body. His grin was returning, though his movements had noticeably slowed.

Tori let him land one last good one: a kick to her gut that sent her flying across the cage. She landed hard on her stomach, though not as hard as it appeared.

Tori lay still, letting him feel the foolish assumption of victory.

The beast staggered over, exhausted, ready to finish her off. He wasn't ready when she sprang, lithely, as though she were a child leaping from bed. Tori used the low-hanging dome to her advantage, launching into the air and swinging from the thick iron mesh, letting her momentum carry her boot into the back of the brute's head as he came up with his final empty attack. He collapsed to the ground. And now it was time to join him there.

Tori leapt on top of him, landing blow after blow to his face. Her knuckles were raw and trembling by the time the Crooked man slumped unconscious upon his back.

When it was over, there was a palpable silence.

No one expected me to win, Tori realized. Not the Watchers, and surely none of the Ytalan villagers. *Are they suspicious now? Furious about their lost bets?*

All eyes were on Tori as she staggered to her feet, blood drenching her tunic, her knuckles aching as her body slowly healed itself. Mischa smiled and raised her fist in a sort of salute. Tori raised her fist in return.

And then, the whole village cheered.

Tori had passed the test.

CHAPTER TWENTY-SIX

There were three more fights that night, but none were quite as exciting as Tori's. Only one other Watcher fought—Joran, a Regenero boy. And he was pummeled. It was his turn, according to Dajha.

"We can't be coming down 'ere and pounding 'em to bits every time. After a while, they'd get suspicious. Lucky 'e's a Regenero. Sahra don't heal wounds from such *barbaric altercations*."

Sahra had not joined the group in Ytala that night. Her husband, Vonn, smiled knowingly. "She hates needless violence."

"Ironic, en't it?" said Dajha. "The trainer of a bloody army! Ha!"

When the fights were over, the two Ytalan taverns filled with rowdy villagers, hyped up on adrenaline and *gnasch*, reenacting their favorite moments from the fights. More than a few were attempting to mimic Tori's swing-from-the-cage knockdown, which led to an amusing amount of spilled *gnasch* and two overturned tables.

Tori, Mischa, Vonn, and Dajha gathered around a table in the corner of the Wolf's Fang tavern, laughing and drinking as the villagers got progressively crazier. Despite not wanting to come, Tori enjoyed the frivolity, forgetting for a moment all her training, Kale's and Scelero's disappearances, and especially forgetting about Ren.

Dajha and Mischa made fun of the drunken patrons of the Wolf's Fang, imagining ludicrous conversations the Crooked folk might be having as they howled and cheered and fought and flirted. The Crooked folk spoke an ancient dialect of the Common Tongue, which had become muddled by the amalgamation of cultures that fled to the Teeth and formed the hardy people at the end of the Old World. It made the Crooked folk difficult to understand at times, but Tori enjoyed the differences. Many had, in fact, descended from old tribes of the Yan Avii—as well as from Morgath, Faere, and the Southern Isles. The mountain people formed their own tribe, safe from the influence of the empire.

The Crooked folk reminded Tori, in many ways, of her own people, her childhood upon the Steppe. The Tomb fights were not unlike the wrestling matches and saber duels that often rose up around evening fires in the Yan Avii tent cities. The people of Ytala were close in a way that Oshans were not. Oshan families were an entity unto themselves, consumed with their own familial accomplishments, but here in Ytala, much like the Burodai tribe of her childhood, the people felt like one big family, with all the bickering and hard work and laughter to go along with it.

A broad-chested man approached a girl with straight black hair who was bustling around serving drinks. Dajha's eyes had been following her every time she returned with another *gnasch*, and Dajha eagerly mocked the man as he made his move. "Ar, little love, look a me. Ima big an' strong. I can break this 'ere table with me own head!"

"Well," said Mischa, imitating the girl's husky voice. The serving girl gestured at the wall of mugs and shook her head. "Tell ye what. If ye can break this 'ere log bar-top, I'll leave with ye right now."

Tori chuckled at the enactment.

The broad-chested man followed the serving girl's tattooed hand. And then, he took hold of it and beseeched her. "Ah!" Dajha exclaimed. "On second thought, these logs be a mite thicker than me skull. Reckon I'll need me wits about me to handle a night with ye. Why don't we skip the show, whadda ye say?"

The serving girl wrenched her hand free of the man's grasp, shaking her head and scowling, and Tori and Vonn erupted in laughter.

"Ah, please!" cried Dajha, clutching at his chest. "Me heart tis breaking."

"Ye'll break more than that, if ye don't beat it!" cried Mischa, as the woman gave him a good shove.

The man staggered away, tripping on an outstretched leg in the aisle. The man rolled. A scrawny boy tried to help him, and they both collapsed. The whole room erupted in laughter, including the rejected Crooked man, who rose to his feet and bowed.

"All part o' the show!" cried Dajha. "All part o' the show."

Tori smiled and took another long pull from her mug. She was glad she'd come. She discovered that, though the taste of *gnasch* was rather bitter, it had managed to completely lighten her mood, and helped push away thoughts of her confusing interactions with Ren that night. *It's stupid to think about, anyway. We have a war on our hands.* A war Tori was eager to begin, and which seemed to be placed on hold with the death of Vashti's father.

Vashti... she thought with disgust.

"Think you got an admirer, Tori," Vonn said, pointing to a handsome young village boy across the room. Tori had caught him staring only a few minutes ago. He turned away sheepishly as Vonn called him out.

"The Crooked men love a woman who can kick their ass," said Mischa, patting Tori's shoulder. "Every boy in this room has his eyes on Tori."

"Not like this one," said Vonn. "He's got it bad."

"Ah, please," said Dajha, with a laugh. "We all know Tori's got eyes for only one man."

"And *who* would that be?" said Tori defensively.

"The captain, obviously," said Mischa.

"I don't have eyes for Ren." *And he certainly doesn't have eyes for me.*

"Ah, Ren," Dajha said in a sing-song voice. "Sweet Fly-Me-Up-the-Mountain Ren. Aha! Sure as the gods are dead, yeh know none o' *us* are on first names with the captain. Nothing to do with those late-night lessons, yeh don't suppose?"

Everyone laughed but Tori.

"Come on, Tori," said Mischa, poking her. "You're telling me there was nothing going on when I came to bring you here?"

Tori fought off a blush. It was all *shenzah*. Even if Tori entertained the idea, Ren had no eyes for her. He'd sent her here to this madhouse, where the Crooked boys were *mighty handsome*. What did Mischa care, anyway? She wasn't usually one to pry into Tori's love life. And Tori had given her the same courtesy. She had not inquired about why Zaya Shalvar seemed to frequent their room less often lately. Nor had she pointed out that the girl had not joined them at the taverns after the fights.

"They're just lessons," said Tori irritably.

"Aha! What sort o' lessons, I wonder?"

"Gods, enough!" said Tori. "There's nothing going on between me and the captain! Just leave it alone, will you?"

"*Shenzah!*" Vashti took up a chair at their table, smirking darkly. She hadn't been at the fights. Likely, Ren had just told her about her father, and she had the humor to show for it. "Tell me, Gallows Girl, has Ren flown with you up the mountain? Has he kissed you in the ruins of Orran's temple?"

"No! He hasn't!" Tori flushed with anger. But Vashti had hit her mark.

Vashti smiled spitefully. "You are not the first to be thrown from Orran's mountain, or fly to his balcony."

He trained Vashti the same way? Suddenly, Tori felt even more foolish for entertaining thoughts about the captain. "It doesn't matter how he trained you, because there's nothing going on!"

"Prove it," said Vashti.

Perhaps it was her anger. Perhaps it was because Vashti was speaking directly to Tori's fears about Ren. Or perhaps it was the effects of the *gnasch*. But Tori didn't think about what she did next. The Ytalan boy across the room was staring again, and this time Tori held his gaze and smiled. He grinned back foolishly.

"All right, I will," Tori said.

Tori crossed the room to join the Ytalan boy. A little flirting couldn't do any harm, and the Crooked boy *was* mighty handsome.

The boy's face was coppery and smooth, but when he spoke, his voice was deep. He was a man grown, sixteen or seventeen at least. He spoke the Common Tongue well for a Crooked boy, and with charm and confidence for his youth. "That cage move, that was good," he said.

"Glad you enjoyed it." Tori smiled, letting a hand brush his shoulder.

"I'm Fallon."

"Tori."

"Want another drink?"

Tori shouldn't have done it. She knew she shouldn't have. She should have pecked Fallon quick on the lips, made her point, and headed back to join the others. But she was already feeling light from the *gnasch* and the adrenaline from the fight. She was frustrated with whatever was or was not going on with Ren—whether she wanted him to have eyes for her, whether she was just the next Vashti to him, or worse, less than Vashti. *He's not looking for me to be his queen, and Ren was the one to suggest a Crooked boy in the first place!*

Tori took the seat beside Fallon. She wanted to forget about Ren, about being the Gallows Girl, about everything. Fallon was grinning expectantly, his eyes only on her. And it felt good for someone to have eyes for her, without any wondering. Tori laughed and took hold of Fallon's hand. "I'd love another drink!"

One *gnasch* turned into three, and Tori's walls slipped farther away with each drink. She had never had so much liquor in her life.

"Didn't think monks were supposed to drink so much," Fallon said, handing her a fourth.

Monks? Tori wondered foggily. *Of course, that's what Ren lets the villagers believe we are.* The Watchtower was a monastery in service to the old gods in the eyes of the people of Ytala. It made the superstitious folk revere the Watchers and keep their distance at the same time.

Tori's words were growing more drawn out, but she liked it. Becoming more carefree made her feel good, made her forget about all the things that had been weighing on her mind. Tori thought she would play into the monastic role a bit more. "Well, we're not exactly s'pooosed to come down here, yuh know. But sometiiimes monks have to let looooose."

This got Fallon rocking back with laughter. His arm was draped around her, and they laughed and talked some more about monk life, which he found fascinating, though not nearly as fascinating as the rebel girl who snuck away from the monastery to fight and drink.

Tori basked in the boy's attention. It was nice, for once, to be fawned over for something other than the bloody gallows, even if it was all a fraud. She let herself slip more and more into the rebel monk persona. Let herself move closer to Fallon, her hands wandering from her mug to grasp his hand, which was already on her knee. Then her fingers ventured up his back, lingering at the soft, brown skin of his neck. Fallon was beautiful, there was no denying it. His curly black hair drifted across deep brown eyes. *I bet he's got some Yan Avii blood in him.* Fallon's hands were smooth as they teased her neck and tangled in her hair. He reminded her of Darien in a way—a boy of the mountains.

The rest of the room was loud and raucous around them, but all of it was slipping away in the background. All Tori was aware of in the world was Fallon's warm hands, which somehow managed to induce shivers.

"Where'd you learn to fight like that?" he whispered in her ear. His breath was warm and made her skin tingle. "I thought monks were supposed to be peaceful."

"Maaybee…I haven't aaalways been a monk," she said confidingly. "But yuh know what, Faaallon?" He drew nearer. Tori hiccuped. "I've never beeeen this drunk before. I feel like I'm floooating."

"Well, *gnasch* is very—"

"And yuh know what else, Faaallon?" Tori interrupted.

"What?" His lips brushed her ear as he spoke.

"I'm tiiired of all this taaalking."

Tori moved in so quickly, the boy almost fell over in his chair. His lips were warm and tasted of *gnasch*, but Tori didn't notice the bitterness. She pulled him in, and they kissed in the corner of the Ytalan tavern. His hands pulled her closer. Tori's whole body rushed with warmth, and suddenly, she wanted to sneak away from the tavern and be alone, and forget everything else. They were in another world, warm and light, like a good dream that didn't let any of the cold, bitter real world slip in. Tori wanted to feel warm and light and desired like this forever. She never wanted this to stop.

She didn't know how long they spent kissing in the dream world. But it ended abruptly, with a jarring, intrusive voice.

"Tori!—Gods!—TORI!"

And then the voice became a hand, jerking her back to reality.

It was Mischa.

Tori pulled away from the Ytalan boy, slowly, as though woken from a deep slumber. Her limbs felt detached, floating around the room without control. As she tried to stand, her legs buckled. Fallon caught her, but his mug of *gnasch* spilled in the process, and the two of them fell into foolish hysterics.

"We have to go back to the monastery. Now!" Mischa sounded like she was speaking underwater.

"I don't wanna gooo," Tori protested. She held onto Fallon's arm as Mischa tried to pull her away. Fallon was grinning drunkenly at the whole ordeal.

Tori pulled back so hard she and Mischa both went tumbling to the floor. Tori kept jerking her arm away as Mischa held tight. But then, a sharp pain in her cheek caused her body to slacken. Mischa had slapped her. Several of the villagers *whooped*, thinking a brawl was starting. Mischa slapped her again.

"Quiiit it!"

"Come back home with me now, or I'll slap you all night!" Mischa slapped her again. Tori tried to block it, but her movements were slow and stupid.

"Fine! Fine! Fiiine!" Tori shirked her friend's grip, and Fallon helped her to her feet.

"Will I see you again?" he said, a boyish grin stretching wide.

"I doubt it," said Mischa.

Tori shot her a glare, then gave Fallon a final kiss on the cheek, before Mischa yanked her away. Mischa's breaths were heaving as she dragged Tori along after her, out of the tavern and into the cold night. Tori quit fighting and followed obediently. The sharp bite of the wind awakened her some. Her legs began to regain their sense, and her face stung in the cold. At the edge of the village, they passed a trough.

"Should I throw you in, or are you ready to act your age?" said Mischa.

"I'm here, aren't I?"

"Gods, I can't believe you, Tori!"

"What? Am I the only one who can't have fun? Dajha ran off with that serving girl, and I didn't see you dragging him away."

"You made a fool of yourself, Tori. You're the Gallows Girl."

"So, the Gallows Girl *is* the only one who can't have fun."

"Let's just get you home, all right?"

Tori didn't answer, but she followed Mischa out of Ytala. They were well up the pass before Tori realized they were alone and not riding back in the sleigh. She was more out of sorts than she'd thought. "Where's everyone else?"

"They left, Tori. Everyone else has already gone back."

"Why didn't you?"

Mischa turned to her, fire teasing from her fingertips like angry butterflies. "I stayed because I wasn't ready to face Zaya! All right?"

"What?"

"I... I ended things with her," said Mischa, the fire dissipated, her lip trembling. "You'd know that if you hadn't run off. I wanted to get drunk with my friends and forget it all. But you left, and then Dajha. And Vonn went home to Sahra. And Vashti was acting strange as ever, and..."

"I'm sorry," said Tori. "I didn't know." *I didn't ask. I should have asked.*

Mischa stopped in her tracks. "That wasn't you in there, Tori."

"I wanted to forget too," Tori said. "I know it went too far, but I... I wanted to make my point to Vashti."

"Well, you damn well made it, didn't you? Gods, what are you going to tell Ren?"

"There's nothing to tell, because there's nothing going on. So, I'm not going to tell Ren anything."

There was a soft thud behind them, and both girls spun around with a start.

"What aren't you going to tell me?" It was Ren.

"Don't sneak up like that!" said Mischa, clutching at her chest. She'd released more flames, and the cuffs of her cloak were singed.

"Sorry, I came looking when the sleigh returned with three missing. Vashti said she lost you in the taverns. Where's Dajha?"

"He found a… distraction for the evening."

Ren didn't notice when Tori shot Mischa a look, implying her double standard.

"Well, then, I've found who I'm looking for," said Ren, leading the way down the path. "So, what weren't you going to tell me, Tori?"

"About how she… can't hold her *gnasch*," said Mischa, returning Tori's glare. "I found her spewing in the troughs. That's why we missed the sleigh."

Ren laughed and took Tori's arm. "Well, if the Crooked folk know one thing, it's how to brew a bloody drink. Believe me, you're not the first to make that mistake. Come on, let's get you home."

Tori didn't protest and was ready to return to the Watchtower, when a cry echoed up the canyon. All three of them spun. There was no one in sight.

"Must be Dajha," said Mischa. "Hey, Daj! Up here!"

There was another cry. Though unintelligible, it was most certainly human.

"We're up here!"

"Hey-ooo!" The voice was youthful and deep, and distinctly not Dajha's. A young man stumbled into view, trudging through the snow, nearly falling as he approached. "Toooriiii!"

It's Fallon, Tori realized with horror.

"Oh gods!" said Mischa.

"Who's that?" said Ren, a dark tone rising in his voice.

"I'll explain later," said Tori. "I'll handle him." She ran back down the canyon, nearly stumbling herself. The speed made her head feel light. *I am never drinking gnasch again!*

"Toooriii!"

"Fallon, what are you doing?"

"I came back for you."

"Go back to Ytala," Tori said firmly.

"Only if you come with me." He grabbed her hand. "Just for tonight. We had so much fun. Just a bit more fun."

"I can't go back with you. Look back there! That's my cap—er, that's the High Priest of the monastery. Now, go! Do you want a curse placed on you?"

Fallon looked taken aback. "A curse?"

"The High Priest is very angry with me. You don't want him mad at you too." Fallon looked a little hurt as he let go of her hand. "I'm sorry, Fallon. I shouldn't have—"

The still night was pierced by an ear-splitting shriek. The sound was unlike anything Tori had ever heard in her life, echoing off the mountains, seeming to come from all around. Her first thought was a kendrak bear. But she had never heard a bear sound like that. It came again. Closer. High-pitched and thunderous and filling every void of silence, it reminded Tori of the time a man had been burned alive in the Fringe pyres. He had been deathly sick, but not quite deathly enough, and his dying shrieks had filled her with the same sickening dread that came upon her now.

The trees around them shook violently, some of them toppling over like saplings in a summer storm. The creature emerged from the woods, a hundred-foot snowpine crashing down in its path. It was larger and more terrifying than any of the tales could capture. But at the sight of the massive white monster, there was no doubt in Tori's mind what it could be.

Its shriek pierced her ears, reverberating from two sets of jaws large enough to snap her in half. Tori's vision filled with the flash of fangs at the end of two furry, serpentine necks.

It's a Rulaq!

PART TEN
THE CASTING OF
THE LOTS

The ritual by which the Great Soltayne was chosen was performed by the priests of Arayeva. Through a series of divinations, the twelve tribal chieftains were narrowed to one. This way, the Yan Avii priests could ensure that the leader of the tribesmen was the one chosen by the will of the sun goddess.

Of course, this was all a facade. The way the lots fell was, in truth, the result of bribes, trickery, and murder. It was a game. The winner was always the most ruthless and conniving player.

—from Dawn of the Third World

CHAPTER TWENTY-SEVEN

The Choosing was held in the temple of the Red Palace. Located at the pinnacle of the dome above the Great Soltayne's halls, it was only used by the Great Soltayne except on the day of Choosing. The golden dome was set on pillars, leaving the horizon exposed in all directions so that the Sol might radiate upon every inch of the temple. At the eastern and western ends stood statues of Arayeva, identical to the graven image in Salla's chambers but more than twice the size. At the center of the dome was a flaming golden Sol intricately etched into the floor.

As they entered, Salla removed his fine robes, handing them to Ashi, and joined the other tribal chieftains, who wore simple white tunics and knelt in reverence around the golden Sol.

Ashi and Kale joined the several hundred attending servants, families, and tribal council members crowded around the *soltaynes*. The rest of the Yan Avii people crowded in the streets of Vlyanii—one great teeming mass radiating from Arayeva's temple like rays of light.

A tense anticipation hung over the entire city. Kale felt as though he could sense it on his skin, breathe it in the air. The temple was a flurry of murmurs as the Yan Avii waited for the High Priest to commence the Choosing.

"According to lore," said Ashi, "the three sets of Choosing stones were etched by the First Soltayne himself, when he was chosen to lead my people from their plight in the Wandering Dunes. The stones are kept in a sacred chest opened only by the High Priest the morning of the Choosing."

"I wonder how high the price was for the sets of stones that came out of the chest this morning," whispered Kale.

"I suspect you could ask Xander Mynah. Now do you sense her, Sky Blood?"

Kale reached out with his sense. Kirra was a Lumeni. She had discovered her ability to manipulate light during her years of slavery in Jurka. In a desperate attempt to hide from her abusive master, she had discovered how to bend light around herself, in order to walk the earth unseen.

It was important that Mynah believe his plan was working until the very end. So, according to Salla's plan, Kirra would switch the stones, invisibly, only before Salla's lots were cast. She must have been somewhere in the temple, but he could not sense her. The cloud of minds around him made it difficult to fixate on anyone in particular. "If all this is a farce—"

Ashi grabbed hold of his wrist. "Kirra is here, Sky Blood. Now you must be silent."

Light poured into the dome, and the room grew quiet as death. At the apex of the dome hung a fixture of mirrors, which captured the midday light of the Sol and beamed it to larger mirrors set between the pillars supporting the dome, making the entire temple glow. Flashing light shone upon all their faces, and Kale had to close his eyes it grew so intense. When he opened them, the light had passed. It was midday, and time for the Choosing to begin.

The High Priest strode to the center of the golden Sol. Three temple maidens followed, dressed in flowing golden silks with a pair of golden Sol medallions covering their otherwise bare chests. Each maiden carried a black satchel containing one set of Choosing stones. The High Priest took each satchel, and the maidens moved to the edge of the circle.

The priest held the stones above his head and looked to the sky.

Everyone in the room, wordlessly, dropped to their knees and gazed up. Priests standing at the edge of the dome lifted their hands, signaling below for the entire city to kneel in prayer. The Red City was still, as though the entire world had drawn its breath.

"Our beloved, Arayeva!" The High Priest's wispy voice filled the room and carried out to the city beyond. "Light of lights, who came to us at the edge of the world, who led us up out of the Wandering Dunes. May your light shine upon your Chosen this day, and may he lead us into many more years of prosperity."

A great moaning sound rose up from the streets and filled the room: "*Arayeva, elenyal Soltayne! Arayeva, elenyal Soltayne! Arayeva, elenyal Soltayne!*"

The entire city recited the prayer as one, asking that Arayeva select her Chosen. The Priest dropped his gaze to the chieftains kneeling at the edge of the golden Sol. "Let the Choosing begin."

Silence abandoned the temple in a great rush, replaced with loud speculation as the *soltaynes* were paired up for the first round of divinations. There were only ten surviving *soltaynes*—one having died in the night, the other deathly sick (which was viewed as the curse of the Sol). This meant that the Mynah and Rajii chieftains won their respective rounds by default. Salla Burodai was first paired against Dol Yarah. Salla's stones fell with three *sols* and two *luuns*, and Yarah with only one *sol*. Salla won, and Yarah cursed angrily as he left the circle.

"The former Great Soltayne's successor usually goes out in the first round, unless paired with especially unblessed chieftains," said Ashi, smiling as her triumphant prince returned to his spot at the edge of the circle. "Yarah will be seen as a disgrace among his tribesmen. I told you Kirra was here, Sky Blood. She is doing her job well."

Kale nodded curtly, but he was frustrated. He could not sense her. However, while a Morph might be able to mimic a Lumeni outwardly, one could not take on her Lumeni ability. The stones had fallen in Salla's favor. And Kirra was the only Lumeni he knew who could have switched the stones in the middle of the entire temple.

"You must believe me and focus on what is most important," said Ashi. "Do you sense the chancellor's Morph in the temple?"

"No," said Kale, again frustrated. He had always thought his gift inadequate. It was so dependent on the openness of the mind he was trying to infiltrate. "She is well trained. And she could be anyone here. Do you really think the chancellor would attempt an assassination so publicly?"

"This is his greatest opportunity. If Salla should die, it would be seen as a curse from Arayeva for seeking to succeed his father. All the chancellor must do is make it look like a curse."

After the first round was complete, the losers competed for the remaining two slots in the second round, a chance to correct any human error in the divinations. When the final eight had been chosen, the lots were cast for the second round pairings. Two of the three sets were identical—five stones, each containing a *sol* and *luun* rune on either side. The third set contained only two stones, each with eight runes.

"This is as important as the castings," said Ashi. "The pairings can determine everything. This is when the *soltaynes* begin to see whose bribes were the greatest, and whose spells came out strongest."

"Spells?" said Kale.

"How else did you think the stones could be made to fall at command?"

"Something with their weight, I suppose."

Ashi chuckled. "You Sky Bloods are so full of yourselves. Your magic is not the only kind in the world. Ours is simply more subtle."

Other kinds of magic? Yes, Kale knew this to be true. His mother had told him so. His search for the godstones was rooted in this belief. But he had never known the Yan Avii wielded a magic all their own. For centuries, the chancellors' Morphs had hunted down Watchers around the world, and yet magic had persisted in other forms. It seemed spells were beyond the scope of Metamorphi senses.

Salla was paired with Yuli Bartol, the only tribe that had never borne a Great Soltayne. Salla shrugged as heads began to turn his way. "The Sol must be playing games," he joked, inspiring several chuckles from the other chieftains. Salla had clearly been better liked among the *soltaya* than his father.

Salla cast his stones, and won again, arousing laughter from the whole room at Yuli Bartol's expense.

It was in the middle of the laughter that Kale noticed the pair of servants standing behind Xander Mynah's attendants. The two stood with marginal distance between them, whispering. They bore the Mynah insignia tattooed on their left shoulders, as all Mynah servants did, but Kale sensed something awry. The boy's skin was brown and blended in, but the girl was pale, her hair nearly silver it was so fair. A Southern Islander. It was not unthinkable that a fair-skinned slave would wind up in the Red Palace. Kale himself was posing as one, and yet…

"You ever see those servants in the Red Palace before?" he said, gesturing across the room.

Ashi shook her head.

"I think I found our Morph."

Kale threaded his way along the edge of the crowd, near the pillars of the temple. Xander Mynah won his round against Ferdan Zora, and the Mynah tribal representatives cheered. The two servants followed suit. In the midst of the cheer, Kale felt a mind open up to him.

You didn't kill him, Kale.

The Southern Islander stared forward as she cheered, eyes watching intently as the High Priest began casting the pairings for the third round. The field of *soltaynes* was now down to four. When Kale turned back, the boy she'd stood with remained, but the girl had vanished. He retreated to the outer edges of the crowd. There she was, the Southern Islander, standing beside a great pillar.

Keep your eyes on the lots. It was Kirra the Morph, only in a new form. She sidled up near him, close enough to speak, and they watched from the back of the crowd.

You didn't kill Salla.

"You lied," Kale murmured. "Kirra's not dead."

Well, I needed you to feel desperate. But it doesn't matter now.

"True, because there's no way you're getting anywhere near Salla now."

"No, Kale," the Morph hissed out loud. He wondered if she had intentionally used a voice so like Kirra's. "It doesn't matter now, because you had to be the one to do it." *Now the lots are in motion, and*

I cannot give away my identity. But you can still do something. Just let Mynah win.

"And why would I do that?"

Because an alliance between the chancellor and the Yan Avii might be the end of the world.

"Why would a Morph want anything less?"

The traitorous Morph did not answer the question. She kept her head low and faced away from the Mynah servants.

I must return to my post. And then, she was gone.

Kale weaved back to Ashi's side and silently considered the Morph's intentions. This time, he had been ready when she opened her mind to him. He could tell that she believed what she said. The Morph was not doing the chancellor's bidding. She was attempting to undermine him. Kale noted the caution with which she regarded the Mynah boy as she returned to his side. Kale sensed that he, too, was a Morph.

Kale was so tired of all the games. The Watchers would deal in due time with the chancellor. But they could not do it without Kirra and the godstones.

"You spoke with her?" said Ashi.

"I was mistaken. The chancellor has not betrayed Salla."

Ashi moved forward. "That's it, I'm telling Salla what's going on."

Kale took hold of her wrist. "Do you trust the Sol?"

Ashi glared at him. "You know I am a believer, Sky Blood."

"And you believe she has chosen your prince?"

"You know I do."

"Salla has two more lots, and then he will face the ultimate test. The last piece of Mynah's plot. His mortality is already plaguing his mind."

"How do you know?" said Ashi.

"Because the wall around Salla's mind is not as strong as it once was. He is strained, and his acting must be at its very best. We cannot place another burden on him. The Morphs will not harm him, I promise you."

Kale hoped he was right. Still, he could not determine the Morph's full intentions. Why couldn't she kill Salla herself? Who was she working for, if not the chancellor? Was this all some ploy of Xander Mynah? Or someone else?

The stones were cast, and the crowd cheered. Xander Mynah would advance to the final round.

Ashi hissed. "If this turns out wrong—"

"It won't," said Kale, clasping her hand. "You told me to trust, not hope. Now it is your turn. Trust the Sol. And trust me."

"Trust you? Pah!" Ashi shirked his grasp with a jerk of her arm, but she remained where she stood.

Kale stole a glance at the Morph. She was speaking with her comrade in adamant hushed tones. He could sense vaguely that he was upset with her for disappearing. And he sensed she regretted upsetting him. "I win only if Salla wins," Kale said. "That is the only way I get Kirra."

Ashi muttered to herself in her native tongue. The stones were cast, and the crowd cheered, laughed, murmured. Salla Burodai would advance to the final round. The temple maidens collected the stones and returned them to their satchels.

Salla raised his hands, chuckling, and approached the High Priest, who surveyed him with a raised brow and ever-stoic eyes. "Good Priest. You have served my family faithfully these many years. You taught me to pray. Taught me the truths of Arayeva from my boyhood." Kale could detect a hidden meaning: Salla despised this priest, and not just because he had his hand in Mynah's purse.

"That is the man who condemned Vashti to death for practicing sorcery," whispered Ashi.

"And so," said Salla, "I ask that you allow me to withdraw from the final lot. The stones have fallen strangely in my favor. But I do not wish to appear zealous for the throne that could never rightfully be mine. Tradition is tradition. No successor has ever been Chosen."

Salla acted the scene brilliantly, and even Kale was half-convinced of its verity for a moment.

The High Priest smiled with thin lips. "The lots fall exactly the way Arayeva wills them to fall. Our Sol has chosen her final chieftains. Let the final lots be cast."

"Very well," said Salla, with a bow.

Mynah smiled. Everything had gone exactly as planned. Mynah had hoped for this outcome all along. But only Kale, Ashi, and Salla knew that things were about to change course.

Salla and Mynah knelt at the center of the flaming golden Sol. The High Priest handed one satchel of stones to each of them. Mynah's eyes sparkled. His lips moved inaudibly to all but Salla, but Kale could sense the unmasked meaning: *A rousing speech, Burodai. But you know Arayeva curses liars.*

Salla simply smiled innocently. The world had gone still with anticipation. Every eye was on the two men in white robes at the center of the temple. Below, the streets might have belonged to a ghost city they were so silent. Over a month of prayer and supplication for the right outcome ended now. In unison, the *soltaynes* cast their stones upon the floor.

For Salla Burodai, three *sols* and two *luuns*.

For Xander Mynah, five *sols*.

While the temple cheered, Mynah's deep bronze face turned pale. All observing must have thought it surprise, or even joy, at his victory. But Kale knew Mynah had not intended to win this round.

The High Priest's face was similarly ashen. Salla's was fixed in a modest smile of relief. The High Priest recovered and addressed the people. "Arayeva has chosen Xander Mynah, chief of the tribe of his name, to be our next Great Soltayne!"

The priests at the edge of the dome relayed the message to the city below, and the entire city chanted a prayer of gratitude to the heavens. Smiling, Salla stood and raised Mynah's hand high in the air. "Your Great Shepherd!"

A cry rose up in the temple and the city below. But as the people cried out, the temple maidens came to the center of the golden Sol, each carrying a golden goblet.

The final divination, Kale thought.

The High Priest shook his head at Mynah, but there was no going back now. The High Priest addressed the temple, masking as best he could the quaver in his voice. "To ensure there has been... er... no human interference in the casting of the lots, the Chosen must pray and select the goblet blessed by our Sol. Two of the goblets of wine are poisoned, and will bring an… agonizing death to any who approach the Great Saddle against Arayeva's will."

Mynah lifted his hands in prayer and lifted his gaze toward the heavens. The prayer was not long, for it was futile. Xander Mynah had made sure of that. It was the last piece to his plan. Only Mynah had not intended to be the one to win and drink from the three equally poisoned goblets of wine. He had meant to let Salla win—and then die—to shame the Burodais once and for all, the curse of Arayeva fixed upon his rival tribe without doubt.

But Kirra had switched the final stones in Mynah's favor.

Mynah chose the goblet from the maiden at the center, raised it high, and drank deeply. The effects were immediate. Mynah lowered the goblet, and the poison began to take hold. His hands trembled. The goblet clattered to the floor, spilling wine upon the golden Sol. And then Mynah, his mouth frothing, lurched forward, upon the High Priest, grasping desperately at the belt of the holy man's robes. The priest shoved him away, but Mynah stumbled back holding the priest's sacrificial knife.

If Mynah could not have the throne, then he would be sure not to let a Burodai have it either. Kale and Ashi each sprang into action, but they were attendants and were far from the center of the temple. Kale shoved his way through the swarm of panicking tribesmen.

Mynah leapt at Salla, who, like all the *soltaynes*, was unarmed and kneeling in his white tunic. He tried to scramble to his feet, but he stumbled, and Mynah was upon him. There was nothing anyone could do, it all happened so fast.

But then, the Morph boy—the one who had stood at the Southern Islander's side—appeared as from nowhere. He moved so fast, so unexpectedly, Kale did not even realize who it was until it was over.

The Morph boy, wearing Mynah's insignia—the one tribe who stood still as their chief tried to murder Salla Burodai—drew a guard's blade and leapt into the center of the temple. In one swift movement, he deflected Mynah's sacrificial dagger, sending it flying across the temple. And then he ran the *soltayne* through the chest.

Xander Mynah bled out on the golden Sol, his mouth bubbling

with poison and blood. With his last breath, he muttered, "Burodai bastard."

The Mynah servant boy helped Salla to his feet. The High Priest was shaken for a moment, but he managed to recover quickly. He strode over Mynah's body to Salla. He raised the prince's hand in the air.

"There can be no denying what the will of the Sol must be. I present to you the Chosen of Arayeva, your Great Soltayne, Salla Burodai."

CHAPTER TWENTY-EIGHT

What followed was largely a blur for Kale. Guards rushed into the temple. Ilya, masked as members of the City Watch, swarmed around the newly crowned Great Soltayne. Salla instructed his followers to bring the Mynah servant boy and his female companion with them.

Kale found himself being ferried along with the Ilya leading Salla Burodai from the Red Temple. Great doors opened to a long hall—the throne room of the Red Palace. The Ilya formed ranks at the door, leaving Kale and Ashi, the Mynah servant boy, the Southern Islander, the High Priest, and Salla alone in the royal hall.

Salla grinned, gazing up at the Golden Saddle, the throne of the Great Soltayne. He turned upon the High Priest, his hand flying to the holy man's throat.

The priest spluttered a plea, and Salla released him with a shove. "Surprised, are you, Jondif?" said Salla.

"My chief, I implore you—"

"Spare me your groveling. We both know you had your hands in Mynah's pockets long before the Choosing. You've been stabbing my family in the back for a decade. But I wanted you to see how I managed to thwart your schemes. Boy, step forward."

Salla addressed the Mynah servant boy who had saved his life. The boy bowed his head respectfully.

"Not even my Cerebro foresaw that sacrificial blade, my friend. The Sol has blessed me with your skill."

"Thank you, milord," said the boy.

Salla turned to the priest. "Meet Darien," said Salla. "The one who thwarted Mynah's attempt at my life."

"I swear to you, my chief," the priest pleaded. "I tried to wrest the blade from Mynah. I would never defy Arayeva's Choosing. The boy was right to kill him!"

Salla smiled, regarding the priest coolly. He turned to Kale. "You will remember him as the guard who brought Kirra to you last night."

Kale had paid the boy little attention then, but now he realized he should have recognized the inconsistency. The boy was not Yan Avii. He had brown skin and brown eyes, but his dark hair was too straight for a boy of the Steppe. This boy came from the mountain tribes of Klavash. But even more disturbing was the sense of familiarity that came over Kale as Salla took the boy's hand. He had seen this Morph in Tori's dreams in the Haunted Forest of Ghen. He was the Gallows Boy.

Salla turned to the Southern Islander. "Meet Valeria," Salla said to Jondif. "The boy's comrade, and the woman you saw as Kirra yesterday," he said, turning to Kale.

The High Priest regarded the Morphs, not with shock, but with anger and disgust. His eyes fell upon Kale like a pair of searing suns.

"Meet Kale," Salla said. "My Cerebro, who detected Mynah's full scheme and concocted the idea of letting your precious chieftain drink his own poison. Your service will be repaid as promised, I assure you, old friend."

"You are a disgrace, Salla," said the High Priest, finally. "How dare you defile these halls with Sky Blood filth?"

Salla's loftiness fell away briefly, revealing a vicious hatred toward the priest. Then he smiled. The hate, which lingered in Kale's senses, seemed to drip from Salla's words. "Oh, I am not done defiling!" Salla took hold of the holy man's shoulder, roughly, and turned him toward the empty Golden Saddle. "Now, Jondif, let me introduce you to the final piece of your undoing. The one who switched your stones for the final lot. The one who made all of this possible." He gestured toward the Golden Saddle.

Kale's heart raced, his eyes following Salla's gaze up the high steps to the throne. Kirra was here in the palace. Right here.

"What exactly should I be seeing?" said Jondif, his timidity apparently having left him with the revelation of the Morphs.

Salla chuckled. "Reveal yourself, old friend."

The invisible person upon the Golden Saddle unmasked and descended the steps from the throne.

It was not Kirra.

It was a man with pale skin and glacier-blue eyes, clothed in fine Oshan robes, who walked with the most assured and commanding stride Kale had ever seen. His lips spread in a wide smile.

"Meet Cyrus Maro, the sixteenth Chancellor of Osha, and my closest ally." Salla and the chancellor clasped shoulders in a warm greeting.

The High Priest lit with rage. "You traitorous bastard, Buro—"

Jondif's protests were stopped short by Kale's fist. The priest collapsed in a heap, unconscious, blood trickling between his teeth.

"Enough!" said Kale. He strode straight at Salla, who backed away timidly, with a glance at the chancellor. But the chancellor stood back, an amused expression teasing his lips. Before the Ilya could descend upon him, Kale had a blade at Salla's throat.

"Stand down," Salla cried, and the Ilya lowered their weapons. "It's no hard feelings to your brother," he said to Kale, "but I must pick wars my people can win."

"I don't give a damn about your alliance," said Kale. "Where is Kirra?"

"Come now, old friend. Lower your—"

Kale pressed the blade hard on Salla's neck, drawing a line of blood. "You bastard! You never had her!" His hands were shaking.

"Don't be absurd, Kale." It was the chancellor. Cyrus Maro spoke with a smooth, steady voice that seemed to fill the room with a wisp of calm.

Kale's grip slackened. "W-what are you talking about?"

"Kale Andovier. The Exiled Lord. Yes, I remember you. Got your own mother killed, and then you fled Osha to save your own skin. And now you've joined up with your traitorous brother and his little Shadow Watch. Don't tell me that after your time with the Gallows Girl, you don't know how I derive my powers. I used Lumeni power to switch the Choosing stones, just as Kirra would have done. I could only have attained that ability through the blood of a Lumeni."

The room was suddenly filled with a chill that shook Kale with shivers. A swirl of mist had formed around the Golden Saddle. Kale's grip fell away from Salla's neck. From the mist, as though stepping from behind a waterfall, two figures appeared. The first was a strange-looking woman with ghostly skin dressed in dark silks.

The second figure was thin and haggard, but there was no denying who it was. As soon as he saw her, Kale felt the presence of the mind he had so longed to sense again.

Kirra.

Kale forgot about his hatred for Salla entirely. He rushed to Kirra as the mists swirled and evaporated away. Kirra's face was drawn, and her eyes were dark and seemed to sink into her skull, as though she had not slept in weeks. Kale wrapped her in his arms. Her body went limp. Kirra slumped to the ground, and Kale went with her to cushion her fall. Leaning against the Golden Saddle, he held her, tears blurring his vision. But he had her back, finally. Kirra was here. She was alive.

"I'm so sorry," Kale sobbed, stroking matted hair from Kirra's face. Her eyes were closed, but she was shaking her head back and forth, muttering unintelligibly.

"Shh, shh," Kale murmured. "It's all right. Everything will be all right."

The strange pale woman, who had brought Kirra through the mists, descended the steps. "Welcome to the festivities, Medea," said the chancellor.

Medea gazed about the room as though there was much more to see than the sandstone walls, as though she was looking beyond them. "Your stones, my lord," she said at last. Medea's voice was airy. She held out a pair of green gemstones to the chancellor.

The godstones!

The chancellor had found them. That was how Salla had known about them, how he had enticed Kirra, how she had disappeared so completely from his sense, and how she had now appeared from nowhere. The legends were true. His mother had been right all along. And this knowledge filled Kale with sick dread.

Kirra's grip went suddenly tight on Kale's arm and her eyes went wide. "You shouldn't have come!" Her voice was but a fragile whisper. "You have to go! Now, Kale!"

Kale held her tight. *Gods, what have they done to you?*

He delved into Kirra's mind, and she did not resist him. Kale saw the chancellor harvesting her blood through long tubes of something like intestines. But there was more. The woman, Medea—Kirra bore incredible fear of her. Kale kept sensing an image of the woman's bony hands clasping around Kirra's forehead, and then a rush of memories. She had been tortured, as the woman probed her mind for something Kale could not place.

"I am not going anywhere without you," Kale whispered.

Kirra's eyes closed again, but her head kept wagging back and forth.

"What have you done to her?"

"She will be fine," said Salla. "Her body is weak from the bloodletting. A few days with one of your healers, and she'll be better than ever. I am a man of my word, old friend. I am sorry for the theatrics, and I am sorry she is weak, but I couldn't very well have you communicating with her through your mind, could I? So, the chancellor had Medea take her someplace far away, until all the madness was over."

"Where did she come from?" said Kale, pointing at Medea.

"From the Old World, of course." The chancellor smiled, stepping to Medea's side. "Medea has merely confirmed what you already believed to be possible. That the godstones might lead anywhere." He laughed. "You are not the only one who wishes they could change the past. My ancestors were fools to exterminate magic. But we can change all that. Even... bring back the dead."

Kale held on to Kirra, who was muttering incomprehensibly again.

Could it be possible? Death was permanent. Of course it was. There was no coming back from that! Was there?

"That is why you sought the stones, Kale, is it not?" said the chancellor. "Yes, you told your brother it was a weapon. The key to your revolution, I don't doubt. But you longed to undo the past. To bring poor Lady Andovier back." Kale did not respond. His grip tensed around Kirra's fragile form. "You and I both know that your brother is no king. You have doubted his little resistance from the start. Your brother is a charismatic fool, and he will lead all those Watchers to their deaths. Which would be a shameful waste of magic. And that is why I am prepared to spare them, Kale. If you lead me to the Watchtower."

Kirra stirred in Kale's arms. Her grip went tight on his wrist, and her eyes opened wide. "No, Kale. You have to... fight!" Her eyes closed. She coughed violently, a trace of blood trickling from her lips, and her body went limp once more.

"You can see where resistance got Kirra," said the chancellor.

Kale shook with anger, but he knew he could not resist. He lowered Kirra to the floor of the throne room and stood to face the chancellor. He descended the steps from the throne. He glanced at the Morph named Valeria, but the girl who had wanted to prevent this alliance, who had wanted him to kill Salla, now would not meet his gaze. She stared forward, the boy, Darien, at her side. The Gallows Boy. This was where resistance had gotten him.

Ashi stood beside Salla. She looked up and watched him. Had she known all along that the chancellor would not break his alliance? About what he was doing to Kirra?

Everything had been part of the game. All so he would give up the location of the Shadow Watch. Ashi looked down at her feet. He had been a fool in their hands. And they had all been fools in the hands of the chancellor. There was nothing he could do.

But then, Kirra's mind reached out to him.

And he saw the Isle of Jallaa, the commune of newly discovered Watchers. He saw the garden where they'd spent their first night together—the night of the slaughter. In his memories, the garden had always felt dark and cold, tinged with guilt and blood. But when he saw it through Kirra's mind, the garden glowed like something from a dream. It had felt like the very best of dreams that night. *It wasn't a mistake*, he felt her say. *That night was the last light before the darkness. We couldn't stop it then. But we can now.*

Kale turned back to her and saw her lips form the silent words: *I love you, Kale. Now, run!*

And then Kirra was on her feet. She'd not been as weak as she had let herself seem. Her body flickered and disappeared.

The room fell into chaos as the chancellor bellowed for his Morphs to find her, as Medea shrieked, as Salla stumbled back and fell to the floor. And in the chaos, Kale took to the air. He soared over them all, landing at the ledge of a high window above the throne, ready to fly to freedom, when he heard Kirra cry out in pain.

Darien had not been so easily fooled. Kirra knelt, now visible, beside the chancellor, the godstones in her hand.

Gods, why did she go back?

Darien had a vicelike grip on Kirra's wrist, and Valeria rushed forward and took hold of the other. The chancellor took the stones and struck Kirra across the cheek, launching her head back. Blood poured from her emaciated face.

"Please, no!" cried Kale.

"Kale, run! Warn the—" The chancellor punched Kirra again.

Kale leapt to the floor of the throne room. "Please, I will do what you want! Just spare her! Please!"

"Kale, n-no," Kirra said, through sobs.

"I've had enough of these games!" roared the chancellor. "Release her!"

Darien and Valeria obeyed, and Kirra slumped to her knees. A burst of energy emerged from the chancellor's fingertips like a bolt of lightning, a light greater than anything Kirra could ever have manipulated with her Lumeni power. The bolt struck Kirra's face and launched her back. She writhed on the floor in pain. When the next bolt came, she shrieked like an Old World heathen set aflame. Her body seized violently and then went still.

The chancellor let up, and Kale was at her side in an instant. Her face was raw with burns. He felt at her neck. She was unconscious, but alive. Thank the gods, she was alive.

Kale did not resist when the two Morphs took hold of his arms.

Nor when he felt Medea's long, needlelike fingers clasp around his head.

"Medea is a Cerebro far more powerful than you, Kale. She is going to enter your mind. And you are going to reveal the exact location of your brother's stronghold, or by the gods, I will wait until Kirra wakes, and then I will torture her again, and again, and again. Until she dies, slow and in agony, before your very eyes. And I will let you live so that you remember the look in her dying eyes until the day it drives you mad, knowing you could have saved her."

There was no hesitation in Kale's mind as he knelt with Kirra lying prostrate before him, the look of agony still etched on her face. She was alive yet, and he had to save her.

"I will hold nothing back," said Kale feebly.

He felt Medea's mind enter his own, like water through a hole in the side of a dam. Slowly, the water seeped in, and the hole expanded, and the dam broke. Medea's mind filled his own, and he let her see everything. All his walls were destroyed in the deluge.

When she was finished, Kale's mind was an empty vessel. When she released him, his body slumped to the ground in a heap beside Kirra's.

The last thing Kale heard before he lost consciousness was the chancellor's delighted voice. "Now the Watchtower will fall."

PART ELEVEN
NIGHT OF GODS & MONSTERS

In the Old World, the Rulaqs ruled the White North. The proud race of monsters was matched by no creature nor god, and few dared venture into their harsh domain. The Rulaqs' return to their kingdom could mean nothing but death to those caught in their wake.

—from *New Histories of the Old World*

CHAPTER TWENTY-NINE

The creature's shriek split the night as the Rulaq lifted its two enormous heads to the sky, its fangs glinting in the glow of the Sisters. Its twin necks were the size of trees, supported by an immense body of muscle and thick white fur, and its paws were as large as Tori's entire body. Wicked claws the size of daggers extended from each paw.

The beast was more terrifying than any tale Tori's mum had ever told, for the tales had been but ancient myths. No one alive had ever seen a Rulaq. The creatures had endured only in terrible memory, passed on from generation to generation since the end of the last age of the world. But this was no myth. This creature was very, very real.

The Rulaq crushed a felled tree beneath its weight, with a crack like thunder, and lumbered into the clearing.

"RUN!" Tori screamed. She grabbed Fallon's arm and jerked him after her. This was her punishment for acting like a prissy noble girl back in the tavern. Now she had to make sure this poor Ytalan boy didn't die, along with dealing with a savage monster from the Old World. Tori and Fallon darted across the clearing, the ground shaking as the beast pursued them.

"Come on!" cried Mischa, whose face had gone as pale as the

midnight snow that had begun to fill the sky. Ren stood beside her, at the edge of the clearing, but his face was calm and set, his eyes focused on the creature.

Suddenly, the rumbling of the earth ceased.

"TORI! DUCK!" cried Mischa.

Tori threw herself and Fallon to the ground. A cold wind rushed over them, and then, without warning, it stopped. Tori looked up. The creature was frozen in the air.

Ren had summoned a power stronger than Tori had ever seen, holding the creature in mid-attack with his Conjuri power. Mischa took hold of Fallon's other arm, jerking him to his feet. Ren's face scrunched with sheer willpower as he strained to hold the beast.

"Take your time, *please*," he grunted. Tori and Mischa dragged the Ytalan boy to the edge of the clearing. With a surge of magic, Ren launched the Rulaq away, and it slammed into two trees, knocking them over like they were kindling.

The Rulaq shook itself off, stood, and roared. Ren brought a tree down on the beast's head. It was still for a moment—stunned—and then charged again.

"Get that boy out of here!" Ren cried. He flew toward the Rulaq, keeping it distracted, drawing his saber and attacking with incredible courage. Tori sprinted up the path cut by the Watchtower sleigh only an hour ago, jerking Fallon along after.

The poor boy was shaking. "W-what is—"

"Shut up and run!" said Tori.

"Up there!" shouted Mischa, pointing to the cliffs towering above them. There was a small ledge a hundred feet up. "We'll fly him up there!"

"You'll what?" cried Fallon.

"Right," said Tori, ignoring him. She gripped his arm, and Mischa took hold of the other. Together, they leapt from the earth. Tori did not have time to think the process through; her body reacted, and the three of them landed safely on the ledge moments later. Fallon collapsed. The shock of flying had the effect of the wind being knocked out of him.

Another shriek pierced the night. In the clearing below, Ren was facing off with the creature. It thundered toward him. At the last moment, Ren flew to the side, swinging his saber.

"The boy's safe!" shouted Ren. "Now help me!"

"You can't leave me up here!" cried Fallon.

"Sorry," Tori muttered. And together, Tori and Mischa leapt from the ledge, leaving Fallon alone. They landed in the trees behind the Rulaq, and Tori marveled at how easily flight came to her now. Ren drew the Rulaq close, then weaved between the attacking heads, swinging his saber as he flew. But the blade did little damage against the creature's matted fur and thick skin. *We'll never beat this thing with blades,* Tori thought. An idea came to her. It was crazy, but it was worth a shot. They needed to be quick. Tori could tell Ren's strength was low because he had stopped using magic.

Tori and Mischa sprinted through the woods and hid behind the trees at the far end of the clearing—the ones that got the most sun and bore no lingering snow on their branches.

"When Ren lands, set these trees into the biggest fire you've ever set!" Tori said.

Ren shifted, mid-flight, and headed straight toward them.

"Tori, I've never set a fire that big all at once!" said Mischa.

Tori grabbed her wrist. "You're a Fieri, Misch! You can do it!" Ren landed and ran straight at them. The creature galloped after him, roaring. "NOW!" Tori screamed.

Mischa closed her eyes, focusing with all her might, and she struck the flints around her wrists together. Instantly, the spark exploded and flames shot forth. A dozen trees lit up, forming a wall of fire. Ren leapt through the lapping flames, and Tori concentrated all her power on the trees. The Rulaq reared up at the flaming wall. Tori ripped the trees from their roots with her Conjuri power and sent them crashing down on the creature.

The Rulaq collapsed beneath the weight and writhed in the searing flames. The air stank with burning hair and flesh. But in the midst of the violent thrashing, the creature managed to free one of its necks. It picked up a flaming tree between its jaws and flung it aside. Ren cried out and flew toward the inferno. Mischa withdrew the flames at the last moment, and Ren stabbed his saber through one of the eyes of the beast's pinned-down head, submerging the blade up to the hilt. Blood spewed, and the Rulaq lurched in pain, sending Ren flying into a nearby tree. He did not stir.

Tori's stomach roiled. She wanted to fly to him at once, be sure he was alive. But there was no time. The Rulaq's free head latched onto another felled tree, no longer ablaze, and heaved it aside with ease. It snatched another, then shook its whole body free from the remaining logs. It removed the sword from its eye and roared as it cast the blade away.

Mischa leaned against a rock, breathing heavily, her body weakened from the expiration of so much Fieri power at once. Tori feared her own power would deplete soon as well. Ren lay unmoving across the clearing. There was nothing but the holes where the uprooted trees had been between Tori and Mischa and the Rulaq. Tori grabbed Mischa's arm and they sprinted, dodging the charging beast. Tori reached out with her sense, and Ren's sword flew to her hands. She handed it to Mischa.

Tori gripped her arm. "Are you strong enough to fly?"

The Rulaq stood at the center of the clearing, its massive necks swinging violently.

"I-I think so."

You'll have to be or we're both dead. "Distract those heads, Mischa. I've got to get close to the body."

"Tori!" Mischa shouted. Her hands were shaking. "If I die, I-I need you to tell Vashti that I'm sorry!"

"Sorry for what?" *Why is Mischa worried about Vashti at a time like this?*

"Just tell her, okay?"

Tori nodded, then squeezed her hand tight. "You're not going to die, Misch!"

Together, they leapt from the earth and flew straight between the Rulaq's heads. Mischa swung the sword, grazing the creature's face, and flew on, but Tori veered and landed on its back. Her fingers latched onto thick, fibrous fur. The Rulaq reared back, but she held tight. It reached with one of its swinging heads band snapped at her—missed.

She was just out of its reach, but the force of its movement nearly sent her flying. *I can't hold on for long. Come on, Misch!*

Mischa was back, swinging the sword at the Rulaq head with two good eyes, and Tori focused all the energy she had left on the beast's heart. If she could start Ren's heart by applying the right pressure with her Conjuri sense, perhaps she could stop the Rulaq's.

One of the heads shot around like a whip, trying to knock Tori free, but she was just out of reach. Her heart felt like it was catapulting off her rib cage. Mischa flew past, slashing at the neck of the other head, but suddenly, the creature lurched back.

Mischa collided with its skull and plummeted to the ground.

Oh gods, oh gods, oh gods.

The Rulaq shook itself and reared up again. Tori felt her grip slipping. Then the beast pitched backward, ready to crush her beneath its own weight.

This is it. Kill or die. Tori focused all her strength on her sense. She felt the beat of the Rulaq's heart, felt the muscles contracting, felt the fibers that formed each chamber. She reached out, with every bit of magic she had left, and ceased their movement.

The heart stalled.

The Rulaq landed on its back, but Tori dove free before impact and rolled away in the snow.

The creature thrashed on the ground, but its heart did not recover. The Rulaq's writhing grew slower, its shrieks fainter. And then the beast stopped moving.

Tori rushed over and helped Mischa to her feet. The body of the dead Rulaq was like a snowy hill beside them. As she stood, Mischa held her head and moaned. "I-I'm alive."

Tori's breaths were sharp, rapid pangs in her chest, but slowly, they calmed. "Yes. We are." Tori collapsed in the snow by her friend's side and gripped her hand. "You're all right?"

Mischa nodded, and her gaze moved to Ren. He had still not moved. "The captain!"

Together, they hobbled past the looming mountain of white fur. Tori's hands shook, and each step jarred her stomach. *Please, be alive.*

Tori knelt beside him, felt at his neck. It was cool to the touch. His breathing was slow but rhythmic. He had been knocked cold by the impact with the tree.

"I'm sorry," Tori murmured, cupping Ren's head in her hands. Blood ran down his cheek, and she wiped it away. If only they had returned with the others. If only Tori hadn't fooled around with Fallon.

Ren stirred. "No, *I'm* sorry…" His voice was weak, but he still managed a grin, and Tori nearly cried with relief. His eyes cracked open.

"Oh, thank the gods!" said Mischa.

"Why are you sorry?" Tori whispered, brushing the bloody, matted hair from his face.

Ren turned over to gaze back at the clearing. The Rulaq's dead eyes were dark chasms, nearly big enough to crawl inside.

"I'm sorry I didn't see you kill that damn beast." Ren chuckled, then coughed. He held his forehead and groaned. "Gods, that thing packed a punch."

They laughed. It felt good to laugh after nearly dying. But there was still much to worry about. *No one has sighted a Rulaq in three hundred years*, Tori thought with trepidation. It seemed impossible for one to appear out of nowhere. "Ren, where did that thing come from?" Tori's voice was the only sound. The three of them stared wordlessly at one another. Ren shook his head.

"EY! OH!"

The frantic cry echoed through the mountains. All three of them shot to attention. The cry echoed again.

"Oh gods," said Tori, chuckling with dark relief. "Fallon is still up on the cliff."

Ren did not laugh. "Tori, why was that boy following you?" The tone of his voice was deep and steady.

"He was… the true reason I missed the sleigh with the others." Tori hated to admit it. It sounded so foolish. Like something one of the noble girls in Osha would have pulled to get an academy boy jealous of her. "I met him in the taverns, and…"

Ren sat up, his eyes fierce, a grimace at his lips. Tori wanted to crawl beneath a boulder. She would give anything to take it back now.

She hadn't realized just how stupid it was until she had to explain herself to Ren.

"He's just a boy," Tori said, rising from the ground, her lips tensing as she pictured herself kissing Fallon back in the tavern. "But at least he didn't die."

"He *saw* us," said Mischa darkly. "Our magic."

Ren still hadn't met Tori's gaze, and she hated it. "Well, bring him down, and we'll figure out what to do with him."

Tori and Mischa leapt from the ground while Ren struggled to his feet and retrieved his saber. Fallon was trembling, standing with his back clinging to the face of the cliff. Tori landed beside him. "You're no monks! You're gods-damned witches!"

"I told you all this was a mistake," said Tori.

"Th-that thing…" Fallon pointed at the dead Rulaq's body in the clearing below. It looked like a mangled white ship had been smattered on rocks and dropped into the forest.

"It's what you think it is."

"Come on," said Mischa. "We've got to go."

The girls took hold of Fallon's arms and jumped. The Ytalan boy cried out like a child as they flew him to the ground. They landed beside Ren. The moment Fallon's feet touched the ground, Ren had him gripped by the neck and thrown up against a tree. "What did you see?" Ren growled.

"Ren!" said Tori. "What are you—" But Mischa held her back.

"I-I-I saw that thing—that creature," Fallon stammered. "And—"

"Wrong!" Ren shouted, slapping the boy's face, peering deep into his eyes. "What creature are you talking about?" Fallon didn't know what to say. He glanced over at the dead beast and then back at Ren.

"Ah!" Fallon moaned. "Your witch priest is going to kill me!"

"Don't you get it?" said Tori. "You can't tell anyone what you've seen!"

"What is in the clearing, boy?" said Ren.

Fallon looked over again. Ren did not follow his gaze, but looked deep into the boy's eyes. "Nothing! I see nothing!"

"Correct." Ren shoved the boy away, and he fell in the snow. Tori was going to help him, but Mischa held onto her arm.

"Let him handle this," Mischa whispered.

Fallon scrambled to his feet. Ren stood tall, with his hands at his belt. "Do not breathe a word to anyone, boy. Or I swear to the gods, I will kill you."

"Y-yes, sir."

"Now, go!"

Fallon nodded frantically. He turned and ran, stumbling over a charred tree branch. When he reached the edge of the meadow, the boy turned back.

And that was when Ren let his dagger fly.

It hit Fallon squarely in the chest, soaring with a flare of Conjuri charm. The Ytalan boy slumped to his knees and collapsed in the snow.

CHAPTER THIRTY

Tori's scream echoed off the cliff walls. The sound seemed to come from all directions, as though it had come from outside of her. It was like the ghosts of Ghen, suffocating her, wrapping their hands around her throat. *Murrrdererrr!*

Ren's face was like ice, and Tori wanted to shatter it, but she didn't have the strength to punch him. Perhaps it was the strangling guilt, or perhaps it was because her body was spent from the Rulaq attack. Ren strode across the clearing toward Fallon's body.

"W-why did you do that?" Tori shouted, finally finding her voice. "He wouldn't have talked!"

Ren stopped and turned. There was no remorse on his face. His eyes burned with fury. "That's not what I was worried about!"

Tori tried to hold back tears, but she could hardly believe what Ren had done. "It was stupid to hook up with him, I know. But he wouldn't have—"

Ren's face hardened. "I don't care that you hooked up with some village rat. I care that you put our entire revolution in danger!"

"He was just a stupid boy!"

"Come with me, Tori!" Ren had never used such a cold tone with her before. Suddenly, he did not seem the same warmhearted captain she had grown close to these past couple months.

"Why did you kill him?" Tori demanded.

"Just come," Ren said again, this time more gently, and Tori followed him to Fallon's body.

The Ytalan boy was bleeding all over the snow, but his chest was still moving with tepid breaths. He wasn't dead. Tori didn't know if she should be relieved or horrified that his death was not over yet. Fallon's eyes cracked open, and the boy laughed, blood spurting from his lips.

Tori felt chills at the sound.

Ren looked her in the eyes. "I did it because this stupid boy led that monster straight to us." Ren dropped to his knees and held his blade to the boy's throat. "Reveal yourself, or by the gods, I will let you die slow and in agony."

Fallon's eyes flickered, his pupils turning narrow like an animal's, and then his body followed—he morphed into the warg-like form of one of the chancellor's wingless Metamorphi. Tori could not believe it. Fallon was still chuckling, a seething purr.

No, Fallon was a lie, Tori thought. *He never even existed.*

"Do your worst, Ren," the Morph growled. "They're coming."

Ren cried out and slit the beast's throat. Blood gushed out in a torrent, and Fallon gasped his last Morph breaths.

The clearing was utterly silent. The pale light of the Sisters seemed to hang in the stillness. Horrified, Tori could not take her eyes off the Morph. The Morph she had kissed, and then brought straight to them. *I nearly killed Ren and Mischa. I nearly led the Morph straight to the Watchtower.* Slowly, Ren rose and wiped his blade off on his trousers. He didn't say a word.

"Ren," Tori finally managed. "I'm sorry. I-I didn't—"

Ren would not meet her gaze. Tears streamed down her cheeks, biting her skin in the cold. *How could I have been so stupid?*

There was a loud rustling in the forest. Ren drew his saber, Tori pulled her dagger, and Mischa readied her flints to strike flame.

Dajha sprinted into the clearing, nearly a blur with the speed of his Enduro power. His face was twisted with terror. At the sight of the dead Rulaq, he slipped in the snow, launched himself back up, and scrambled toward them even faster.

"Ren!" Dajha shouted. "We're under attack!"

Ren closed his eyes slowly, then opened them. "What happened?"

"Rulaqs, a whole herd of 'em! They're destroying Ytala!"

"Oh gods!" said Mischa.

"The chancellor is looking for the Watchtower," said Ren. "We've got to be gone before they find it! If we fly, we'll lead them right to us. We'll have to run!"

Ren led the way, hurrying down the mountain path, trudging through the deepening snow. Flurries were coming down harder by the minute. Tori, Mischa, and Dajha followed, struggling to keep up with Ren's brisk pace. Tori's head was throbbing from the lingering *gnasch* and the expended energy from the Rulaq attack. *A whole herd of Rulaqs. How is that possible? Where did they come from?*

After some time of hard running, they reached the entrance to the narrow canyon the Watchers called the Birth Canal. Tori feared it was not quite narrow enough, though. A piercing shriek echoed up the valley.

"*Shenzah*!" said Ren.

A second shriek followed, then another, and another. The night filled with the cries of the hellish beasts, resounding off the alpine summits like a horde of banshees. The snow began to fall harder, stinging Tori's eyes. The ground trembled as the beasts neared.

"A herd of them," said Tori. "They've found us."

"What do we do?" said Mischa.

"The three of you fly back to the Watchtower," said Ren.

"But that'll lead them straight—"

Ren cut Mischa off. "It's too late for that now. They know where we are. Find Sahra and tell her to take everyone out through the catacombs."

Tori didn't know what the catacombs were, but Mischa nodded without question.

"What about you?" said Tori, though the knowledge of what he had planned was already gnawing a hole in her gut.

"I'm going to give you time," he said, looking out on the field of jagged boulders below. The shrieks were rising up from the forest beyond. The sound was piercing, sending shivers through Tori. The ground thundered beneath her feet. The first creature emerged from the trees, bringing a pair of trunks down with a crash. "I'm going to let them get close. And then I'm going to bring this entire mountain down on those bastards."

Dajha nodded solemnly. "We'll get everyone out safe, Cap'n."

Mischa and Dajha headed down the tunnel. Ren held Tori back.

"Ren, I—"

"Don't." Ren squeezed her hand. His other hand drifted to her face and touched her cold skin lightly. "You're not the first to be fooled by the chancellor."

A sense of understanding seemed to pass between them, and Tori knew he was talking about himself, the days he and Scelero had vied for the chancellor's graces. She gripped his hand. "Promise you won't die."

Ren smiled grimly. "Get the others out, Astoria. I'll find you."

Tori nodded to her captain. This time, she would not let him down. She could see five Rulaqs marching across the boulder field. Their long necks towered like battlements. More shrieks filled the valley. *How many of them are there?*

Tori could not let herself think what might happen to Ren. She obeyed his orders, leapt from the ground, and flew farther and faster than she'd ever flown before. She soared through the bitter night air, praying Ren would be able to hold off the attacking horde of Rulaqs before it was too late. She caught up to Mischa and Dajha as they neared the Watchtower. They landed within the gates and crept through the silent lanes of the ancient stronghold. Everything in the Watchtower, everything in the entire Valley of Orran, was still. It was late, long past midnight, but Tori expected someone would be waiting for their return.

"What do we do?" said Tori.

"Split up," said Dajha.

"Daj, you find Sahra. We'll round up the others," said Mischa. "We'll meet in the courtyard."

Dajha went running, his form blurring again, and Tori and Mischa hurried toward their central spire chambers. But as they reached the main courtyard, they heard a voice.

The girls ducked behind a corner. The voice was approaching from across the courtyard. It sounded vaguely familiar, like something from a dream. But this was not because it belonged to someone from the Watchtower.

Tori had last heard the voice in a dream—back in the Haunted Forest of Ghen. Her heart thundered. It had been so many months since she'd last heard it, she could hardly believe it.

"They should be here by now," Darien said. "Something's gone wrong."

After all this time, all the horrors they'd both been through, all the time spent wondering if it might be possible he was still alive—here Darien was. As though the gods had brought them back together. Tori's heart filled with warmth.

Until she heard the other voice.

"Everything he's planned has fallen into place," said a strange girl. "Trust him."

"Of course I trust him."

Tori peeked around the corner. Darien and the strange girl stood at the edge of the courtyard, looking away, toward the valley below. Tori wanted to leap out and shout, but Mischa's grip had gone tight around her wrist.

"That's him," Tori whispered. "The Gallows Boy."

Mischa clapped her hand over Tori's mouth and pulled her deeper into the shadows, shoving her against the tower wall. "Wait," Mischa whispered. "Listen."

Together, they waited and listened to Darien and the strange girl, whose silver hair glimmered in the moonlight. Tori tried to push away the agonizing sense that this was too good to be real.

"I wish he would have let us go to the village," said Darien. "Not stay back here with the bloody Legions."

The Legions... Tori thought. *He's part of the attack, but... he could help us.*

"You're sure that's him?" whispered Mischa.

Tori nodded, though fear had begun to replace her joy at hearing

Darien's voice. "I'd know his voice anywhere." And yet it did not sound like anything Darien would say.

"I mean, are you sure that's the Gallows Boy you *knew?*" said Mischa.

Tori was not sure. Darien was a Shadow of the Night Legions. *But surely he's the same boy I knew. Surely he's here for a reason.* Tori feared this was only wishful thinking. She knew what happened to soldiers in the Legions.

"This is the most important part," the silver-haired girl said to Darien. She touched his arm, which made Tori tense up all over. "That's why he chose us. To secure this tower until—"

"You don't get it, Valeria," said Darien. "I wanted to be the one to capture the Gallows Girl. The last test to prove myself."

"The chancellor knows where your loyalties lie," said Valeria.

Tori could not believe what she was hearing. She felt like she might be sick. "No," Tori whispered. "He wouldn't…"

"No one is invincible to the conditioning of the Legions." Mischa took her hand and pulled her deeper into the shadows. "We've got to get out of here."

"What about the others?"

"It's too late for that now," said Mischa. "The Legions are already here. The chancellor is coming for *you*, and I'm not going to let him have you."

They made for a narrow passage into the Watchtower, but there was someone standing in their way, waiting to meet them.

It was Vashti.

"Oh, thank the gods! You're okay!" said Mischa. She hugged the Yan Avii princess, but Vashti returned it stiffly. "We need to get Tori to the catacombs. The Legions are looking for her."

Vashti regarded Mischa with a strange look of sorrow. "You're wrong, Mischa," Vashti said. "For once, our beloved Gallows Girl is not the center of everyone's attention."

"Vashti, what are you talking about? We need to go!"

"They're not here for Tori. They're here for me, Misch. The chancellor is here for me. SHADOWS!"

Before Tori could fully comprehend what was happening, Darien and Valeria were upon them. A company of Legions appeared behind the girls, torches suddenly lighting up all around.

Darien stepped forward, the torchlight glinting off his copper skin. Tori felt weak at the sight of him in Legion uniform. *He looks the same as ever, and yet…*

Darien's face had hardened, and he was built thicker, filled with muscle. And his eyes—there was something off about his eyes. He met Tori's gaze, and she could not move. After so many months, she and Darien stood face-to-face, and Tori's body seemed to have forgotten how to function.

She was relieved to see him alive, and something told her he was going to help them. Maybe not at once. But surely he would not let the chancellor have her.

Darien looked Tori over, and his eyes lit up as recognition dawned on him. "Good work," he said to Vashti. "You brought me the Gallows Girl. Tori, I was hoping I'd be the one to find you…"

"Darien!" Tori said weakly. She wanted to rush to him, to pull him into an embrace. Tell him that a day had not gone by she hadn't thought of him, wanted to find him, wanted to free him from the Legions. She had never forgotten him.

Tori had to believe that he'd wanted to be the one to find her so he could help her escape. But Darien's eyes betrayed him. Just like Fallon's had right before he died. The pupils narrowed. And then his body shifted, and he took on the form of a dark, winged Metamorphi. Long wings stretched out like a dragon's, claws stretching out. They brushed her shoulder.

Tori jumped back in disgust. "What have you done with Darien?"

The terrible creature smiled, and then it spoke. And even behind the rasp, Tori could still hear the true timbre of Darien's voice, and it filled her with dread. "I *am* Darien. This is me, now. Thanks to the chancellor, this is what I have become."

Darien pointed a taloned finger at the guards. A pair of them clasped their hands around Tori's arms. Two more took hold of Mischa. Tori tried to resist, but it was useless. *This can't be happening. It can't be real.*

"Hold them with the others," Darien said, shifting back to his human form. The form Tori had leaned on, depended on, all their years as slaves. "The chancellor will be here shortly."

Darien's voice belonged to that same boy from Scelero's estate, but Tori's friend was worse than the dead ghost of Ghen that haunted her nightmares. By defying the chancellor, by thwarting Darien's suicidal rebellion, Tori had turned him into the very thing he had raged against.

A mindless soldier who did the chancellor's bidding.

A monster.

CHAPTER THIRTY-ONE

Tori and Mischa were escorted to the Great Hall of the Watchtower. The dim room was lit only by a torch at either end, but even in the low light, Tori could see the bodies littering the floor.

"No!" Mischa shrieked, resisting the soldiers holding her. One of them slugged her in the gut, and she crumpled to the ground, only to be jerked back to her feet.

"Let her go," instructed Darien firmly. "Let them both go."

The Shadows shoved Tori and Mischa into the center of the room, beside the bodies of their friends. Tori's nails bit into the palms of her hands. *He killed them. He killed them all!*

Darien's face remained hard and his eyes cold. Without a glance in Tori's direction, Darien left, his comrade Valeria right behind him. Vashti remained in the hall, and four Morphs stood guard at the door. Mischa and Tori hurried over to the nearest body—Zaya Shalvar's. Mischa was trembling, and she held onto Tori's hand. Tori steeled herself and felt Zaya's neck for a pulse.

Tori breathed, and her body relaxed slightly. "She's alive."

"Thank the gods," Mischa whimpered.

"Of course she's alive. All of them are." Vashti strode forward, holding up a vial filled with a dark liquid. "A sleeping draught developed by my brother. This was how Salla managed to get me out of the Red Palace after my father burned me alive. I would have been shrieking in agony when I woke, as they were smuggling my body away. This draught saved me then, and it saved every Watcher now."

Tori wanted to punch the Yan Avii princess. "Saved them?"

"W-what are you talking about?" said Mischa.

"The chancellor's men were able to enter without shedding a drop of magical blood," said Vashti. "While everyone slept safe and sound."

Mischa had gone completely pale. Her jaw tensed. "Why, Vashti? How could you betray us?"

"Betray? I am *saving* us all from fighting a battle we never could have won." Vashti knelt down and placed her hand on Mischa's shoulder, tenderly. Tears were streaming from Mischa's eyes. Vashti looked away, but Tori noticed the pained expression the princess fought to hide. "The chancellor is not a monster," said Vashti. "He doesn't want to kill us. He wants to bring magic *back* to the world. Can you imagine it, Misch? We wouldn't have to hide anymore."

"You know what he did to me in his citadel," said Tori. She could not believe that Vashti could be so naïve. "He harvested my blood, Vashti! He used me to build *his* power. You really believe he intends to spare us?"

"I don't have a choice," hissed Vashti.

"There's always a choice."

"Oh, how foolish of me. Thank the Sol I have the Gallows Girl to remind me what I have! Look around you, Tori. We lost Ren's little revolution before it began. My brother was smart enough to take the chancellor's side before the war came to the Yan Avii. And now I have the same chance, to save the Watchers."

"Vashti, what are you talking about?" said Mischa.

"My brother, Salla, has been chosen as the new Great Soltayne of the Yan Avii, and he's formed an alliance with the chancellor. He promised my hand in marriage in exchange for peace. For my people. *Our* people." Vashti turned to Tori with scathing eyes. "If that means anything to you."

"Of course it does!" Tori snapped. She had always felt loyal to her people, but she had not lived among them in eleven years. Her people were here at the Watchtower. "The Watchers are our people too."

"And the chancellor has promised the same peace for the Watchers if we do not resist," said Vashti.

"You believe that *shenzah?*" said Tori.

"My brother saved my life," said Vashti, meeting Mischa's gaze again. Her voice grew softer. She took hold of Mischa's hand. "I spent all my childhood suppressing who I was. When Salla sent me here, he found a way I could embrace who I was. Now he has found a way for a dead princess to become queen of the most powerful nation in the New World. And besides, what other choice do we have?"

Tori thought the choice to kill Vashti was sounding very appealing. But she never got the chance to entertain it further.

The doors to the Great Hall flew open. The first to enter was Dajha, shoved to the ground by a pair of Morphs. The creatures had found him. Darien and Valeria marched in after, Darien bearing a limp form in his arms. He set the body, roughly, on the floor beside Dajha.

It's Ren's body, Tori realized with sick dread. The captain of the Watchers was covered in blood and the dust of rubble. "No!" Tori rushed forward, fearing what she would find.

"He's not dead," Darien said as she knelt beside her captain. Tori searched Darien's face as he spoke, but there was no expression, no hint at what was going on inside his mind, no revelation as to where his loyalties truly lay. It killed her to see Darien this way.

Ren's hands were cold, but Darien had not lied. Tori could sense Ren's life before she even checked his pulse. It was the same way she had known when she revived him in the courtyard. His mind teemed with magic, and she could feel it.

Ren stirred. His eyes cracked open and then grew wide when he saw where he was. His gaze locked on the Morphs, and he shot up from the ground. But he had no strength to stand, let alone wield magic. His legs gave out, and he crumpled to the floor.

"Captain," Tori whispered, gripping his arm.

Ren groaned. "I… failed. The Rulaqs… broke through."

"You're alive," said Tori. "It's all that matters."

A slight grin creased Darien's lips as he watched them. It was not his true smile. Not the one Tori had known. Not the one that had kept her fighting in the Fringes. This was not the face that had helped fuel her training to lead a revolution against the chancellor, that had kept her mind from thinking that all had been lost the day of the Gallows. Now those fears swept upon her like a rogue wave, capsizing her fragile resolve to keep hoping. *Darien's gone. There's nothing of that boy left anymore…*

The doors flew open again, and this time the chancellor appeared. He regarded the scene with delight. "What a sight! The Gallows Boy and the Gallows Girl, reunited at last. What, no tender embraces?"

Darien smirked, and Tori said nothing. There were no words for such treachery.

"I really should thank you, Astoria," the chancellor continued. "When you defied me before all of Osha, little could I have known you were actually saving me from executing my finest and most dedicated soldier. What a shame that would have been!"

Tori wanted to scream. To call the chancellor the bastard he was, but she restrained herself. She had to wait for her moment. *If there are any moments left to wait for.*

Ren struggled to sit up, anger flaring at the sight of Cyrus Maro. "How?" he rasped. "How did you find us?"

The chancellor smiled. "Ah, you have your pathetic brother to thank for that, Lord Andovier."

"What?" Pain was written all over Ren's face. "He wouldn't!"

"Come now, Ren," said the chancellor in a patronizing tone. "You know you and your little rebellion are no match for my Morphs and Legions. It was almost too easy to force the Exiled Lord to give you up."

"Where is he?" Ren growled, rising to his feet. "I'll kill that *skazha!*" It was a curse from the Old Tongue, reserved for the vilest of creatures.

The Morphs had their hands on the hilts of their blades, but the chancellor laughed. "I don't imagine you'll get the chance. That *skazha* is tending to her, of course, back in the Red City. To Kirra. Though I must say, he sees to his love life better than you, Lord Andovier."

The chancellor regarded Vashti, who had not looked at Ren since he'd entered. And then his eyes fell to Tori.

"Vashti was only too happy to help. And Tori... well, let's just say that Morph didn't have to try very hard to keep you all distracted while we infiltrated your Watchtower, did he?"

It was Tori's turn to look away from Ren. *The chancellor played us all. This whole army, this whole revolution was an illusion. We never had a chance.*

"Yes, Ren," said the chancellor, "you could learn a thing or two from your spineless brother."

Ren's strength was waning. He slumped over, supporting himself against a pillar.

"But Ren, you're not who I'm really here to see," said the chancellor. His eyes passed from Ren to Vashti to Tori.

Tori stood so that she could look the chancellor in the eyes. Cyrus Maro strode across the room, took hold of her hand, and held her gaze, much to Vashti's chagrin. His skin was warm, and Tori hated how intoxicating his glacier eyes were. Despite all she knew, deep down, there was something about his eyes that made her think he couldn't possibly be as purely evil as his ancestors.

"Come, Astoria. I'd like to show you something." The chancellor's voice was sweet to her ears, like the rush of a brook in a meadow. *No, it's his spell, his magnetism. Just like the first day I met him.*

But Tori followed him out the door. Darien and Valeria made to follow, but the chancellor bid them away. "Don't worry, comrades. The Gallows Girl is no threat to me. In fact, she never was."

Darien and Valeria obeyed.

As she left, Tori overheard Mischa mutter, "I hope being queen is worth it!" And Mischa stormed to the other side of the hall to tend to Zaya, who remained unconscious. Ren followed her. "I'm all right too, by the way," Dajha said derisively, following after them.

Vashti was left standing alone, amidst the unconscious forms of the Watchers she had betrayed.

The chancellor escorted Tori by the hand through the halls of the Watchtower, up a narrow staircase, to an intricately carved set of doors —Ren's chambers. Ren kept a pair of blades above his hearth, and Tori entertained the brief notion that she could summon one and attack the chancellor. But she knew it was futile. She was spent from all the magic she had already used, and she knew the chancellor was fueled by replenishable blood.

"Don't be foolish, Astoria," said the chancellor, leading her past the hearth. "Resistance would only result in death, and not just for you."

Tori did not respond, but she dismissed the notion. She would have to play his games for now.

The doors to Ren's balcony flew open, propelled by the chancellor's magic. The curtains blew in the wind, and the chancellor led her out. Outside the walls of the fortress, a herd of gargantuan two-headed beasts stood still as statues.

"How?" said Tori, trying to hide the fear that was tearing at the last shreds of hope she had left. The might of the beasts was beyond comprehension. There were at least a dozen of them. Their massive necks plunged into the sky like war towers.

"The greatest folly of the Old World was to mistake monsters for mindless brutes," said the chancellor. "The Rulaqs are a race like any other. Their home was ripped from their grasp by a man—my ancestor —who thought them beneath his own race. I promised to give the Rulaqs back the Crooked Teeth, and in exchange, they agreed to ally themselves with the descendant of their greatest adversary."

"That's not what I meant," said Tori shortly. "How have so many of them remained hidden all these years?"

The chancellor grinned. "I always did like your spirit, Astoria. The Rulaqs remained hidden because they weren't *here* all these years."

"W-what do you mean?"

It was then Tori noticed the woman walking amongst the beasts. Her face was as pale as the snow, and she wore a dark hooded cloak. She crossed the field of monsters, weaving between the pillared legs of the beasts. She glanced up at them, her eyes seeming to cut across the distance. Tori remembered Ren's story earlier that night of the dark witch that the chancellor had been learning from, and she knew this must be her. The witch rose from the ground and flew to join them. Her flight was slow, and she landed on unsteady feet, gripping the edge of the balcony. Tori swore the air grew colder as she landed.

"Astoria, meet Medea," said the chancellor.

The witch's eerie gaze unnerved her, but Tori held her head high as the woman looked her over. It felt as though Medea were looking through her, to her soul. "Ah, the infamous Gallows Girl. Yesss."

Tori said nothing, but she felt her senses surging within her. The woman's very presence made Tori want to lash out and fight. Medea reached inside her billowy cloak and retrieved a pair of shimmering emerald stones. She handed them to the chancellor, and he grinned, holding them up for Tori to see. Tori feared she did not have to ask what they were.

Medea left them, then, without another word.

"You asked how the beasts have returned to the world after hundreds of years," the chancellor said, his fingers playing with the gems. "The answer: I let them in. Or rather, Medea did."

Tori felt a dark chill run across her skin. "Let them in from where?"

"There is magic in the world far greater than that of the Watchers, Astoria. Believing that they were the lone wielders of the powers behind the world—the gods' chosen saviors of humankind—that arrogance was what led to the Watchers' demise in the Old World. The First Chancellor, for all his blunders, didn't despise magic. He was a Watcher himself, and a devout follower of the Order. The problem was he couldn't control the others. Magic doesn't play favorites. Look at yourself. A slave girl who suddenly possesses the strength to cast a ripple in the pond of power. The lowborns of Osha would follow you to their deaths if they ever had the chance. Magic is the great leveler of the world in the right hands. And so, my ancestors banished magic entirely from our world."

The chancellor held the stones out for Tori to see. She had seen highborn ladies in Osha wear stones such as these around their necks. But as she eyed them, she noticed something subtly different. There was a glow to them, not like that of a flame, but more like the glow of primal life.

"My ancestors ushered in our magic-less, monster-less New World with one final act of incredibly powerful magic." Cyrus Maro held up the stones. "With the godstones."

Powerful magic, thought Tori. It was just like the draft, the way he used sterile words to describe the deaths of innocent people. It made her sick. "Sure, if you call slaughtering all of my kind a mere act of magic," said Tori.

The chancellor laughed to himself. "Ah, but he didn't slaughter them, Astoria. Not all of them. That's what people thought, of course. How else could you explain the disappearance of every magical creature, every savage monster?"

"How would *you* explain it, then?"

"The First Chancellor sent them away from our world to ravage another one." Tori's face must have borne the puzzlement she felt, because the chancellor laughed once more. "What if I told you that the New World is not all there is?"

That made no sense to Tori. "What are you talking about?"

"Would you like to see?"

The chancellor did not wait for a reply. He pressed the emerald stones, now glowing intensely, into Tori's palm. A swirl of mist engulfed them, until the valley and the Rulaqs disappeared. Tori was filled with the sensation that her insides were being turned inside out. Searing pain filled her senses. The stones burned through the skin of her hand, sending waves of pain through her bones.

The burning spread from her palm to the rest of her body, as though she'd been set aflame. And then the pain changed. At first, Tori thought it was her body healing itself. But that was not *this* feeling.

I feel… numb…

The mists swirled around them, then dissipated, and Tori knew immediately that she had arrived somewhere else. Somewhere utterly different from the world she had always known.

CHAPTER THIRTY-TWO

Tori crumpled to the ground in a field of grey grass. The searing pain had become a throbbing ache that permeated her entire being. She lay in the grass and let the pain wash over her. Slowly, the intensity ebbed away, becoming a lingering ache that made her feel hollowed out. After a few minutes, she found the strength to sit up and take in the world around her.

She lay in a meadow. There was a vast forest at the edge of it, but the trees were different from the ones in Osha. The snowpines and everwinter trees of the North were tall and slender and covered in needles. But these trees were broad and had leaves as large as she was. Tori had seen such trees in the Bay of Trium, but there was something different about this place, something that told her there was no way she could be anywhere near the Trium'vel.

The trees were alive, but they were not green like trees in the New World. These bore a dull grey color like the grass. Though the sun shone bright, it seemed washed out, almost too bright. What's more, Tori did not feel the warmth of its rays, nor did she feel cold.

I feel... nothing, Tori thought dimly.

The place stirred no sense in her at all. The world was utterly silent. There were no leaves rustling. No birds chirping. No rodents foraging. It unnerved her how quiet this place was.

The chancellor stood, unfazed, a short distance away, atop a small grassy knoll, gazing out to a world beyond the meadow. Tori hobbled through the grass to him, and he turned and met her halfway down the hill, taking her arm. She only realized her body had been weakened from using the chancellor's godstones when he aided her.

"How is your hand?" Cyrus Maro said.

Tori stretched out her fingers, and pain shot up her arm again. The skin was swollen and tender. Each movement felt like the skin was being stretched over a bed of broken glass. But if she held her hand still, the pain subsided.

"Fine," she lied. "Where are we?"

"Come see." The chancellor led her up the grassy knoll. From the top, they looked upon a great valley, and beyond, the ocean stretched out to the edges of the world. Yet the water did not flow in waves like it did in the New World. It stretched flat and motionless, like a great grey plain, reflecting the grey nothingness of the cloudless sky.

On the rocky shore lay a vast city. At least, it had once been a city. It was now a field of bramble, shards of jagged stone sticking out in all directions like the bones of a long-dead beast, wrenched and splayed open at the chest. Tori had heard tales of the Necropoli of the Ruined Empire, ancient ghost cities that had fallen to ruin after the Elyan races arrived from the Lost Continent. The fair-skinned invaders had conquered the Faere Dynasty of the ancient world, and then gone on to take over the whole continent, leaving death and rubble in their wake. The Necropoli were said to be haunted, infested with plagues.

Is that where the Rulaqs came from? Tori wondered. *But then, why is everything so strange? Why does it feel so… otherworldly?*

Outside the necropolis, a horde of Rulaqs stood peacefully. There must have been a hundred or more. The chancellor had apparently only let in a portion of the beasts. Every one of them stared at an empty archway at the edge of the rubble.

"Is this the land of the dead?" said Tori.

The chancellor smiled, not darkly, but in an enduring way, the way mothers smile at naïve children. "This is the Old World, Astoria. Or rather, this is what's left of it after the First Chancellor was through with it. A gloomy shade of our own world."

"What are they doing?" Tori said, pointing below at the statuesque Rulaqs.

"This world is the most dismal place you can imagine. It echoes the beauties of our world, but with no sensation. Grass without color. A sea with no waves. Sunlight with no warmth. Eating with no hunger to satisfy. This place is worse than the land of the dead. It is nothingness. The Rulaqs lived in this nothingness for three hundred years, but one day, a door opened and took a few of their own away. These poor beasts are waiting, desperate for that door to open again and take them away from this wretched place."

Tori stretched out her hand again. It still hurt. The skin was raw from the searing godstones, and she thought she could see bone peeking through. It made her cringe, and she was surprised she was not in more pain than she was. *Why aren't I healing?*

"To open the door to this horrid world, the stones require payment," said the chancellor. "A blood tithe. A Regenero is very handy for using the stones. Without your blood, I would have died after my first trip."

"That's why you kept me alive—why you harvested my blood," said Tori.

"I kept you alive because killing you would have been a waste. I did not know how great a waste when I first drank your blood. You were not the first Watcher I spared. Once I discovered what could be done with Watcher blood, I began preserving them when possible. This was after my family died, of course. My father despised Watcher gifts. He got what was coming to him, I suppose."

The chancellor spoke of their deaths nonchalantly, as though talking of what he ate for dinner. *It was his father's Morphs that killed Mum,* Tori thought.

"But you were different than the others I collected, Astoria. Most died after a few months. But a few months went by, and you did not die. At first, I thought you were simply stronger than the others, but then I was wounded in a battle against Morgath. I should have died. I did not heal as fast as you, but two days later, I woke without pain. No wound. No scar. And I knew it was your blood. It explained your resilience during the bloodletting. That was when I realized it. You are a Mage—legend of the Watcher orders—a wielder of more than one magical gift.

"I had been experimenting with the godstones, but I did not dare venture beyond our world until then. Oh, I sent a few Morphs to their deaths trying, but the tithe was too great. They could get here, but they could not get back without dying. It was the curse of the passage. But with your blood, though the pain was arduous, one could survive the passage. This discovery was what led your precious Commander Scelero to finally free you from my dungeons."

"He knew about the stones?" Tori asked.

"No. He never knew quite how great a weapon I had. But he had his suspicions about my experiments, and he knew I'd found the company of a practiced sorcerer."

"Medea," Tori said.

The chancellor smiled. "Scelero suspected something awry about her, and he knew I was dabbling with ancient blood magic. He was bred to sense power, after all. Scelero knew what *you* really were before anyone. That traitorous bastard."

Tori did not know what to say. Scelero had truly known what she was all along, just as Ren thought?

"You didn't think he set you free simply because of you, did you?" The chancellor laughed. "Because he cared for one of his slaves enough to risk his own life?"

But that was exactly why Tori had thought Scelero rescued her. *That's why he came to see me in my cell, wasn't it? Why he hid my true nature during my years in his household? Why he chose me? Helped me escape?*

"You were nothing special to him, Astoria. Your blood was the key to a great new power, and he orchestrated your escape to prevent that power. Why do you think he let you bleed out in that cell for over a year?"

Tori hadn't let herself consider anything other than his care for her. *Did he choose me for that very reason? To be some sort of magical pawn?*

"The commander left you to die until he realized you were a threat.

But even in his rebellion, Scelero was weak, and he deserved the punishment he received."

Tori felt tears streaming down her cheeks, but she felt no sadness for Scelero, nor anger about the shattering of the image she had preserved of her kind master. She felt only enough to know that this dullness was not how she should be feeling, to know it was this place already having its effect on her—a feeling of nothingness that slowly seeped into her very being.

"What did you do to him?" said Tori.

"I brought him here, of course. And left him. Somewhere, Commander Scelero is wandering this abyss, desperately longing for a lost world from a nearly forgotten dream."

Tori shuddered at the horrible thought. And suddenly, she realized why the chancellor had brought her here. "You mean to leave me as well."

The chancellor did not answer immediately. He looked out at the great expanse before them, out to the edge of the world. Tori imagined herself trapped in this land of nothingness forever. But she did not feel the terror she knew she ought to feel.

Already, Tori felt different. It was as though she had stepped into a dimly lit room, and her eyes were slowly adjusting to the darkness. The grey world was growing less and less strange every moment she spent here. She wondered how long it would take for all this to feel like the real world—to forget how color brightened all things or how bitterness and passion burned inside her.

Perhaps it won't be so bad, Tori thought vaguely. *I won't feel pain or sorrow or regret again.* Perhaps nothingness was not the torment the chancellor described. *No! That's this place poisoning your mind.*

The chancellor touched her shoulder and he smiled, almost sadly. "I am afraid I will not be leaving you here, Astoria. That would be too great a mercy, and too great a risk. You've spent too much time in the Crooked Teeth. You don't know the problems you've caused since your escape. I made the mistake of letting you live once. But rumors have spread of your miraculous escape from my dungeons. Despite my victories in Morgath, the Council of Osha doubts my supremacy, thanks to you. Now, there are tales of a strange Witch Queen gaining followers in the Southern Isles. And with the slave uprisings across the empire... No, I won't make that mistake again."

"You won't kill me," said Tori straightforwardly. "You need my blood. That's why you brought me here."

"If only that were true, for your sake, Tori. It is true the harvest from your time in my dungeons has run dry. But I have another Regenero now. One who will be my queen, and whose devout love for her people will keep her in line, should she think of changing her allegiance."

"Vashti."

"I am afraid your usefulness has run its course, Gallows Girl. I will show the people of Osha, once and for all, what comes from hope in gods and Watchers. This time, it *will* be your body hanging from my citadel."

"What if I fly away?"

The chancellor laughed. "If you could use your powers in this place, you would have done so already. Look around you, Astoria. There is no magic in this world."

That's why my hand isn't healing. The skin of Tori's hand was raw and bubbling, making it look more like scales than skin, though the pain was fading along with all other feeling.

The chancellor took hold of her hand and led her along, down the hill, toward the horde of waiting Rulaqs.

"You are looking much better than Scelero did when I brought him here. Your body must already have been healing during the passage from the New World. But even if you wanted to resist, you will not."

"Why? What do I have to lose?"

"You won't resist because I hold the lives of all your friends in my hands. Mischa, Ren... even Darien."

Tori could not bear the thought of being responsible for the deaths of the other Watchers, nor for Darien's. Despite what the chancellor had turned Darien into, the thought of him being dead...

"Y-you wouldn't! He's your finest soldier! One of your Morphs."

"No soldier is too great to sacrifice. But since I am a gracious ruler, and because I despise the magical wastes of my ancestors, I will spare them all, Astoria. If you do not resist what is to come."

Tori did not answer. But she feared she had no true choice, and the chancellor had known it all along. She had no magic here. And even if she did, could she really risk the lives of everyone she cared about for one last attempt at resistance?

The chancellor led her across the valley, and she followed without protest.

They weaved between the massive Rulaqs outside the ruined city. Tori expected, at any moment, the beasts would notice, and one of the giant serpentine heads would come swooping down to devour them, and part of her wished it would happen. But the beasts were as innocuous as a herd of fawns that had lost their mothers, cowering in the tall grass at the edge of a meadow.

When they reached the immense archway of the necropolis, Tori noticed the film that spanned the space. It was like a thin wall of water stretched tight in the air. From here, she saw blurred resonances of color. And she understood why all the Rulaqs were staring at the gateway.

It was a door to the New World, and it was utterly beautiful. It filled her with a twinge of light and hope.

"People long for the Old World," said the chancellor, gesturing at the nothingness around them. "They pray to dead gods and place their hope in Watchers. Well, if the people want the Old World, I will give it to them. In all its glory. We'll begin with the rest of the Rulaqs. The time has come for monsters to reign over the Crooked Teeth once more."

The chancellor placed one of the glowing godstones in Tori's burned hand. She tensed, but the pain did not come. He kept the other in his own hand. "To open a gate this wide, it will take both of us. All of your blood I have left."

Tori could see the Watchtower beyond the gateway. Its mighty towers filled the sky. A world of refuge and hope for so many like her. *And now,* she realized with growing dread, *the chancellor will destroy that world.*

"Stretch out your hand," the chancellor instructed, pointing toward the water-like wall. "And be brave. This is going to hurt like nothing else in this world."

Tori steeled herself and obeyed. Her hand penetrated the passageway. It passed through easily. The film felt thick between her fingers, like the eggs she used to prepare in the kitchens at Scelero's estate. Her senses awakened, and she felt anger and terror once more.

And pain!

It shot through her anew, and again, she felt as though she were on fire. The chancellor stretched out his own hand, the watery passage vaporized, and Tori could clearly see the glorious harshness of the world beyond. The jagged black rock of the Teeth and the starkly contrasting snow of the valley. A cold wind swept through the passage, and the ground began to quake.

Tori stood fixed in place. The gateway between the worlds held her fast as the Rulaqs lumbered through the door she and the chancellor had opened. She stood, helpless, as the terrible creatures from the Old World gathered speed on the other side, life and ferocity returning to them for the first time in hundreds of years. Their massive necks swung like battering rams, and the outer walls of the Watchtower began to crumble. More Rulaqs poured through the gateway to join the fray. Dozens more waited, pawing the earth with intense anticipation.

But amidst the pain and the horror of standing between worlds, strength returned to Tori as well. Her senses were on fire, and a desperate idea formed in her mind. If the chancellor needed her to open this door, then she could stop this. She had to stop this. She could not stand by while her magic brought back this horror into the world. She could still save the others. The longer she stood in the doorway, the more her pain intensified, but the stronger her resolve became.

With one frantic burst of Conjuri energy, Tori freed her hand from the gateway, and she threw the godstone through the opening into the New World. The emerald gem landed in the snow with a rush of steam. Tori leapt through the opening between the worlds and collapsed in the snow. Pain and cold and guilt filled her with a fury no longer held back by any trace of the Old World. She had never felt such an overwhelming onslaught of feeling at once. She screamed as the blood tithe took its toll. Her vision blurred with tears.

Back in the Old World, the chancellor cried out in pain, crumpling to the ground, his hand still fixed to the gateway. The strange film began to close over the door.

Despite the pain, Tori felt relief. *I've done it.*

But to her horror, the door did not close instantaneously. The chancellor still had one stone, and the film descended slowly from the top of the archway.

The Rulaqs, realizing their chance at freedom was nearly lost, stampeded through the diminishing opening. One beast arched its necks with a roar of triumph as it passed through. The film brushed against both necks, severing them clean. The Rulaq's body crumpled beyond the door, its heads tumbling in the snow. This only intensified the horde's rage. The remaining monsters stormed through the gate, trampling their fallen comrade, lowering their heads to avoid decapitation.

Tori braced to be crushed to death, but none of the monstrous paws landed on her. Only a few more beasts passed through before the gate was rendered impassable for them. Several threw themselves desperately at the door and fell dead. In the New World, the beasts had worked themselves into a mad frenzy. Rulaqs roared and thundered across the valley, joining the others in their attack on the Watchtower.

Tori glanced back. The chancellor was still trapped. The Watchtower might fall, but he would at least be left behind in that hell world.

With a shriek, a shadow passed Tori.

It was Darien in his Morph form, Tori realized with dread. He flew low, snatching up Tori's godstone from the snow, and shot through the narrow opening. With the stones reunited, he managed to free the chancellor from the gateway. The door was nearly closed, the murderous film only feet from the ground.

Tori tried to get up, to stop them from crossing, somehow, but she was too spent from the trip between worlds. Her hand was searing with pain, and her head felt light. She crumpled in the snow, watching helplessly as the chancellor crawled back into the New World with the help of the boy she had once loved. The boy who had betrayed her. The chancellor collapsed safely on the other side.

The world became a mad blur. It rocked and swirled like a sick dream. Tori's mind was fading.

The last thing she saw, before she passed out from the pain, was the central spire of the Watchtower crashing down as the Rulaqs took back their realm.

CHAPTER THIRTY-THREE

When Tori woke, the pain from the godstones had subsided. Back in the New World, her body had healed as always. For a brief moment she basked in the absence of searing pain, but she soon jolted upright. *What happened to the others?*

She had seen the crumbling walls of the Watchtower. She knew the devastation the Rulaqs must have caused. But as far as she could tell, she was nowhere near the Watchtower. The place Tori woke in was dark and smelled musty, like air gone stale across centuries. Was this dark place the land of the dead?

The pain of the stones had been so severe, Tori had longed for death before everything had gone black. Tori tried to raise herself, but she was held back by a taut chain. Shackles were fixed at her wrists. Her hands had gone numb, though whether because of her wounds or from cold, she did not know. Her limbs were dreadfully weak, and she collapsed on the stone once more.

A flame pierced the darkness, appearing around a corner. Voices broke the silence. A torch entered the dank chamber, followed by a second. In the light, Tori could see milky wax coating the walls. *I'm not dead*, she thought. *I'm in a cave.*

As the intruders neared, Tori could make out the faces of Darien and a young soldier carrying a bucket and a length of tube. Elements that Tori knew all too well. She swelled with anger, reaching for her magic, but she felt only a dim sense. And then, it was gone altogether, as though it had slipped from her grasp.

"This her?" said the strange soldier eagerly as they approached.

"Yes, Jujen," said Darien. "This is the Gallows Girl."

At the sound of his voice, Tori tensed all over. *Why did he save the chancellor?*

"Ooh, rah!" said Jujen. "The most wanted criminal in all of Osha. Gods! But why's the chancellor keeping her alive? He wants her dead, don't he?"

"Course he wants her dead." A third voice. It was familiar, though Tori could not place it. "She's the bloody reason we're all down here. But you know the rumors spreading. The chancellor can't afford there ter be any doubt this time about her death. He's waiting for the right moment. Waiting till we get out o' these damned catacombs an' return ter Osha."

So that's where we are. The catacombs. But why?

"What are you doing here, Merri?" said Darien coolly. "You're to be standing watch in the main chamber."

"I know you don't yet trust me with her, Darien."

It pained Tori to hear the cook's voice. She was relieved Merri was alive. But was she as far gone as Darien?

"He's your bloody captain!" said Jujen. "You'll address him so."

"Let her speak, Jujen," said Darien.

"I've seen the way you measure me… Captain. Ever since we been in the North. Like you're worried I might be up ter something. I saw you gauging my reactions ter the destruction o' the Watcher stronghold. An' truth be told, I don't blame you. I'm here ter prove where my loyalties lie."

Tori had to fight to control her breathing, to keep listening in secret. They didn't seem to know she was awake.

"And how do you wish to prove your loyalty?" said Darien.

"Let me bleed her out, Captain," said Ol' Merri. "Let me harvest the Gallows Girl's blood."

"Bleed her out? That's my job!" complained Jujen.

"Shut up, Jujen!" snapped Darien. But his voice softened as he addressed Ol' Merri. "If all you want is to prove yourself, Merri, there is no need. I have no doubts of your loyalties."

Merri's voice lowered, the way it once had when she would talk of something dark and serious, like the Watchers and the old gods, back in the kitchens of Scelero's estate. "Ah, but there *is* need. I don't want ter prove nothing for *you*, Darien. I need ter prove it for myself."

Tori cleared her throat and opened her eyes wide. In the torchlight, she locked eyes with Darien and then Ol' Merri. Their faces were hardened and unreadable, but Tori made no attempt to hide her disgust.

"So, this is what it's come to, is it?" said Tori icily. "The greatest believer I ever knew, and the greatest rebel. And you both are just mindless followers now... You do whatever the chancellor says, no questions asked. No bloody thoughts in your heads at all."

"Now, child," said Merri, putting on the warm tone Tori had always known. "You've spent too much time with that loony Watcher captain, my dear."

"We didn't know anything back then," said Darien. "It was foolish talk."

"Foolish talk?" said Tori incredulously. "That was why you stood up to die the day of the Gallows?"

"Tori, you don't understand now," said Darien. "But you will."

"I doubt that," Tori said. "I'm a dead girl walking."

Darien met her gaze and then looked away. For a moment, Tori let herself believe there was some spark of the old Darien in those eyes. But she wished she hadn't thought it.

"You killed good soldiers," said Darien carefully. "Good men and women. Like me and Merri."

"What are you talking about?"

"When you tried to fight. When you tried to leave the chancellor in the Old World. It worked the Rulaqs into madness."

"They destroyed the Watchtower! That was the chancellor's plan all along."

"No!" Darien shot back. "You stirred them up. No one was supposed to die! But those monsters didn't stop at the Watchtower. They turned on us all, and killed *my* soldiers. That's why we're here in these damned catacombs. The Rulaqs are destroying the North, Tori. Because of you."

Tori could not believe what he was saying. These were not Darien's words. "How is it that *I* turned out to be the only one of us who kept their head?" said Tori.

The room was silent. If there was a time for them to show their true colors, surely it was now. They were in some cavern, all alone, except for Jujen.

One last time, Tori tried to reason with Darien and Merri, the slaves she'd known long ago, before they were turned to mindless soldiers. "One day, you'll end up useless to him too, you know. And then you'll be here like me, waiting to die. But we can get out of this! Set me free, and we can escape. We'll run away from the chancellor and Osha, and all of this madness. Whatever you've been forced to do in the Legions, you can still make it right."

Again, there was silence. Darien and Merri smiled. They were not smiles of hope, but of pity.

"Ha!" cried Jujen. "Listen to her. She's gone mad!"

Darien did not tell Jujen to shut up this time. He held Tori's gaze. His brown eyes had never seemed so empty before. Tori had never thought she would detest looking in Darien's eyes, but she did. She felt like she might be sick.

"Jujen," said Darien, "give Merri the harvesting tools. We have orders to attend to." The young soldier looked aggravated to be taken from the duty, but he did not protest again. "Merri, she's all yours."

Darien clapped Jujen on the shoulder and made to leave.

"For a year, I prayed I'd find you alive again," Tori shouted after him. Darien stopped and looked back. "Now… I wish I had never been gifted with magic. I wish I had stood back and let you die on that gallows."

Darien shook his head. "Darien did die on that gallows. And Tori must have died too. Because the Tori I knew never would have risked the lives of her friends for some damned fool act of rebellion. Watchers died in that attack too." And with that, he left.

Tori's eyes welled with tears as she watched him leave. *Watchers died? Oh gods! Who?* She prayed it was not Ren or Mischa or Dajha. A sick dread twisted in her gut.

Ol' Merri strode forward, and Tori met her with a hard glare. "I was a fool to ever believe the things you used to say," Tori said. "Your tales. The gods and their damned Watchers."

Merri looked away and began preparing the needle and tube that had been Tori's world just a few short months ago. Merri said nothing. She drew a cord tight around Tori's arm and held out the long needle.

"Do your worst, you old bitch," said Tori.

And Merri did. Once again, Tori's world became blood and pain and nothing else. As the blood drained from her, she looked straight in Merri's eyes and let her see the pain she was inflicting. But there was no remorse hidden there.

When it was finished, Merri jerked her to her feet. "Come along, Gallows Girl."

"Where?"

"To atone for the lives you took."

Tori had nearly forgotten the toll that bloodletting took on her body. She staggered along, Merri's grip firm on her wrist, or else she would have likely fallen. They passed through a series of passages and emerged in an expansive chamber brimming with soldiers and Morphs. At the center of the room, the Watchers were gathered in a cluster. All were in chains, kneeling. The chancellor stood at the center of the room. Vashti stood at his side, looking angrier than ever. Cyrus Maro looked terrible. His eyes were dark and his skin was deathly pale.

Atone for the lives I took. Tori feared the worst as she took in the sight of the Shadow Watch in chains. She had not forgotten the chancellor's deal in the Old World. She had broken it, and she realized how foolish that last desperate act had been. She had risked the lives of her friends, and not just from the Rulaqs.

"You look worse than me," said Cyrus Maro, his eyes alighting with a dark fire as they settled on her.

Tori did not speak. Merri led her forward and shoved her to her knees before the chancellor. Tori was relieved to see Ren and Mischa and Dajha and many of the others. But her stomach churned at the faces that were missing. She caught Mischa's gaze. "W-where's Zaya?"

Tears streaked Mischa's cheeks. Blood still trickled from the crook of her arm where the needle had stolen her magic. She could barely manage to shake her head before she began sobbing.

"No, no," Tori murmured.

"Your friend is dead," said the chancellor, leaning on a shoddy cane made from a tent pole. "Along with three other Watchers. To say nothing of the dozens of loyal Shadows we lost. All thanks to the Gallows Girl."

Tori felt the intensity of the Watchers' eyes as they looked to her. She shook her head. "You attacked us! This was *your* doing." She looked around the room. There was hate and sorrow and confusion in their eyes, but they did not believe her. "Please, don't listen to his lies!"

But even she did not fully believe the words. Tori choked back tears. Zaya had been one of the kindest people she'd ever known. And she was dead.

"That is where you are wrong, Astoria. I never wished to kill your Watcher friends."

The passage between worlds had taken a harsh toll. The chancellor's voice was more subdued than ever, barely more than a whisper. But somehow, it managed to be even more terrifying. Cyrus Maro looked out at the kneeling Watchers, and Tori realized why they were all gathered here.

This was an execution. Because of her last desperate act of rebellion.

"You were my enemies," said the chancellor. "You plotted against my throne. You cannot fault me for attacking your Watchtower. But I knew that many of you were led astray by the charisma of manipulative leaders. So, I made a deal with your Gallows Girl. If she came quietly, I promised to spare you all. But Tori never cared for any of you. Despite my act of grace, she just *had* to attempt one last act of resistance. An act that killed Watchers and Shadows alike. And now, someone must pay for the lives of our fallen comrades."

The chamber thundered with the cheers of the Shadows and Morphs. The crowd parted, and Darien came forward, shoving Ren Andovier to the center of the chamber. Tori's heart collapsed inside her chest.

"No! Please! Not him! Kill me."

The chancellor's laugh was like ice. "That was always going to happen, Astoria. And when we reach Osha, you *will* die. In front of all the empire. But for now, there must be blood for blood."

The soldiers chanted, "Blood for blood! Blood for blood!"

Ren's head rose weakly, and he met Tori's gaze.

"I'm so sorry," Tori whispered between sobs. All strength had left her. She slumped forward and only Merri's grip could hold her up.

Ren shook his head. "You did good. I would have done the same."

The room went silent. "So say the leaders of your worthless rebellion," the chancellor said, gesturing to the Watchers. "You hear how much they care for your lives. They sound like Morgathian radicals, willing to sacrifice their women and children for one last chance at rebellion."

No Watchers spoke, but Tori knew what they were thinking. She was thinking it too. Tori had risked their lives for nothing. And now, Ren was going to die because of her.

"Captain Redvar, my saber," said the chancellor.

"Milord," Darien protested as the chancellor staggered forward to take his blade. "You're still recovering. Let me do it."

"I uphold my own justice, Captain."

The chancellor raised the saber to his shoulder. A pair of Morphs held Ren by the shoulders so his head drooped in front of him.

"Consider this the dying wish of your Gallows Girl." Cyrus Maro raised the blade above his head, his hands shaking.

Merri held Tori tight. Her entire body felt like it had been filled with lead. It was all she could do not to look away. She held Ren's gaze. She owed him that much. His eyes were beautiful sapphires, glistening in the torchlight. Tori's heart wrung inside her chest. *Oh gods! No, no, no!*

The blade came down.

One of the Watchers shrieked.

But Ren's head did not sever from his neck.

The blade struck the stony ground in front of the Watcher captain with a sharp clang. The chancellor let the blade slip from his fingers, and it clattered on the ground. *Did he miss? Is he too weak to wield the saber?*

The room was completely silent. No soldier stepped up to finish the deed.

All of the Watchers' eyes were on the chancellor, waiting to see what would happen next.

Vashti Burodai stepped forward and turned to face the Watchers she had betrayed. "Our captain and his Gallows Girl would sacrifice your lives for the sake of their radical *shenzah*. Ren had a feud with the chancellor long before he recruited us, and he formed the Shadow Watch because he wanted to use us to seek his revenge. And he set the chancellor up as our common enemy. The enemy of our Watcher kind. But *this* chancellor is not our enemy. He never wished to take our lives. He came to peacefully quell our resistance."

Vashti raised her hands. It made Tori sick to hear her speak. "In exchange for peace, he has offered me freedom and the union between my people and Osha. But that offer is not just for me."

The chancellor smiled and took Vashti's hand, gently. "I offer you all the chance to use your gifts to serve the empire. The time has come to bring magic back to the North. If you join me, you will be free. Not to run and hide, as in the days of my father, and not to fight and die for a hopeless cause, as your former leaders would have you. You will be free to discover your gifts and serve the people of the New World. The time has come for magic to return to the world, and all of you can be part of that future."

The chamber was silent at first.

Ren was the first to speak. "Don't listen to his lies. It's all a—"

Darien silenced him with his fist. "The chancellor spared your life. And this is the gratitude you show?"

"It's all right," said the chancellor. "He'll come around. As for the rest of you…"

Dajha glanced at Tori, then shook his head. He gestured at the saber lying in front of Ren. "If this is justice in the empire, I reckon Ren's been feedin' us *shenzah* all along. I never signed up to be a barterin' chip in some noble's blood feud. I signed up to learn magic. And I reckon I can do that just as well in Osha as anywhere."

Many of the others nodded their heads in agreement.

"I'll serve," said Dajha. He stood to his feet, and Vashti helped him up.

The chancellor patted him on the back. "You've chosen well, son."

The young Fieri boy, Jann, was the next to rise. And then, Vashti's friend, Calla, rose to her feet.

In the end, there were only a few who resisted—Sahra, Vonn, Mischa, and Ren chief among them. In a dark way, Tori wished they all had joined the others. There was no future left for the Watchers but death or betrayal.

CHAPTER THIRTY-FOUR

Tori's blood was drained daily, just enough to keep her body weak and her magic suppressed, and she was not alone in this daily agony. All the Watchers were drained of their strength each night, and in the morning, they were herded through the catacombs beneath the Crooked Teeth, dull aches filling their bones with each jarring step. Those who pledged their allegiance to the chancellor, however, received kinder treatment. They got food and water rations and slept on mats in the main chamber. If they complied until they reached the citadel, then they would go free. Tori and the other dissenters were treated like cattle. Their bloodletting was arduous. They were chained in dark chambers and watched at all times. The Legions and the Morphs surrounded them, kept them apart, kept them from conspiring, or even sharing in their hellish march.

The system of caverns was an immense labyrinth. Tori's mum had told stories of the tunnels beneath the world. It was said they were formed by the Gurlag, a giant worm-like monster of the Old World. Even in her youth, Tori had thought it an outlandish myth. Tori wondered, now, if it was real, if the Gurlag was in the chancellor's abyss somewhere, along with all the other legends of the Old World.

Probably a world of sinking sand, where it could dig no tunnels, she thought.

Every few leagues or so, the catacombs reached an expansive chamber, where the large company made camp. The races of the Old World were said to have used the caves to hide from Rulaqs and other beasts. And now in the New World, *they* had been forced to do the same.

At first, Tori wondered why the chancellor had not used the godstones to escape the catacombs, but the disgruntled murmurs of the soldiers answered her question soon enough. The chancellor was still weak from the unleashing of the Rulaqs, and he had drained his store of the Gallows Girl's blood. And worse, according to the soldiers, the chancellor's dark witch, Medea, had been lost in the madness. And so they were all cursed to wander this underworld maze until they reached the surface.

It was some time before Tori pieced together who else had died in the Rulaq attack—Joran, the Regenero from the Ytalan fights, a Medici named Gany, and a Conjuri named Lera. Every time Tori saw any of the turned Watchers, she was overwhelmed by guilt. Her resistance had been futile; perhaps it had always been so, ever since the day of the Gallows. And if she had complied, the others would be alive. Zaya would be alive. Only once, she caught Mischa's gaze during the march, and her best friend looked away, holding back tears. Tori wished Mischa would join the chancellor like the others. At least, then, she would survive.

After the chancellor extended mercy to the Watchers, Tori noticed a growing uneasiness among the soldiers, even in the apparent safety of the catacombs. The grumblings grew worse by the day. Many felt that the chancellor should have killed Ren. Others were unhappy that their rations were being shared with the turned Watchers. A fight broke out on the third night underground over food portions. A large brute stabbed a younger, scrawnier Shadow for his helping. Darien broke up the fight himself, disarming the brute with a swift flash of his saber. The young soldier was not mortally wounded, but Tori feared it was a sign of worse things to come if they spent much longer underground.

According to lore, the cannibalistic Nosferati inhabited the catacombs. As the soldiers murmured during the marches, Tori found herself remembering the old terror stories that her mother had told around fires on the Steppe. At the climax of the stories—the point when a Nosferati always came to the surface in the night and kidnapped little boys and girls—one of the older children would sneak up and grab the littles from behind. Tori could still remember the thrill, the squeals, and the relieved laughter that had always followed. Because, of course, monsters weren't real. They were only stories.

Tori longed for those innocent days again, before the betrayal of her mother, before life as a Fringe rat and a slave. Before the citadel and the Watchtower. Before Tori had discovered that if some tales were true, then they *all* must be. *There is no magic without monsters.*

Tori saw little of the chancellor and his new queen-to-be during the march. They kept to the front of the company, and the chancellor and his personal guards did not camp in the same chamber as the soldiers and the Watcher prisoners. Tori saw much of Ren and Mischa and the other Watchers who had refused to turn. But always from a distance. The more their blood was drawn and the longer they were herded along, the weaker they became. It was evident in the way they held themselves, heads down, backs hunched, feet shuffling. They looked like poor abused animals resigned to their fate, not Watcher rebels—even Ren had visibly given up.

On the fourth day underground, Tori was kept at the rear of the company, escorted by Darien's companion, Valeria. Tori had noticed the way the female Morph regarded Darien—whether it was affection or comradely devotion, she did not know. But Tori despised the Morph soldier with silver hair.

For the past few days, Darien and Merri had been close by, but they did not regard Tori, except when Merri would come to drain her blood each evening. And each evening, it was the same cold look in her eyes. Darien had not even bothered to look her way since the first night.

Tori often wondered when it had happened. When Darien had turned from rebel slave to mindless follower. *Is it all some dark magic that's taken over his mind?*

But Darien did not seem like he was under a spell. No, Tori imagined it happened when Darien began feeling like he belonged with the

Legions more than anywhere else. And she had the suspicion that Valeria had something to do with that sense of belonging, for Tori had noted the way he looked to *her* as well. She suspected Valeria had become to Darien the Soldier what Tori had been to Darien the Slave —a survival companion.

Valeria kept silent the entire march, occasionally offering a good shove when Tori slowed. But as they reached a small chamber with a pool of water, the soldiers rushed forward to drink, and Valeria held her back.

"He's still in there," Valeria whispered when there was a distance between them and the soldiers clambering for fresh water.

"What?" Tori was about to turn and face her, but Valeria held her fast by her shackles.

"Don't look at me. Just listen. Darien is not much like the boy he was when you last knew him, Gallows Girl. But he's not all gone."

"Why are you telling me this?"

"So you don't lose hope." Valeria paused for a moment. "Not all Shadows are as dark as they seem. Some are still human deep down. And some are… biding their time."

With that, Valeria shoved her, and Tori collapsed to the ground, aches shooting through the hollows of her bones. "Quit your bitching! You don't need a drink till we make camp, like all the other prisoners!" Valeria kicked Tori in the side for good measure.

Valeria did not say anything more the rest of the march. When evening came, the chancellor and his entourage marched on to camp in an adjoining chamber, and the Legions began to pitch tents in a large domed space. If Tori believed the murmurs among the soldiers, this would be their last night in the catacombs. They were near the surface. Which meant Tori was drawing nearer to death with each step. Once they reached Maro'El, she would be executed for all the world to see.

Tori had come to accept this reality. It was like the dull aches that wracked her body as she walked—something she could not change. The chancellor had forced them all into a corner, and there could be no good outcome.

Tori pondered what Valeria said all day, but no matter how much her heart longed for it to be true, she kept telling herself it was a cruel Morph trick. Why would a Morph want to keep her hopes up?

But still the idea teased her. Could it be that Darien was not as far gone as he seemed? Tori kept telling herself it was foolishness, but she could not stop herself from hoping. It was all she had left.

———

TIME MOVED SLOWLY THAT NIGHT. ANTICIPATION HUNG HEAVY IN the air. The Legions were restless, knowing the world above was only a short distance away, and this restlessness was turning them ruthless. Tori shuddered as she watched Sahra be dragged out of the chamber after her blood was drained. Sahra did not have strength to fight. Vonn barked and bellowed at the offending Shadow, only to be knocked to the hard stone by another soldier. Blood poured from his mouth, but he did not stop screaming until a Shadow rendered him unconscious with a blow to the head.

Tori watched, helpless, like all the other Watchers. Her body tensed. She wanted to make it stop, but knew no one could. They were chained and weak. Tori closed her mind to the scene. The sadness was too much to bear.

The Legions were famously feared for their vicious treatment of war prisoners. The raping and ruthless destruction of defeated cities was what made the Legions so notorious in the New World. The Watchers were the latest defeated army, and they would be treated no differently. All Tori could do was listen helplessly to Sahra's muffled cries.

But a moment later, Valeria emerged with Sahra in tow, her saber drawn, traces of blood specking it. The offending Shadow hobbled after, cradling his bleeding arm. A spark of hope surged in Tori once more. *Valeria is saving Sahra?*

"These prisoners are the chancellor's prized possessions! You will not treat them like some Morgathian rat!" Valeria raised her blade in the air. "The next Shadow I catch taking prisoners to the back caverns, I'll run through!"

But it did not end that easily. The Shadows were restless and growing more so by the moment. One Shadow overturned a bucket of Watcher blood, splattering it across the cavern floor. "What's it matter, ey? We're already takin' their blood, what's it hurt to take a bit more?"

This sentiment was chorused by a few others. The room quickly turned into chaos. Soldiers shoved one another, and a second priceless bucket of Watcher blood was overturned.

Darien transformed to his Morph form and roared. The sight of his beastly shape sent shivers through Tori. "That blood is worth more than your very lives!"

Valeria morphed and flew to his side, along with a few others. But it was little use. The tension had reached a point of no return.

In the chaos, Tori went unnoticed, chained at the edge of the room. Unnoticed by all but one.

A hand came from behind, covering her mouth before she had time to make a sound. And then, she was being dragged backwards into a side corridor. Before the dark enveloped her, she caught a glimpse of her attacker's face, and it filled her with fear. It was Jujen, the soldier who had wanted to harvest her blood.

The Shadow shoved her up against a wet cave wall in an abandoned chamber. "The Gallows Girl," he hissed. "I heard a rumor you and the captain tossed around back when you were slaves. But seeing as he's moved on, well, I reckon it's equal shares now, en't it?"

Jujen spun her around to face him, throwing her head back hard against the stone, his hands tearing at her cloak and thick woolen shirt. Dazed by the blow to her head and weakened from the march, Tori could hardly resist. She let out a weak cry, only to be stifled by another blow against the cave wall. She squirmed with what little strength remained, but Jujen was too strong. Her mind went hazy, drifting away from reality, and Tori did not try to come back. She could not fight him, and she did not want to remember what was to come.

Jujen pinned down her arms and wedged his body against her. "Seeing as the chancellor wants you dead, I reckon there's no need to worry about—"

"Jujen!"

The boy's hands fell away from Tori's body at the sudden voice from the darkness. A torch lit up the chamber. It was Ol' Merri. "What're you doing, comrade?" Her voice was soft, but commanding.

Jujen spluttered at first. "I, er, just… It's none of your business, cook!" he snapped. "I came back to drain her blood." His fists were clenched. He reached for his belt.

"Ah," said Merri. "No need ter be defensive, comrade, if you're just bleeding out the prisoner, is there?"

"I, er… I en't defensive!"

"You're a fine soldier, Jujen," said Merri carefully. "But I think you may've forgotten something important." She held up a bucket and tube.

"Oh gods, er—how foolish of me." He reached for the elements, but Merri pulled them back. Jujen's eyes were alight.

"Don't be foolish, son. Fools in this world wind up dead, you know."

"A-are you threatening me?" Jujen said tremulously, hand still hovering near the blade at his belt.

"Why don't you let me deal with the Gallows Girl's blood, as our captain commanded me, an' you head on back ter the main chamber? I reckon the captain could use your help calming down the troops an' their… lust." She held his dark gaze, and finally, he stood down.

Without another word, Jujen darted away into the dark. Tori breathed with relief.

Merri regarded her with cool eyes, and Tori steeled herself for the bloodletting that was to come. She wished Merri would drain all her blood and be done with it. Be done with the chancellor, this march, this unrelenting world.

But the prick of the needle did not come. Merri dropped the bucket on the floor. The clatter echoed off the walls.

"For someone who's been through a dozen hells, you're the most resilient girl I've ever known," said Merri. Her voice was barely a whisper, and it cracked as she spoke.

"W-what?" Tori managed.

Merri smiled. Her face seemed to lighten the room, brighter than any torch. It was the warm smile Tori had known from Scelero's estate. "You survived, Tori. You kept your head through more suffering than any girl should endure. But you're still here. I'm so proud o' you, child."

Suddenly, Tori was wrapped in Merri's arms. And Tori cried desperate tears of relief, soaking Merri's Legion uniform. "Thank the gods," Tori muttered between sobs, her fingers clutching the middle-aged cook as though this reality would disappear if she let go.

Merri brushed Tori's dark, matted hair out of her face. She smiled as tears streamed down her cheeks. "Yes, child, thank the gods."

There was movement in the dark.

Tori pulled away quickly. She would not reveal Merri's betrayal to her comrades, if she could help it.

A face came into the light. But it was not that of a soldier or Morph.

It was Mischa. The small Melanesian girl was gaunt and staggered as she walked, but there was a glimmer in her eyes. "That Morph, Valeria, she was draining my blood when that soldier came back with Sahra. When Valeria dragged him off, sh-she let me go... and then Merri found me."

Merri nodded, her face glowing in the torchlight. "All Shadows are not as dark as they seem." She echoed the very words Valeria had spoken to Tori only hours before. *Some are biding their time... Valeria and Merri were working together?*

Mischa pulled Tori into a tight embrace. Tori had never been so relieved to feel the warmth of a friend. They were alive. They were free.

"What about the others?" said Tori. *Vonn and Sahra and Ren... they're all back in chains.*

Merri pulled them apart, her hands grasping their shoulders. "There's no time, I'm afraid. Come, girls, we must be swift. It is time for the Gallows Girl an' her comrade ter run far away from this gods-forsaken madness."

PART TWELVE
NIGHT OF BLOOD & TEETH

Beware the dark, little children,
With sweet delight, it lures you in.
In dark of night, it lies and waits
For boys and girls to wander late.

Beware the dark, little children,
With sweet delight it lures you in.
Don't go out to tempting night.
It searches there for flesh to bite.

Beware the dark, little children,
With sweet delight, it lures you in.
Do not tarry, and never stray.
It waits beyond for little prey.

—a children's song of the North

CHAPTER THIRTY-FIVE

The chamber was chaos, and sanity hung at the edge of a great precipice. The Legions were losing their minds in bloodlust and restlessness, and if Darien let them have anything now, it would all be over.

Gerdy was the soldier who had tossed up the bucket of Watcher blood after Valeria refused the Legions their spoils. Darien had trained with Gerdy in the Shadow Camps. He was a hothead, but he was a loyal comrade.

He was also inciting this riot, and Darien had to assert his dominance once and for all. Darien did not like it, but he knew there was no other choice. When he was named captain, the Morphs embraced him. If the chancellor had chosen Darien to lead this mission, then they trusted he must be worthy. But when Darien had been put in command over his old regiment for the infiltration of the Watchtower, there was some resistance from his old comrades.

Jujen tried to hide it, but Darien could tell that even his young Faerish friend resented his sudden rise in the ranks. They had been comrades—equals. They had sparred at the Shadow Camps. Jujen had helped Darien become a decent marksman. They had been bunkmates for over a year, and now, suddenly, Darien was a Morph commanding them all.

That was what this riot was truly about. The Legions were testing him, and Darien could not afford to fail this test. They would be marching out of these catacombs in the morning, and the chancellor would parade the Watchers, and most importantly, the Gallows Girl, before the people of Osha. The turned Watchers would pledge themselves to the empire, and the world would be changed. But not if the Shadows descended into madness before they reached the surface.

The chancellor stood at the edge of the chamber, and Darien felt his eyes, as though they were spyglasses, fixed only on him. This was a test of his leadership, and the chancellor was watching to see what he would do, to see if he had made the right choice.

Darien could not let his master down. In his Morph form, Darien took flight, grateful for the vastness of the domed chamber. He landed upon Gerdy, talons at the boy's throat.

It was over in an instant. Gerdy bled out from the gash in his neck, and the chamber went silent.

Darien morphed back to his human form and cradled the boy in his arms, holding him until the last breath. It pained him to feel the boy's warm life draining between his fingers, but if he had learned anything from the chancellor, it was that sacrifices were sometimes necessary for the greater good.

Every soldier and Morph was silent, waiting to see what the captain would do next. When Gerdy had gone still with death, Darien stood, the blood thick on his hands and uniform.

"This is a mission unlike any other." Darien addressed his soldiers coldly, with the confidence of a king whose word was law. "We will not conduct ourselves as we have in other missions. The fate of the empire is in our hands, comrades. I will *not* allow any one of you to put that empire in jeopardy! You will act like the servants you are, and if anyone else breaches command again, you will *wish* you would have been devoured by Rulaqs!"

Jujen was the first to stand at attention. Darien hadn't noticed him during the uprising, but he was grateful he was here now. Everyone in the regiment revered Jujen, and if he submitted, the others would follow. Jujen saluted him. "Aye, sir! You are our chancellor's chosen leader, and we will do as you command!"

Rikken was the next to recite the mantra. And the other Shadows soon followed, saluting and declaring their loyalty to the chancellor's chosen captain.

Darien breathed a sigh of relief. The chancellor caught his eye and nodded his approval. Darien had passed the test.

While the soldiers dispersed and returned to making camp, Valeria came to his side, sheathing her saber. "You did well killing Gerdy, Captain. It was a necessary sacrifice."

He should have said, *Of course! I know what I'm doing. I am your captain, as well.* But truth be told, he needed Valeria Sardona's affirmation to ward off the guilt and insecurity that had plagued him since he'd been made captain. What was it the chancellor saw in him?

He and Valeria had been through so much together, and if there was one person who could make him feel that he had what it would take to get the Watchers to Osha, it was Valeria.

"Thank you, comrade," he said with a nod. The room filled with the smell of porridge as supper was served. But both of them stood back and watched their old regiment go about their nightly routine. The chancellor withdrew to his own chamber, walking slowly and with a slight stagger.

Darien had never seen Cyrus Maro so weak, and it worried him. The chancellor had always seemed so… in control. But he was clearly shaken after the events of the Watchtower. Darien knew the passage between the worlds had taken its toll on him, and Medea's absence surely plagued him. The witch had always unnerved Darien, but he knew she was important to the chancellor's plans, and he feared for her life and for the Shadows who had been lost in their mad flight from the Rulaqs.

But in addition to all this, Darien feared there was more to the chancellor's weakened state. They had defeated the Watchers, and yet Darien felt as though they had been conquered themselves. Monsters had returned to the world, and he feared they never should have been brought back. Darien considered talking his fears over with Valeria, but he thought better of it. It would not do to question the chancellor in front of a subordinate.

"It's strange to watch from the outside now," Valeria said. "To be... something else."

Darien should have said, *Nothing feels strange. We are meant to be what we are.* But instead, he simply nodded.

Valeria grimaced and glanced about the chamber. "One more night, and we'll be rid of this gods-forsaken place."

One more night, and they would be back in Osha. The chancellor would soon be wed to the Watcher princess of the Yan Avii. The Watchers would no longer be a secret, nor a threat. They would not be Watchers to the New World. As the chancellor had told him, the Watchers were a myth born from a lack of understanding of the magic in the world.

Magical beings would be known as the chancellor's servants, just like the Morphs. The Watchers who wished to live would join the Morphs to form a new army—the Sky Guard—or they would join the fate of the Gallows Girl.

Tori...

Darien tried to push the thought aside, but it was difficult. As much as he hated to admit it, he felt no pleasure seeing his old friend suffer. He did not let it show; he knew it was necessary, but—

Valeria squeezed his wrist subtly as she walked away to set up her own tent. Again, he was filled with reassurance that he had what it took to lead. Darien surveyed his soldiers for a while longer, but his eyes wandered back to Valeria. It was nights like these he longed to be closer to her. Of course, it was improper for comrades to think of one another in such a fashion, and for some time, he had managed to keep the thoughts at bay. But lately, the notions had been taking him off guard.

Another thought crept up: *What of Tori?*

Gods, what of her? She was a threat to the empire. And besides, they had never been anything but friends. Very close friends, sure, but... He thought back to their last night together. When she'd kissed his cheek and they had fallen asleep together in Scelero's stables and his skin had felt like it was on fire.

Gods! Where is *Tori, anyway?*

Throughout the march, Darien had kept his distance, but she had always been under his attentive watch. In the chaos of the Legion uprising, he had gotten distracted. Now, he realized she was not chained with the other Watchers. And she was not the only person who was not where they should be.

Ol' Merri! A sick feeling rose up from his gut. Surely Merri was not stupid enough to—

Darien was about to rush to the back reaches of the caverns to find Merri, when a shrill scream filled the chamber. It was desperate and riddled Darien's body with violent chills. The Legions froze where they stood, tent stakes and cookery still in their hands.

There was a second scream.

Someone appeared at the entrance to the chamber. It was Hollen, who had been one of those chosen for the first watch. Hollen tripped and fell to the ground.

"We're under attack!"

Hollen clambered to his feet, his face distorted with fear. The front of his breeches was soaked through. His eyes were wild, skittering about the room like a madman. Darien had never seen a soldier look more terrified in his life.

"Run! Run!" Hollen shrieked.

A creature leapt into the chamber, as though launched from a cannon in the darkness. The thing was deathly pale, its body little more than a skeleton with skin draped loose over its bones like burial cloths. It reminded Darien of the children from the Fringes—their corpses. But this creature was no starving Fringe rat that could barely raise its head. This creature was strong and fierce, and though it looked like death, it was very much alive. It leapt with unconscionable force, crossing a span of fifteen feet from a crouch. It landed upon Hollen's back.

Before Hollen had time to emit a dying shriek, his head had been wrenched free of his shoulders. The creature tossed the head into the middle of the room, and took a ravenous bite from the expanse left behind.

The creature looked up, blood dripping from its lips, and smiled, then returned to devouring Hollen's body.

A second creature entered, and the chamber turned into chaos—terrified soldiers stumbled and panicked and shrieked like village children during a raid.

A third creature entered.

Darien had never thought the legends true. They were ghost stories meant to keep children from wandering too far from their villages. But there could be no denying what these horrid creatures were.

"Nosferati!" cried a soldier, unfortunate enough to have made camp near the chamber entrance. In a moment, he was a carcass, splayed open. More and more creatures entered and swarmed like wolves upon him.

CHAPTER THIRTY-SIX

The shrieks and blood of soldiers filled the air. Muskets fired madly, but lead seemed to have little effect on the Nosferati pouring into the domed chamber. Darien drew his saber, not a moment too soon, decapitating one of the creatures as it leapt at his head.

The attack came in waves. During the first wave, the entire force of at least fifty creatures attacked and devoured the Legion soldiers. But their mad hunger was a blessing in a way, for it gave those who survived time to retreat and form a defense before the second wave.

Once their hunger was sated, the creatures picked their way through the ranks with methodical precision. They worked together, formed diversions. What little strands of humanity might remain of the beasts, their intelligence seemed fully intact. They did not decapitate and feast any longer. They wasted no time, cutting throats with razor claws and taking bites out of jugulars. The more the Nosferati slaughtered, the more creatures there were leaping and tearing apart the Legion ranks. Darien realized the Nosferati were multiplying when he saw Rikken's corpse rise, his skin turned the grey of his Legion uniform. The horde grew larger and larger as the Legion forces dwindled.

During the first wave of the attack, the Morphs managed to move the Watchers to the chancellor's corridor, and the chancellor's armies bravely fended the creatures off. But the catacombs formed a winding labyrinth. All passages might connect somewhere in the dark. Any moment, the creatures might appear from behind, and they would all become grey cannibals.

Darien slew another creature, fighting to hold his balance as he maneuvered over a floor of bodies. Another comrade rose from the dead a short distance away.

Gods, it's Jujen!

Jujen's skin was the color of ash and his eyes were like little holes of night. He leapt with sudden, unfathomable strength, straight at Darien.

Darien hesitated, only for a fraction of a moment, but it was enough. Jujen landed upon him, teeth bared. Darien lost his grip on his saber, and he and Jujen fell, rolling upon the ground. Darien twisted away and managed to land a kick that sent the creature flying back.

Jujen leapt again with renewed rage—

Darien reached for his belt—

His dagger met its mark at the nape of Jujen's neck. Darien fought back tears as he shoved the boy's fully dead body away. He could barely see through the smoke of frantic musket-fire. His ears rang and his head throbbed.

A hand grabbed him from behind. He was about to thrust with his dagger, when he heard Valeria's voice.

"Thank the gods!" she cried, holding out his dropped saber to him.

Without another word, the two formed up, back-to-back, the way they had back at Goran'El, and swung their blades in tandem, taking down one, two, three of the nightmare creatures.

The Nosferati began to tear through the ranks. Several bounded through the entrance to the chancellor's passage.

"The chancellor!" Darien cried.

Together, Darien and Valeria morphed and took to the air, soaring past their comrades. They landed beyond and made for the adjoining passage where the chancellor had made camp. At least three Nosferati had come down this corridor, and Darien prayed the chancellor was already gone, that his master had heard the deathly cries and disappeared with his godstones.

But the chancellor did not flee.

Three of his royal guard lay dead. The chancellor, in his Morph form, loomed over the severed body of one of the Nosferati. Vashti knelt on the ground beside another creature. The tents were a shredded mess. Darien sprinted to his master. The chancellor was bleeding from a wound in his shoulder and shaking.

"Were you bitten?" Darien asked.

"No," said the chancellor. It was the first time Darien had ever seen his master show such visible fear. "J-just a rock. I fell."

"You must flee, milord!" cried Valeria, who helped the chancellor's new queen to her feet. Vashti Burodai was shaken, but alive, a bloodied blade still clutched in her hand.

"Like hell, I must!" said the chancellor.

"Please!" said Darien. "Use your stones. I will get the Watchers out."

The chancellor pulled the stones out of his cloak, eyeing them warily. Darien knew he feared to use them again. "No, I will not abandon—"

"As your chosen captain," Darien interrupted, "I will *not* risk your life and the fate of Osha! You are too valuable. You must use the stones, milord!" Darien could not believe he was defying his master. Momentarily, he worried he had signed his own death sentence.

But the chancellor nodded to him, clasping his fingers around the stones. "I see I chose my captain wisely."

Another creature came bounding down the passage from the main chamber. Darien surged forward and met it, dodging its attack and severing its head in one fluid stroke.

"Go, milord! Now!"

The chancellor took hold of Vashti's hand, and the stones glowed brightly. He grimaced, but his resolve held strong. "Darien," he said. "You must get the Gallows Girl to Osha!"

"I will, milord!"

"The fate of the New World rests upon you, Captain!"

Mists swirled around the chancellor and his queen-to-be, and in a moment, it was only Darien and Valeria in the chamber.

"What do we do?"

"We've only one chance," he said.

Darien rushed over to the mess of tents and rummaged around frantically. It took longer than he hoped to find the explosives. From within the guard tent, Darien heaved up a sack. It was one of the Morgathian firebombs from Goran'El. "We get the Watchers! Then we blow the mountain down behind us!"

They had brought two bombs, leftover after the defeat of the Morgathian rebellion. They had been intended for the destruction of the Watchtower, but had proved unnecessary. However, there was only one left in the tent. Darien tried not to let his terror show, wondering where the other bomb had gone. He could only hope it was hidden somewhere beneath the shredded canvas.

Darien and Valeria rushed back through the winding passages, back toward the main chamber. At the entrance, Commander Zamel had formed the Legions into three lines, bayonets jutting out like spears. As men in the front line were taken down, men in the second line rushed in to take their place, and those from the third line filled in behind them. The Morphs were wreaking as much destruction as they could in the domed chamber, but many of them had fallen.

Behind the wall of Legions, half a dozen Morphs stood guard over thirty Watchers. Several had been lost in the first wave. There were only a few in chains. Darien scanned their faces, but he already knew what he would find. Tori was not among them.

He turned to Valeria. "You have to lead them out!"

"What about you?"

"I've got to find the Gallows Girl."

They locked eyes for a brief moment. She squeezed his hand. "Make it out alive, Redvar."

Darien could not speak. He squeezed her hand back and left. He found Zamel and shouted amidst the madness.

"Hold them off a few more minutes!" Darien said, holding up the firebomb. "Then fall back, and we'll blow them all to the Abyss!"

Darien did not wait for an answer. He left the bomb with Zamel, transformed to his Morph form, and took flight, soaring over the domed chamber, where only an hour before they had been making camp like any other night.

There were four entrances into the chamber. Most of the Nosferati had poured through the same entrance. The creatures that had come this way had come later in the battle, and Darien thought he knew why. It was only a guess, but it was his only shot. It was the chamber farthest away from the soldier uprising before the Nosferati attacked. If Merri had wanted to try to get the Gallows Girl out, that would have been her window of opportunity.

Darien flew through the entrance and morphed back to his human form, landing in a sprint. He raced down the corridor, counting the time before the firebomb would blow.

His instinct proved true. There was a reason the Nosferati had come back from this cavern. A short distance back, Darien reached a dead end. Rubble filled the passage. There was no way past. During the chaos, he had not even felt the explosion. Merri had blown up the cave with the second firebomb.

A single Nosferati knelt at the edge of the rubble. Darien held his saber out before him. The creature's eyes glowed. Its skin was dead, but to his amazement, Darien recognized the face.

"Commander Scelero?"

The creature rose at the name and looked at him strangely. And then it shot to its feet. Darien dropped to the ground, reaching out with his saber, but the creature that had once been Commander Scelero leapt over him and disappeared down the passage.

Darien was about to leave, but he saw an arm protruding at the edge of the rubble, where Scelero had been kneeling. He rushed over, pulling away debris with mad determination.

Ol' Merri lay buried beneath the crumbled cavern. As Darien heaved the rocks from her head, she stirred, moaning terribly. Darien forgot his anger for her treachery. He forgot his rank, and even the chancellor. He took hold of the woman's frail fingers. They were pocked with bite marks. Fighting back tears, he whispered, "It's all right, Merri. I'm here. It's Darien."

"Darien?"

"What happened? Where's Tori?"

"Tori..." It was faint, the weight of the rubble crushing her voice. Darien had to put his ear right up to her face to hear. "The creatures came. Reckon I... held 'em back... didn't I?"

"Scelero?" he asked, his hands running over the lacerations on her hands. How was it that his old master had appeared here in this demon form?

"Nah. He was trying ter get me out. Reckon he came back, didn't he?"

"What are you talking about?"

"Back from that cursed world ter get his revenge on—" Merri broke into a fit of violent coughs.

Darien hated to see her this way. He gripped her hand, but her fingers were weak. She was fading. "Merri, where's Tori?"

"Safe... the other side..." Her eyes drifted, as though they saw nothing. Her grip tightened on his for a moment. "I never turned dark, Darien... I kept strong..."

"It's all right, Merri. I'm going to get you out of here. Quit talking. You got to save your strength."

"Nah..." whispered Merri. "This is it for me... Get yourself safe before..." Her voice faded, and her hand went limp in Darien's grasp.

Her eyes were still open, but stared emptily. She blinked one last time. "Tori still believes in you, Darien... an' so do I..."

CHAPTER THIRTY-SEVEN

It took nearly a minute after Ol' Merri's last breath, and he knew he might not make it back before the explosion, but Darien waited until the end. Tears streaked his world like falling stars, and he waited. Waited until Merri's skin turned ash grey and her breath returned—a horrid, frantic wheeze that made his skin prick with violent shivers. He took his dagger and thrust it deep into Merri's skull. It pained him more than anything he'd ever done, but he would not let Merri become a monster.

Darien felt her second life shudder. Merri's muscles spasmed, her heart fluttered, and then she was gone. He let the blood run over his hands. It was cold. Darien had never felt anything like it. Darien made himself experience every moment, every tremor of her passing. He owed her that much. When it was finished, he retched across the floor. Then he closed Merri's dead eyes, and he ran.

Darien hoped Zamel would give him enough time. How long had it been since he'd left the main chamber? All concept of time escaped Darien in battle, and he could only hope it escaped Zamel as well.

Darien reached the domed chamber where so recently a camp had been set up—now, it was a mess of shredded tents and bodies. But not nearly enough bodies.

The horde of grey-skinned demons was filled with dozens of Legion uniforms. Darien wished he could slay them all, spare his soldiers this wretched end. The shrieking creatures stormed madly at the wall of Shadows blocking the entrance. By some miracle, Zamel's dwindling troops still managed to hold the Nosferati at bay.

Darien morphed and soared on black wings over the devastation.

"Ready the bomb!" Zamel shouted.

Darien flew over the wall, narrowly missing the jutting teeth of the cave roof. He morphed to his human form as he descended. Vaguely, he heard Zamel cry for the Legions to fall back.

And then, the explosion—

The force catapulted him forward—

Darien landed sprawled on his face—

A plume of smoke rushed through the cave like a great serpent, and Darien held his breath for fear of suffocating. The cavern shook as though it were a living thing, its seizing heart raging against an inexorable death. Darien lay still, his arms covering his head as debris cascaded around him. The entire mountain trembled as though it might give way and plunge into the depths of the world. And as he faced the end, Darien prayed.

He had never believed in gods, but still the prayers sprung from him unbidden. He had faced so much death, yet never once had he cried out to the old gods. Never, until now.

The catacombs trembled one last time. It was the shudder of death Darien knew too well. The mountain's breath faded. The great smoke serpent slithered away through the tunnels. The air thinned.

And finally, Darien could breathe. He gasped violently for several inhalations, and then he lay still, panting in the stillness.

The cavern around him was utterly silent. Darien prayed again. That no Nosferati had made it through. That Zamel and the Shadows had made it out alive. That Valeria had led the Watchers to safety. Even that Tori, wherever she was, had not been injured in the quaking of the mountains.

All at once, as though at the press of a lever, the caves filled with the coughs of the living, gasping for precious breath. Somewhere, a torch lit up the passage. A hand reached out and helped Darien to his feet, brushing away the chalky debris from his uniform. "Thank the gods!" whispered Valeria, pulling him close, her hand touching his face.

They embraced, and Darien did not care that there was a host of soldiers around him to witness the affection. They had survived a nightmare, and that was all that mattered.

———

ALL TOLD, THERE WERE TWO HUNDRED SHADOWS, ELEVEN Morphs, and four Watchers lost. Most of the slain now haunted the catacombs beneath the Crooked Teeth, save those who'd had the mercy of being eaten alive in the first wave of the horrific attack.

Exhausted, wounded, and never more shaken in their harsh soldiers' lives, the Legions pressed on, marching through the night. They reached the end of the catacombs by daybreak and fell out of the opening onto late summer grass in the warm light of the rising sun.

Darien had never fully appreciated the beauty of the true light of the sun, never longed more for the sting of the cool Oshan wind, and never been less pleased to see the towering White Citadel plunging into the sky in the valley below.

He had failed his master. The Gallows Girl had escaped. How had it all happened? Where had those monsters come from?

They were a legend of the Old World. There was no record of a true Nosferati attack in the New World, ever. Just as there had never been a Rulaq sighting. And Commander Scelero had been among them?

It made no sense.

A train of horsemen escorted the chancellor from the city to greet them at the edge of the mountains, ready to parade his conquered Watchers before the people of Osha. Darien's heart was an abandoned well in his chest. The chancellor would not have the capstone of his parade.

Tori…

Valeria squeezed his hand, and Darien hobbled out to meet his master. His right leg was bruised and stiff from the explosion, but if that was his only suffering, he counted himself desperately fortunate. It was strange to think what a curse the Morgathian firebombs had seemed a short month ago in Goran'El. Now they were a blessing from the gods, the only reason that any of them were still alive.

The chancellor neared, and Darien filled with dread. To his amazement, the deathly pale sorceress, Medea, rode at the chancellor's side. Her wild gaze flitted about the valley. *She survived the Rulaq attack!*

Though Darien was relieved at this, he also feared the worst. He imagined himself being tortured, the way Kirra had been in Vlyanii, for his failure.

The chancellor's smile turned sour as he rode to them, noting the absence of the Gallows Girl from the huddle of Watcher prisoners. Nevertheless, the chancellor dismounted and greeted the captain of his Morphs. Darien knelt before him, but the chancellor gestured for him to rise.

Darien felt bile rise in his throat, but he stood tall and did not let his voice quaver as he spoke. "I am sorry, milord. I've failed you."

Cyrus Maro paused, his eyes studying Darien as though he were one of the priceless Old World sculptures held in the library of the White Citadel. His eyes seemed to bore through to view Darien's true self. His gaze held for an eternity. Darien readied himself for punishment. Maybe even execution, right here before his comrades.

Finally, the chancellor spoke. "You have much need for sorrow, Captain Redvar. But not on my account. You brought us all through a nightmare. I am indebted to you, as are many others. Tell me, how many of our sorcerers were lost?"

Darien gulped. "Four, milord. Two who were to join the Sky Guard. A Fieri named Mischa. As well as the Gallows Girl. Tori was… lost in the madness. It is likely she was slain by the devils. But… it is possible she escaped in the chaos."

The chancellor was silent for some time. "Only four lost?" he said finally. "Then, I must thank you for your service, Captain. You have done very well."

Darien had not expected such understanding. He had failed miserably, and yet his master was proud? The dread drifted away, and relief swept over him.

The chancellor motioned for a horse. "Ride with me, Captain, as I lead the Watchers before the people. We have much to celebrate."

"But, milord, the Gallows Girl…"

"Is still alive, Captain. Medea can sense it well. And once we've recovered, we will hunt Astoria down and bring her back to Osha."

"Milord, how did Medea survive?"

"It's a miracle." The chancellor smiled at this. "Medea led a company of survivors through the mountains after the Rulaqs left the Watchtower. While we traveled underground, they traveled above. She arrived in Maro'El shortly before Vashti and I arrived using the stones. All is far from lost, Captain."

"But milord… what happened? Where did those… monsters come from? The Nosferati?"

The chancellor shook his head. "From where you think they came from, Captain. Somehow, it seems the Gallows Girl released them from the Old World. And I fear the Nosferati may not be the only ones. I expect there will be more terrors rising, soon enough. The Old World is colliding with our own once more."

A hollow dread tugged at Darien's gut. What did this mean for him? For Osha? For the New World? How could Tori have done this?

"The Gallows Girl…" Darien murmured.

"She is more dangerous than I ever imagined. But for now, we have cause to celebrate. The Watchers are ours, and we are alive. And if worlds are colliding, then the New World has need of our power more than ever before, and we will be the saviors they need."

"We?" said Darien.

"A third age is coming to our world, Darien. It is time we revealed magic to Osha once more. Not as their mythical guardians sent by the gods. We will be the gods of this Third World. We have many new recruits for my Sky Guard, and I am in need of a commander."

"M-me?"

The chancellor reached out and clasped Darien upon the shoulder, like his father once had in the mountains of Klavash so many years ago. Darien flushed with pride. "Come, Darien. Let's usher in a new world, together."

Darien mounted his horse and rode tall at the chancellor's side as they led the Watchers through the streets of Maro'El, all the way to the White Citadel. There was a great ceremony. Magic returned to the world with cheers. Watchers pledged their loyalty to the empire. And Darien was raised to yet a higher station—commander of the Sky Guard. A lowly Klavash boy, now the commander of the first magic army in the New World.

But something nagged at Darien. He should have felt proud. He should have been relieved, honored by the chancellor's promotion. But in the deep caverns of his mind, Darien could not stop thinking of the words Merri had spoken before she died. He kept thinking of the prayers he'd muttered in the explosion. His thoughts lingered on Tori, wondering where she was, somewhere out in the Crooked Teeth, surviving. Was she freezing to death? Being stalked by Rulaqs? Had she made it through, like Medea and the company of survivors from the Watchtower? Had Tori really brought Scelero and the Nosferati back from the Old World, as the chancellor claimed?

And these thoughts—these doubts—filled Darien with a gut-wrenching guilt, as though, any moment now, the chancellor might see into his heart and sense the war raging inside him.

That night, Darien ascended the long steps to his chambers at Commander Scelero's estate—now his own estate as the chancellor's new commander of the Sky Guard. He lay in his old master's feather bed, but he could not sleep.

Darien suspected Scelero himself had once lain in this bed, tossing sleeplessly, in the nights before his great betrayal. Before he freed the Gallows Girl. Before he was cast into the abyss of the Old World, only to come out the other side a monster. A monster that had helped Tori escape once more.

Darien was no longer sure what he believed, nor where his true loyalties lay. And this scared him more than any terror he'd experienced in his young life.

PART THIRTEEN
THE FATE OF THE GALLOWS GIRL

From the ashes of the Old World,
From the depths of the New,
From the Great White plains of the North,
She rises.

Against the beasts of the Old World,
Against the monsters of the New,
Against the Great White shadows of the North,
She rises.

For the lost of the Old World,
For the downtrodden of the New,
For the Great White peoples of the North,
She rises.

—from "The Gallows Girl Rises"
a folk song of the peoples of the North

CHAPTER THIRTY-EIGHT

The tears would not stop flowing. Tori simply could not believe Merri was gone. One moment, they were hurrying down the winding passages of the catacombs to escape the Legions unnoticed, and then horrific shrieks echoed up through the caverns. And in an instant, the world changed forever.

The first creature came at them like a storm from nowhere. Tori was too weak to use her Conjuri power. Before she knew what was happening, Merri was shoving Tori and Mischa away, and leaping out with her blade. The grey creature shrieked as it flew through the air. Merri was quick with her Legion skill and severed the monster's head in one swift stroke, but not before it had landed a bite on the back of her hand.

Blood coated the cave floor. Shrieks rushed from the depths of the caverns beyond, the echoes building to cacophony; the terrifying sounds stole Tori's breath, as though she'd been struck by an invisible force. Without a word, Merri Kyrsted removed a heavy sack from her pack—the firebomb. Merri screamed for them to run. Tori was dazed with shock, but she held onto her old friend's arm. "No, Merri! Come with us! We'll help you."

Merri glanced at her bitten hand, a strange smile teasing her lips.

The wound sent strange grey lines up her arms like veins. "Nah, this is what I been fighting for all this time. I'm so proud o' you, child!"

"Merri, no! Don't!"

Merri shoved Tori away. "Keep fighting, girl! Keep believing there's good left. In Darien, and in all this world! Now, run!"

Those were the last words Merri said before she brought the cave down on herself, just as a wave of Nosferati bore down upon her. But before the end, Tori saw the face of the first grey-skinned creature. It was leading the horde, and it was the only one that stopped. The others shot at Merri with demonic fury, but not this one. It looked as though it'd been struck still by some spell. Even in its monstrous skeletal form, Tori recognized the face.

Commander Scelero?

Before Tori could react, the roof fell. The caverns went dark. The tunnel was engulfed with smoke. And Tori knew Merri was gone forever.

———

It all happened so fast, Tori could hardly make her brain comprehend the truth: *Merri's dead. She died so I could live…*

Merri had endured unspeakable horror in the Legions, killing and letting her masters believe they had changed her. But they hadn't. All along, she had been waiting for her moment.

Tori just could not believe that *she* was the moment Merri had been waiting for.

And Scelero? He had been sentenced to the Old World for conspiring against the chancellor, only to come back to his own world a monster. Tori imagined her old master stumbling around that hellish nothingworld, growing numb and hollow, forgetting all the beauty that made the real world worth living in. Until eventually, he stumbled upon some colony of Old World cannibals, like the Rulaqs at the gates of the necropolis, waiting for their chance to return to the real world. And it seemed he had joined them. *How did the Nosferati show up at all?* Tori wondered dimly as she and Mischa pressed on through the catacombs.

The sight of her old master, transformed into a demon, haunted her thoughts. She prayed Merri had died in the explosion, that she had not joined the ranks of the Nosferati.

For hours, led by torchlight and a quickly fading hope, Tori and Mischa staggered through the labyrinthine catacombs, weak from the bloodletting and the long march and all the horror they'd been put through. *But none of it matters now. Merri is dead. Scelero is a monster. And the others?*

The tears kept flowing, and words would not come. Mischa kept silent. Occasionally, she brushed Tori's shoulder, but she never broke the silence weighing down upon them. It was as though Mischa could feel the gravity of the loss, even though she'd never known Merri or Scelero. As though, somehow, Mischa felt everything Tori felt and knew that no words could express the sorrow plaguing her. *Of course she does. She lost Zaya...*

The caverns stretched on and on. Tori did not have the willpower to choose their path. It was all she could do to keep going. And Mischa sensed this too. As they reached divide after divide in the winding pathway beneath the Crooked Teeth, Mischa paused, giving Tori time to find her voice if she wished—though Tori never spoke—and then, Mischa pointed with the torch, and they continued on.

Tori was too weak and too ravaged with loss to care what happened to them next. In all likelihood, Merri was but one of many of Tori's friends who had died in the Nosferati attack. She had seen at least a dozen of the demons bounding through the chamber toward Merri. And she had heard the horrid wails of what must have been dozens more. *We might be the only ones left.*

Vonn and Sahra and Ren, all of them were too weak to fight, even if they weren't in chains. Tori knew they were probably dead. And if they weren't, what good was it? They were in the hands of the chancellor. All was hopeless, and this truth enraged Tori even more. *Merri died for nothing.*

Mischa led them on and on. If she was filled with dread, she did not show it. She held onto Tori's arm and pulled her along. After hours of plodding—after Tori's legs felt like they might give out at any moment—they came to yet another divide, and this time, Mischa did not choose a direction.

Finally, Mischa's fortitude gave out, and the tears struck her as well.

"I don't know where to go," Mischa said. "We've been here before." She pointed at the ground with her torch. "Those are our prints."

Tori did not know what to say. She felt as though all this was a dream, some dark effect of the bloodletting. Any second, she would wake up, back in her chains. Maybe back in her cell in the dungeons of the White Citadel. Perhaps she'd never left, and all this was an illusion. Some trick of her mind to keep her alive. She did not care anymore. She was so weak, and all she wanted was to lie down and sleep.

Suddenly, Tori was jarred from her stupor by a cold fist. She staggered back. "You hit me?"

"Wake up, Tori!" Mischa cried. "I need your help!"

"I-I don't know anything… I can't help!"

Mischa hit her again. "*Shenzah!*"

"Quit hitting me!" Tori swung back, but she missed and her momentum carried her into the damp cave wall. She crumpled to the ground, landing on soft dirt.

The ground is soft! Tori's fingers closed around fine grains of dirt. There had been no loose earth in all their march through the catacombs. It was all smooth, hard cave stone. But here, the ground was soft enough they had made footprints. Soft enough, she could feel the grains between her fingers.

"We're near the surface, Misch," Tori said. "The dirt. We could only leave prints if we were near the surface!" Tori scrambled back to her feet, a surge of renewed hope rising in her. She took Mischa's arm and led the way down the path they had not yet taken.

There was another divide a short distance off. Tori analyzed the ground carefully. She could feel the slightest movement of air coming from the passage to the right, and she knew that was the way.

It was midday when Tori and Mischa tumbled from a small opening in the side of the mountain, out into the snow, somewhere in the endless passes of the Crooked Teeth. They collapsed in the light of the high sun. With the cold and the Rulaqs roaming free once more, sleep could mean death. But exhaustion won over, and they slept.

———

Tori woke, shivering in the faded light, her stomach wringing with hunger. But she felt stronger. Her blood was beginning to fill her up again. Her senses were sharpening, her power making her more aware of the complexity of the world around her. But that world was nothing but snow and rock and cold for leagues in all directions.

Mischa did not stir beside her. Tori nudged her. Already, Tori's fingers felt stiff and achy from the cold. Night had come, and it would be getting far colder. Mischa moaned, but did not sit up as Tori shook her again. "Misch, we've got to move. We'll freeze to death if we don't." Tori tugged at her friend's arm, and finally, she rose from the snow.

"If I w-weren't so weak, I c-could make a f-fire," Mischa stammered, flicking the flints at her wrists helplessly. A mere breath of flame flickered around her fingers and faded.

Though the thought of a fire was the most glorious thing she could think of, Tori said, "Fire would just bring the Rulaqs straight to us, anyway. Come on, we've got to move."

Tori reached out her hand, and Mischa managed to get to her feet. "D-dying as Rulaq food doesn't sound all that b-bad anymore." Mischa chuckled darkly.

"We're alive, Misch. We made it out. We're not going to die." Tori did not believe it, but she had to keep Mischa's spirits up.

Mischa smiled, though her lips trembled with shivers. "That sounds m-more like the Tori I know. G-guess I knocked some sense into you back in that c-cave."

They trudged into the darkening night. The sky was clear, and the stars began to creep out from their hiding places. It was true, they might be devoured by Rulaqs, but at least they wouldn't freeze in a blizzard.

Tori fixed her gaze on the Eldest, the brightest star in the northern sky. It would lead them east, out of the Teeth to the rocky plains of the

Grey Waste. Though Tori had no idea how far they would need to travel.

———

It was nearly daylight when Mischa finally dared to voice the wrenching question that had been eating away the silence between them for so long. "Do you think the others survived?"

Tori trudged through the thick snow, grateful for all the hard exercises Sahra had put them through. That hard-earned stamina kept them going now, through their weakness and the cold. It had been a long night's march, but the horizon was beginning to turn grey with the coming morning, and the sharp wind was dying down. Tori had needed to focus so much on moving forward, on surviving the night, she hadn't let her mind settle long upon the thought of what the Nosferati might have done to the others. "I... I don't know, Misch," said Tori, at last.

"The chancellor wouldn't leave them to die, right? They're too valuable to him."

"Nothing is as valuable to the chancellor as his own life and power." Tori knew this all too well. A sick dread picked away at her hollow stomach.

"We can hope they're alive," said Mischa. "We have to hope."

Tori nodded. She thought of all their friends in those caves, of Sahra and Vonn, even Dajha and the others who had turned. She thought of Ren... how foolish it was to think that only a few nights ago she had been stupidly worried about his attention. Now, all she wanted was to know he was alive.

Tori thought of Darien... what she would give to go back to the day of the Gallows. Yet Tori knew she could never take back what she'd done that day. It meant he was still alive. Even if he was a monster now, Tori could never have chosen otherwise. Merri had sworn that the real Darien was still in there, beneath the uniform and the morphing skin. *And Valeria said the same thing...*

Tori hoped it was so, but even more, she hoped that Darien had survived the attack in the catacombs, whether still a monster or not.

She hoped that the chancellor would not take her escape out on him, or any of the others.

"I feel torn about the others," said Tori, after some time. "As though my heart's been ripped in two. If they all died in those catacombs, then all is lost, Misch…"

"All is not lost," said Mischa firmly. "Merri told you as much before the end. 'The Gallows Girl is the hope of the New World.' That's what she said. There are people who will help us."

"But where?" said Tori. "We're all alone in the middle of the mountains. Rulaqs are ravaging the world, and the others…"

"Some survived," said Mischa, determined. "They had to survive."

"I hope they did too, Misch. But the Shadow Watch is done. They betrayed us. And…" Tears began to well up in Tori's eyes. "And I don't blame them."

Mischa stopped and took her hand. "You did the right thing, Tori."

"Our friends died because of me. Zaya died… I'm so sorry, Misch."

Mischa pulled her tight, and Tori sobbed into her thick cloak. Mischa held her for some time before she spoke. Her voice was firm. "Zaya died because of the chancellor. Maybe the others can't see it yet. But it is true. And don't you dare believe otherwise, because I don't."

Tori nodded, and they pushed on silently toward the crest of a steep pass. Tori did not know where they were going. They were bearing east to leave the Teeth, she knew that much. But beyond that? With Osha in the west, and the Yan Avii now allied with the chancellor… their paths were virtually blocked anywhere to the south.

Perhaps the North? Tori pondered the idea. Sahra had spoken highly of the Alyuts of the Great White North, but little was truly known about them in Osha. They were a mystery. Old World savages, according to Oshan lore, supposedly the original inhabitants of the western continent before the arrival of the Elyan races, driven north during the ancient conquests. Tori had once seen an Alyut trader in the Trium'vel when she was a young slave girl. His hair had been formed into long, thick locks, and his beard had been immense. He dressed in strange white furs and spoke of bear riders and cities of ice.

Tori pushed the thoughts aside. *Once we're safe, we can figure out what to do next. First, we have to stay alive, which means we've got to get out of the Crooked Teeth as soon as possible.*

Her fingers felt raw, and Tori knew the cold would kill them both if they spent another night exposed to the elements. It had been a warm night for the Teeth. She doubted they would be so lucky again.

Mischa was quiet for some time, before she voiced a painful question. "Do you think Vashti is still valuable to the chancellor?" Her voice quavered.

Tori cringed at the thought of the Yan Avii princess, especially after her betrayal of the Watchers. A dark part of her hoped Vashti had died in the catacombs. But she could not hope that, for Mischa's sake. Vashti might have betrayed them all, but it was not out of spite. Tori knew that. She had sensed the pain when Vashti explained to Mischa what she'd done.

It was out of desperation for her people, and even for Mischa and the others, that she'd betrayed them. If she was honest, Tori wondered if Vashti had been right, that all this was truly a hopeless war. And Tori hated the princess all the more for this.

Regardless, Tori felt sure Vashti was alive. Tori knew more than anyone how much the chancellor valued her Regenero ability, how much he needed her to cross between the worlds. And besides, if Vashti were dead, Tori would have to feel more guilt for still hating her so much.

"I think," Tori said at last, "if there was anyone the chancellor valued in those caves, it was Vashti. I'm... well, I'm sure she's still alive."

Mischa nodded, and Tori could tell she was holding back tears. Tori felt a kinship forming between them, something deeper than before. She gripped Mischa's hand. Tori knew exactly how it felt to be betrayed by someone she loved. She knew the confusing twist of emotions that surfaced, hating them and yet praying they were alive. She'd learned first from her mum, and now Darien.

"How did you..." began Tori. She was not sure how to say it.

"How did I come to love someone like Vashti?" said Mischa. "Someone you despise so much?"

"I didn't mean it that way."

"I know," said Mischa. "I don't blame you for hating her, Tori, but… well, you two had a lot more in common than you were ever willing to see. You were just set against each other from the start. Vashti was different when she first came to the Watchtower. She was strong and brave. We… we got on from the start…"

Mischa's voice faded into memory. When she spoke, her voice croaked. "But—I mean, everyone liked her. Especially Ren. He wanted to make her his queen when the Watchers rose up. He thought she'd be perfect. A phoenix rising from the ashes. The girl who came back from death. And she…"

"She thought it would be best for her people," Tori finished. "She sacrificed her love for you, for the sake of her people."

Mischa nodded. "I couldn't hold that against her, but… it hurt. Like nothing I've ever felt."

"But after I came, why did she hate me so much? I mean, why couldn't you two…"

"After the hope of an alliance with the Yan Avii dissolved, Ren moved on," said Mischa. "But things couldn't be the same. It started as something for her people, but Vashti fell in love with Ren. She was crushed when it ended. We just… we couldn't go back. She broke my heart. Ren broke hers. It never felt right. You saw how we were. Things were always strange between us after she decided to become Ren's queen."

"And now she's going to be the chancellor's queen…"

"You can't choose who you love. I wish I could. I tried. I liked Zaya…" Mischa kept her head down as she trudged on through the deep snow. Tori could only imagine her friend's tangled web of emotions about Zaya.

"All hope isn't lost for Vashti, you know." Tori could barely believe she was saying it, but she was trying to see Vashti through Mischa's eyes, and she knew Mischa needed hope. Tori's body was healing itself, and despite the cold, she was feeling stronger, but Mischa was moving slower, growing weaker the farther they trekked. "She doesn't have to be his queen, not if we kill the chancellor. And we're going to, Misch. We have to kill him."

Mischa squeezed Tori's hand. Her fingers trembled. "Maybe we should focus on surviving another day in these mountains, before we plot any assassinations."

That was exactly what Tori feared for Mischa, though she tried not to let her concern show. They needed food, shelter, fire, but the world stretched out white and bleak before them, and Tori feared for Mischa's survival.

The girls spoke little as they trudged on. It was morning, but the sun still hid behind the towering mountains for several hours before they finally felt its warmth. As the sun rose over the jagged peaks, they reached the edge of a great valley. Below, the remnants of a Crooked settlement lay scattered in the snow like branches splayed out across a meadow after a summer storm.

"Oh gods," said Mischa. "They're dead. All these innocent people."

Tori felt guilty, but she saw the ruined settlement for the blessing it was. "There may be provisions left in the rubble."

The settlement was a crushed skeleton of splinters and debris. No bodies. It seemed the inhabitants had all been devoured by Rulaqs.

How many did I let through? Tori wondered, a pang of heavy guilt pressing in her chest. It was more than the Rulaqs. She had been avoiding the thought ever since she had seen the first Nosferati, but now, looking at all these ruined homes and the blood staining the snow, it overwhelmed her. *Where did those creatures come from in the catacombs? Were the Nosferati hidden all these years? Or did I let more than Rulaqs through, somehow?*

Tori's experience in the Old World felt like a faded dream. She remembered the horde outside the gateway to the New World. She remembered how poor and timid the Rulaqs had seemed there. She remembered them roaring back to life and stampeding when she tried to close the portal. Could she have let something else through in the madness?

Tori knew that was where the chancellor had banished Scelero. *The Nosferati must have come from the Old World. But how?*

As she walked through the devastated settlement, Tori wondered whether the stories had gotten it all wrong. Perhaps the Old World was not the paradise of magic and freedom it sounded like in all her mum's stories. Perhaps the First Chancellor had made the right decision to rid the world of magic and monsters.

Tori and Mischa searched through the rubble of several buildings with no luck. Finally, they found the remains of a tavern. The storehouses in the North were always underground, and after some effort, they cleared away the trapdoor. A ladder led down to a vast storeroom. With hope reviving her strength, Mischa managed to tease a flame and let it hover in front of them, lighting their way. The room was stocked with shelves of potatoes and unleavened bread and jars of preserves and, best of them all, barrels of water.

"Thank the gods!" Mischa cried, lapping it up from cupped hands. Tori had been so cold, she hadn't realized how thirsty she was, and she, too, drank greedily.

When they'd drunk their fill, they began stuffing their mouths with bread and preserves. Mischa found a lantern and jars filled with oil, and shadows soon flickered on the walls from the soft flames. *We can build a fire and cook some potatoes before it gets dark,* Tori thought ecstatically, *maybe even find some salted venison for a stew.* They could sleep down in the storeroom, protected from the elements and the monsters, and Mischa could regain her strength for a day or two before they pressed on.

Consumed by the joy of the treasure they'd found, Tori did not stop to consider that they might not be the only ones seeking shelter. Tori did not notice how quiet it became in the storeroom as she filled herself with glorious sustenance. She did not realize anything was amiss until she turned to search for some meat on a shelf by the entrance. As she turned, horror shot through her.

Standing at the base of the ladder, a young man with olive skin and long black hair towered over Mischa. A massive hand covered her mouth, and the other held a blade at her throat.

Tori reached out with her mind, grasping for her powers, but nothing happened.

The young man's dark gaze shot through her. "Your powers have no place in the North, Darkling."

Tori felt as though her chest had collapsed. She could not breathe. The Alyut man pressed his jagged shank into Mischa's skin, and Tori was completely helpless to save her. A trickle of blood eased down Mischa's neck as he pressed the blade harder. The Alyut man blocked the only way to the outside world and escape.

And Tori's magic was gone. It was unfathomable, but somehow, her powers had vanished. Tori felt no awareness of the intricacies beyond the visible world. Her line to magic had been severed. She felt nothing. Tori felt entirely ordinary, and entirely helpless.

"Don't move, Darkling," the Alyut man instructed, and Tori obeyed. He guided Mischa forward with a shove. "I've been waiting for you, ever since you set those monsters loose."

How could he know that?

"You returned our world to the Abyss, and now you will—"

But the young man's threat was cut off. Mischa trembled in the man's grasp, but that did not stop her from one last attempt at resistance. She bit deep into the man's hand, and he roared in pain, his hand jerking away from her mouth. The blade fell away, clattering on the ground. Mischa arched her body back. The man lost his balance, stumbling over something on the dark storeroom floor. Shelves of provisions collapsed on him.

"Run, Tori, run!" Mischa screamed.

Mischa hurled herself at the man. She was sacrificing herself for Tori, just as Ol' Merri had.

Tori hesitated. Could she really flee and leave Mischa to the whims of this Northman? *No! I've already lost too many. I will not lose Mischa too!*

Tori spun back to help, but she had paused too long. The Alyut man recovered himself. He leapt to his feet, hurtling Mischa into one of the barrels of water. As Tori launched herself at him, the man's hand flew to his belt.

Tori never reached him.

His blade lodged itself at the base of her neck.

A perfect throw.

Ren would have been proud, Tori thought strangely.

Mischa screamed, but her voice was stretched thin. Blood rushed from Tori's body like a fountain. She slumped to the floor, and already she could feel it. Her body was not healing itself. The blade had struck an artery, and life was gushing from her wound, and she knew she was dying. A calm acceptance washed over her.

"Noooo! Oh gods!" Mischa hurled herself at the man, and they fought in a blur. But Tori was fading away. Sound felt as though it was drifting from leagues away, from far mountain passes, from another world. The blurs morphed into little more than shadows against a bright light.

Tori envisioned her mum at the end. Her warm face and bright green eyes shone in the sunset light upon the Steppe. Her smile was filled with warmth. Her hands reached for her. It felt like a glorious reunion. *I'm coming back to you, Mum…*

The light grew brighter, washing out her mum's beautiful features. And then there was nothing.

CHAPTER THIRTY-NINE

T hank the gods."

It was Mischa's voice, slipping through the fog of Tori's consciousness as she stirred from death.

By some miracle, Tori was alive. She sensed the warmth of a fire nearby. Slowly, the fog cleared away, and she found herself still in the storeroom beneath the ruined Crooked village. Mischa clutched her hand, smiling down as Tori squinted against the light. *It's still daylight. And I'm alive. But how?*

A bandage coated Tori's neck. It was wet to the touch, and Tori knew she had lost much blood. She had known the instant the blade lodged in her throat that she was going to die. Yet here she was. A fire crackled near the base of the ladder, set so the smoke would escape through the open hatch. A shadow passed in front of the flames, and Tori shot up. It was the Alyut man.

Tori jumped to her feet and had a blade to the man's neck in an instant. It was too easy.

The Alyut man chuckled. "If your reflexes had been so swift earlier, I might never have had the devastating realization that I nearly killed the Gallows Girl."

Tori raised an eyebrow, but did not remove the blade from the man's throat. He did not resist her, and he was still smiling. "What do you want with us?" Tori demanded.

Mischa was at her side, touching her arm softly. The man was still not resisting. And then, the light-headedness caught up with Tori, and she slumped forward. The Alyut man caught her, and he and Mischa helped her lie back down beside the fire.

"You've healed," said the man. "But you are weak. You should rest."

"What happened?" Tori's head hurt and her vision was foggy.

"It's all right, Tori," said Mischa. "He's not our enemy. He... he saved you."

"Saved me? He nearly killed me!"

"Thought you were Darklings," said the man, or boy, rather. Up close, Tori realized he could be little older than she or Mischa. "I can't tell you how truly sorry I am. As soon as I realized who you were, I withdrew my barrier from your magic. And not a moment too soon. You were near death, but your body healed remarkably."

Still, Tori regarded him with suspicion. *But if he meant us harm, surely there could be no purpose in sparing my life.*

"What are Darklings?" Tori asked.

"Darklings... that's what we call the chancellor's servants up here in the North."

"The Morphs?" said Tori.

The Alyut man nodded. "I've felt many Darklings in the Crooked Teeth this past week."

"Y-you felt them?" said Tori. "Who are you? What did you mean about lifting a barrier from my magic?"

"My name is Alyk dul Baruk. A shaman of the Alyuts of the Great White North. We have learned to render magic useless when we must. I was sent as the lone spirit protector for a party of my kinsmen. We were trading with the Crooked villages before the Darklings unleashed hell upon the North once more. Thank the All Mother, we managed to rescue many survivors after the annihilation the Rulaqs left in their wake."

"You were with a party of traders?" said Tori.

Alyk gazed at her for a long moment. Tori's suspicion began to wane, and as her vision cleared, she took stock of the young man. The hood of his fur-lined parka was down, revealing dark, straight hair pulled back behind his head. The ring of his face was darker than the rest of his olive skin, likely from when his hood was drawn tight. His jaw was muscular and smooth. His deep brown eyes invited her to hold his gaze, and he smiled broadly, which annoyed Tori.

"What are you looking at me like that for?" she said.

"It's just—well, I never believed my grandmother, that you might actually be alive."

"Your grandmother?"

"Mala dul Baruk, the High Shaman of the North. She has been praying vigilantly that the rumors would prove true, that the Gallows Girl was still alive. And here you are. I cannot wait for her to meet you."

"Meet me?" said Tori.

"The rest of my company is holed up in a cavern a short distance from here. We raided these same stores last night. As morning came, I felt you coming. So, I sent the others away and remained to kill you. Little did I know the Darkling that I sensed was the Gallows Girl. The Saint of the North."

Tori did not like where this was going. "I'm no saint. It will be far better for your people if I remain as far from them as possible. The chancellor will be hunting for me."

"Let him come. We will be ready."

"What do you mean?"

"While you were unconscious, Mischa told me what you both endured in the catacombs. You feel shame for the people you've lost. I sense that clearly. But you don't understand, Astoria. Their deaths were not in vain. You have brought hope to a desolate world, where there has been little hope. Even in the Great White North, we have heard of you. My people were driven to the Icelands by the kingdoms of the Old World. We have survived a harsh and cruel existence for hundreds of years, waiting for our time to reclaim the land of our ancestors, to reclaim Osha.

"Many years ago, my grandmother received a vision from the All Mother. A vision of the day of our Restoration. On that day, she saw a winter lily breaking through the thaw. It was the day when Osha fell, when the world was made right. I believe that lily was you, Astoria Burodai. My grandmother believes a third age of our world is approaching. An age of peace for the oppressed. You *must* come north to meet the High Shaman, and see the army in the North."

"Army?" said Tori. A note of fear resounded through her.

Alyk dul Baruk stood tall as he spoke. "Ever since you resisted the chancellor on the day of the Gallows, there has been unrest building across the New World. And now, here you are, right before my eyes. My grandmother was right. The day of our Restoration is near."

"I'm not... I can't be..." Tori began, fumbling for words. This young man might be amiable, but he was a fool, just like Ren, and the Watchers, and the lowborns of Osha who put hope in the Gallows Girl. All of them had thought she was going to come to their aid, but she had failed them all.

"Look, I'm not some saint," Tori said. "I wasn't even trying to resist the chancellor on the day of the Gallows. I was just trying to save my friend. And now he's one of the chancellor's servants, one of your Darklings, and all my other friends are probably dead. That's what happens when I save people. I can't be what your people long for. That's what got all my friends killed. I can't do that again."

Alyk was silent for a long time, but his smile never wavered. His olive Alyut skin glowed in the firelight, and his eyes glistened. Tori had to look away. *Why is he always smiling?*

"You long for revenge," he said finally. "I can sense it in you. I can see it in the way your fists tremble when you speak of them. The way your eyes darken at what happened to those you love. You long to see the chancellor dead. You long to see the fall of the White Citadel, like we all do."

Tori sighed. "I do. But my revenge is not what your people need."

"My people need justice, Astoria. For centuries we have prayed for it. A war is coming to the New World. But we in the North are few and inexperienced. We're hunters, not soldiers. We cannot win Restoration alone. And neither could your Watchers. But together... with the Gallows Girl..."

"No," said Tori. "You don't get it. The Gallows Girl is only a myth."

Alyk remained irritatingly calm. "Perhaps she is. But perhaps that is okay. Perhaps what you really are is not the point."

"It's the only point!" Tori's throat throbbed with pain. She leaned back and closed her eyes.

When she opened them again, the young shaman was still smiling. "You don't know the hope you bring others because you haven't seen them. There are thousands who will join you in the North. We may still be little match for the chancellor's Legions, it is true, but there are others. This Witch Queen in the Southern Isles is gathering followers. For the first time in centuries, many of the Isles are uniting under one banner."

"What does that have to do with your Restoration?"

"This queen does not come from a highborn family, and rumors suggest she has her eyes set on the mainland, on Osha, just as we do. The refugees fleeing the Teeth are coming north for refuge, and with the destruction of their homeland, they long for revenge. And ever since your escape from the White Citadel, slaves are stirring all across Osha. There have been several major uprisings. The time is ripe for change. And who better to unite them all than the Gallows Girl?"

"You want me to start a war?" said Tori.

"I want you to come with me," said Alyk. "I want you to meet the people who dare to put their hope in the symbol of the Gallows Girl, in the return of magic to our world. What you do after is your decision."

"You *did* say the North might be our best path," said Mischa, who had been smiling throughout the conversation. Tori knew it was because the notion of a resistance had rekindled her hope. Hope of rescuing the others. Hope of being reunited with Vashti.

But Tori felt hesitant to hope. She was responsible for what happened to the Watchers. If there were even any left alive. The chancellor would not have attacked the Watchtower if not for her. Tori did not bring hope. She brought destruction wherever she went.

"I will go above and ensure the Rulaqs have not returned to these ruins," said Alyk. "It is nearly nightfall. When darkness comes, I will be leaving, with or without you. But Astoria… I really hope you'll come."

"I like him," said Mischa, when the shaman had left.

Tori gritted her teeth. "You like what he says. You like that he gives you hope."

"We need hope, Tori! Perhaps he is the very reason we escaped. Maybe we were meant to meet him here."

"Meant by who? The gods? A vision of some lily? This doesn't sound like *shenzah* to you?" Mischa just smiled, and Tori shook her head. She knew her friend's mind was already made up. "What if he's lying? What if there is no resistance? What if he's dangerous?"

Mischa crossed her arms over her chest. "You didn't see him when he realized who you were. I did. I trust him. And I think we should go. Besides, what other choice do we have? To wander the Teeth until the Rulaqs find us? Or worse, the chancellor? We need Alyk's help."

As much as Tori hated it, she knew Mischa was right, at least about that. Deep inside, as much as her mind told her to flee from anyone interested in the hope of the Gallows Girl, Tori felt they *were* supposed to go with Alyk dul Baruk. She could not explain it, and part of her screamed to resist it. But something in her heart told her it was the right path forward. Tori sighed. "All right, we'll go. But the moment something seems wrong, we leave."

"Deal," said Mischa. "But it won't go wrong."

"Won't it?"

Mischa gripped her hand. "You feel it too. I can tell."

"Feel what?"

"Hope."

———

WHEN DARKNESS CAME, THEY SET OUT FROM THE RUINED Crooked settlement. The rest of Alyk's party was camped a league away in a small cavern. Tori remained wary throughout the journey. She did not like the idea of trekking alone with a man who could incapacitate her powers. *Although, if he'd wanted me dead, he could have just let me die already. Which means he wants me alive because he's trustworthy, or because he is up to something...*

The cavern opening was small enough they had to crawl through, and it consisted of only one large chamber, which did not seem to connect to any deeper passages. Still, going underground again immediately brought back nightmarish images of the Nosferati leaping upon Ol' Merri, and Commander Scelero's twisted face. Tori shuddered at the memories.

Within the chamber, a host of about fifty people sat huddled around small fires. When Alyk led the girls in, the entire place hushed to complete silence.

There were about a dozen Alyut men and women, dressed in coats with fur-lined hoods encircling their faces. The rest were Crooked folk, evident by their weathered, high altitude skin—survivors of the Rulaq attack that Tori had made possible.

Everyone in the chamber rose as Tori and Mischa entered. Their eyes grew wide. The silence transformed to faint murmurs.

Alyk raised his hands at the center of the chamber, and all fell silent. "My friends," he said, grinning and gesturing to Tori. "This is Astoria Burodai, the Saint of Osha, the Hope of the North—the Gallows Girl."

Every eye was fixed upon her. Wordless mouths hung open, and Tori did not know what to say or do. Were they glad to see her? Angry? Did they know she was the one who had brought the Rulaqs upon them? Had Alyk tricked her? Brought her here only to let this group of refugees slaughter her out of revenge?

And truth be told, Tori felt she would deserve it. The North was in ruins. And she had caused it. She had not been strong enough to fight the chancellor, and she had not even thought what the greater effects of her resistance might be. *All these refugees are fleeing the Teeth because of me.*

The chamber remained silent. Tori looked to Alyk. He took hold of her hand and raised it, and the room erupted in cheers.

Mischa took Tori's other hand, and the cheers grew louder. Without thinking, Tori released their hands and let herself rise from the ground by magic.

A young mother at the front of the crowd dropped to her knees, and the others followed suit. Soon, the entire room knelt before Tori, as though she were royalty, as though she were a god. The room fell silent.

A young girl clutched her little brother's hand. Both had seen fewer than twelve summers. The little boy's face was streaked with happy tears. All eyes remained expectantly fixed upon Tori as she returned to the ground, but still the kneeling crowd was silent.

Alyk leaned close and whispered in Tori's ear. "You are the hope of the gods to these people. They are waiting for you to speak."

Then Alyk knelt as well, and Mischa followed his lead.

Tori was the only one left standing in the chamber. She felt uncomfortable. She wished she could escape her own skin and disappear. These people were fools to put their hope in her. Tori could do nothing for them. She was the one who needed *their* help to survive, to escape the Teeth.

Finally, she found words. "Thank you, good people of the North, for letting me join you here in the safety of these caverns. I am honored."

"It is *we* who are honored," said Alyk, "that she who was sent by the gods would grace us with her presence."

And it was then Tori realized how much bigger than her all this was. This band of Northern refugees had lost everything, but at the sight of the Gallows Girl, they were smiling, hopeful. She had heard it said so many times, from Ren, from the chancellor. But she had never understood. Not until she saw their wide, hopeful eyes.

The Gallows Girl was a symbol of hope for these people. Their livelihoods had been stripped away from them, casualties in a war they never asked for. The Alyuts and the Crooked folk had all fled the Oshan Empire, turning to harsh, secluded environments for the semblance of freedom. But they were not free. And for hundreds of years, they had possessed little to put their hope in.

Tori understood now. She was not just a girl who could wield magic. To these people, she was the hope of Restoration, sent by the gods. The Gallows Girl was an idea that transcended the bounds of reality. She was larger than life. Perhaps in the same way the old gods had been. Maybe the gods had symbolized that same hope, all those years ago. The same hope that the Gallows Girl gave these people now. Maybe the gods had merely been people like her. Ordinary people with extraordinary destinies.

Tears filled Tori's eyes. Looking out at the wide, hopeful faces before her, she could not help but be filled with an overwhelming sense of awe and duty. She felt a responsibility to these people to become the hope they needed, even if she did not believe in it herself.

They needed her. The surviving Watchers needed her. Darien needed her. This was why she had felt led to the North. She knew it now. This was her path. Whether it was a destiny set by the gods or not, she knew it was what she was meant to do.

Finally, Tori found words. As she spoke, it was all she could do to keep her voice from cracking. She raised her hands high, the way the gods did in all her mum's old stories. She wondered if her mum had known. If that was why she had abandoned her all those years ago. So that, one day, she would be here.

"Good people of the North, I will journey with you to the Icelands. You have been trodden upon, left alone in this world for too long. But your prayers have been heard. The time of the chancellor is drawing to an end. The age of the Restoration of the North is now!"

The words were not her own, Tori felt sure. They seemed to come from outside her, from some other person, from the Gallows Girl. The refugees of the North cheered and rose to their feet. As Alyk led her through the crowd, hands stretched out, just to touch her and know she was not an illusion, that the Gallows Girl was real. They swarmed around her, offering her food and water, which she took eagerly, though she tried not to let her frailty show.

To the people of the North, she was a god, invincible. They did not know that her neck was still sore, still healing in the place where Alyk's blade had nearly taken her life.

Tori was *not* invincible. She gave these people hope, but in reality, they were the very source of the hope welling inside her own heart. The hope that things might still become better. That her friends might still be alive. That they might be set free. That the chancellor's vicious reign might truly come to an end.

And with the help of the North, and anywhere else where hope remained, they would rise up against the chancellor's empire of cruelty and injustice.

———

THE COMPANY OF ALYUT TRADERS AND CROOKED REFUGEES rested for two days in the chamber, and then Tori marched alongside Mischa and Alyk dul Baruk into the Northern night. A procession of hope-filled followers streamed through the snow behind them. Together, they left the Crooked Teeth and set out across the expanse of the Grey Waste, toward the snowy plains of the Icelands.

The Sisters shone down like twin torches from the gods to light their way. Their thousand daughters twirled their nightlong dance across the sky, an intricate choreography that led Tori and her followers on, to the Great White North.

END OF BOOK ONE

APPENDIX ONE
MAGIC OF THE WATCHERS

In the Old World, magic was partitioned according to the dominant gift of each Watcher. This helped bring order for the purposes of sorting and training young Watchers in their budding abilities. Each were separated into two schools of knowledge:

Corporeal - magic that manipulated the bodily elements
Material - magic that manipulated the physical elements

On occasion, a Watcher would defy the neatly segregated orders of magic. These multifaceted Watchers, known as Mages, were gifted with multiple abilities. They were seen as especially blessed by the gods in the eyes of the people they served.

However, the Watchers did not look upon these Mages so fondly. To their fellows in training, they were seen as threats, Watchers who sought to rise above them. To the masters of the Order, they were seen as overly ambitious, even dangerous.

Contrary to common belief, the magic of the Watchers did not belong only to them. Though the Watchers were the most famous and practiced wielders of magic in the Old World, they were not the only ones with access to such knowledge and power. Magic could not be confined to the realms of the Watchers, nor to their orderly systems. Before the fall of the Old World, one Watcher sought to defy this system. It did not end well.

Nevertheless, here are the orders of magic, as they were known in both the Old World and among the remnant at the Watchtower:

<u>CORPOREAL ORDERS</u>

Medici: the healers
Regenero: the regenerators
Cerebro: the mentalists
Metamorphi: the shapeshifters
Enduro: the ultra-swift

<u>MATERIAL ORDERS</u>

Conjuri: *the manipulators of matter*
Fieri: *the manipulators of fire*
Lumeni: *the manipulators of light*
Sonora: *the manipulators of sound*

APPENDIX TWO
REGIONS, CITIES, AND NATIONS OF THE NEW WORLD

<u>Osha and the North</u>

Alyut: a tribe of native Northmen, who first inhabited the region now known as Osha; when the first Elyan invaders came, the Alyut people fled north; little is known about their whereabouts, except for the rumors spread by the few Alyut traders that venture to the southern realms of the world

Crooked Folk: the wild peoples of the North populate the few remote settlements in the mountains of the Crooked Teeth; they come from a variety of nations, but hold no real political loyalties; known for being a hardy people, fitting of their environment

Crooked Teeth: remote mountains of Osha; the highest range in the New World, and serves as the eastern border of Osha

Forest of Ghen: the large haunted forest on the eastern border of Osha; it is said the severity of the ghosts' torment is dependent on the state of the soul who dares enter the forest

The Fringes: a sprawling slum city at the northernmost edge of Greater Osha

Glacier Sound: a narrow channel, fed by the glaciers of the Crooked Teeth and the fjords that line the western coast of Osha

Greater Osha: the nation of Osha is partitioned by Glacier Sound; Osha proper resides to the north of the body of water and contains the capital city of Osha, Maro'El

The Green Sea: an expanse of grass and farmlands, composing much of Greater Osha

Hatia: a small Oshan village at the easternmost edge of Greater Osha, near the edge of the Yan Avii Steppe

Maro'El: capital of the Oshan Empire; named after Darius Maro, of House Maro, the First Chancellor of Osha, whose family has served as chancellors of the empire since the dawn of the New World

The Meridian: a large bridge that spans Glacier Sound near the Fringes

Osha: a fragmented nation in the New World, ruled by the chancellor and a high council composed of highborn nobles; though the Oshan Empire once spanned the entire continent, the nation now struggles to maintain power as conquered nations have slowly withdrawn or rebelled

Ytala: a little known mountain village in the Crooked Teeth

<u>The Yan Avii Steppe</u>

The Great Spillway: a long river that runs south from the Grey Waste, all the way across the continent of the New World; the Spillway runs through the Steppe, and the Wandering Dunes lie across its eastern banks

The Grey Waste: an expanse of barren tundra to the north of the Steppe

The Steppe: the great expanse of rolling hills where the nomadic tribes of the Yan Avii make their homes

Vlyanii: the capital city of the Yan Avii, commonly called the Red City, due to the sandstone bricks used in its structure; it is the home of the Red Palace of the Great Soltayne, as well as the Golden Temple of Arayeva; it lies on the border between the Steppe and the Wandering Dunes

Wandering Dunes: a large desert to the east of the Steppe; according to Yan Avii folklore, after the fall of the Old World, the Yan Avii were once exiled to wander the desert of the Wandering Dunes, but were rallied and unified by their First Soltayne, who was purportedly visited by Arayeva herself

Yan Avii: the twelve unified tribes who inhabit the Steppe; each tribe is led by a *soltayne*, and all pay tribute to the elected Great Soltayne; since returning from their exile, the Yan Avii have warred with Osha over portions of the high plains for centuries

<u>Morgath</u>

Fangsport: a coastal city on the northwestern border of Morgath

Goran'El: capital city and fortress of the newly-formed kingdom of Morgath; formerly a city of the Oshan Empire, named after Magnus Goran, of House Goran, one of the great houses of Osha

The Klavash: a small tribal society organized in small villages high in the Klavash mountains; one of several native peoples who populated the region in the Ancient World, before the arrival of the Elyans

Klavash Mountains: a massive mountain range that seals off the nation of Morgath along northern, eastern, and southern borders; most noted for their dark appearance due to the abundance of star rock, which is used in most Morgathian architecture

Morgath: a rebel kingdom which was, until recently, part of the Oshan Empire; under the leadership of King Hollsted, the Morgathians formed their own kingdom, and ever since, they have been in a state of war against Osha

Ravencrest: a small fortification near the northeastern borders of the kingdom

APPENDIX THREE
YAN AVII PRONUNCIATION GUIDE

Arayeva [air-uh-YAY-vuh]: the sun goddess of the Yan Avii

elenyal [el-EN-yuhl]: a Yan Avii word meaning to elect or choose

Ilya [IL-yuh]: an insurgent group of assassins, bent on rescuing the Yan Avii from the corruption of the soltaynes; they were formed and led by Salla Burodai

luun [LOON]: a Yan Avii reference to the moon, seen as far inferior to the Sol

lynti [LIN-tee]: a female slave garment of the Yan Avii, fashioned of leather; tailoring varies, but typically worn to cover the chest, while leaving shoulders and midriff bare

sera [seh-RAH]: a formal address given to a Yan Avii woman of noble birth, akin to "My Lady" in the Common Tongue

shenzah [SHEN-zuh]: a vulgar Yan Avii exclamation conveying disgust or anger; something that is seen as an obvious lie; also a reference to literal excrement

Sol [SOLE]: a common term used to refer to Arayeva; also a reference to the literal sun

soltaya [sole-TAH-yuh]: a broad term referring to all noble-born members of the Yan Avii, from any of the twelve tribes, who would reside in the Red Palace during gatherings in Vlyanii

soltayne [sole-TANE]: a chieftain of one of the twelve Yan Avii tribes; each tribe is led by their own soltayne; however, the twelve tribes are ultimately led by the Great Soltayne, the Chosen of Arayeva

sorenyi [soh-REN-yee]: a Yan Avii word meaning to surrender or yield to an opponent

terasi [teh-RAH-see]: a Yan Avii word meaning to accept or thank

xadjar [ZAH-jhar]: a billowy, woven pant, commonly worn by slaves of the Red Palace

ylkii [IL-kee]: a buttered flatbread, a staple of Yan Avii cuisine

APPENDIX FOUR
DRAMATIS PERSONAE

The Watchtower

Astoria Burodai [uh-STORE-ee-uh BOOR-uh-die]: a Watcher of the Regenero and Conjuri orders; Oshan slave of Yan Avii and Oshan heritage; also known as the Gallows Girl, the famed sorceress rebel of Osha

Dajha Bhati [DAH-jhuh BAH-tee]: a Watcher of the Enduro order; son of a notorious Parjhan privateer in the Silver Sea

Jann [Jan]: a young Watcher recruit of the Fieri order

Mischa Sufai [MEE-shuh soo-FIE]: a Watcher of the Fieri order; daughter of a Melanesian merchant

Ren Andovier [Rehn An-DOE-veer]: a Watcher of the Conjuri order; former Oshan noble of House Andovier, one of the great houses of Osha; self-proclaimed Captain Andovier, leader of a small magical army set on resisting the Oshan Empire

Sahra Elra [SAH-ruh EL-rah]: a Watcher of the Medici order; of Alyut descent; and one of the trainers at the Watchtower

Vashti Burodai [VAHSH-tee BOOR-uh-die]: a Watcher of the Regenero order; daughter of the late Great Soltayne, sister of Salla

Vonn Elra [Vahn EL-rah]: a Watcher of the Conjuri order; from the Kingdom of Malai; and one of the trainers at the Watchtower

Zaya Shalvar [ZIE-yuh SHAHL-vahr]: a Watcher of the Medici order; from the Klavash mountains

The Night Legions

Cyrus Maro [SIE-russ MAH-roe]: the eleventh Chancellor of Osha; second-born of Aleksander and Lysette Maro, ascended to the throne of Osha after his entire family tragically died

Darien Redvar [DARE-ee-uhn RED-var]: a soldier in the Night Legions; raised among the tribes in the Klavash mountains; also known as the Gallows Boy and Captain Redvar

Jujen [JOO-jehn]: a soldier of Faerish descent; member of Darien's regiment in the Night Legions

Merri Kyrsted [MAIR-ee KER-sted]: a soldier in the Night Legions; of Morgathian descent; served House Scelero for most of her adult life

Commander Scelero: [Seh-LAIR-oh]: former commander of the Metamorphi; secret conspirator against the chancellor; Tori's former master

General Thrain [Thrayne]: leader of Darien's regiment in the Night Legions

Valeria Sardona [vuh-LEER-ee-uh Sahr-DOE-nuh]: a soldier in the Night Legions; of Southern Islander descent; chosen alongside Darien Redvar to join the ranks of the Metamorphi

Commander Zamel: [ZAY-mehl]: one of the highest-ranking officers in the Night Legions; commander of the attacks on Goran'El and the Watchtower

The Red Palace

Ashi Burodai [AH-shee BOOR-uh-die]: a slave of the Red Palace, and the only female member of the Ilya; deeply devoted to Prince Salla Burodai

Jerrah Mynah [Jeh-RAH MIE-nuh]: a captain of the Ilya

Kale Andovier [Kayl An-DOE-veer]: a Watcher of the Cerebro order; former Oshan noble of House Andovier, one of the great houses of Osha; also known as the Exiled Lord, after he fled the empire in the wake of unwittingly betraying his mother's magic to Chancellor Aleksander Maro

Kirra Fehn [KEER-uh FAIN]: a Watcher of the Lumeni order; close companion and former lover of Kale Andover, who has gone missing

Salla Burodai: [SAHL-uh BOOR-uh-die]: son of the late Great Soltayne, brother of Vashti, and leader of the Ilya

Xander Mynah [ZAN-der MIE-nuh]: chieftain of the Mynah tribe and sworn enemy of the Burodai

APPENDIX FIVE
BEASTS OF THE NEW WORLD

**the following bestiary notations are taken from*
Dawn of the Third World

Metamorphi

Morph soldiers take on two typical forms. Though Morphs can also take on other transformations with blood magic.

The winged Morphs were a favorite of Cyrus Maro, retaining most human capabilities with the addition of flight.

The warg-like beasts were terrors in battle, known for losing their minds to predatorial instincts.

Rulaq

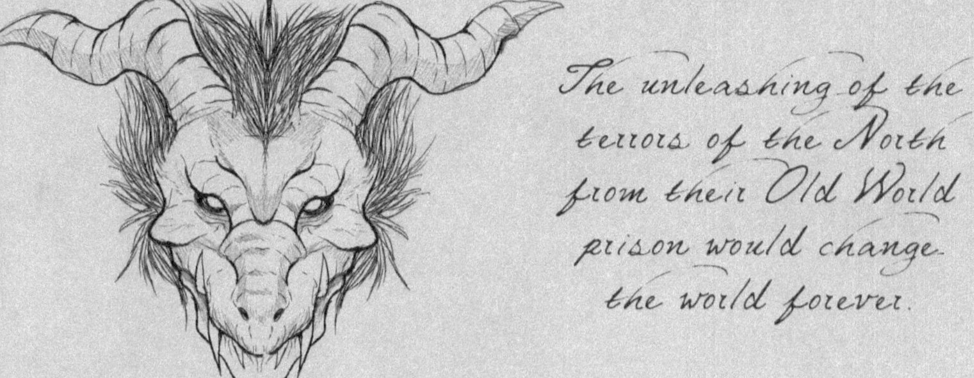

The unleashing of the terrors of the North from their Old World prison would change the world forever.

Teeth the size of large daggers.

And hide is thick as leathern armor.

Rulaqs are large enough to trample trees.

Nosferati

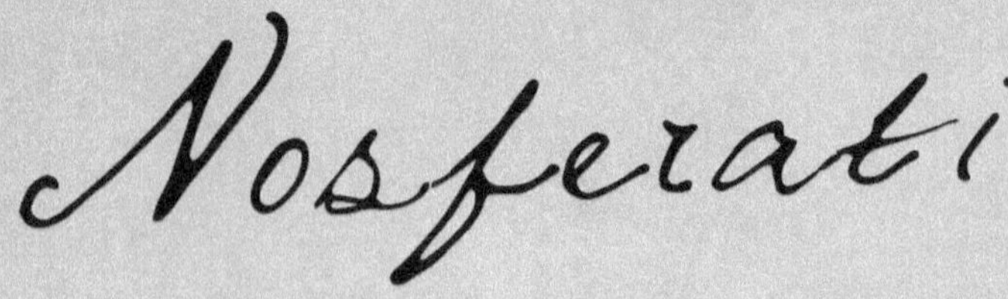

Long sharp claws are remarkably strong. Capable of ripping a man in half.

Glowing red eyes and razor sharp teeth betray the demon within.

Maintains a deceptively human form. But make no mistake. There is no humanity left inside. Only savagery.

STREET RATS OF THE FRINGES

(A SHADOW WATCH PREQUEL)

ONE
BRAWLERS

The Year 318 N.W.
Four years before the Day of the Gallows

Darien Redvar's body ached from the arduous march from his boyhood home in the mountains of Klavash. In the wintry conditions, the ice-cold shackles on his wrists and ankles had worn swollen red rings into his skin. He'd hardly eaten, and the water he drank was spoiled and foul, making his stomach roil with each step. But all this was no match for the turmoil in his heart.

At the outskirts of the sprawling slumlands of the Fringes, the Night Legion commander raised his hand for the slaves to stop. A host of slavers emerged from a crumbling brick building—one of few Fringe structures Darien had seen that didn't lean on the verge of toppling.

A Legion soldier shoved Darien's chin up with a cruel twist.

"Look alive, Redvar! Or face the chopping block!"

Darien fought the urge to tremble. From rage. Terror. Sorrow.

This sordid churning of emotions had left him raw and aching and empty. But he had resolved to never give one of these Oshan bastards the satisfaction of breaking him. At least not in front of their eyes.

The soldiers of the Night Legions had been hard and cruel over the past few weeks, but Darien expected nothing less from the monsters that had slaughtered his family. His entire village.

Yet, they had spared him. For reasons he would never fully understand. And now, Darien stood outside the Fringes of Osha, a teeming cesspool of slave hovels and workhouses.

Two dozen men and women, collected during the long march, stood in a line of newly-minted slaves in a grimy square that reeked of sewage.

The taskmasters made their way down the line as Lord Tamra offered words about each prisoner, touting all their potential as slaves.

A gruff Oshan man with a thick greying beard stopped in front of Darien.

"I think you'll find this one most enticing, Fletch," Lord Tamra said. "A fighter, this one. Killed a pair of my best soldiers in Klavash."

The bearded taskmaster named Fletch guffawed. "And yeh bloody spared 'im?"

Lord Tamra clapped his hand on Darien's shoulder. He winced at the contact from the cruel man.

Fletch looked him over like a predator surveying his latest kill. Darien stared past the man.

"How old are you, boy?"

"Fourteen," Darien responded, deadpan.

"A child," said the taskmaster.

"Look at his shoulders, Fletch," Tamra said. "Mountain boys aren't like the pissant lordlings. Redvar would make a fine addition to your lot. In a few years, he might make a bloody damn good soldier."

"If he survives!" Fletch cackled.

"Toughen the boy up, and the empire will pay you handsomely."

Fletch grabbed Darien by the chin and pulled him close, so Darien could taste the ale on his breath. Darien did not meet his gaze.

He pictured the meadow near his home. His mother's eyes. Willing himself to remain—

THUD!

The punch took his breath away. Pain blazed through his body. He doubled over, then quickly straightened, glaring fire at the bastard. His nails dug into his palms.

"Aye," said Fletch, rumbling with sick laughter. "Reckon there's some fire in him. With the right motivation. But if he loses…"

"I'll bet on Redvar's first gods-damned fight," Tamra said.

The men shook hands, and Fletch fixed his own chain to Darien's shackles, then a giant of a guard jerked him from the line.

———

THE FRINGES WERE THE GUTTERS OF THE OSHAN EMPIRE. BUT across Glacier Sound in the towering city of Maro'El, nobles lived in comfort and extravagance. Even from the plains approaching the Fringes, Darien had been able to glimpse the shimmering White Citadel towering in the distance.

The palace could shimmer, he understood now, because all the grime was shoveled off into this hellhole.

The stench of death and rot hung over the streets like an invisible cloud. Darien thought he had stunk during the long march, but he nearly retched on more than one occasion as Fletch led the way through the winding, muddied lanes to the far side of the sprawling ghetto.

"So, I'm to be a fighter?" Darien asked. "What kind?"

Fletch chortled. "The kind that wins, boy." He gestured to a rotund building ahead, with walls several stories high, no roof.

"That's my lord's stadium. No rules. Just two brawlers. Whoever has the guts, comes out alive."

"And the losers?"

Darien did not tremble at the thought. Death no longer scared him. It was the cost of survival that tugged at his insides. *You've already paid the price once,* he thought.

"There's no place for losers in the Fringes," Fletch said. "But we're not complete barbarians. Brawlers are matched according to size and experience. So, make damn sure you're ready."

They entered a small compound near the stadium, with an inner courtyard where, even in the winter chill, bare-chested men sparred with wooden blades. As they entered, the brawlers turned around and glared at Darien. Sizing him up for slaughter.

"Meet Redvar," Fletch announced. "Our newest recruit. I trust you'll… make him feel welcome."

The wicked grins that stretched the fighters' faces offered Darien little comfort.

The giant guard removed Darien's shackles, then stepped away to stand beside his master.

"I treat my fighters well," Fletch said. "You'll be fed, given a bed. No chains, unless you're outside the compound. If you win… well, then you'll earn an even better treat. How's that for charitable?"

A chorus of chuckles filled the yard.

Darien nodded and took in his new "home."

The compound was three stories high, and on the upper level, several guards paced a wall walk between towers. Each man carried a long musket against his shoulder.

Charitable, Darien thought. *The bastard actually believes that.*

Darien rubbed his aching wrists as the brawlers gathered round him. He held his head high and took note of each man. A skill his father had taught him every time they encountered traders from other villages. Especially foreigners. The worst ones were always the Oshans.

And Fletch had conditioned all these men.

A short Jurkan stepped from the crowd. He was not built like one of the Morgathian prize fighters Darien had heard tales about. He was scrawny, but what meat he had on his bones was all muscle. His eyes were wild. Predatorial. Without provocation, he drew *very* close.

Darien backed away, but the giant shoved him forward. The Jurkan swung his fist, and Darien barely managed to roll away, as the other fighters jeered.

So, it's like that, is it?

Darien scrambled back to his feet, quickly scanning the muddy ground for any signs of a rock. Anything he could use for a weapon. A sweeping kick to the ribs sent him rolling again.

The brawlers roared with laughter.

The Jurkan's face twisted into an evil leer.

"Come on," shouted one of the fighters. "Show us what yeh got, kid!"

Darien's heart thundered in his chest. He fought to remain calm, the way his father had taught him. The thought of his father's death steeled his resolve.

Just like the soldiers Darien had killed, this man was stronger. But he under-estimated Darien. The poor village boy whose family had been slaughtered while he watched. Helpless. Weak.

The Jurkan leapt forward throwing a huge right hook. Darien managed to brush it away with a sweep of his left arm, but not without jarring pain, as the man's fist glanced off his elbow. Darien spun, just in time to deflect another punch.

He backed away again, bumping into the giant guard.

"Touch me again, and I'll—"

Darien leapt forward before the giant could shove him again, ripping a pair of shackles from the guard's belt. Clamping one around his own wrist, Darien gripped the other clasp in his fist.

The Jurkan glanced at Fletch, but the taskmaster shook his head. "No rules, Raz!"

Raz let out a fierce roar and charged, fists flying. Darien ducked one blow, and parried another with his free hand. He swung the shackle at the man's head. Instinctively, Raz blocked the attack with his hand, but howled as the jagged iron struck the back of his hand.

"Don't get your face knocked in!" one of the fighters hollered.

The Jurkan spun away, gritting his teeth in pain. One of the other fighters tossed him a wooden staff.

Raz brandished the weapon eagerly.

He leapt forward. The first strike missed, but as Darien scampered out of the way, a stray foot shot out, and Darien slipped in the mud, falling hard on his knee.

The second strike hit him across the back and sent him sprawling forward.

His fingers clamped around fistfuls of mud. Raz raced toward him. Darien ducked the attack and let mud fly. Right into the Jurkan's eyes.

Raz roared, swinging his stick blindly. Darien swung his chain around the stick. He snatched the loose shackle and twisted with all his strength.

With a furious cry, the stick went flying out of reach.

Raz pawed at his muddy face. And Darien leapt in, tackling the man to the ground with a jarring thud. An elbow to the gut nearly sent him reeling, but he held tight. He absorbed blow after blow as he scrambled to maneuver his body around the man. Teeth sunk into his left forearm, and Darien took the abuse, while he swung his shackle around and clamped it onto his other wrist.

He jerked backward, pulling the man back on top of himself, wrapping his legs round the man's waist. The chain pulled taut against the Jurkan's throat.

Raz gasped desperately, clawing at the chain. At Darien. Anything. But there was no way for him to move without pulling the chain tighter.

Raz's movements slowed as his screams turned to muffled rasps. His movements weakened, but Darien did not relent.

He envisioned his sister's tiny form, lying in the dirt, a bullet through her chest. Soldiers congratulating one another.

His entire body tensed.

"All right, all right! You bloody won!"

The voice belonged to Fletch.

The Jurkan had gone limp in Darien's grasp, and someone behind him was pulling at his shoulders.

Darien snapped out of his revery and released the Jurkan.

The man had gone completely still.

Darien drew the chain up and over the man's head as the giant knelt down to investigate.

"Did I—"

The giant shook his head. "Nah, he's breathing. Barely."

Raz spasmed. Then coughed up mud and bloody spittle.

Darien sighed as the other brawlers gathered around. The yard filled with excited murmurings.

A large hand clasped his shoulder.

Darien flinched. But the touch was not meant to harm.

Another hand clasped his chain and tugged him up to his feet.

Fletch shook his head with a grin. He unlocked the shackles once more. The man stooped down to look Darien in the eyes.

This time, Darien held his gaze.

"Lucky you didn't kill him, boy."

Darien nodded. "Yes, sir."

Another fighter helped a barely conscious Raz to his feet, but all eyes in the compound were on Darien.

"I reckon Tamra was right," Fletch said, giving him a soft shove toward the other fighters. "I'd bet on your first fight too."

TWO
SPECTATORS

I don't give a damn about the bloody fights," Tori said, shoving her way through the teeming masses of Fringe rats.

Curly haired Cera gripped her wrist tight and continued to tug Tori along, as though she hadn't heard.

"Come on, Tori, I'm not going to that place alone!"

At sixteen, Cera was three years older than Tori, and much stronger. She was also the daughter of Tori's taskmaster at the textile houses, and the only reason Tori was allowed to leave her duties before nightfall. This was the first time Tori had seen the sun in a week.

"*Oooor*, we could do something actually fun," Tori said.

A large greasy man shoved his way past them, and Tori nearly fell over as she spun around the massive body.

"Watch yerself, little wench!" the man growled.

"Oh, sorry, milord," Tori murmured.

"Go to the Abyss!" the greasy man shouted, his voice diminishing into the crowd.

Tori waited a few moments, then, held up the man's shoddy-looking iron dagger for her companion to see.

Cera blanched. "You'll get yourself killed lifting off bastards like that."

Tori shrugged. "I thought you liked that sort of *shenzah!*"

"Gods, we're not on the bloody Steppe, horse girl! We're in Osha. The greatest nation in the world. Is it really so hard to swear like it?"

Tori offered the older girl a smirk. It was almost comical the degree to which Cera embraced the propaganda of Osha. Even here in this cesspool. Sure, Cera enjoyed a little more comfort in her life than the rest of the Fringe rats, because her taskmaster father served a kinder lord.

What did that amount to?

A shanty with brick walls for a home, rather than the typical rotting wooden shack. Cera shivered through every winter night, huddled up against her father. When he wasn't working through the night. When someone hadn't stolen their blankets.

And yet, Cera still thought of their masters with blind patriotism. Typical Oshan.

Cera was still a slave, just like Tori, and no slave in all of Osha had a good life, no matter their heritage.

Tori and Cera continued on their way to a sparring stadium where Cera's Oshan boyfriend was going to fight to the death against some brawler from Jurka or the Southern Isles.

Cera barely batted an eye at the boys Taven had killed. Nor did she seem to fear for Taven's life either.

Perhaps Cera wasn't that blind, after all.

Tori herself was growing numb to the reality of the Fringes of Osha, and she hated herself for it. It was a jarring contrast to life under her former master in the Trium.

Such was the tenuous fate of all slaves.

One bad deal, and Tori's "comfortable" life in the Southern World was over, and off she shipped to the Fringes.

It was hardly the first cruel twist of fate the gods had dealt her.

But she would survive this one too. She would adjust. She would do whatever it took.

Tori led Cera into a narrow lane between shanties and pulled her close.

"One of these times, Taven's not going to win," Tori said softly.

Cera shrugged and rolled her eyes. But there was a slight tell in her eyes. "If you'd rather go back to the workhouse…"

Tori shoved the girl in the shoulder. "Don't be a horse's ass!"

"I thought horses were supposed to be majestic."

"No ass is majestic," Tori said. "Not even a horse."

"Give it a couple years, and we'll see what you think," Cera said, with a wink.

"Gross!" Tori said, shoving her again. She gripped the girl's hand. "Let's just get this over with already."

———

THUNDEROUS ROARS MADE TORI'S ENTIRE BODY TREMBLE AS slaves dragged the decapitated Parjhan man's body from the arena. Blood streamed across the stone and attendants rushed to mop it up.

Tori's stomach lurched at the sight.

But Cera raised her fists in the air and screamed her head off with all the rest.

They watched from one of the middle rows. The entire place smelled of sweat and bodies not washed in months. Some of them, probably years. Tori'd thought she was growing used to the stench. But she'd never seen so many Fringe rats in one place before.

Except on burning nights.

Tori pushed the haunting images of the pyres from her mind.

"Bloody savage!" Cera shouted as the victor raised two swords over his head and roared. Cera clapped Tori on the shoulder and laughed. "Beats the Abyss out of work, doesn't it?"

Tori had to laugh. The girl had one of the softest jobs on the line. Packaging finished garments. Tori worked one of the machines, constantly replacing needles and clearing thread from jammed mechanisms with split-second speed. After a month, her fingers were just starting to build calluses thick enough to manage the constant discomfort.

But Tori forced an eager grin. She'd learned enough to know you had to play the game with anyone who could make your life better.

"He had a lucky break! Both those swords were placed closer to him from the start. Bit boring, really."

Cera shook her head with a chuckle. "The blood's the fun, Tori! Who cares how easy it flows?"

And if it were Taven's? Tori wondered.

"Oh, oh, look!" Cera's eyes widened as blond-haired Taven Thorne emerged from an arched doorway across the arena.

His shirt was removed to reveal lean muscles and porcelain skin. He wasn't exactly built like a Morgathian prize fighter, but his body was all muscle.

Cera howled with glee as Taven's opponent emerged after him.

The boy's skin was light brown. Hair darker than Tori's own. Even from a distance, she could tell he was younger than Taven. Barely a man grown. But his shoulders were broad, legs thick as tree trunks. A mountain boy.

"Darien Redvar!" announced the fight master from his box seat overlooking the arena.

"Oh, this is gonna be a gore-fest!" Cera shouted, squeezing Tori's hand.

The boy, Redvar, was not as tall, but he surely matched Taven's strength at a glance.

"I don't get it," Tori said. "Looks like an even match."

"He's a Klavash boy," Cera said disdainfully.

"I don't—"

"Gods! You *are* a bloody foreigner! I don't care if your mum was Oshan. The Klavash are weak. Peace-loving. Whatever you wanna call it. Bet that boy's never fought a man in his life."

The girl giggled eagerly.

Tori's stomach churned as the two young men squared off. Two thick poles of wood were set on opposite ends of the arena. The boys made their way to the starting blocks.

Taven hefted his arms in the air, eliciting roars from the crowd. He'd been a crowd favorite in his first matches, according to Cera.

The Klavash boy remained calm. Concentration fixed on his opponent. His brown eyes shone, and Tori was struck by a sense of sadness.

She did not know why. But she did not want this boy to die.

It was wrong.

A burly guard took a long dagger and jammed it into the frozen ground directly between the two fighters and stepped back.

"Aha!" Cera cried. "Only one blade!"

THREE
THE PRICE OF LIVING

Darien took one long slow breath as the guard stepped away. Time slowed. The stadium disappeared. The roars of the crowd faded. The world was Darien and the Oshan fighter named Taven. And the dagger between them.

Taven was tall and lean. Quicker than Darien. He could tell at a glance.

Take what's given to you, Fletch had told him. *You can't change it. The dead ones fall trying to force what they want rather than using what they got.*

Darien would not reach the blade first. To try might be the death of him. His next move would determine everything.

The Oshan boy eyed Darien like a savage predator. He saw Darien as weak. As the typical Klavash mountain lad. Strong, but inexperienced in combat. Hardy, but hesitant to kill.

Fletch had told him as much. But Darien already knew from years of experience. His father had taught him to use this to his benefit during their journeys to Morgath for trade.

The world always under-estimated the Klavash. And Darien used this to his advantage against the Night Legions. Against Raz.

This Oshan boy had no idea what Darien was capable of.

A horn blared.

The reverberations hung over the arena the same way the Night Legion horns had announced the fall of his village.

Taven pushed off from the starting block at a dead sprint, and Darien raced to meet him. His bare feet were numb on the hard ground. His breaths were knives in his lungs.

A full body length ahead, the Oshan boy snatched up the dagger and braced himself for the attack.

Right before he met him, Darien dropped, ducking the boy's slashing attack. He slid feet first, gripped a stone with his hands, and swung his feet hard.

Taven expected him to go for the blade.

That would have been his death.

The boy's feet dropped out from under him, and he met the ground with a jarring thud. But he held on to the blade.

Taven spun, dagger raised, as Darien met him.

Again, he did not go for the blade.

Taven lashed out. Darien shirked the attack, gripping the boy's elbow and letting his momentum carry him past, while Darien's knee drove into his thigh.

The Oshan boy tumbled onto the ground.

Darien's hands trembled. The cold amplifying the pain of every jarring impact.

Taven leapt forward, swinging the blade at Darien's neck. He dodged it, sweeping the attacking hand away with his forearm, and punched the boy in the throat with his other hand.

The boy staggered back. Reached for his neck.

Darien grabbed the boy's wrist and wrenched it in a hard twist that snapped bone.

The wrist went limp. The blade clattered to the ground. Darien swept his foot, and the ground fell out from under Taven's feet. His head jolted on impact. Darien leapt on top of him. Driving knees into his shoulders. He took a weak punch to the face as he grabbed Taven's hair and throttled his skull against the ground. Once. Twice.

Taven's hands went slack at his sides. His body twitched.

Eyes wide with terror as death neared.

Darien's mind flooded with memory.

His mother's eyes. Brown like the boy's. Going still forever. Snow falling. Mind screaming. The world swallowing Darien into a realm of bitter, helpless fury.

He froze.

The Oshan boy looked up at him with fearful tears streaming. The roars of the crowd struck him like an avalanche, jolting him back to reality.

They longed for blood. This world longed for blood. It had taken his parents. Stolen his old life. Just as this crowd lusted for him to steal this boy's.

Darien would not let them steal his soul.

He released his grip on Taven, and eased back.

The boy's entire body shuddered.

Darien rose to his feet, with the shouts of the angry crowd raining down on him.

And he stalked back to the arches at the edge of the arena.

———

Tori watched, transfixed. Cera gripped her hand so tight she could barely feel her fingers, and let out a gasp as Darien Redvar backed away from Taven's body.

The crowd went utterly still.

At first, Tori thought the boy must have already died from the blows to his skull. Then, Taven's feet twitched. His chest heaved.

The Klavash fighter marched away, never glancing back.

A burly soldier marched to the center of the arena and jerked Taven to his feet. The boy nearly collapsed. He clung to the guard's shoulder and staggered as they crossed the arena.

The crowd turned into a shouting mob, and Tori tugged at Cera's arm. All these Fringe rats were screaming for the death of her boyfriend.

Everyone's attention was fixed on the arena. Attendants scrambled to ready for the next fight. A Morgathian prizefighter was brought out the moment Taven was out of sight. Attendants wheeled out an enormous cage with a north bear. Its roar filled the stadium. And the crowd's anger subsided.

"Let's go," Tori murmured.

Cera nodded, unable to speak between sobs. The girl covered her mouth with her hand, and Tori led the way down a back set of stairs and the roars faded to a din.

"He's still alive," Tori said softly.

Cera shook her head as they reached the bottom level, a long wide corridor that encircled the base of the stadium. Enormous stone pillars lined the path like the trunks of socha trees. The weight of the entire structure converging upon them. Tori felt as though the place might crush them at any moment.

Ahead, the corridor was blocked by an iron gate, monitored by a pair of Legion soldiers.

"I-I've got to go to him!" Cera said, suddenly, and in an instant, the girl's hand slipped from Tori's grasp, and she raced toward the gate.

Both guards bore muskets over their shoulders. They held their bayonets out as a warning, but Cera didn't stop. Blessedly, the guards drew back their guns. One of them caught Cera by the shoulder as she tried to race past and shoved her against the gate. She shrieked as her head banged against the metal, and she slumped to her knees.

Tori's gut wrenched as she caught up. She raised her hands in the air as the other guard jutted out his musket toward her.

"Please! I'm just trying to help my friend!" Tori knelt down and gripped Cera's hand. The older girl knelt on the cold stone, shaking.

"What in the Abyss are you thinking? Shoving a girl like that?" Tori demanded, glaring up at the offending guard.

She'd seen the look of horror in his eyes as Cera's head hit the gate.

"She's a bloody taskmaster's daughter!" Tori added.

"I meant no harm," the guard said, a trace of worry crossing his face.

"No spectators allowed," insisted the other. "I don't care who she is."

"She's shook up, okay?" Tori said. "Her boy just lost his fight."

The guards nodded. Perhaps not sympathy, but understanding.

"Th-there he is!" Cera shouted.

Down the corridor past the gate, a pair of guards shoved Taven Thorne forward. He collapsed on the stone ground. A tall wiry man in fine clothes followed, glowering as a guard kicked Taven in the back.

"Her boy lost," said one of the guards, "and still lives?"

Taven howled in pain as the guards grabbed him by the chains. The well-dressed man—Taven's master, Tori was certain—grabbed a long wooden rod from an attendant and the corridor echoed with a sickening crunch.

The boy crumpled on the ground.

FOUR
THE WAY THE WORLD IS

All at once, Cera flew into a fit of hysterics. She wrenched away from Tori's grasp and scrambled towards the gate. The guards, distracted by the beating, reacted too late, and Cera slipped past.

Tori watched in horror as Taven's master swung the rod once more, cracking against the boy's skull. His entire body shuddered and went still.

The hall fell silent, and Tori's gut ached. Cera froze in her tracks, waiting for Taven to move.

The guards made to pursue her.

"Leave her!" Tori held up a small purse of coins, and the guards stopped. She handed the purse over to them. It was all she had. Lifted off a few Fringe rats over the past week.

"It's too late, anyway," the guard said, shaking his head. "No loser lives."

"Then, let her mourn," Tori muttered coldly.

Tori strode past the men and hurried to catch up to Cera. The taskmaster's daughter threw herself on top of Taven's body. No one stopped the weeping girl.

Taven's master handed the beating rod over to his attendant, and without another word, turned away and left his servants to clean up the aftermath. He strode out a corridor that led back to the stadium.

The corridor resounded with Cera's cries.

Three attendants stood around, watching. One waved Tori away, but she ignored the man and knelt beside her friend. She reached for Taven's wrist and checked his pulse.

But it was as she'd feared.

Tori hadn't even known the boy, but tears traced down her cheeks. She'd seen bodies before. But not like this.

Taven's blood was warm. His body had yet to stiffen. But in one instant, his spirit was worlds away.

Tori couldn't help thinking that it would have been better for the boy to die in the arena. There was nobility in that. She'd learned that much in her short life.

This was not a good death.

It was a tragedy.

"You can't be here," said a guard, drawing closer.

Cera shook with silent sobs. Her hair, her clothes, everything was coated in blood.

Tori gripped her friend's shoulder. "We need to go. Now."

Cera shoved her away, mumbling something incoherent.

"He wouldn't want you to die too," Tori said.

The guards closed in around them. A hand clasped Tori's shoulder.

She spun around, fire in her bones. "I'll get her out! Don't make this worse. You want to kill a girl too?"

The burly man glowered down at her. "I'm not getting beaten so some girl can cry. We need to clean this mess up. "

Cera turned to face the man. "Mess? He's bloody dead!"

The man crossed thick arms over his chest. "He was a brawler. He lost. Welcome to the Fringes, kid."

Cera nodded, whimpering, her hand over her face.

"No one else needs to die," the burly man said with a nod to Tori. "So I suggest you make your peace and get home."

Tori realized now, even a lifetime in this place, even the loss of her own mother, had not driven out Cera's hope. She'd never fully accepted the fact that Taven was always a dead man walking. For all the tough-girl front that Cera had put up since Tori'd met her, she was just a scared child now.

Tori gripped her hand and pulled the girl to her feet. Cera wrapped her in a tremulous embrace. Completely enveloping her.

It was strange to comfort a girl so much older than she.

Cera had spent her whole life here in the Fringes, and yet it was Tori who held her. It was Tori who remained strong. She wondered if, deep down, that was why Cera had latched on to her. Why she'd insisted Tori come today.

"Come on," Tori murmured, and she led the girl away.

Cera said nothing, but she didn't resist. Tori wrapped her arm around the girl and urged her back toward the gate. The guards stood tall, muskets draped over their shoulders. They didn't even turn as Tori and Cera approached.

A cry resounded from the chamber, and Tori glanced back.

Her heart thundered as the other fighter, Darien Redvar, was shoved out from the same hall they'd brought Taven.

She stopped.

Cera spun around too. Her voice was ice. "Oh, I hope they beat his bones to bloody dust!"

Tori didn't know what to do. She suppressed the inexplicable urge to race back down the corridor.

Redvar held his head high. His face betrayed no expression as a giant of a guard led him out. An Oshan taskmaster with a thick greying beard emerged from another corridor. They stood around Taven's body.

The Oshan looked up the corridor. "Ay! Get those gawking girls out of here!"

The guards at the gate spun and fearfully motioned the girls through. "Mourning's over. Get lost quick, if you know what's good for you."

"What in the Abyss did you think would happen?" the Oshan shouted at Darien.

Tori glanced back to find the taskmaster shoving Darien to his knees.

"Kill him," Cera muttered.

"Heh!" one of the guards said, as they reached the gate. "That's Fletch. He runs this bloody place. And that boy was one of his own fighters."

Tori shuddered. The boy had defied his master's rules in his own stadium.

"Whatever happens to the boy, it'll happen back at their training compound," the other guard said.

The guard motioned beyond the stadium. A small crowd had formed at the gate, and the guards barked orders for everyone to disperse.

Tori and Cera hurried to the end of the corridor and exited the stadium, while the roars from another finished fight erupted behind them.

The square outside was filled with Fringe rats. Tori shoved her way past a man peddling charred rats impaled on wooden spikes.

The grimy lanes beyond the square were empty, and Tori and Cera slowed when they escaped the throng outside the stadium.

Cera's head hung low. The girl's terror had turned to a bitter rage.

"Gods, I hope they bleed him dry."

"He didn't kill Taven."

Cera met her gaze, eyes ablaze. "No, he left him to die in shame! Taven was a warrior. That boy's a bloody coward! And if you can't see that, you won't last any longer in this hellhole than he will!"

The girl's words pierced straight through her. She merely nodded.

Nothing Tori could say could bring Taven back. Nothing she could say would change the pitiful way the boy Cera loved had died.

Cera's rage blinded her to the true enemy—the Oshans who built these slumlands.

But it didn't matter.

Cera was right. That Klavash boy wouldn't last. Perhaps not even this night.

Tori released Cera's arm as they reached the large walls surrounding the textile houses.

"What are you doing?" Cera asked.

Tori gestured for the main servant's entrance a few hundred yards down the wall. Cera's home was close.

"I should get back to work," Tori said.

"Y-you're going to leave me?"

Tori felt a pang in her gut, but there was nothing for it. "Get home, Cera," Tori said.

"Look, I'm sorry for what I—"

"No, you were right. No one survives this place by going soft. And that goes for you and me too."

The girl's eyes brimmed with tears.

"I'm sorry about Taven. I'm sorry about all the people that've died in this place. But that's the way the world is. We all do what we got to survive."

With that, Tori turned away. She strode along the wall, waiting till she was halfway to the gates before glancing back. Cera was gone.

Tori knew she'd never have another daytime escape from the textile mill again. Not by Cera's doing.

But she'd make the most of what she had.

Tori turned down a narrow lane between ramshackle huts.

She did not return to work.

FIVE
DEATH WISH

Darien's wrists ached as the giant jerked him forward. Night had descended on the Fringes like a shroud of death. The streets were vacant but for a few guards stationed outside the stadium gates.

All Fletch's fighters marched out in a line, shackles attached to one long, heavy chain that dragged between their legs with an incessant clanging.

Darien marched at the front. Spiteful mutterings echoed behind him. Most he couldn't distinguish. His mind seemed to hover somewhere outside his own body. Lost amidst a crowd of ghosts.

But when they stopped outside Fletch's compound, Raz's sharp whisper cut straight through him, jolting him back to the real world. They were now back within the walls of Fletch's training compound.

"I hope it's me who's matched with you next games," Raz muttered. "I ripped the throat out of mine today. I can still taste the blood."

"Shut your traps!" the giant guard bellowed. "The day's done. And you've won honor for this house. Tomorrow, it's back to work. But tonight, enjoy the spoils of your victories."

A crowd of servants in white tunics emerged from an archway that led to Fletch's own home. The women bore trays of food and flagons of wine, and their attire suggested other festivities might ensue.

All at once, it was as though Darien were invisible. The brawlers howled with excitement and triumph.

The giant strode down the line, unlocking shackles. As they were freed, the servants escorted the men back toward the cell block.

When the giant reached Darien, he untethered him from the chain, but left the shackles on.

"No feasting for you," the brute said.

The giant strode down a narrow hall lit by lanterns, motioning for Darien to follow. The others had all retreated to the inner sanctum of the compound. Raucous laughter echoed through the corridors, somehow leaving Darien feeling even more alone.

A pair of guards opened the gates at the end of the hall, and the giant led Darien out into the harsh exposure of the training arena. The thick mud had frozen over and snow fell from the heavens in slow swirls.

The giant jerked Darien's head to look to his right. Across the arena, Fletch sauntered over, dressed in a thick fur cloak. Darien wore only his tattered shirt and trousers, still stained with blood. The frigid shackles dug into his wrists, biting like a circular blade.

Fletch stopped a few feet from him and eyed him up and down. Darien looked the man in the eyes, waiting for him to draw the saber at his belt. He'd known what he was doing when he let his opponent live.

"Bloody Klavash fool," Fletch muttered, shaking his head. "And for what?"

Darien glanced away, picturing the body of the boy, his life's blood pooled around him.

He had killed once. And the shame of it enveloped him. He could still see the sorrow in his mother's dying eyes. No matter how he strove to justify his actions, he knew he could not. He'd struck before the Legion soldiers could fight back. It was the coward's path. A duel of shame.

"Do you have a death wish, boy?"

Darien did not answer.

"Course you don't," Fletch said, clapping him on the shoulder. "Else, you would've let that boy run you through. Nah, it's that bloody mountain thinking and your damn god of peace."

Darien had stopped believing in Rivka the day his family was slaughtered.

"You know nothing of my people. Or their god."

"Their god," Fletch said. "You see, your transformtion's already begun."

Darien stared past the man. "Leave me with what honor I got left, sir, and kill me."

"Heheh!" Fletch's cackle echoed off the stone walls of the compound. "And waste a good investment?"

"What do you mean?"

"You're a scrapper, boy. And I mean to take full advantage of it." Fletch motioned to the main gate. The wrought iron doors spread wide and another guard dragged a boy along after him.

Darien's blood chilled. The boy was his own age, maybe younger. Certainly smaller. Short and scrawny, still coming into the body of a man. And like Darien, he wore no cloak.

Fletch gazed up into the streaks of falling snow. "Storm's coming. Give it an hour. Maybe two. When it sets in, neither one of you will survive the night. So, that leaves you with a decision to make. Only way you leave this arena is with the body of the other at your feet."

The guards unshackled the boy. He bore high cheek bones and olive skin. Long dark hair, pulled back in a thick braid suggested a horse boy from the Steppe. The boy's eyes were full of fear as he faced Darien.

"You decide, Redvar. Do you have a death wish? Or will you accept the world as it is?"

Fletch and the guards backed away leaving the two fighters alone in the arena.

Darien planted his feet in a crouch as the Yan Avii boy sized him up. The boy's jaw trembled. Darien had never seen the boy before, so he must be new to Fletch's lot.

Did that mean he was new to the arena too?

Taven had learned the hard way about underestimating Darien. He wouldn't make the same mistake. The horse boy circled him, eyes wide.

Darien's gut twisted at what he had to do.

"Go to the Abyss!" the Yan Avii boy shouted.

And he sprinted at Darien.

———

Tori clambered her way up the outer walls of the compound. The stones were nothing like the perfectly-fit bricks of Trium buildings.

Far as she'd seen in the past month, there was no such thing as a well-constructed building in the Fringes. The mortar was crumbling away from every seam between stones, and her fingers and toes wedged in easily. But in the snow and cold, her fingers throbbed with each move. Slowly growing numb against the stones. As Tori reached the top of the wall, she wrapped her fingers in scraps of cloth.

The very edge was lined with glass. She gripped it gingerly with one hand, keeping the pressure on her feet as much as she could. As she maneuvered one foot higher, stone crumbled beneath her other foot.

She gripped hard with her fingers. Even with the cloth, the pain was excruciating. But she was light and strong. Gritting through the pain, she planted one foot and heaved herself upward. Her other foot caught the next stone up and she threw herself over, tumbling onto the wall walk between towers.

Her chest heaved. Palms stung. She shook her hands violently, biting back a scream, as she glanced up and down the walk. But there were no guards on patrol.

Because what mad girl would try to break into a brawler compound in the middle of a stormy winter night?

There were no footprints along the wall walk, and the snow was falling harder. Tori followed the wall until she reached a set of stairs, and crept deeper into the training facility.

Laughter echoed from the towers at either end of the walk, illuminated by blazing fires. And other sounds too. Tori had watched them bring the nightlings to the compound.

But whatever gods watched over the Klavash, perhaps they were watching tonight.

SIX
NO MARTYRS

I *had no choice, gods damn it,* Darien told himself over and over.

Unmoving, the Yan Avii boy lay at his feet. Darien's own body had gone numb, as though his spirit were drifting away on the winter wind, leaving only a shell behind.

The giant guard knelt in the snow and shook his head. "Still breathing," the gruff man said. "Just finish the damn job, boy, and come inside."

Darien's teeth rattled in his skull. He couldn't feel his fingers, even tucked into his armpits. His eyes streamed with half-frozen tears. He shook his head.

"He'll die out here," Darien muttered. "What's the difference?"

"You know the difference," the giant said. He gestured to a large stone nearby. "There's no saints in the Fringes, boy. No martyrs neither. You got talent. The master can see that. This is your chance at a life. Take it."

Darien dipped his chin against the cold and turned from the man.

The gate clattered in the distance as the giant returned to the warmth of the compound.

He'd used a sleeper hold on the horse boy. It was all Darien could think to do, when he attacked. But Darien could not bring himself to kill him. He already had the blood of those Legion soldiers on his hands.

And yet, Darien refused to be killed either.

He eyed the horse boy with terror. Snow coated his entire body now. But his chest still rose and fell tepidly.

"Better to die with your soul in tact," his mother had told him before she died. One last plea after she watched him kill those soldiers.

All of it had amounted to nothing. His family died, regardless of his resistance. Taven died in the arena. And this Yan Avii boy's soul would be lost in this storm, the same as Darien's.

Deep down, he wished he would have relented. Let the Yan Avii boy bash in his skull with that same stone the giant had pointed out.

Darien feared his soul had already drifted away.

He couldn't take back what he'd done. Couldn't reason it away as self-defense. But every time he tried to picture himself finishing the deed, he saw only his mother in the boy's face. Watching as the soldiers murdered his father. Putting up no fight as they stole her honor. Stole her life.

Anger surged through him at how gently she'd left this world.

Kneeling beside the Yan Avii boy, Darien shook him, hard.

But it was no use.

The wind howled above the arena. Snow whipping around, as though the night had brought all the ghosts of Ghen upon him in a torrent. Darien could not even see the guard towers in the raging storm. And he did not care. Let the storm whisk him away to join the throngs of tormented spirits that haunted the forest outside these slumlands.

He closed his eyes to the storm. His mind to the cold and retreated deeper and deeper within himself.

Returning to the mountains of his boyhood. His first stag.

He and his father kneeling beside the majestic fallen creature.

"Death begets life," his father said. "It is nothing to fear. But never to be taken lightly."

His father leaned over and whispered the prayer of departing. And in the middle of the arena, kneeling beside the Yan Avii boy, Darien murmured the same prayer. Though in his heart, he knew there was no life in this for either of them.

A sudden gust of wind nearly sent Darien reeling. His eyes sprang open. A sharp hiss filled his ears.

The gust struck again. And again.

As though rousing from a stupor, Darien dimly realized it was not wind at all.

"Come on, come on. Stay awake, damn you!"

Darien spun, nearly toppling over. Small hands steadied his frozen body. He looked up into shimmering green eyes. Wild dark hair darted in the wind. And those hands shook him again.

A girl.

It was a girl. Here in the midst of the storm. Impossible.

"Arayeva!" she murmured.

The goddess of the Yan Avii. Darien was surely drifting into madness.

But the girl shook him again, tugging at his arms.

"Come on, you have to get up! You won't last much longer. You have to MOVE!"

Darien's legs shifted. The surprisingly strong girl heaved her weight beneath his arm with her shoulder.

And he was on his feet, gazing down at a scrawny girl who barely reached his shoulders. She glared up at him with fire in her eyes.

"They can't see *shenzah*!" she murmured. "I can get you out of here!"

———

THE KLAVASH BOY SQUINTED AT TORI THROUGH NEARLY FROZEN eyelids. "Y-you're real?" He looked as though he were greeting a spirit from the Aether. He shook his head, eyes flickering. He began to slump back to the ground.

Tori slapped his face. "Yeah, I'm bloody real. I'm Tori Burodai, and we have to go. Now!"

Sorrow and anger raged in her gut. She feared she was too late.

But the slap roused something in the Klavash fighter. He forced his eyes wider.

Tori gripped his hand. His fingers felt like ice, but somehow, they closed around her own. Then, he pulled away.

"What are you doing?" Tori hissed.

Darien motioned with his entire hand toward a form on the ground. Tori shuddered.

"I c-can't l-leave him," Darien said, shivering. He trudged toward the boy.

Tori pushed past him and knelt beside the second boy, nearly covered in snow. Yan Avii, just like her father.

She checked his wrist for a pulse, but his life fire was gone. More anger surged through her at the cruelty of this world. Tears blurred her vision. She blinked hard and focused. There was nothing for it.

Darien looked down with hope in his eyes.

It killed Tori to see it. The same goodness she had witnessed in the arena that afternoon, despite the terrible hand he'd been dealt.

"I'm sorry," she whispered, rising to her feet.

Darien shook his head back and forth, back and forth.

"Better to die with your soul in tact," he muttered, pulling away from her.

Tori slapped him again. "You didn't do this!" she hissed, seizing his hand. "They did! Don't let his sacrifice be for nothing."

A change dawned in Darien's expression. His fingers gripped her own. "Okay."

Tori held on fiercely, as though he might slip away into the storm if she let go for even a moment. She trudged against the biting wind back the way she'd come. Into the swirling wall of whiteness. The first steps felt like she was pulling an entire ox cart all by herself, but as they moved, the Klavash boy grew stronger, his movements more lucid.

Tori's body was cold, but a warmth filled her from deep within. Perhaps it was her own determination.

They reached a gate to the arena and Tori pushed past into a corridor. Best Tori could guess, it was where servants unloaded goods for the compound. One wide hall exposed to the elements from above, halfway between two guard towers. The guards had retreated indoors, either from the weather or to steal a moment of frivolity with the others.

The corridor at least sheltered them from the wind, but the snow still pelted down from the skies. Despite his near-death experience, Darien kept up with Tori as they moved. Ahead, Tori spotted the lone guard outpost beside an outer gate to the compound. Nothing but a small enclosed room with no light emanating from within.

As they neared, Darien stopped.

"Th-that gate'll be locked."

Tori looked up at him and grinned. She held up a key.

Darien's eyes grew wide. "How?"

"Magic," she said, then chuckled at his expression. "Obviously, if it was magic, the chancellor's Morphs would already be ripping our throats out. There's lots of wine going around this place tonight. Didn't take long to find a guard who'd had too much."

Darien shook his head. "All this seems like m-magic. Or a d-dream."

"Well, it's not over yet," Tori said, and tugged him toward the gate.

There were only three keys on the guard's ring, so it didn't take Tori long to find the right one. Carefully, she turned it. When the lock gave, there was a loud clink that made them both jump.

Voices filled the night somewhere behind them.

"*Shenzah!*" Tori muttered. "Come on, hurry!"

Heart racing, Tori shoved the gate open with all her might and slammed it shut as soon as Darien was through.

More voices.

She hurled the keys into the snow, and took off.

Darien stumbled, but managed to keep his feet as they raced across the main road and slipped into a narrow lane between shanties.

Shouts and the clanging of metal resounded in the distance. Tori dared one last glance back, to find several guards scrambling out the same gate they'd left.

SEVEN
STREET RATS

The Fringes were desolate this time of night. Any Fringe rats not working the late shifts in the factories were huddled in their hovels. Tori and Darien raced past a seedy ganglord's tavern, but even that was quiet tonight.

The only tracks close to the compound were their own, and Tori knew she had to think of something quick. Darien was already struggling to keep pace.

A dark pillar of smoke loomed to the west.

The pyres!

Tori weaved in and out of narrow lanes, but the guards remained close behind them.

Images of her first burning night haunted her memory. The smell of incinerating dead, the living huddled close for the one good thing that could come from the tragedy—

Warmth.

And it could be their refuge now.

They were near the western edge of the slumlands. The paths were caked black from soot. Even the fresh snow was stained.

Hope burned in Tori's chest as they neared the pyres.

They turned another corner. A mound of bodies was heaped at the center of a small square outside the walls of a large workhouse facility.

One glance, and Tori's heart sank.

The pyre was not the source of the smoke at all. No flames. No huddled masses.

Perhaps another night, they might have hidden themselves in the pile of bodies at least, but tonight, their tracks would give them away in a moment. Tori had hoped that the weather might bring an early burning night, but she knew in her heart that was always a fool's hope.

All things, even burning nights, were a matter of economy, and it would be a waste to burn the bodies now, when so many more would surely be added to the pyres by the time this storm was over.

The square was cast in a hellish glow. Fiery light hung over them, as though it were trapped in the storm the same as them.

Tori came to a stop beside the pyre. All at once, she had no idea where to run, or what to do.

But Darien didn't stop. He huffed straight past her, to the edge of the factory wall.

"Give me your cloak!" he said.

There was no time for questions. The guards were closing in again. Tori pulled her cloak over her head.

"Now, give me a boost!"

Tori knelt on the ground and cupped her hands. Darien heaved the cloak up, draping it over the top of the wall. Then, with a grunt, he launched himself up the side.

————

Darien heaved his body up the wall. Even with the cloak, shards of glass lining the top pierced his stomach. He was so numb, it barely registered in his mind.

Cries echoed across the square. A chunk of wall exploded to his right. Tori let out a shriek.

Fletch's guards had rounded up members of the Night Legions, dressed in thick coats and grey uniforms. And they were firing at them!

Darien shifted his freezing body and reached his hands back down.

More shots pinged off the stone around him. Fletch's guards sprinted across the square as the Legion Shadows let loose another volley of musket-fire.

"Now!" Darien shouted.

With remarkable agility, Tori took two steps and jumped. Her feet hit the stone and launched her body upward.

Darien snatched her by the wrists and threw his body back. This time, the pain raged as his stomach lurched back. Tori flew over the top of the wall.

She landed on top of him and rolled. Pain shot up Darien's back.

He'd landed on what felt like a sea of glass. All around, the snow was coated black. Shards of dark rock stretched in all directions.

Coal, he realized.

Huge mounds of coal darted the bleak expanse like hay in a farmer's field, except these were everywhere, scattered every ten or twenty yards. Strange metal tracks weaved in between them. The grinding sounds of machinery echoed from a massive building in the distance, where enormous smoke stacks towered into the stormy skies.

There was no time to waste. Darien gritted his teeth and turned over. A hand pulled him to his feet, and together, he and the strange girl raced across the dark fields toward the factory compound.

He glanced back. A face peered over the wall. Curses rang out.

Darien and Tori weaved between hillocks of coal, and when Darien glanced back again, the wall was out of sight. And so were the guards.

His lungs ached from the cold and the storm and their long flight.

The grinding sound of shovels and the groans of grueling labor echoed from somewhere ahead.

"Fill it to the brim, you vermin!"

The voice stopped them in their tracks.

They'd lost themselves in the maze of coal, somewhere in the no man's land between the Fringes and this factory.

Tori motioned to a metal cart set beside a nearby heap of coal. It was the size of a small skiff, and seemed to be a means of hauling the coal to the factory along those strange metal tracks.

No words were needed. They clambered up the side and dropped into the bed of the cart. The sides rose a couple feet above their heads while sitting.

The taskmaster barked more orders. A whip cracked.

"Now, heave!"

A loud creak and the grinding of metal on metal. The taskmaster's voice faded into the night and all went still.

The cold of the metal cut straight through Darien's clothes.

"W-we should stay here for a b-bit." The girl was shivering violently without her cloak. "M-make sure those g-guards don't come after us."

Darien nodded. His hands trembled. His shirt was torn across his stomach. He felt at his wounds, relieved to find little blood.

Tori drew close to him. He jolted.

"W-we'll freeze to death if we d-don't keep close."

Darien nodded, wrapping his arms around her.

As they waited, her shivers abated. The storm ceased at some point, but Darien had no idea when. Their entire flight from the compound was a haze in his mind.

"Where did you come from?" he asked.

"The gods," she said with a soft huff of laughter.

"I'm serious. You could have gotten killed. Why in the Abyss did you help me?"

"Why did you let Taven live? In the arena?"

"You were there?"

Tori nodded against his chest, looking up at him. He could barely see her in the darkness.

He shook his head. "It doesn't matter. He died. Just like that Yan Avii boy tonight."

"Of course it matters," Tori said softly. "The Fringes turns everyone to monsters. You kept your soul. And I knew they'd kill you for it. So… I don't know… I had to try and help you."

Darien shook his head and shook with laughter. "Thank you."

Tori nodded.

The snow stopped falling, and the skies filled with plumes of smoke, but Darien could see the first traces of dawn approaching.

"We should go," he said.

Tori eased away and helped him to his feet. His limbs were stiff, and his stomach throbbed, but best he could tell, his injuries were relatively minor.

Carefully, they climbed out of the cart and began to navigate their way across the fields of coal. Back toward the Fringes.

"We should split up," Darien said. "As soon as we're back in the Fringes."

Tori stopped. "No, we stay together."

"Those guards will be looking for me."

Tori chuckled.

"What?"

"I thought I was the one new to this place."

"What are you talking about?" Darien asked.

"You're a rat of the Fringes now. You'll be forgotten by lunchtime. People fall into the cracks every day in this hellhole."

Darien didn't know how to respond. The moment he'd arrived in this place, he'd thought he was a dead man. Was it possible he might eek out some sort of life after the tragedy he'd left behind?

The grey pre-dawn gloom offered just enough light for them to find the walls of the Fringes, and climb over once more. With no cloak, Darien's stomach took an even worse beating.

But he would survive.

Blood splattered the snow as they strode back into the maze of lanes. Bodies poured from the buildings as Fringe rats filled the lanes and made their way to wherever they worked.

"I can get you something to wrap that wound with," Tori said.

"How?"

Tori drifted into the crowd. Darien kept pressing forward. All of a sudden, Tori bumped back up against him, holding a strip of linen.

"Not bad," Darien said.

Tori grinned and kept moving. Fringe rats swarmed all around them, and Darien suddenly felt lost, in a good way. No one cared who he was. No cared about his tragedies. No one cared about what he'd done. He was no one.

And that was strangely freeing.

"What now?" Darien asked as they reached the walls outside a workhouse in the heart of the Fringes.

"Well, I got to work," Tori said with a yawn. She pulled up her left sleeve to reveal a weave of thorn-like tattoos. "Textile houses."

"Would I be able to work there too?"

"My taskmaster's daughter was seeing that boy you fought in the arena yesterday," she said. "That's why I was there in the first place."

"You're her… friend?"

Tori shrugged. "I don't think she'll want much to do with me anymore. I kind of ran off on her right after he died."

"Oh…" Darien said.

Tori gripped his hand and smiled. "We all do what we got to survive in this world."

Darien smiled down at her. He was pretty sure he hadn't smiled once since his family died.

"Anyway, no way you'll be able to work here. Cera would make sure of that. But you're strong. You ever worked in a mine?"

Darien shook his head. "I'm a bit new to forced labor."

Tori smiled. "You're from the mountains though. You got what it takes to survive. And besides, now, you've got me."

Darien couldn't explain it. All at once, his fate had turned. All because of this strange Yan Avii girl. It was as though someone had crossed their paths somehow. To survive together. He sensed that deeply.

"I've got to go inside," Tori said, motioning toward a guarded gate a short distance away.

"I'll find you when you're done," Darien said.

Tori smiled. "You better."

And with that, the girl walked away.

Darien ventured back into the crowds. A sea of scrawny bodies in tattered clothes. He knew his life would be hell, and yet, he could not shake the sense of hope filling his chest.

For the first time since he'd left the mountains of Klavash, Darien knew he was not alone.

ACKNOWLEDGMENTS

Kaitlin is my wife, best friend, first reader, art wizard (witch?), and the most incredible mother our boys could ever have. She's been a part of this writing adventure every step of the way, and I am deeply grateful.

Logan and Parker are a reminder that the best stories are found in the real world.

Thanks to my family for nerding out about books all my life, and for always supporting my writing.

I'm indebted to the incredible artists whose illustrations and designs made this edition a work of art: Andrew Maleski, Rachel St. Clair of Claymore Covers, Sebastian Breit, Sabzdunz, Sutthiwat Dechakamphu, and Ömer Burak Önal.

A special thanks to Petrik Leo and Johan from Library of a Viking, for helping spread the word about the campaign.

A project like this would have been unmanageable for me alone, and would not have happened without Andrew Cobble's guidance and the help of Merrick Books with distribution.

And none of this would have been possible if not for the incredible backers who funded the project on Kickstarter. Thank you for making this a reality! In alphabetical order, they are:

A-E

Emma Adams | Matt Allen | Walter E. Alvarez Jr. | Hank Alward | Jerome Anello | Maria Angell | Anonymous | Alyssa Arce | Jon Auerbach | Helena B. | Callum Barber | Chris Bernardo | David Berry | Zeb Berryman | Jack Bilton | Felicia Bisson | Brandon Black | Brett Blakley | Peter Blomberg | David Bobbitt | Travis Brannan | Justise Briones |

Carter Bristol | Shanon M. Brown | Adam Bryant | Karen Bulgarelli | Robin Busch | Ashley Byrd | Rob Campbell | Jaden Canencia | Franchesca Caram | Meredith Carstens | Tyler Cheek | Scott Chisholm | Tonje Christoffersen | Gianna Christopher | Christopher Clayton | Zach Cooper | Heather Cooper | Alexandra Corrsin | Kathryn Craig | Tim Cross | Andy Culver | Lulu D. | Graham Dauncey | Daybreak Treasures Boutique | Chase de Groot | Andrew Deans | Patience Deaton | Rhel ná DecVandé | Dave DeHaan | Julián Delgádo | Monica Dempsey | Jarda Deneš | Amanda DiAlessandro | Ben DiDonato | Angelo Drakontaidis | Alex Dummer | Eric Dunlap | Lucas Edwards | Amy Elliott | Troy Erickson | Hugo Essink

F-I

Amber Ferguson | Irinel Finco | G. Fischer | Emma Flaws | Kimberly Florendo | Jacob Fox | Athena Franks | Caleb Friesen | Christi G. | Morgan G. | Mike Galligan | GhostCat | Katrina Gilles | Eric Gossett | Alex Grade | Vance Green | Connor Grove | N Gustafson | Ryan H. | Joshua Hair | Jonathan Hamm | Matias Hansen | Kathryn and Alex Hastings | Andrew HAUG | L. Haymond | Matthew Hechel | Cady Henry | Emalei Henry | Billye Herndon | T. Hise | Thomas Hodges | Christopher Hofer | Liana Houdershell | Terry M. Hulett | Ashton Hurley | John Idlor | Corbin Igoe

J-M

Ryan Scott James | Joe Jimenez | Brad Johnson | Fred W. Johnson | Eddie Joo | Kala Judd | James Kaylor | Christian Kegley | Katie Keith | John Kern | Christopher Kirke | Callie Klopfenstein | Susie Klopfenstein | Alex Kuczwara | Ian LaBrecque | Megan Lagarde | Dakota Land | Samantha Landström | Ivan Lee | Mathieu Lefebvre | Nicolas Lobotsky | Makayden Lofthouse | Rhys Lowcock | Yoliany Maceiras-Gooze | Ben Madeley | Rachel Maifret | In loving memory of Basil Martin | Craig Mayne | Allison Mayo | Writer MBA | Rory McCabe | Larry McConville | Gerald McDaniel | RC McKinney | Cathy McLoughlin | Michael McMullen | Sancho Melis | Agnès Metanomski

| Sean Mills | Kevin Miraglia | Angela Mitchell | Michael Mitchell | Annarose Mitchell | Zach Monroe | Cristiana Monteiro | Nathan Morgan | LaToya Moritis | Janet Moule | Jay Mullen | Joshua Murphree | Adriane Myers

N-R

L. Nabeta | E. Nabeta | Brandon Neal | Korbyn Nelson | Señor Neo | Benjamin Newton | Adam Nooney | Jason Nugent | Mike Olson | Toby Otto | Brendan Papz | Anthony Paulino | Jonah Pavlicek | Paul Perez | Neil Phillips | Sarah Phillips | Ellen Pilcher | A. Pueppke | Marea Quijano | Jason R. | Marcos Ramirez | Morgen Raney | Stuart Karl Renz | Annie Richer aka Lawrichai | Nancy Richey | James Richmond | Joe Rixman | Todd Roark | Caitlin Roberts | Michael Robinson | Gina Rochester | Roseking | J.D.L. Rosell | Matthea W. Ross | Daniel Rowell | Natasha Rueschhoff

S-Z

Colin S. | James S. | Jessie Sanders | Seamus Sands | Luca Leo Schneider | Armin Schopfer | Megan Scrivens | Sal Scullstreet | David Shaffer | Megan Shelton | Akul Singh | Mike Smid | T. J. Smith | Heather Smith | Kent Smith | Clayton Smith | Paul Smith | Ethan Smith | Richard Sorden | Anders Sørensen | Siona St. Mark | Kelsey Stenberg | Sarah L. Stevenson | Kelly Stirling | Michael H. Sugarman | Viola Tempest | Zach Tomlinson | Atakean Trishria | Arild Tvedt | Christoph van Dommelen | Kristy VanWyhe | Cédric Voglet | Evett Voyles | David Walters | Ken Warner | Jackie Warrior-Strong | Lisa Watson | Jacob Watt | Heather Webber | Russell Weeden | Kenyon Wensing | Kyle Westjohn | Duncan Wilcox | Spencer Wright | Troy Young | Zeth